THEOWLING

Other books by Robert Elmer

The Shadowside Trilogy:
Trion Rising (Book One)

The Wall series:
Candy Bombers (Book One)
Beetle Bunker (Book Two)
Smuggler's Treasure (Book Three)

THE SHADOWSIDE TRILOGY

THEOWLING

ROBERT ELMER

ZONDERVAN®

ZONDERVAN.com/
AUTHORTRACKER
follow your favorite authors

ZONDERVAN®

The Owling
Copyright © 2008 by Robert Elmer

Requests for information should be addressed to:

Zondervan, *Grand Rapids, Michigan* 49530

Library of Congress Cataloging-in-Publication Data: Applied for
ISBN 978-0-310-71422-4

Published in association with the literary agency of Alive Communications, Inc., 7680 Goddard Street suite #200, Colorado Springs, CO 80920. www.alivecommunications. com

Interior design by Michelle Espinoza

Printed in the United States of America

08 09 10 11 12 13 • 22 21 20 19 18 17 16 15 14 13 12 11 10 9 8 7 6 5 4 3 2 1

THEOWLING

You yourselves are our story, written by the Numa
on the scroll of our hearts for all to read.
~ Codex 32:4

Oriannon jerked awake, jolted by the shuttle's sudden dive and the high-pitched whine of ion boosters. The unseen hand of several *G*s squeezed her squarely back in the padded seat, and she gasped for breath.

Where were they?

Off course, without a doubt, and certainly not heading home. The fifteen-year-old managed a glance out a tiny side viewport, though her eyeballs hurt to focus and her stomach rebelled at the sudden drop. Outside, space appeared cold, dark, and colorless — not the dense, bright violet atmosphere she would have expected to see above irrigated farms and the well-watered surface of Corista, her home planet.

Just across the aisle, her father unstrapped from his grav seat with a grunt, gathered his gold-trimmed ceremonial robe, and struggled down the narrow aisle of the shuttle toward the pilot's compartment. Several passengers screamed as they banked once more, sharply, and the engines whined even more loudly. He seemed to ignore the panic; he put his head down and tumbled the last few feet to the flight deck.

"What's going on here?" Father always remained polite, even when he was pounding on doors. "I'd like a word with you please."

The pilot would have to listen to an Assembly elder, one of the twelve most important men in Corista, aside from the Regent himself. But Oriannon's father kept pounding, and Ori gripped the handle in front of her as they made another tight turn. Light from the three Trion suns blinded her for a moment as it passed through the window and caught her in the face. When she shaded her eyes, she saw something else looming large and close.

"Father?" She tried to get his attention over all the noise. "I know where we are."

But he only pounded harder, raising his voice above braking thrusters as they came on line. She felt a forward pull as the shuttle engines whined, then seemed to catch. Still they wagged and wobbled, nearly out of control. Outside, a pockmarked asteroid loomed ever larger, while sunlight glittered off a tinted plexidome built into the surface.

From here the dome didn't seem much larger than Regent Jib Ossek Academy back home, but Oriannon knew it covered what would have been a deep impact crater on the near side of the huge space rock's surface. This was obviously no planet, only a remote way station called Asylum 4 — one of twelve ancient Asylum outposts. Why had their shuttle diverted here?

By this time everyone else on the shuttle must have seen the asteroid out their windows as well. Now it filled each viewport with close-ups of the tortured surface, scarred by thousands of hits from space debris and tiny asteroids. But instead of an announcement over the intercom, shuttle passengers were met only with a strange silence from the flight deck.

"I insist that you — " Oriannon's father couldn't finish his demand as he was thrown from his feet by the impact. Oriannon's forehead nearly hit the back of the seat in front of her. A loud squeal of scraping metal outside told everyone they'd made full contact with Asylum 4's docking port.

And then only silence, as the engines slowly powered down. Her father rose to his feet, and no one spoke for a long, tense moment. Air rushed through a lock, and they heard the pilot's emergency hatch swing free. Still, the twenty-one passengers could only sit and wait, trapped in their sealed compartment without any word of explanation and without any fresh air. A couple of men rose to their feet and pushed to the front.

"We need to get out of here!" announced one, but Oriannon's father put a stop to it with a raised hand.

"Just be patient," he told them. "I'm certain we'll find out what happened in a moment."

Or two.

Several minutes later they heard footsteps and a shuffling before the main hatch finally swept open and they were met with a rush of cool air—and a curious stare.

"Are you people quite all right?" A small man in the rust-colored frock of a scribe looked nearly as confused as Oriannon felt. "Where's your pilot?"

"We were hoping you would tell *us*." Oriannon's father tried to take charge of the chaos that followed as everyone shouted at once, trying to find answers in a place that only held more questions. Why were they brought here, instead of back to Corista?

"Please!" The scribe held up his hands for silence. He didn't look as if he was used to this much company—or this much shouting—all at once. And how old was he? Oriannon couldn't be sure, though he appeared wrinkled as a dried aplon, and wispy white hair circled his ears as if searching for a way inside. Yet his pleasant green eyes sparkled in an impish, almost pleasant sort of way, and judging by the way his eyes darted from side to side, he seemed to miss nothing.

"I'm very sorry for the confusion," he continued, "but all are welcome here at Asylum Way Station 4. As you probably know, it's the tradition of the Asylum outposts to welcome all visitors. Although I must say ..."

He glanced at the hatch beside him, where trim along the bottom edge had bent and twisted during the rough landing. The ship's skin, though gouged and damaged, appeared not to have been breached. It could have been worse.

"Whoever piloted your craft here was either in a very great hurry, or perhaps in need of a bit more practice in the art of landing."

No doubt about that. But as her father introduced himself, Oriannon noticed the hatch hydraulics hissing a little too loudly while an odd thumping sound came from inside the craft's wall, weak but steady.

"I'm Cirrus Main," the scribe went on, bowing slightly to her father. "And we're especially honored to greet a member of the Assembly. I cannot recall the last time we enjoyed a visit from an elder, though I should consult our station archives to be sure. There was a day, several generations ago, when —"

"But what about the pilot?" interrupted another passenger, a serious-faced man a bit younger than her father. "Didn't you see him? We didn't fly here ourselves, you know."

The scribe seemed taken aback by their rudeness, blinking in surprise.

"Please pardon my lack of an immediate answer for you," he replied, holding his fingertips together and his lips tight. "Most of us were otherwise occupied in the library when this incident occurred. However, in time I will inquire as to whether your pilot was seen disembarking and attempt to discern his or her disposition."

"The pilot will answer to the Assembly," replied Oriannon's father. "We were returning from a diplomatic mission to the Owling capital on the other side of the planet and on our way back to our capital city of Seramine. We should never have been brought all the way out here."

"Ah, but do not all things work for good to those who are called according to …" The scribe forced a shy smile, opened his mouth to say something else, then seemed to change his mind. "But never mind. Our protocols here on Asylum 4 require us to offer sanctuary to all, you see, no matter the circumstances."

"Sanctuary?" barked the serious man. "We need some answers, and you're—"

"As I said." The scribe raised his hand for peace. "We simply cannot say who brought you here, other than the Maker himself. However, we are quite pleased it appears you're all unharmed."

Yes, they were. But then the shouting started all over again, most of it to do with who was to blame for this unscheduled stop, who was going to be late for their appointments, and how soon they'd be able to get home. Finally their host had to raise his hand once more.

"Please let me assure you that despite the apparent confusion of the moment, we will extend every effort to make your stay as comfortable as possible, so that you may return to Seramine in due course. In the meantime, I trust you'll agree to observe our protocol."

"Remain silent before the Codex." Oriannon quoted an obscure, ancient commentary. "And at peace before all."

"Who said that?" Cirrus Main searched the crowd with a curious expression. She shrank behind another passenger so he wouldn't see, but couldn't quite hide her head of tousled black hair.

"My daughter is an eidich," explained Oriannon's father, taking his place at the front of the little crowd. "Oriannon remembers everything she reads in the ancient book. Every word."

That was true most of the time, with certain annoying exceptions over the past several months that no one needed to know about.

"I'm familiar with eidichs," answered the scribe, raising his eyebrows at Oriannon. She couldn't really hide. "Although there were once many more than there are today. In fact, when I first came from Asylum 7, years ago, we knew of several ..."

His voice trailed off as he seemed to put aside the memory with a sad shake of his head.

"I'm sorry." His face reddened. "You didn't come here to hear an old man's stories. But perhaps you'll find clarity here. That is, after all, the purpose for which this outpost was created. So if you'll follow me, I would be most pleased to show you the facilities."

"We do appreciate your hospitality," said her father, looking around at the group, "but we can only stay a short time, until we get another pilot and the shuttle is prepared to return."

Oriannon shivered—but not because of the cool, musty air that smelled of far-off worlds, aging dust, and something else she couldn't quite identify. She followed as Cirrus Main led them through narrow hallways blasted out of rough, iron-stained rock. They walked through a network of prefabricated but obviously ancient modules anchored to the surface of the asteroid at three or four levels. Chalky rust tarnished most of the walls. And through viewports she could see the sheer face of the crater rising up on all sides around them before finally meeting the umbrella of the plexi-dome above. This place had obviously been constructed generations ago. She craned her neck to see hanging gardens and flowing plants cascading from terraces cut precariously into crater walls. The scent of cerise and flamboyan joined rivulets coursing over small water-falls as moisture condensed on the inside of the dome. She found it odd to discover the faint perfume of Coristan flowers at such a remote outpost.

"I suppose it's a bit like living in a greenhouse," their host admitted, ducking past a stream of spray. "It is an environment, however, to which one becomes accustomed."

They paused for a moment to watch a viria bird flitter across the upper expanse inside the dome. Here, under the plexidome and against the cold void of space, the freedom of small fluttering wings appeared strangely out of place.

"Remain close behind me, please," he told them. "Our environ-ment is rather fragile, as I'm sure you can appreciate."

By now Oriannon had made her way to the front of the group, where she could hear everything Cirrus Main told them about the water recycling system and the gardens, and the delicate balance of work and study that made their home livable. Here and there other residents, each one dressed in red work coveralls, quietly tended the gardens, harvesting fruit and adjusting irrigation controls. None seemed to notice that this group had been brought here under strange circumstances, or even that they had been brought here at all. Oriannon saw a young face staring at them from the far end of the dome, but the little girl ducked out of sight behind a humming generator.

"Some of us have families here." Cirrus Main must have noticed the little girl as well. But he didn't stop as he led them up a stairway, through a set of noisy airlocks, and finally back into a large, high-ceilinged room where ten or twelve other red-frocked scribes sat at tables, leaning close to each other in animated discussions. Here the polished stone floor contrasted with the worn look of the rest of the station, while the dark pluqwood trim and carefully inlaid ceiling of planets and stars in copper and stone suggested a different type of room. Certainly it looked less utilitarian than the rest. Cirrus gestured at a wall filled with shelves.

"Our library." He crossed his arms with obvious satisfaction and lowered his voice, as if they had entered a holy place. Oriannon carefully picked up a leather-backed volume from a stack on a nearby stone table. "Mainly theological, but also a bit of the fine arts," he said. "Some of Corista's finest ancient philosophers, Rainott, Ornix ... You know them?"

Of course she did—at least every word that had ever been digitally transcribed. Oriannon nodded as she riffed through the pages, sensing something entirely different among them. Here the carefully inscribed words came alive in a way that the ones in her e-books never could. Each page appeared hand printed, in a script that flowed carefully across each line with a sort of measured serendipity. Here a real person with hopes and dreams had actually written the words on a page—laboriously, lovingly, one letter at a time. Some of the pages even showed flourishes and highlights, making the book more a work of art than merely a collection of thoughts.

"I've never ..." She held back a sneeze. "... seen so many old books in one place. Back home they're all under glass."

"Like everyone else," he told her, slipping the book from her hands and holding it up for the others to see. "You're accustomed to words in their digital form. Here we study the Codex as it was first recorded—in books and on pages, scribed by hand many generations ago, in a day when we still had calligraphers among us. They brought us words from the Maker's heart, straight to the page."

He sighed deeply as a couple of the other passengers stood off at a distance, arms crossed and muttering something about how old books weren't going to help get them off this rock. But he smiled again as he lovingly smoothed a page before returning the book to its place on the table.

"We seek the Maker in these pages," he said, closing his eyes and rocking back on his heels. He paused as if actually praying. "Sometimes, if we're very quiet, we can hear his whisper."

In the books? Oriannon thought she might hear such a whisper too, as she listened to water tinkling from outside and the gentle murmur of scribes discussing their wondrous, ancient volumes. In fact she could have stayed there much longer, but their silence was interrupted by hurried footsteps as a younger scribe burst into the room and whispered something obviously urgent in Cirrus Main's ear. The older man's face clouded only a moment before a peaceful calm returned.

"Your pilot seems to have been found," he told them. "Locked inside a storage compartment in your shuttle. We have yet no idea how he came to be there, only that one of our maintenance people located him."

"Alive?" asked Oriannon. She shuddered at the thought.

"Oh, I'm alive, all right."

Oriannon and the others turned to see the Coristan shuttle pilot in his cerulean blue coveralls standing at the entry through which they'd just stepped. He rubbed the back of his neck.

"But I'll tell you something," he added, his voice booming through the library. All the scribes froze at their seats. "When I find the Owling who hijacked us, he's going to wish he'd stayed on his side of the planet."

2

Oriannon had no idea how so many black-suited securities made it to Asylum 4 so quickly, all the way from Corista. In any case, within minutes they had docked their ships and swarmed through every passage and study room of the little way station. Their round, black security probes filled the air as well. Each probe, the size of a small head, flew around illuminating corners and under tables, checking for signs of its prey.

Meanwhile the scribes stood with their opened books, looking as if a horrible flood had overtaken the peace of their home and they had no idea how to make it go away.

Oriannon ducked into a corner as another probe flew by at shoulder height, and she shivered. By the way they flew, she knew these probes were different from the irritating, but mostly harmless, mechanical sentries that for years had harassed her in school, checking hall passes and keeping track of schedules. Or even those on the streets of Seramine, conducting routine security checks and announcing special prices at local cafés. She assumed these probes were similarly enhanced with an animal's eyeball plugged into a titanium socket in the side of the biomechanical hybrid. That part looked the same, at least. She just wondered how the aggressive new probes had all come on line so quickly and completely, and what had happened to the old ones.

One of the probes paused briefly, scanning her face with a red beam before hurrying on. She brought a hand to her cheek where it tingled and stung. They would know instantly who she was and where she was—probably her heart rate and what she'd had for lunch on the shuttle as well.

"Please!" Cirrus Main stepped forward and held up a shaking hand. "I must object to this ... this *intrusion*. I told you we were making every effort to locate your hijacker, if that's what really happened. What you're doing is entirely out of proportion."

"You think so?" Their pilot crossed his arms across his blue coveralls and gazed around the library. But he didn't move as helmeted securities with silver visors and black jerseys pushed open storage doors and hurried past bookshelves, tipping several volumes to the stone floor and kicking them with their black boots. "I don't think it's out of proportion at all. In fact, this isn't the first time a criminal has found asylum here, is it now?" He turned to face their host, who swallowed hard but kept his ground as he replied.

"We've been under charter from the Corista Ruling Assembly for more than a hundred generations as a place of safety and study, on the planet surface and up here. You know that as well as anyone. And you have no right to—"

"No right?" interrupted the pilot, his face reddening and his voice heating up. "Let's talk about rights then. You're saying those Owling terrorists had a *right* to tie me up, a *right* to commandeer a Coristan vessel, a *right* to throw me into the storage area, a *right* to divert my craft to this rock?"

"No, of course not. All I'm saying is that you can't just rush in here and—"

"And what? These people are simply responding to my distress call." He smiled and waved his hand across the room. "And doing a fine job, wouldn't you say?"

Cirrus Main did not reply; he only stooped to pick up some of the fallen books as the pilot continued.

"But we haven't found the hijackers yet, which tells me they probably had help from you or your people to hide. Isn't that right?"

"I told you this is a place of asylum for all," the scribe finally replied, only this time his voice was a soft whisper. "You've broken our peace and our protocols."

"To tell you the truth, I'd like to break something else." The pilot raised a finger of warning. "Only I'm afraid the honorable elder and his esteemed daughter in the royal white tunic might find it objectionable."

By this time Oriannon was ready for the awkward face-off to end, and she looked for a way out of the library. As the pilot railed on about Corista Security's obligation to protect its citizens, she stooped behind a shelf, picked up a stray book, and held it out to Cirrus Main. He whispered his thanks ... and something else.

"You remember the waterfalls outside?" he asked, turning aside to make sure no one else noticed.

She nodded, unsure how else to answer. What was he saying? She bent a little closer to hear, placing another book in his hands.

"Waste no time," he went on, his hands trembling and his face bowed as if pleading. "Go to the twin waterfalls without delay. Only be certain no one sees you. You are the only one who can—"

As another scribe happened by, he changed his voice.

"—help. Ahem. Thank you for helping. Most kind of you."

Now he smiled again, divulging none of his earlier fear, and backed away from Oriannon with a bow to replace his books on the shelf. Meanwhile, her father and the pilot still argued on the other side of the room.

"Jurisdiction?" Oriannon's father crossed his arms and turned his head to the side in a challenge. "We're talking about a technicality. Surely it's not necessary to do things this way. I'm sure you'll find your hijacker without—"

"Pardon me, sir." This time the pilot didn't smile, and he narrowed his menacing eyes at them. "Up here it's best if you let Corista Security do their job, the way we've been trained, and then we'll be sure to get you back safely to Seramine, where you can do yours. Does that sound all right with you?"

He didn't wait for an answer.

"Oh, and something else you should know, Elder Hightower. If we don't find this Owling hijacker within twenty minutes, I'm obliged to take more drastic measures. In fact, I am not authorized to wait, nor am I here to play an extended game of hide-and-seek. I say this as a courtesy, if you catch my meaning."

Oriannon had no doubt the man was deadly serious, and she couldn't help wishing for a moment that he might have stayed a little longer where the hijacker had left him, back inside the shuttle. She scolded herself for the thought, even as she wondered how a normally small-statured Owling could have wrestled the broad-shouldered pilot into hiding. She would find out, and she would get away from this nasty man. When her father wasn't looking, she slipped out the doors, back out to the atrium, and away from the chaos.

I can't believe this is happening, she told herself. But then perhaps it should not have come as a surprise. She looked around the atrium for signs of probes or securities. It seemed as if the search had moved to another part of the way station. Still her heart pounded as she found her way slowly to a quiet spot between a wall of furry three-ferns and two cascading waterfalls, a place where she could catch her breath.

What did Cirrus Main have in mind?

Her hand still shook as she reached out to pull a cerise bloom closer. She didn't hear the footsteps on the gravel path behind her until it was too late. A scribe grabbed her hand and pulled her behind a dripping curtain of water, cascading over both of them.

"What are you doing?" she started to ask, but the small man clamped a strong hand on her mouth. She would have kicked and screamed had she not seen the unmistakable look of fear on his face, the wide-eyed expression that peered out at her from behind the olive-green hood of an apprentice scribe.

Only this was no scribe. Close up, the huge, dark eyes and the olive complexion gave him away, along with the fact that he stood no taller than Oriannon herself.

This was an Owling.

"Please, there's no time." He pleaded with his eyes. "Will you listen to me for just a moment, and not be screaming? Just be hearing what I'm telling you. Please. I promise not to be hurting you."

This could not be good, no matter what he promised or how sweet his Owling accent sounded. On one side, the curtain of water screened them from the rest of the way station, and light from outside glittered through. On the other, behind them, a gaping hole in the rock wall led only to darkness. He might pull her into the cave, and she would never be found.

But something in his words kept her from panic, and despite herself she nodded slightly. She would not scream. Yet.

"I've seen you before," she told him, as soon as he finally lowered his hand. "Back in the Owling city. In Lior."

He nodded quickly, still keeping a lookout in all directions. A probe could happen by at any time. Or worse yet, a security.

"It's good you're remembering," he told her. "But that's not mattering now."

So what *did* matter?

"What's mattering is you're a follower of Jesmet." He went on. "You and your friend Margus Leek. This I'm knowing."

"How?" she asked. "How do you know? Did Cirrus Main send you?"

A flicker of a smile crossed his lips and then was gone.

"Listen to me carefully, if you're caring about Jesmet and the Owlings. I'm trying — "

"No, wait a minute." Oriannon tried to reverse course in this strange conversation. "Why are you doing this? Did you hijack the shuttle? How did you do it? How do you know my name? And Margus too. Why did you bring me here?"

"There's no time to be explaining all of this to you." He shook his head and grabbed her by the shoulders, which seemed a very odd thing for an Owling to do. She had in fact never seen the gentle Owling people do anything of the sort. "I'm trying to tell you. Your friend Wist is in danger back in Lior. All the Owlings are in danger."

"That's not true anymore. Weren't you there when my father came with the Assembly's peace delegation? He really wants to help find a way for Coristans and Owlings to live together."

The Owling sighed as if he was trying to explain higher physics to a pinchbeetle.

"You're not understanding, young lady. The Assembly is not what it used to be, and not now what it will be. They debate theology and set their policies, not knowing there is a new energy ready to destroy them and Owlings both. And facing it, your father is powerless."

"What are you talking about?" she asked. He had to be mistaken. "The Assembly is the most powerful council in Corista."

"Was and no longer is. Deceived by their own advisor. But I'm not here to be arguing with you. The Assembly will soon fail, so our time on the planet is short, and my job now is to be finding a safe place for Owling believers. And safekeeping for the Pilot Stone."

"The Pilot—"

"Please be letting me finish." He held up his hand. "We thought the scribe Cirrus Main would help us, but we were mistaken. He feared for his life and for this place if he received such a priceless relic, and I don't condemn him. Perhaps it was an ill thought on our part. But now I'm seeing Jesmet brought you here, and you're the one who will be helping."

Oriannon shook her head in confusion, not sure how much she liked being a back-up plan.

"Help you? You don't even know me. And Jesmet—"

"You're an eidich, are you not? You will add to the Stone what you remember and what you experience of Jesmet."

Still it made no sense—not yet. At that moment, a red beam flickered through the waterfall, as if it had been searching for them, and she ducked aside barely in time. Oriannon knew that this curtain of water could not shield the Owling from the searching eye of a probe for long. He also ducked his head and took Oriannon's hand, looking her straight in the eye.

"I must go now, Oriannon Hightower of the Nyssa clan. They must not be finding me here. But now take this."

He pressed into her hand a smooth, polished black stone, like a flattened skipping stone. A simple leather strap went through a small hole drilled in one end. It felt heavier than she would have guessed. Gleaming bands of red, violet, and green seemed to oscillate in the changing light. Even odder, a faintly crimson light shone from within the Stone, like a heartbeat. Though it seemed silly, she couldn't help thinking this Stone was living, breathing . . . alive.

Or was it just a reflection on a pretty rock?

She wasn't quite sure, but when she held the Stone, she felt a sure but strange pulsing sensation, a warmth she didn't understand. The kind of warmth she might feel talking to a good friend or laughing at days shared, and it warmed her to the core. When she ran a finger across it, she heard voices, clear but far off, like in a dream, and she couldn't be sure what they were saying.

"The Pilot Stone?" She might have forgotten everything else for another look at the strange treasure, had the Owling's urgent tone not jolted her back to face the danger at hand.

"Listen to me," he told her. She opened her mouth, but he shook his head in warning. "Once there were many, but now this is the last one, and they will do anything to keep it from being used. Do you understand? Anything. We thought it would be out of reach here; that was our mistake. Now above all you must keep it safe from them. You must promise me."

In this case she well knew who he meant by *them*. "But—"

"A vow and nothing less!" He would not let go of her now, gripping both her hand and the Stone. "Will you keep it or not?"

She held the pulsating Stone, wondering how she had been chosen for something as strange as this. And though she wasn't at all sure what she was agreeing to, she could do nothing but nod and agree.

"I'll keep it," she whispered. That was apparently good enough for the Owling. He took a step back, leaving her clutching the Stone. Another red light from a probe swept through from a different angle as the Owling backed into the darkness behind them. They were obviously catching up.

"Wait a minute!" Oriannon started to follow, but thought better of it. She had no idea where the honeycomb of tunnels or lava tubes might lead, but one thing she knew quite positively: she did not care to find out. "You can't just run away. What exactly do you want me to do with this thing? You still haven't explained."

Her words fell flat; by that time he had slipped into the darkness, leaving her alone. She heard his voice echo from the tunnel.

"A pilot guides, does it not? Time is coming when Jesmet will be telling you more. For now you'll be keeping it safe until it's to be used. This I'm knowing."

He sounded so sure in his curious Owling way. A moment later two dark probes splashed through the water curtain, pausing only a moment to scan her face. She clutched the Stone behind her back, shivering, while something very strange about their single eyes stopped her cold.

"Hightower, Oriannon," intoned one of the probes. "Evacuation order One-A. Confirm your identity by saying yes."

For a moment her most peevish instinct held sway as she confronted this new threat, and it took all her will to ignore the probes as she stepped back through the water and back out into the atrium. By this time several other probes had also gathered around, and the first probe pursued her as if on a leash.

"Hightower, Oriannon," it told her, more loudly this time. "Evacuation order, priority One-A. You must confirm your identity immediately."

She wondered how far the mysterious Owling could get into the caves while she slipped the Stone into a deep pocket in her cloak and hurried back to the group. Perhaps with her silence she could distract the probes, even delay them a few moments. Her father waved and pointed at her as she approached the library building.

"Where have you been, girl?" He parked his hands on his hips. "The shuttle's ready again, and we have to get out of here. Now!"

He didn't say anything about her wet hair, but under the circumstances he might not have noticed.

"Hightower, Oriannon!" screeched the probe, flying in front of her face. "Confirm immediately!"

"Yes, of course," She finally batted at the pest like a veno hornet down on Corista. "Who else would I be?"

That would satisfy the probe as she followed her father at a fast jog through metaloid-paneled corridors back to the docking ports and the boarding area where they'd first entered the way station. Others ran past as if they were escaping a theater where someone had shouted "Fire!" Even the black-suited securities hurried past to the other three gates, herding scribes into the open maws of waiting transports.

"Is that everyone?" asked one of the underling securities, while another security with three silver stripes on his shoulder grunted.

"Not our concern," he answered back. "If it is, it is."

Just behind them, Cirrus Main stumbled into the loading zone, arms full of ancient books. At the last moment his toe caught on the platform edge, sending him sprawling and his books flying.

"You were told to bring nothing!" growled the security in charge, but the flustered little man still tried to grab several of his treasures. On his knees, he looked back at Oriannon with tears in his eyes.

"I'm very sorry," he whispered, and Oriannon caught a glimpse of his sorrow's depth. "And I pray you're not in danger."

"Wait." Oriannon grabbed one of the books and handed it to the scribe—just before he was shoved into another shuttle and the doors shut behind him with a whoosh of air.

"There's nothing we can do, Oriannon." Her father motioned for her to hurry. But before following him into their own craft, she stooped to scoop up one of Cirrus Main's books. Whatever was not digital here could be lost. So she hid it in another fold of her flowing (but damp) white tunic and bent over so no one would notice. If the scribe had thought them so precious, she might at least save one.

"That's it; let's go." Their pilot wasted no time closing the doors behind them and disengaging the boarding tunnel. In fact, he blew it off as if it might never be used again, and Oriannon watched it tumble out of view as they backed away with a jolt from Asylum Way Station 4.

"What's going on?" Oriannon finally asked her father as her seat's force field kicked in and she felt her back and head pulled into the plush of seat 2a. Without the usual safety announcements, the pilot engaged the ion drive afterburners and they leaped away from the asylum. "What was all the panic about? Did they find the hijacker?"

A moment later she witnessed the answer to her own question as she strained to pull her neck just a few centimeters away from the headrest to see out her viewport. In the distance she saw the way station falling behind them as they once again laid in a course for the surface of Corista. And she blinked at the sudden flash of light just ahead of an oddly beautiful ring of destruction rising from the asteroid.

It couldn't be! She pulled away completely from the force field, pushing her nose against the plexi viewport, wishing she had imagined it all. A moment later the angle of their flight made it impossible to see anymore.

But she had seen so much more than she'd wanted to.

"Father!" she gasped. "Did you know that would happen? Because of the hijacker? How could they?"

Judging by the grave look on his pale face, she guessed he already knew. He sat silently, nodding slightly against the lightened pull of the seat's force field, while a dark expression of pain wrinkled his forehead and he bit his lower lip. He knew.

He knew why Asylum Way Station 4 had been destroyed, and along with it anyone who had been left behind. She fought back tears of unbelief, thinking of the Owling who had risked his life to bring the Pilot Stone to this place—to her.

At the same time she recalled the Owling's words about Cirrus Main wanting to protect his home, refusing to take the Stone she now hid in her pocket. Too dangerous? Now the station had been destroyed anyway, and the Owling killed with it. She hadn't even known his name.

"They'll take the scribes to another asylum station." Her father's voice and the touch of his hand made her jump, but she could not pull her eyes from the view of empty space. "Maybe Asylum 2 or 3."

She nodded her head, still numb from shock. She held close her two treasures, hiding them in the folds of her tunic. Now even without touching the Stone she could feel its pulsing. In the distance she heard its voices, still strange and too far off to understand, though she listened intently.

"Asylum 2 or 3," she repeated, and she wondered if the next asylum station would see the same end.

"Let's just get you home now, all right?" he pulled down the sliding window shade. "I promise we'll be okay."

Still damp from the waterfall and thoroughly confused, Oriannon nodded again and fell back into her seat. She just wasn't sure how her father could keep such a promise.

3.

hat's that?

At first Oriannon thought the noise had come from the media screen hovering just over her bed. Leaving it on as background noise helped her fall asleep more easily. With the volume turned up she could drown out the ugly flashbacks of what had happened to them just the day before.

She adjusted the bedside control, upping the volume three more clicks.

"Coristan scientists are still trying to assess the long-term effects of the planet's axis shift," said the announcer, a pretty woman named Meela Rhon who wore too much makeup and who normally did the entertainment news. "Obviously daytime temperatures have dropped dramatically, since we no longer experience exclusive daylight. But even ten days since the planet began wobbling and changed life as we know it, authorities are still not sure what is happening."

"Them and me both," Oriannon talked back to the screen as she rubbed her eyes. It flashed up shots of quake-damaged homes and businesses in Corista, dramatic footage she'd seen over and over again in the past week. She reached over the edge of her bed and brushed her fingertips across the reader panel on the face of a drawer. It glowed a faint green when it recognized her biosign and her mental "yes" before unlocking the drawer in her bedside stand with a soft click. She felt inside the drawer, assuring herself that the book and the Stone were still safely hidden. She had not just dreamed what she'd experienced on Asylum Way Station 4.

As her hand brushed the smooth Stone, she once again felt the odd sensation of warmth, the strange connection, and she let it linger as she wondered again what she had been given. What kind of stone could be alive, like this one? But her heart jumped at a rumbling sound outside, and she quickly slipped the drawer shut before anyone could walk in on her. The media screen continued.

"While some believe there's little serious effect from the darkness that now descends on Corista every ten point two hours, many mental-health experts insist it's too soon to tell what kind of dangers we're really facing ... now that the Trion don't always shine overhead. I'm Meela Rhon, Media240 Reports."

"Whatever." Oriannon shook her head and waved at the hovering screen to turn off Meela Rhon's report. "You forgot to mention the Owling side of the story though."

Another low rumble shook her bed again. She bolted out of bed and grabbed a nightshirt before padding down the hallway, trying not to shiver in the chill and doing her best to shake off the confused grogginess that had gripped her ever since their light patterns had changed. What was it now, the middle of the dark time? They hardly had words for what was happening.

Maybe a breath of fresh air would help — though she wasn't quite sure if she wanted to wake up all the way or go back to sleep. Either way, she slipped to the back patio door, hoping her father wouldn't wake. She touched the sliding panel and waited for it to slip to the side with a quiet rush of cool air. Before she could even step outside, her eyes were drawn to the night sky.

They moved overhead in groups of three and four, sometimes more, not much higher than treetop level. Oriannon could only look up in wonder at the parade of transports and shuttles, their engines roaring and blue lights flashing as they gained altitude and finally passed out of sight into the darkness. Not just two or three, but one after another after another.

"So many." She wondered what could have launched such a force. Maybe they were heading to Shadowside, where residents of the Owling city waited for the peace her father had promised. She wasn't sure peace would materialize quite so quickly after all these years of Coristans treating the Owlings like animals, pumping Shadowside dry of water, and pretending the simple people didn't exist.

Another group roared overhead.

In between waves of transports, she thought she heard something else, closer to home. She turned her head to see a dim light from the window of her father's study at the far end of the house.

Father?

What would he be doing still awake at this hour? The patio door slid shut behind her when she stepped outside to the tiled patio. Even after hours of darkness, the tiles still held the last of the day's warmth. Outside, the sweet scent of orsianthius blossoms filled the cool air in a way they never could when Corista knew no darkness. Perhaps this was how they were meant to smell. She breathed in the heady perfume.

But she wasn't strolling in their terraced hillside garden to smell the flowers. Ducking at the sound of yet another group of transports, she hugged the side of their low stucco house and slipped along its deepest shadows, closer to the partly open window where her father's voice drifted out into the night. The guilty feeling of spying on her father wasn't enough to outweigh the curiosity that drew her close enough to hear what he was talking about, and with whom.

"I understand the official explanation for the incident." Her father's shadow stretched through the half-open window to the ornate tiles at Oriannon's feet. "And I understand Security was simply following their directive. But that still doesn't excuse what happened up there."

He paused to listen to the other person on his comm link.

"Yes, but they completely obliterated the way station!" he continued. "How long has it been up there, and under the Assembly's charter? They only barely evacuated the scribes, not to mention me and my daughter. If they wanted to make an example of the hijacker, well, they certainly accomplished that much."

He paused again, tried to interrupt, and listened some more. Oriannon couldn't help drawing even closer.

"Of course I know he was a criminal, and I assume there was more than one. Two or three, probably. No, Oriannon didn't see anything. Of course she's not to blame in any way. I'm glad you feel that way. But really, Sola, why do you keep asking about her?"

Oriannon's ears perked at the mention of her name. What were they saying?

Her father answered. "That's right. What I'm really worried about here is that Security is overstepping their bounds in ways they've never dared before. That's what I want you to tell them! I was swept out of there like a ... like a refugee. Do your people no longer respect the Assembly?"

As her father spoke, the Owling's words came back to Oriannon.

The Assembly is not what it used to be, he had told her. *Your father is powerless.*

Her father's questions forced her to wonder again if the desperate Owling had spoken truth after all. The possibility stuck in her thoughts, bitter and difficult to accept. Surely her father remained one of Corista's most powerful men, a member of the Ruling Assembly of Elders. It had always been so, for as long as she could remember.

Why then did he sound so worried?

For a moment she thought of stepping out of the shadows and telling him everything: the odd meeting under the atrium waterfall back on Asylum 4, the Owling's words, maybe everything she and her friend Margus had seen back in the Owling city of Lior weeks earlier.

But what good would it do now? Certainly she couldn't say anything about Jesmet to her father, not after the part her father had played in Jesmet's death. He might already know what Margus had done, but that was another story. She wondered if she could ever forgive her father for being a member of the Assembly that first banished her mentor, then condemned him to death for returning across the border to save her life.

In another way, she couldn't blame her father. He was only following what he believed was written in the Codex, only doing what he thought was his duty as a member of the Assembly. Did he have any other choice?

Meanwhile, she couldn't tell her father everything she knew — not yet. Not about the Stone, and not that Jesmet lived once more. But when she backed away from the window she tripped over a clay flowerpot, tipping orsianthius flowers and potting soil all over the patio. She froze as her father halted his conversation and came to the window.

"Of course I've heard," he told the person on the other end, lowering his voice and drawing the curtain closer. "We're right under the flight path. It's probably keeping her awake."

If he only knew. Once again she felt a pang of guilt for hiding in the shadows, listening to a conversation not meant for her ears. But now his voice grew muffled as he pulled the window in to close it.

"No! I don't want her involved in any way. Yes, I understand, but ..." He sighed, or perhaps it was just the window as it clamped shut with a soft hiss of air, leaving her with just the low sound of his voice. She no longer understood the words, but she could tell he was talking about her, and he did not sound at all pleased.

She scrambled to her feet and slipped to the back door, glancing skyward once more to watch the stars, which reminded her of

Asylum 4 exploding. The memories played over and over, like the door buzzer that now sounded insistently. At this time of night?

Oriannon slipped back inside, nearly colliding with her father in the hallway.

"Ori! What are you doing up?" He tucked the corner of his robe around his waist as he headed for the entry. Oriannon couldn't be sure who was at the front door, but she remembered the Owling's words: "Keep it safe from them."

So while her father answered the door, she hurried to her room, slipped open the drawer in her bedside stand and wondered.

Why am I doing this? I still don't know what the Stone is all about.

Even so, she slipped it into a pocket of her nightshirt, glanced at the ancient book, and closed the drawer again.

Just in time.

"Now you wait just a minute!" Her father's voice filled the house. "You can't just come pushing in here in the middle of our sleep cycle. Do you know who I am?"

Oriannon peeked out into the hall in time to see a tall security glance at his handheld e-pad.

"Hightower, Tavlin." The black-suited security's voice sounded flat. "One daughter and one Owling housekeeper. Your housekeeper is on the premises?"

"We have no Owling housekeeper. You should know that."

The security shrugged. "Are you sure? My database says here—"

"I don't care what your database says, and I refuse to answer any more of your questions." Oriannon's father crossed his arms. "This break-in is outrageous."

Two more securities pushed in behind the first, and Oriannon heard the sound of a stun baton charging.

"Look, Elder Hightower." Now the first Security almost sounded apologetic. "There's been a security breach, and we're just doing our job. Every home with an Owling has to be searched. Now, we can do this the hard way or the easy way."

"I just want to know what you're looking for, and who authorized this."

By this time the other securities had already jumped into action, rifling through drawers and running hand-held scanners around each corner of the kitchen and den.

"If you're on the Assembly, you already know who authorized this, and if you like you can ask *her* what she's looking for. I'm not at liberty to say."

Oriannon shrank back into her room once again, digging into her pocket to clutch the Stone. It warmed and sang in her hand even as the securities worked their way through the house, searching every corner. She heard the voices and worried that others might too.

"Do you have to search in here too?" asked her father, agitation bleeding through his voice. "This is my daughter's room. Surely she doesn't have anything you want."

The security just grunted and pushed his way into Oriannon's space. She sat down on the foot of her bed, pulled her robe even tighter, and pretended this wasn't happening. At least her bedside drawer was good and locked. The security nearly broke the treb bear figurine her father had given her on her tenth birthday. After a few moments of searching, pulling things out of place, and waving the scanner here and there, he pointed to the locked drawer.

"Open it."

She clenched her jaw and hesitated, but her father nudged her quietly.

"Better do as he says," he told her.

Reluctantly she obeyed.

"There's nothing in there you want," she told the security. But he ignored her as he reached in and picked up the ancient book.

"Hey, what? We've got something," he told the others, who came in to examine his find.

"It's just a book," she told them. "You've seen one before?"

He ignored her. Instead he just tossed it at the leader, who riffed through the pages of ancient, scholarly script before confronting Oriannon.

"Where did you get this?" he demanded.

"A souvenir from Asylum 4, before it was blown up," she snapped back, but now her father took her arm and held her back from being too flippant. "It's the Prophet Joeb. You know, 'And in the later days people will no longer listen to the truth, but will take for themselves that which only belongs to the Maker.' Or maybe you don't—"

"Ori, hush!" Her father whispered at her. "Let me do the talking."

The security stared at them through his one-way visor, then finally tossed the book to one of the others and motioned for them to follow him out.

"You can't take that!" Oriannon objected, but her father held her back.

"No?" answered the security, sounding unconcerned. By then another security returned from the other end of the house. He showed the readout of his scanner to the search leader. It made no sound, only blinked its green "all clear" light.

"No unusual readings," he reported. "No Owlings. No rocks."

"What did I tell you before?" The leader snarled as he grabbed his underling's instrument. "Keep your mouth shut."

But the word had already slipped out. No *rocks*. Now she knew for certain, and it made her grip the Stone even more tightly.

"Of course there are no Owlings," retorted Oriannon's father. Maybe he hadn't heard the slip, or understood it. "I told you that before. Now, if you're quite done ..."

"All right, then." Security number one clicked his instrument shut and motioned for the others to follow him to the door. "Looks like this place is clean."

Oriannon looked around the den, where the invaders had piled up blankets and furniture and wall paintings of the Trion system in large piles on the floor. A hand-spun crystal vase had been turned upside down and cerise blossoms were strewn across the floor.

"Depends on what you call clean," she replied, and this time she probably should have kept her mouth shut, the way her father had told her. Because instead of leaving, the first security turned around to face her father.

"I'd keep your daughter on a tighter leash, if I were you," he grumbled, "since all this goes in our report, and you don't want to be seen with disfavor. Even the old book. Questionable."

Her father didn't flinch, just stared straight ahead before the security finally turned to go. She kept a grip on the Stone, squeezing it so hard her fingers ached. Though she knew without doubt that's what they'd been looking for, she wondered why they had not found it.

4

He said *what?*" Oriannon's friend Margus Leek stopped in the middle of the shaded boulevard the next morning when she told him what had happened the night before. The early sun already glinted off his stringy blond hair and would soon make it too hot to stand in the street.

"Not so loud." She sidestepped a passing lev-scooter, which came close enough to raise her hair on account of its plasma field. "I'm just telling you they searched everywhere."

"But you still have it, right? Let me see. After everything you told me about Asylum 4, that's got to be some rock."

"Not here," she whispered, pausing at a corner to let a herd of small transits buzz by. Here in the heart of Seramine, the day's traffic channeled across four or five levels, through hillside tunnels and past ancient white stucco buildings topped with gleaming solar collector roofs made to look like red tiles. Brightly colored blue and green transit tubes carried small pods filled with people and products up and down the city's hillsides, opening here and there with puffs of compressed air. But wherever people were going, they all seemed to be in too much of a hurry to admire the stately curve of a streetside archway laced with climbing lonicera vines, a tiled fountain filled with bright red sargeonfish, or a tucked-away plaza paved in blue and green marble.

Yet even with all the quaint hideaways and back alleys of the city, Oriannon knew of just as many security cams and roving probes. Even more, of late. No, they would need to go somewhere else.

"Come on, Ori. After all the things we've been through these past few months?"

True, Margus was the only one who understood what had happened to her on the other side of the planet, back in Lior, back with the Owlings—and with Jesmet. Who else had seen it all? Who else would believe it?

"I know, Margus. But we can't talk about it in public."

"That's my point!" He pumped his fist impatiently. "We can't even tell anybody on this side of the planet. I mean, for all they know, Jesmet is just dead, right? Executed in the star chamber, broadcast on every media feed. Did anybody not see it? So what would people think if we started telling them we saw him over there at a party on Shadowside, and alive? How completely insane would that make us?"

She didn't have to answer; he'd made his point and they both knew it. Without a word they passed an open-air café tucked between leafy flamboyan trees covered with their signature orange blossoms and filling the air with their sweet perfume. Here lev-scooters and transports crowded the narrow transit lanes, while people crowded the terraced cafés, sipping strong, foaming cups of tea and nibbling sweet pastries. Everyone seemed to be buzzing about the searches and watching the latest media reports projected on a 3-D vapor screen inside a patio area.

"Updates now on a story that has all of Seramine talking," said Media240's news anchor, looking around at them as if she actually were sitting at a nearby table, instead of tucked away in a dark media studio. Meela Rhon's three-dimensional image hovered on cool sprays of mist. "An outlying way station in high orbit has reportedly been destroyed. We suspect Owling terrorists with ties to Jesmet ben Saius, the former mentor executed as a faithbreaker. However, swift reaction from Security forces …"

Twisted lies, all of it. The reporter went on about how the so-called terror group undermined Corista's vital water-mining efforts on Shadowside, and how Mentor Jesmet had incited the Owlings to violently resist Water Transfer Protocols, unchanged for generations. Before he'd been put to death, of course. Margus looked at her with a serious expression, arms across his wiry frame.

"The Owlings didn't blow up the station, did they?"

She shook her head, while he kept up his questions.

"And you're sure they don't know you have that Stone?"

"I plan to keep it that way, but there are probes all over here, so …" They stepped down a walkway and through a vine-covered arbor, keeping a careful eye out. "So I'll show you after school—in the Glades."

They continued on until Margus slowed and stopped for a moment to look out over the city from a balcony. She paused with him, hardly seeing the vast sweep of terraces and gardens, covered in blue haze below filmy sunlight.

"What?" she finally asked, and he seemed to swallow hard.

"You trust me now, don't you?" he finally asked, looking away. "Even after … you know."

She knew too well. Even after the way he had once betrayed Mentor Jesmet to the Assembly. Even after the Assembly had put their music teacher to death. Even after they'd been to the other side of the planet together and seen the Owlings attacked.

Of course, so much had happened since the planet had convulsed and wobbled, and since the ancient dividing line between the always sunny side of Corista and the always dim Shadowside had been breached—after Jesmet had come back. Who understood everything that had happened? Had it only been three days ago?

Three days ago she'd danced and celebrated with the Owlings, and now she couldn't forget how the celebration had marked a fresh start for everyone.

"It's all behind us," she managed to tell him. She walked backward a few steps, not realizing what was behind her. "Jesmet trusts you now. So do—"

"Oriannon! Watch it!" Margus must have seen the transit before she did; he leaped at her like a yagwar after its prey, grabbed her arm, and yanked her away.

"I'm going to fall!" Oriannon laughed as the circle of dancers picked up speed, faster and faster, spinning in circles across the grand plaza of Lior, the Owling cliffside city. A warming Shadowside breeze had caught her in the face, making her smile, and she'd caught the scents of flowers and grasses coming alive.

Just like her.

Owling girls were on either side of her—her friend Wist and a cousin. They all laughed and managed to keep up, tripping and giggling and singing songs about the return of the Living One and what a day that would be. Wist's long black hair flew out behind her, and the Owling girls seemed to know the words, as if they'd been singing the song all their lives.

Well, and hadn't he returned, just as the Codex said?

"We are celebrating . . ." The lyrics tangled on Oriannon's tongue as she tried to follow the wonderfully intricate ancient melody, tried to match their distinctly musical accent. The tune rippled and rose, bubbling and sprightly and full of joy.

There could be no mistaking their meaning this time. Because the Living One, Jesmet ben Saius, danced with them today as never before, though he certainly wasn't like this when he served as an ordinary music mentor at the Jib Ossek Preparatory Academy. Now, though, it seemed as if he had created every rhyme, every tune, every step . . . just for this occasion.

Never mind all that he'd been through in the weeks leading up to this grand celebration that spontaneously spilled out onto Lior's grand plaza, its largest gathering place. Now the music of laughter echoed from every wall of their cliff city, as if daring the barren plains far below to celebrate. Newly lit bonfires crackled and blazed from copper urns set on every rooftop, bright even in the virgin sunshine. Festive garlands of woven myrtling sprigs graced arched doorways and tiny patios, decorating the air with a spiced, nose-tickling scent.

"The Living One . . ." Owlings of all sizes clapped and sang from their shops and studios, even from their tiny whitewashed apartments — most of which seemed plastered to the sheer cliff walls, piled on top of each other and carved into solid rock. Narrow passages ran between the whitewashed adobe buildings, sometimes widening out enough to provide a level open walkway, other times disappearing back beneath canopies or into the cliffs for safety. But everywhere laughter rang throughout the bright new face of Lior, connecting its Owling people with the reason they celebrated. Even the snow-white hunting owls had been let loose for the occasion, and they looped about, high overhead, watching their masters spin themselves dizzy with joy.

What choice did they have? What else could these people do but celebrate when they sighted Mentor Jesmet walking across the Shadowside plains, alive, the rising suns at his back for the very first time?

He had survived, and perhaps he would explain exactly how someday. For now, though, Oriannon supposed these Owlings probably had every right to call him what they liked, as they danced their hearts out — holding hands, twirling in circles, skipping sideways, and hands lifted to the sky . . .

No, such a thing had never been allowed back home — never been dreamed of! Here, though, even Margus was catching on, a little clumsy at first, but making up for it with enthusiasm. From across the square she heard him whoop as his line of dancers crossed under the outstretched arms of another, all in time to the haunting, celebratory songs that would never again leave her head. How did they do it all at the same time?

"Time out." Oriannon finally broke free of her circle, gasping for breath as she stepped over to lean against a stone wall on the edge of the city square. She could follow the celebration better from here, and she watched as the three distant suns cast their golden shadows across

Lior for the first time in generations, across lands wholly unaccustomed to the brightness of sunlight and the warmth of brightness. It lit up the stones with a warm yellow glow as the people danced and sang.

As Regev, Saius, and Heliaan lit up the sky, she could think of no better way for the Owlings to celebrate, even if she didn't recognize the songs — or the ancient words. She had seen them on parchment before, just never heard them spoken aloud, much less sung. Now these words resonated in her heart as they came to life in the lilting minor keys of these sad-eyed people, only now not nearly so sad as they had been when they'd been living in the always dark.

"Come on, Ori." Wist joined her and tugged at her hand once more. The Owling girl's large brown eyes sparkled an invitation, but Oriannon could only shake her head no.

"You go ahead." Her chest still heaved. "Let me just rest for a couple more minutes."

"What's the matter, don't you ever dance on your side of the planet?"

Again Oriannon felt the playful tug, the challenge. Wist and her Owling people might be small, Oriannon had discovered, but they still had a whole lot more energy than she ever did.

"You know we don't," answered Oriannon. "Not like this."

"Oh, that's right. I remember you told me. No Chanak and no Feast of Dor, not even the Seven Days of Toradin! I don't know how you people can read your Codex but not know when to be celebrating."

"I don't know either." By this time Oriannon was getting used to Wist's good-natured teasing, though she did wonder why her people had never followed the festivals like the Owlings. This time she knew what Wist would say next.

"Well, you know what Jesmet was saying about the difference between reading and —"

"And understanding," Oriannon finished the quote. She turned to watch the dancers once again. Her bearded music teacher stood in the middle of the crowd with his ear-to-ear smile, hands raised, clapping in time to the singing. Or perhaps they sang in time to his clapping, because just as he had back in her music class, he kept a perfect beat. Wist linked her arms around Oriannon's elbow and leaned a little closer.

"I wish you'd be telling me more about what happened," she said, and then she must have felt Oriannon stiffen at the prospect of reliving the nightmare she'd lived through. "I mean, when you want. You don't have to right now."

Oriannon untangled herself and tried to look casual, though she wasn't quite sure how to tell anyone about what she and Margus had been through at Ossek Prep Academy. Like the time her girlfriend Brinnin Flyer had fallen from a tall ladder and died, and Mentor Jesmet stepped over and pulled Brinnin up by the hand — alive. Who could explain that? And who would try to explain what Mentor Jesmet was doing here in Lior, dancing and singing, after he'd been executed in a star chamber, in front of thousands and thousands of Coristans? She wished she didn't remember that part so well.

"You know they put him to death." Oriannon finally whispered, and her friend nodded. "But you know why?"

"They were calling him a faithbreaker." So Wist knew more than Oriannon expected. A faithbreaker — one who opposed the teachings of the Codex, the way the Elders interpreted them. Despite all the dancing and celebrating, despite all the cheering now about Jesmet the Living One, Oriannon still wrestled to sort it out.

"That was only part of it. The way he talked about the Maker, like he actually knew him? I don't think the Elders liked that. I know my father didn't. That's why they banished him."

Again Wist nodded, and she rested a hand on Oriannon's shoulder as if she knew what was coming. Here in this little city where buildings didn't fall to the ravine below but clung to the sheer face of the cliff almost by faith . . . well, the Owlings turned out to be pretty good at the faith thing.

Oriannon wasn't so sure about her own people back in Corista — despite their Temple with the beautiful spires and the moor-doves that flew about the way they probably would in the hereafter. Back home in Corista, faith meant something entirely different — an indescribable something that surrounded the Temple like the heady smell of incense that clung to her father's robes. As a little girl she had sneaked one of his robes to bed with her, just so she could snuggle under the scent of the Temple.

There she'd wanted to believe, once. Why else would she memorize every word of the Codex and all its hundreds of pages? But here they actually lived the book, and here they celebrated as if their lives depended on it. Here they sang and danced with each other; here she believed.

What would happen when she had to go back home?

She didn't really want to know, and she didn't realize that tears ran down her cheeks until Wist squeezed her, her arm around Oriannon's shoulders.

"He knew he would be sentenced to death if he ever came back to Corista," Oriannon said. She sniffled and ran the back of her hand across her nose. "He knew. But when he saw the yagwar attack me, he came running. Straight across the border. Right into their trap. It was all my fault."

Wist didn't seem surprised.

"But you see how it turned out?" She gave Oriannon another squeeze and waved at the dancing crowd. The dancers now stepped into an intricate set of moves, like a beautiful colored tapestry in motion. "Jesmet always turns it around."

"Okay, but listen." Oriannon hated to be serious at a time like this, but she couldn't help it. She held her friend's attention as Wist gave her an amused look. "Seriously. We're dancing today, but if anything bad ever happens — "

"Don't get morbid on me, Ori. Not now. This is a party, remember?"

"No, let me finish. All I'm saying is that if anything bad happens, we're going to stick together, right? I'll always be here for you, no matter what. I'll come back. I want you to know that."

"Of course." Wist smiled, but with none of the heaviness Oriannon felt. "That goes both ways."

46

"Promise?" Oriannon held up a hand, and Wist matched it with hers, palm-to-palm.

"My life for yours," Wist responded. And when Oriannon echoed the words, her spine tingled. She knew she could do no less. But a moment later, yet another Owling relative dragged Wist back into the dancing ring, and it was back to celebrating. The clapping now sounded louder than ever.

"Coming?" Wist asked over her shoulder, her eyes sparkling.

"In a minute."

Oriannon nodded in time as she watched the celebration, listened to the beautiful singing with levels of harmony she'd never heard before. She didn't want to feel gloomy and contemplative in the middle of all this celebration. But before long she thought she heard something else — a low rumble at first, then louder. It came from somewhere behind them, higher, and behind the top of the cliff. She looked up and saw the unmistakable colors of the Corista Ruling Assembly painted across the gleaming silver alum-lithium of a shuttle, the violet stripe overset with the three familiar golden star-suns of the Trion. Unannounced and unin-vited, Corista's most powerful men and women had come calling, and their arrival cast an instant damper on the celebration.

Clapping tapered off and voices faltered as the entire city paused to watch. Almost in a panic, Owling hunters called back their birds with shrill whistles, and mothers gathered their children with shouts. As the sleek craft's landing thrusters cut in, it drifted slowly past the city, almost as if suspended on a leash, on its way to a landing spot at the foot of the cliff. As it did, Oriannon thought she caught a glimpse of a familiar face peering out a viewport at them. She could not be completely sure, but even at a distance she believed it so.

47

"Father," she whispered. The shuttle blocked out the suns for just a moment, casting a huge shadow over the celebration.

Oriannon couldn't help shivering.

"Are you okay, Ori?" Margus helped her to her feet as she dusted herself off. The two-seat transit that had knocked her down had already disappeared down the lane, not slowing down at all. "I thought you were going to step backward right in front of it!"

"Almost, but not quite. Thanks." She smiled and rubbed her shoulder. Better pay attention next time. But now she looked up.

"Look at that!" said a passing man, pointing at the darkened sky. A dozen lights flickered on without warning, like stars but far brighter. Moments later the sky was filled with floodlights, casting new light on both the gathering crowd and the surrounding city. Before long, new stars grew too bright to look at directly.

"Coristan Security reports that reflective satellites are just now coming on line ..." A media announcer's voice drifted out to the street, where people here and there applauded spontaneously. "Bringing back some of the day-round brightness we were used to here in Corista. There is no danger to anyone on the surface. However, the light will continue to be adjusted as new satellites are brought on line and others are repositioned. Until orbits are stabilized, schools and many businesses remain closed as part of a mandatory planning period ordered by Coristan Security."

Oriannon didn't miss the irony of this moment. The satellites that had once focused Trion's rays on a single spot to take away Mentor Jesmet's life now spread the same light across the surface of her planet, bringing brightness where there was darkness.

She almost preferred the dark.

5.

The next day Oriannon quickened her pace past their empty school building, past terraced flower gardens and pools accented by rippling fountains, and past the sign that read, Restricted Access: By Permission Only.

She and Margus kept to the shadows, and she glanced around to be sure they hadn't been noticed by the school's security probes. She prayed they would not set off any proximity alarms with their steps or their voices.

"You have it, right?" asked Margus, his voice lowered.

"Wait until we get inside the Glades."

Just to be sure, she slipped her hand into the pocket of her tunic where she'd kept the Pilot Stone safe these past several days.

"And you told them to meet us?" he wondered again.

"They'll be there."

Oriannon did her best to sound sure of herself, even as she tiptoed over a garden path of crushed pink rock that would take them past reflecting pools and flower gardens behind the school and deeper into the Glades—a circular buffer of thick, watered forestland. Where else could they go? These hectares of wild gardens and fern grottoes, overgrown stands of elephant leaf and wild orchids would provide a safer place to meet the others ... and decide what to do next. "Hold up." Margus paused to adjust the volume on a wafer-thin comm nested in the sleeve of his green jersey. "You're going to want to hear this."

Now? He tapped a tiny button to up the volume so they could both hear, just barely.

" ... Security officials are raising their alert status after credible reports have come to light of a plot to attack Coristan public facilities. According to Sola Minnik of Central Security ..."

"I've heard that name before." Oriannon wrinkled her nose, thinking back to the time she'd overheard her father.

" ... an Owling terror cell has apparently stolen the body of convicted faithbreaker Jesmet ben Saius, whose body is now believed to be at the center of a strange but dangerous cult."

"Stolen the body!" Oriannon couldn't believe what she heard. "How can they think that?"

"In related developments," continued the reporter, "officials are still working to confirm the identities of Owling hijackers who commandeered a Ruling Assembly shuttle returning from the earthquake-damaged Owling capital where they were rendering humanitarian aid. Eyewitnesses say—"

Oriannon leaned in to hear better, while Margus tapped the volume button just a little more. In response, a high-pitched alarm sounded from the direction of the school building.

"They heard us!" Margus instantly snapped off his comm. They both knew one of the school probes would be sent out to investigate.

"Sorry!" Oriannon whispered, knowing it was just as much her fault as his. They shouldn't have stopped so close to the school. She motioned with two fingers for them to separate, and Margus nodded.

"Meet you there!" Without another word, he ducked around a bush and disappeared into the gardens.

Oriannon wasn't in the mood to deal with another curious probe, so she sprinted in the opposite direction, around a patch of furry ferns and into heavy underbrush that grabbed at her ankles. Was that the sound of an approaching probe behind her? She didn't want to look back as she pressed on. But a minute later a root caught her toe, sending her sprawling.

Ohhh ... she groaned at the pain that shot up her ankle, and she rolled once before struggling back to her feet. If a probe was after her and not Margus, it might be upon her by now. And how would she explain what she was doing?

Oh, just out for a walk. We're terrorist sympathizers, and we're just looking for ways to help the Owlings.

But now she had another problem—not being able to put much weight on her right ankle. Pain like fire brought tears to her eyes, but she gulped and hobbled on. The good news was that the clearing was just ahead—though she hardly wanted to lead a probe to where Margus, Brinnin, and Carrick were probably waiting. Breathing hard, she flattened herself behind an ancient flowering flamboyan tree and listened.

The faint sound of a tree frog's *co-kee* made her jump, but she held her breathing steady and didn't move. A soft breeze rustled leaves around her, and she filled her lungs with damp, heavy air.

There! From somewhere up in the high, leafy canopy, a pair of viria burst into exuberant song, filling the Glades with music. From even higher above, reflected light from the satellite mirrors filtered through the trees like artificial sunlight. From back in the direction of the school, Oriannon thought she heard a distant crashing, as if someone else had followed her into the underbrush.

"Margus?" Oriannon took a chance at calling out, then held her breath as she listened for an answer.

Nothing. She counted to sixty before moving out from the shelter of the giant tree trunk, even as the viria continued to serenade her. She winced again at the pain of her turned ankle, but managed to hop toward the clearing once again. Maybe the crashing was just an animal of some sort, a little razor-toothed treb bear, which when threatened could turn nasty indeed. Out of habit she checked her pocket once again for the Stone, then froze.

Where is it?

"Oh, no!" She turned her pockets inside out, forgetting for a moment who — or what — might be following her. "I can't believe I lost it."

Without hesitating, she limped back the way she came, eyes glued to the forest floor, not caring who might catch up with her but only looking for the gleam of the Stone. Oh, but it could be anywhere!

Five minutes later she fell to her knees at the spot where she'd tripped. She sifted through leaves and sticks and slimy mossy things. The approaching footsteps no longer mattered, not compared to the missing Stone. A small brown terramole eyed her from its perch on a tree trunk, turning its head from side to side and swiveling its eyes at her in the way only lizards can.

"Don't just sit there," she whispered, blowing a wisp of hair from her face. Her heart raced faster and faster. "Help me find it."

Instead the terramole skittered away at the sound of approaching footsteps. Oriannon looked desperately for a way to follow the terramole into his little hole in the ground. Of course she wasn't quick enough; before she could dive for cover, a pair of legs came to a stop right in front of her. She almost couldn't look up, but when she finally did, she couldn't hold back the gasp.

"What are you doing here?" she whispered. His face appeared scarred and mottled behind his dark beard, and he wore the same plain gray Owling robe he'd worn the other day at the celebration. The only thing that hadn't changed since he had been their mentor back at Ossek Prep were his eyes — deep blue, smiling, sparkling — as if they might see through anyone he looked at.

"What else would I be doing?" Mentor Jesmet smiled as he rested his hands on his knees and looked down at her. "Looking for you."

Which could not have been true, but Oriannon surely wasn't going to argue with him as he straightened up. She could have asked him a thousand questions, but a part of her couldn't even be sure this was even a real man. Had he really danced with the Owlings on the other side of their planet back in Lior? But that was the point, because Oriannon knew there was no way he could have traveled all this way so quickly, unless he'd ridden a shuttle. Right now that seemed as unlikely as the fact that she was seeing him here and now.

"Speaking of looking," he added with a little nod of his head, "you might want to look over there, instead."

She followed his glance and wondered, *How would he know that?* But once more she bit her tongue, holding back the flood of questions. In the past couple of weeks she had already seen much stranger things than this, and she had a feeling things might yet get even stranger.

"Go ahead," he urged her, pointing now at a thick bramble of roots and decayed leaves. "Trust me."

But he could not have known, and he could not have seen. No one could have. Still, she could not believe she was actually following his directions and reaching into a hollow.

Yet that was not the half of it. Because as soon as her hand closed around the Stone, she knew without even looking that she had found it. Its peculiar warmth and its distant songs shot through her hand and up her arm, once again calling to mind something much, much deeper than just a sliver of rock with a temperature. But whatever had brought this Stone alive would still only dance on the fringes of her knowing, as if it had a mind of its own, and she had no idea how to coax it any closer.

"Hey!" She nearly burst out laughing before catching herself. "I found ..."

Her voice trailed off, and she was again left wondering what had just happened, or how. But Mentor Jesmet had already started out the way she'd come. He paused only a moment to look over his shoulder.

"You found it? Good. I didn't think you'd want to lose it. The others are waiting. Oh, and don't worry about that ankle. I'm sure it will be fine now."

"Uh ..." She stood there with the Pilot Stone in her hand, working hard to wipe the sheepish grin off her face. A glance back at the path told her no security had yet arrived, and no probe. Just this man who had once been her music mentor—and very dead besides. And was she going to follow him deeper into the Glades, perhaps all the way to the Outlying? Well, yes, as a matter of fact.

"I'm coming!" She hurried after him, forgetting all her earlier plans and pains. What mattered anymore? She just wondered how the others' faces would look when the two of them stepped into the clearing.

She didn't have to wonder long, and she covered a grin to see the same slack-jawed expression from Margus. Funny how much she enjoyed seeing his shock, though she was only a few short minutes past the same reaction herself.

Brinnin, on the other hand, stood with her back turned. She raised her arms the way she did when she was ready to bawl someone out.

"What happened to you?" she asked, pivoting slowly and flipping back her shoulder-length hair with that usual sideways expression of hers. "We thought you were never going to—"

Before she could turn all the way, she caught sight of who now stood in the clearing, while Mentor Jesmet acted as if he'd just shown up for a picnic. Which, come to think of it, perhaps he had. A white-faced Carrick gathered up the four ripe aplons that had rolled out of her hands and looked totally confused.

"Oriannon told us," she squeaked, "but I didn't believe it."

"So good to see you." Mentor Jesmet stepped up to greet them. "I must admit that for once I'm glad you're thinking about lunch,

Carrick. Of course, you're always thinking about lunch, aren't you? Is anyone else as hungry as I am?"

"I don't know about you three." An hour later Carrick wasn't afraid to offer her opinions. "But I'm still confused about what he said back there. And slow down, Ori, I'm getting a side ache."

Oriannon slowed her steps as they continued single-file down the path between overhanging yoob tree branches laced with thorns and seed pods. Though Jesmet had left them only minutes ago, his words still swam in her head.

Tell Corista what you've seen.

Only how? She offered an opinion over her shoulder. "I think he was just telling us to be ready for what's about to happen."

"The question is," replied Carrick, "what's about to happen?"

Margus had a ready answer.

"They're going to find Oriannon's Pilot Stone, and we're going to be arrested for hanging around with Mentor Jesmet and his Owling terrorists."

"What?" Oriannon paused in a small clearing and turned to face the others, her hands parked on her hips. "After all this, and that's all you can say? Whatever happened to 'no worries'?"

"I'm just kidding." He shrugged. "But you heard what the media said about terror cells and strange but dangerous cults."

"You're strange," Carrick pointed first at Margus, then at Oriannon. "And you're dangerous."

"Get serious, Carrick." This time Brinnin spoke up. "Margus is right."

"I am?" Margus looked surprised. He snapped a bitter yoob seed in his mouth to chew.

"Yeah. Either we run back home to hide and pretend everything Mentor Jesmet told us about the Maker was a joke, or ..." They all looked at Brinnin as she paused to finish her thought. "Or we go out and tell people the truth."

"About ...?" Carrick wanted to know.

"About Jesmet, about the Owlings. *Someone* has to." Brinnin's challenge hung in the thick garden air, daring them to answer. An unseen bird twittered from a nearby branch, and Carrick tilted her head to the side as if she still didn't get it.

"Okay, but what about this: Even if people did believe us—and I don't see why they would—I still don't see how he could walk away from that execution. You know what I mean? Maybe it wasn't him that was cremated alive in the star chamber after all. Or maybe we just had lunch with a wraith."

"You know he's not a wraith, Care." Brinnin shook her head. "Wraiths don't eat three aplons and a cirit-bun. Wraiths don't have lunch with their former orchestra students. And everybody in the world saw the execution. Ori and Margus were in the front row. They should know."

Margus frowned and sniffed at the aplon core in his hand before finally pitching it into the bushes.

Carrick wasn't done wondering. "Okay, but what about the Numa stuff?"

This time Brinnin looked to Oriannon for help.

"Well ..." Oriannon picked at the yoob tree's rough bark, collecting her thoughts. "The way I heard him, Mentor Jesmet said that Numa is like a breath from the Maker, only it really *is* the Maker ..."

Carrick groaned and brought a palm to her forehead.

"That's what I thought he said. This is so totally strange, it gives me a headache. Am I really the only one who doesn't get this?"

"None of us really gets it, Carrick," said Brinnin.

"But the other thing is," said Oriannon, "we're supposed to wait, not go anywhere until it comes."

Of course that explained ... not much. Besides that, Oriannon still wasn't sure what the Pilot Stone was all about, only that she still had to keep it hidden. They stood in silence for a few long moments, until Margus spoke up again.

"Well, that's okay for you girls." He took the lead this time, pushing aside branches and holding them so they could all pass more easily. "But I'm not into waiting. I say we *do* something while we're waiting."

"Like what?" asked Carrick. He had an answer for that too.

"Get on the media, maybe." Margus shrugged. "Any better ideas?"

Oriannon wasn't sure how to answer . . . until she felt the Stone in her pocket.

"I just can't help thinking." She let the warmth climb through her hand once more. "Don't you think it all fits together somehow? The Stone, what happened on Asylum 4 with Cirrus Main, Jesmet being here . . . there has to be a connection, right?"

"Maybe, maybe not," said Margus. "But if this Numa is really as important as he says, he wouldn't be asking us to just sit around. *Important* means urgent, and *urgent* means now."

Brinnin and Carrick seemed to buy the argument, and maybe Margus was right. He jabbed at the air to make his point. "All I know is we need a plan. That's what I think Mentor Jesmet would want us to do. Otherwise, we're just—"

Oriannon couldn't make out his next words. Through the green canopy overhead she counted three jet-black Coristan Security craft, maybe more, streaking over the treetops, low and loud. Trees shook all around them, scattering a flock of birds, while leaves swirled in all directions.

"Stay low!" shouted Carrick, crouching behind a tree. Her short dark hair stood on end, and Oriannon choked on the overpowering sulfur smell of the exhaust from the ion engines. But no one had a chance to move before the ships made another pass. No doubt they were looking for someone—and getting closer to finding them.

"We need to get out of here!" Margus screamed in her ear, and she could barely hear him over the roar of engines. Two of the craft slowed to a hover almost directly overhead, while Brinnin grabbed Oriannon's hand and nodded toward the path ahead. From here it wound through a thick copse of low-hanging trees, a tunnel through the woods. Even Carrick got the idea, and she held up a hand before turning away in the opposite direction.

"I'll go with her!" shouted Margus. A branch shattered overhead, causing them to duck as more leaves flew in all directions. But Oriannon held on, and they dove for cover away from the roar. Margus yelled something about "tomorrow," but she couldn't be sure.

All she cared about now was getting away.

esterday was just a start." Margus craned his neck to watch another ten shuttles roar past the tall triple spires of the Coristan Temple, obviously in a hurry to get to where they were going. "And don't look now, but there's a whole lot more probes up ahead."

"I see them." Oriannon clutched her package more tightly and lowered her voice as they neared the Temple gates, the doors through which they would approach a maze of peaceful garden courtyards clustered below the sparkling white Temple. Above their heads moordoves looked for a place to land on the red tile roofs or in the towers, disturbed by all the bustling traffic above and below.

In fact, she had never seen so many probes buzzing about, stopping people on the city street and scanning them for identification. Never seen so many securities, either, always in their intimidating black helmets. Some raced about in lev-scooters, others patrolled on foot in twos and threes. Of course they all carried a brutish and potentially deadly stun baton.

But Oriannon just lowered her head. Securities would not stop her.

"No worries," he told her.

"Who's worried?"

To prove it, she led the way to the main gate in the Temple courtyard wall, still clutching her package, not even checking to see if Margus followed. He could come, or not. Maybe it would have been better if he'd stayed home. But as it turned out, it really didn't seem to matter one way or the other to the probes that stopped them at the gate that had just been added in front of the ancient double doors always left open before.

"Name and purpose." The one-eyed probe hovered in front of her face, instantly scanning her eyes before she could flinch. It would know who she was before she could even mouth the words "Hightower of Nyssa, Oriannon, 9907–2236–0021." The scan stung more than it should have, between the eyes and then across the temples. She raised her hands in self-defense, but by that time two more probes came from behind to encircle her. She couldn't move more than a few centimeters without bumping into one of them. A glance to the side revealed that Margus had been surrounded in the same way. She could do nothing to help him either.

"Hey, back off," he sputtered. "We're just here to bring her dad some lunch, okay?"

Oriannon waited quietly while the probes scanned her package. She held it out in front of her and felt more than ever like a prisoner. Something had gone way wrong. This was the city where she had grown up.

I don't recognize this place anymore.

She was fairly sure the probes couldn't read her thoughts. Not the way Margus once did when they'd still had their thought transceivers, before they'd lost them on Shadowside. And not the way Jesmet had, even without the transceivers.

Or could they? She closed her eyes and waited, willing herself to think of something else, just in case. But when she could not stop the memories from popping into her mind, she decided instead to think of a song, the words of which would drown out everything else.

Unfortunately, the only song that came to mind was one Mentor Jesmet had sung, and she snapped her eyes open in time to see the lead probe pull away to the side while the gate slid open with a hiss of air.

"You may proceed," said the probe. The door nearly caught her heels when she stepped through.

"Wait a minute," she objected. "My friend."

"Your friend will wait." The probe led the way through a tiled courtyard, and she stepped across an alternating pattern of rose and gold tiles set with tiny glittering stones that reminded her of the stars she had never really seen until she visited Shadowside. She wondered who had set the tiles in place and how long ago.

"This way!" The probe took her past manicured plumeria bushes framing an ornate stone fountain set in the exact center of the courtyard. A cool curtain of spray issued through the opened mouth of a life-sized carved yagwar, and Oriannon could imagine every detail of the real thing, from its thick black fur and its two rows of wicked-sharp teeth, to its glassy, red-orange eyes that hypnotized its prey. She shivered at the way it crouched in the waters—even if it was only stone.

Beyond the fountain, a vine-covered breezeway led into the part of the Temple where her father and the eleven other Assembly elders usually met. But along the way she was stopped two more times, each time forced to recite her name and ID number. And each time the laser scan made her wince more than the first. Finally they reached the tall chamber doors, but she hardly recognized the gaunt man standing in the hallway outside.

"Father?" She shivered, waiting for him to open his eyes. Had he really grown so thin in just the past two days? He rubbed the stubble on his face and gazed at her from behind the dark circles under his eyes.

"You shouldn't have come here," he managed, his voice hoarse. The probe hovered nearby, no doubt recording every word.

"Why not?" She looked around for a clue, but they were alone in the long marble hallway. Alone, except for the probe. Her father rubbed his forehead and sighed, but didn't answer her question.

"I'm sorry, Ori. Is Mrs. Eraz taking care of you? Are you getting enough to eat?"

"I'm fine. You know they cancelled school for a couple of days, until things settle down." He acted surprised, raising his eyebrows, but she also noticed how he glanced at the probe without moving his head.

"Hmm, well look, I'm very sorry you've had to go through this. We've been meeting around the clock, but I'll be home soon. We'll get this straightened out."

Still he didn't explain further, so she held out her small parcel.

"I didn't know if you were able to get anything to eat here. And since you hadn't been home, I brought you some biscuits and jam. Hope they're not stale."

He nodded as he accepted the package and offered a wan smile, dead weary from whatever he had been through in the past several days. The weight of it seemed to hang on his face, his dropped shoulders.

"Father." She lowered her voice, knowing the probe would still be able to hear every whispered word. "Can't you tell me what's going on? All the new security doors. The probes. And they're so much nastier than before. The eye scans hurt. Are you all right here?"

"Of course I'm all right," he answered a little too quickly, and his weak smile remained unconvincing. Oriannon could have cried to see her father like this, and she wanted to tell him everything she'd seen in the past week. Everything about Jesmet—what her mentor had said and done, from strange to stranger. Just the fact that Jesmet was alive was, well, strange enough. Even in front of the probe, and even after what her father had once said about Jesmet, she wanted to spill everything right then and there. But her father's wristband glowed amber. In an unguarded moment she saw him wince and look back toward the door.

"That's my summons; I've got to get back to the Chambers." He patted her cheek and smiled again. "Thanks for the snack."

She looked at his eyes and tried to understand what he would not say. But his wristband glowed once more, and he turned away.

"We're working on a big humanitarian project, honey, after all the earthquakes on Shadowside. I'll tell you more when I can."

There was that word again — *humanitarian*. She wondered what was so humanitarian about security checks and media reports, even about canceling classes. She wondered what was so humanitarian about the haunted look on her father's face.

"Father." She would try once more; never mind the probe. "I'm scared. I've never seen you like this before."

For a moment he paused, leaning against the door frame and rubbing his forehead. He opened his mouth as if to tell her something, then changed his mind as a clicking of heels and a hubbub of voices echoed from down the hall. Instead he reached out and pulled his daughter close.

"Don't say anything," he whispered, as if he knew exactly who approached. A small crowd of media types and Temple officials reached their door. Oriannon couldn't help noticing the young woman in the center of all the attention — attractive and bright eyed, tall and well dressed in a trim-fitting black tunic and with her bright red hair, not at all like the bleary-eyed men with robes that made up most of the Temple staff and Assembly elders. She couldn't have been more than thirty-five years old, a few years younger than Oriannon's father, though with her perfect skin and perfect face it was a little hard to tell. What's more, she wore an infectious smile that had already rubbed off on all those around her. She didn't wait for an introduction.

"This is inspired. Absolutely perfect!" Her smile grew even warmer when she turned away from the others to squarely face

Oriannon. "You must be Elder Hightower's daughter. Oriannon, is it? I simply love that name, and he's told me so much about you."

"He has?" Oriannon shook the woman's outstretched hand and wondered what was so absolutely perfect and how this stranger had heard of her—all the while fully aware that at least ten media cams focused directly on them. At the same time she couldn't help feeling as if she and this young woman were the only two people in the hallway. What was going on? Oriannon looked quickly at her father for a clue, but he had already been blocked out by several of the media people.

"I'm sorry." The woman talked to Ori as if she was an old friend. "My name is Sola Minnik, Special Security Counsel to the Assembly elders. They've asked me to help them think through the current crisis; come up with fresh solutions. We're reinventing ourselves in a sense."

Though she spoke directly to Oriannon, the words were loud enough for all the media cameras to record every word. Flashing red lights on every cam told her they weren't missing a thing.

"Good to meet you," Oriannon managed to squeak out the words. Like a politician, it took several more moments for Sola to release her grip on Ori's hand. When she did, she caught her breath, looked away for a moment, then focused back on Oriannon.

"I hope I don't startle you by saying this, Ori, but I believe we're meeting like this for a reason. Don't you feel that too? I was just coming to the Assembly chambers for a press conference, but this is even better. Nothing ever happens by chance, you know."

Oriannon heard cam lenses zooming in, recording the encounter. Though no one called her Ori except her father and her best friends, Ori smiled back and nodded. A reason? Nothing by chance? This sounded just like something Jesmet might have said. And Sola Minnik was going to tell them what she meant, after Oriannon stuttered and tried to say something intelligent.

"Here for a reason. Sure. Uh … you mean, to bring my dad his lunch?"

The media people all laughed, and no one laughed harder than Sola, who slipped an arm around Oriannon's shoulder and straightened the two of them slightly toward the cams.

"That too. But you've been to Shadowside and back. And today you can help us discover the goodness in everyone on the planet. Right, Ori?"

Well, of course. Sola paused. Oriannon had no choice but to say yes. She did agree, anyway. Sola addressed the cams like a seasoned leader before a cheering crowd. The funny thing was, Oriannon felt as if every word was meant for her, and it warmed her almost the same way as when Jesmet spoke, only in a little different way. She wondered if her own mother might have been anything like this, had she lived. Maybe, yes. For a moment it felt good, very good, to let down her defenses and just nod at Sola's words.

"It's because of people like Ori that we're building new policies that offer assistance, security, and opportunity for all Coristans. We see young people on the streets today, looking for better answers, and I don't blame them. So we'll be outlining our new policy in the next few days at a planet-wide conference called *Peace Begins Here.* Young people want to see one Corista, not a divided planet. But the bottom line is we're saying there's a place for everyone — for Coristans and for the Owlings as well."

Applause broke out, and Oriannon realized for the first time how large of a crowd had gathered in the wide hallway, just outside the ring of media cams. Where had they all come from, and how had they crossed Security to get here? She looked over at her father, who stood to the side and who had closed his eyes once again.

Oriannon knew it was just a quick first impression, but already she was certain she liked Sola Minnik very much. After all, Sola was obviously nothing like the older men on the Assembly. The only other person remotely like Sola was Jesmet himself, though Oriannon would never dare to compare the two—except that Sola was here and Jesmet was ... not. She guessed he might like her though. What was not to like? Surely he would like what she was saying about making peace with the Owlings. Even so, the woman's next announcement caught Oriannon off balance.

"Now, I said you're here for a reason, Ori, and here's the rest of the story. Neither of us planned this, did we? But I happen to believe in destiny. I believe destiny put you here in this hallway just now. And since you are both a respected Assembly elder's daughter and one of the only people in Corista to have actually spent time living with the Owling people, we need your perspective—and your insight."

She paused for effect as the crowd leaned closer, and the entire hallway crowd hushed.

"We need young people like you to help us build a new society. One where we leave violence behind, and where the Owlings are treated with the kind of care and friendship they deserve. After all, you are—this is—the future of our planet. Peace begins here!"

With that she took Oriannon's hand and raised it in the air to the enthusiastic applause of the gathered crowd. Though her heart beat wildly at the shock of what was happening and her cheeks flushed in embarrassment, Oriannon couldn't help smiling as broadly as did Sola Minnik.

Finally here was someone important who made sense in all this craziness. Maybe Sola was even an answer to her prayers. Didn't the Maker work this way? With serendipity? Just like that?

She should have known! Oriannon smiled at her father, who had worked his way clear by this time, and who was politely putting his hands together, but without the same fervor of the crowd. What was that in his eye? He smiled and waved at her, but she couldn't quite read the look.

Maybe he was just tired from all his meetings, and he still had more to come. He nearly stumbled as the crowd around him pressed through the double doors like a tide, sweeping him into the Assembly chambers. Oriannon hugged the amber-stained paneling as the people moved by, but Sola managed to turn once more and catch her eye.

"You'll be at the conference next week." She smiled again, and Oriannon couldn't help but nod. Of course! It was not a question. "Remember: Nothing by chance."

7

I totally don't understand, Margus." Oriannon turned to face her friend as they walked away from the fortified Temple gate. "You're the one who said we had to do something. Now I'm doing something, and you say you're not so sure."

"Yeah, I know." He sighed and paced around her with his arms crossed and pointed with his chin toward a nearby outdoor monitor. "I saw everything on the screen, and you looked like an android with a pasted-on smile."

"You don't get it," she told him. "Nothing happens by chance. Didn't Jesmet tell us that?"

Actually, those were Sola's words, and she knew it for a fact even if Margus didn't. But the point was, they might just as well have been. She put out an arm to hold him back from stepping right out into traffic on Jib Ossek Way.

"You tell me." He kept his arms crossed and didn't back down. "Whatever happened to 'We have to wait, the way Jesmet told us'? All of a sudden Sola walks up to you and says you're her girl, and now you're going to a peace conference. Does that sound right to you?"

69

She chewed on the question for a moment. This time it didn't seem to matter much that a couple of probes hovered nearby. Hadn't everyone in Corista just watched her and Sola on a special Media report? Margus added with another question of his own.

"I guess I don't understand what you're trying to prove, Oriannon."

"Who says I'm trying to prove anything?" she snapped, and Margus backed off as they continued down a narrow walkway, weaving around mid-day shoppers and workers out for lunch.

"Okay, let me put it this way. We go to the Temple to bring your dad his lunch, some stranger walks up to you, and you totally jump on board, trade in everything you were saying before about waiting."

"But that's just it. She's not a stranger, and I didn't trade in anything."

"Well, what do you know about her?"

"Uh ... I don't think she has a family or anything like that. But she treats me like a sister, and when she says things, it all just ... clicks."

"Didn't it click with Jesmet?"

"Of course it did, but ..." She sighed. How could she explain that Sola seemed to be doing everything Jesmet told them? "You don't understand."

"I understand it's like you did a complete one eighty in the space of a half hour." He pointed back in the direction of the Tem-

ple. "Are you even the same person who walked into the Temple courtyard?"

Well, that seemed like an overly dramatic way to put it. She glanced up at the media screen mounted under the awning of a sweet-smelling fruit market. She watched the replays of Sola walking down the Temple hallways with her people, watched the scene where she and Sola held up their hands to the cheers of the crowd, and she liked the funny kind of butterflies she had felt at that moment. She liked them much better than she might have guessed.

"Ori?" Margus asked again with a wave of his hand, trying to get her attention.

"Yeah." She picked up a fuzzy green loanfruit, inhaled its aroma, and set it back in the stacked display before a tiny market probe with a basket could float over to help. "I mean, no. I don't know if I really am the same. I know you think it sounds silly, but I think I was meant to be standing there, right at that time."

"Sounds more like a set-up to me."

"You're so cynical, and she's just trying to do the right thing. You weren't there."

"I still think you need to be careful, Oriannon. I have a bad feeling about this."

He took her by the shoulder as he spoke, but she shook free and marched out of the market.

"Will you stop it?" she told him. "Now you're being paranoid!"

"Whatever." He balled his hands into fists. "I still think she might be using you. All that hooey about building a new planet, and peace, and being nice to the Owlings."

"You don't think we ought to be nice to the Owlings? You don't think we should work to help save them? That's what this is all about."

"Okay, sure. But from what I could see, that's not what those Security guys had in mind."

"She's not a Security guy."

He shook his head. A nearby shopper gave them a wary look.

"Ori, something doesn't add up. She's a ... what? An advisor to the elder Assembly? Head of Security? How come we're seeing her on the media all the time now? I mean, every few minutes, seems like. And what did she mean by all that 'destiny' business? That doesn't sound like the Codex, and it doesn't sound like something Jesmet would say."

Oriannon rolled her eyes. "That just shows what you know."

"Well maybe I haven't memorized all 857 pages like you have, but —"

"Eight hundred fifty-two."

"I knew that. But what makes her the expert?"

"I don't know what makes her the expert, but Sola is the only one around here who's actually putting the Codex into practice." The words spilled out of her mouth as if they didn't belong to her. But still they came, and now she hurried to out walk Margus. "I think her solution is the same thing Jesmet was talking about. Getting people back together again. Maybe she's the Numa we're supposed to wait for!"

"You don't really believe that." He huffed along beside her.

"Yeah, well I'm just shocked it's me saying all this and not you. I'm shocked you're so cynical, that you're not giving Sola a chance."

"*You're* shocked?"

"That's right. And you know what else? I think you're bent out of shape because things aren't happening the way you want them to happen. Like it wasn't your idea, and you're not at the front of the parade."

"That's the dumbest thing I've ever heard." He spit out the words and finally turned away with a red face. "Look, I've got to go. I'll see you later."

He crossed the busy shopping lane and doubled back the way they'd come. Oriannon watched a Security probe follow him at a distance but said nothing.

Let him figure it out himself, she thought, even as she brushed away a trace of guilt for not warning him. *He's a big boy.*

But he sure didn't understand. She turned back to the nearest media screen to watch the images of Sola Minnik's smile, and she saw what Margus obviously could not see, or what he stubbornly refused to see: that Sola was the real thing, that she was helping the elders get straightened out, that she was the one who could really help the Owlings. Maybe the only one. Why did it matter where she'd come from? She was here, wasn't she? Oriannon smiled inside when the media reader mentioned the upcoming *Peace Begins Here* conference — the one she would be going to in just a few days.

A few days later, Oriannon still couldn't keep from smiling at the way things were going for her, as a stretch lev-transporter picked her up outside her home. Obviously she'd never before ridden in anything so fancy, with tinted windows and reclining seats for six.

"You're sure you're not going?" she asked her father when he escorted her to the waiting ride. He shook his head and crossed his arms.

"I wasn't invited, Ori. None of the Assembly elders were, not even Regent Ossek."

What? That seemed strange. He hadn't told her that before.

"And besides," he went on as if nothing was wrong. "I'd probably fall asleep in the middle of all the speeches and embarrass you. You know I need some rest after all the meetings I've been to."

True, her father needed to rest before they called him back to the Temple again. She paused at the open door, glanced in at the plush black leather seat.

"Go ahead," he told her with a peck on the cheek. "Blessed are the peacemakers. Sola thinks you're a good example to the world. And you look great in that blue tunic."

She tried to forget the glimmer of worry in his eyes as she rode alone to the opening banquet of the *Peace Begins Here* conference. Probably he was still tired from working such long hours. So she contented herself with sitting in the plush compartment, watching the city go by outside her windows and pretending for a moment she was someone very important. Minutes later, when she arrived in front of Justice Hall, she had to hide her grin as media types crowded around the stretch.

They must think I'm someone else.

In fact, she could hardly make her way through the cam-wielding crowd toward the front steps. Moments later she couldn't help smiling at the way Sola recognized her through the crowd from across the high-ceilinged ballroom of important-looking older people in gold-threaded tunics and robes, showing their high station in Coristan society.

This, however, was obviously not the usual upper-class gala social gathering, as the ballroom was peppered by tall, stern-faced men in black Security uniforms, minus the standard helmets. Some lined the wrap-around second-floor balcony, speaking urgently to each other on shoulder-mounted comms. Others lurked behind floor-to-ceiling burgundy drapes, while many more stationed themselves around a perimeter of marble columns (and they looked every bit as stiff). None blended into fanciful murals of the jagged red Sorian mountains, luminous under violet Coristan skies and the three Trion suns. In fact, each security seemed to wear the same blank expression, as if totally unimpressed by beautiful artwork or gracious buildings. Or perhaps they'd just been ordered to look hard, bored, and terribly out of place.

They might have looked even more out of place than she did, as the youngest person in the room. But Oriannon didn't shrink at the sight of the securities this evening as she normally might have. This time she just enjoyed the same butterfly feeling as when Sola held her hand up in front of all the media cams the other day. Who wouldn't feel rather important being singled out in an upper crust crowd like this?

"There you are!" Sola flashed her signature smile and slipped through a knot of people to greet her. She wrapped Oriannon in a warm hug. "I'm so glad you could make it!"

Had there been any question? Oriannon looked down at her own rather plain blue tunic and wondered if she might have come a little under-dressed, despite what her father told her.

"You look just fine." Sola held Oriannon out at arm's length, as if she might be talking to a favorite niece. "Now come with me to the head table. There's a place reserved for you."

And there was, along with more rich, fancy food than Oriannon had ever seen in one place at one time: Curried meyaplant quiche smothered in tart citron glaze, mounds of sweet pawl buttons roasted in a tangy gorall butter, stringy-sweet loanfruit pies, and trays of light doan biscuits speckled with powdered azucu, all washed down with steaming pots of sweetened clemsonroot tea. She was so busy eating, it didn't matter much if anyone noticed her or that she didn't know any of the important-looking people sitting on either side of her.

"More aploncakes, miss?" A server held out a platter loaded with baked delicacies, and she would have eaten more if she could. Well, all right. Just one more. She popped it in her mouth, covered her puffed cheeks with a napkin, and scooted her chair back as a black-suited man stood up to a clear plexi podium at the front of the crowd. His starched, dark uniform reminded Oriannon of the legions of securities that lately filled her city, though it looked softer. His voice boomed over their heads as the erhu trio in the corner paused at their instruments and the entire banquet hall fell silent.

"Our speaker today needs no introduction," he told them, his eyes gleaming. "But I will offer one just the same. Because the most difficult of times bring up our finest leaders. We are about to hear just such a leader. Like all of us in this room, she holds Corista's security as her top priority. Already her initiative in guiding the once-powerful Assembly of elders brings us back from the brink of disaster, restores our light, and returns us to the direction for which we all know we were destined!"

Oriannon shifted uncomfortably when he spoke of the Assembly that way, but no one else seemed to notice, and she didn't have time to worry about it. As he spoke a giant Coristan flag unfurled in the background, dark violet emblazoned with the three golden stars of the Trion. A light breeze from the ceiling whispered to its memory fabric, causing it to ripple and wave, while a stirring national hymn rose in volume, bringing everyone to their feet. Even Oriannon felt her heart beating out of her chest, and she cheered at the top of her lungs along with everyone else as a reddish spotlight came up and the introducer stepped aside with a flourish, holding out his hand.

"Please welcome First Citizen Sola Minnik!"

Oriannon could feel herself going hoarse from all the cheering, her palms sore from all the clapping. But still they kept it up, and in the front Sola beamed in the spotlight even as she waved for quiet and thanked them more than once.

"I have to agree with my friend here about the future of our planet," she finally told them, and she was looking straight at Oriannon as she spoke. "And I believe we're all here for a reason—you, me ... all of us. I believe in the destiny of Corista. And I believe here in Corista we all long for peace with greatness, as we forever leave behind the evils of religious fanaticism ..."

She went on like that for the next twenty minutes, bringing the crowd to their feet over and over again with ovations and cheers. Clearly the crowd liked what Sola had to say about making Corista great once more, about building bridges between Corista and any others they might discover in their outward expansion, and about Corista leading the way in this part of the galaxy.

"In fact," she said, standing to the side of the podium, "there's a young lady I'd like to recognize for her contribution. She's a bridge between our people and the lesser race from the side that was once dark, and her courage has already caught the attention of all Corista."

Oriannon's throat went dry when she realized where Sola was going with this speech. Was this why she had been invited here?

"She is this generation's peacemaker, the daughter of a distinguished Assembly elder who was unfortunately unable to be here tonight with us. She, however, is. Please, I'd like Oriannon Hightower of Nyssa to join me here at the podium for a moment. Ori?"

The room broke into polite applause as Oriannon felt her heart stop and her legs stiffen. Sola hadn't said anything about this. She didn't really want her to step up there in front of everyone, did she?

Fortunately Oriannon didn't have to rely on her own legs. She felt strong hands on her shoulders that nearly lifted her out of her seat, and two black-suited securities escorted her through the maze of tables to the podium. And Sola never slowed down her speech. Oriannon felt her cheeks flame brighter and redder than an over-ripe aplon left out to burn in the suns.

"This young woman is a model for others to follow. I know she will inspire and provoke many to seek peace, especially in the coming Month of Peace that I propose we all celebrate together. I believe with all my heart that this is her destiny. Oriannon, don't be shy!"

The applause grew even louder when Sola placed a delicate titanium medallion suspended on a beautiful silver chain around Oriannon's neck. Oriannon ran her fingertips across the medallion's laser-engraved moordove, the Coristan symbol of peace, and felt a small relief that at least Sola wasn't asking her to say anything.

"Oriannon is going to be working with me in the weeks to come on the Ultimate Solution to our planet's problems," Sola told the cheering crowd. "And she's going to be wearing her peace medallion to remind everyone what we're all working for, aren't you, Ori?"

Ori nodded and smiled as the crowd cheered once more, louder this time. The clapping continued while the two securities escorted her back to her seat. The good news was that Sola still had more to say, and the dinner crowd shifted their attention back to her mesmerizing words. Oriannon sat quietly the rest of the evening, still fingering her medallion. She could have listened all night, as Sola spoke of the Ultimate Solution, the Peace Initiative, the birthright of all loyal Coristans.

Sola called it destiny. Jesmet might say it was only what the Maker would allow. But with the heady sound of applause still ringing in her ears, Oriannon honestly wasn't sure she could explain the difference. One way or another she was here, in the right place and at the right time, just the way Sola said. She couldn't wait to get home, to tell Margus and the girls.

8

ell, I don't care what you guys think." Carrick Trice had a funny way of wrinkling her nose. "I mean, look at that cool medal she gets to wear. I'm proud of Oriannon."

"Thanks, Carrick." From one side of her basement rec room, Ori held up a game paddle and nodded. "At least *you* are."

In other words, at least Carrick recognized the new Ori, if no one else did. Margus, for instance.

Margus hunkered down as he served the virtual game ball once again, banking it off the far wall, shaded green for this game. Oriannon returned it with a spin, and Margus grunted as he reached and volleyed. Carrick followed the game from a safe distance.

"Nobody said we weren't proud of you." He swung fiercely, barely making contact. "It's just that for the past few days ..."

He backhanded a loping shot.

" ... every time we talk to you it's Sola this ..."

Wham! Into the corner.

" ... and Sola that. Sola, Sola—"

A vicious return, low and sizzling.

"—Sola!"

He just didn't understand. Oriannon looked to the corner of the room where Brinnin was curled up with a vid projector, watching a dull romance story. Ori finally let the ball slip by her on purpose, giving Margus the point.

"See, that's what I don't get." Oriannon caught her breath. "Sola's one of the good guys. She's working to help the Owlings and bring our planet together again. Didn't Jesmet want us to do what Sola's saying we should do?"

"Maybe." Margus served once more, a straight shot that Oriannon had to duck. "But what about the Stone?"

"Hey!" she countered, ignoring the question. The Stone was still safe in her drawer, and he knew it. "You're trying to distract me."

"I just want you to hear what you're saying." He faced her with a hand on his hip, panting for breath. "You're talking like Sola's the same person as Jesmet. You're confused."

"You haven't met her up close. She's much different in person."

"And you think that's a good thing?"

Oriannon pressed her lips together and fought away the tiny doubt.

"Okay," he finally conceded. "So how about this. Maybe I'm not going to convince you that you're wrong, and you're not going to convince me. But next time you see her, ask Sola what she thinks of Jesmet."

"I'm sure she just thinks he's, you know, no longer alive. Just like anybody else would. So what?"

"And that doesn't bother you?" Margus held up his hand in a question. "That's my point! What about all this stuff she's saying about the Owlings? Have you seen her on the media lately?"

Dumb question. Had she seen anything else? Five hundred channels carried live reports, each one of them falling over the next one to get the latest Sola scoop.

"I saw her on Food 34," said Carrick. "They interrupted a show on how to make loanfruit cobbler. I was halfway through mixing the ingredients, and then it was just her talking again about the boring old peace thing."

"The Peace Initiative," Oriannon corrected her. "And it's not boring. She talks to me about it all the time."

"Does she know how to make cobbler?" asked Carrick. "Mine was ruined."

"So why don't you ask her what's really up with the Owlings?" asked Margus. "Better yet, why don't you ask her if you can go see for yourself? I'll bet she wouldn't let you."

"She would too." By this time Oriannon was wishing this conversation would just go away.

"I think you should ask her too." Brinnin raised her head above her vid. "Just to see what she says. You are going to see her again, aren't you?"

"Yeah, actually." Oriannon glanced at a chrono on the wall. "She said she was going to send someone to pick me up."

"What is it this time?" asked Margus. "Another 'Girl of the Year' award?"

"You know what the problem is?" She stepped up to him, toe-to-toe. He wasn't going to get away with being so sarcastic. "You're jealous."

He narrowed his eyes at her.

"Give me a break." Finally Margus shook his head slowly from side to side, and his voice softened. "If you really think this is all about me being jealous and you being famous, you don't know me at all."

She thought it might have been easier if he'd responded with a little more fire, and for a moment she even wondered if he really could be right and she could be wrong. But of course not! Sola treated her like a sister. She wasn't going to turn her back on Sola, just because Margus was acting like an immature brat.

"Miss Oriannon?" Their housekeeper's voice drifted down the stairs as the front doorbell sounded a pleasant duotone. "Looks like your ride is here."

"Oh, no!" Oriannon grabbed the side of her head, wondering how she looked. Was it already time? She couldn't keep Sola waiting.

"It's okay, girl." Carrick opened the food prep door on the far wall of the room. "Do you mind if we finish our snacks here?"

"Carrick!" Brinnin scolded the other girl. "I can't believe you just said that."

"No, it's fine, really." By that time Oriannon was hurrying for the stairs. "Stay as long as you want. Eat all you want. I'm sorry I have to leave in such a hurry."

"We're getting used to it," Margus replied. "Even if we *are* jealous."

"Here, you try." Oriannon tossed Brinnin the game paddle. "Maybe you can beat him."

● ● ●

Ten minutes later Oriannon's ride zipped in and out of traffic on Seramine's busy streets, up a level and then down, through hillside tunnels and past busy marketplaces filled with shoppers carrying bags of fresh fruit and bread. Had she wanted, she could have powered down the window and reached out to tag people on the sidewalk. Instead she gripped the handle in front of her with white knuckles and tried not to look when the driver boosted their mid-sized lev-transporter up and over the backs of stalled traffic, which was slightly illegal but would probably keep them from arriving late. Her comm buzzed.

"Are you in a place where you can talk?" asked Sola, as the driver of a lev-scooter they had just passed (in the wrong lane!) gestured angrily at them. Oriannon winced and assured her she would be there in just a few minutes.

"Good. Then let me brief you on what you're going to be telling the media today. This is all about the Peace Initiative, and you're going to be explaining how poor the conditions are in Lior. Understand?"

"Actually, they're not that bad. In fact, in—"

"That's not what I mean, sweetheart," Sola interrupted. "We're talking compared to Corista. All right? So you explain as an eyewitness how poor the living conditions are there, and how much help the poor Owlings need."

"Oh. I guess if you put it that way."

"Exactly. You talk about the earthquake damage, that kind of thing, but you take your lead from me. Can you do that?"

"Sure. No problem. But, Sola?"

The comm line had already gone silent. By that time her ride had pulled up in front of the imposing Corista Bureau of Security building. At three stories, it seemed somewhat tall by Coristan standards but without many of the columns and outside ornamentation that set apart many of the other government headquarters.

"Miss?" The driver looked over his shoulder at her, as if wondering why she was still sitting in the backseat.

"Right." She took a deep breath and reached for the door. "Here I go."

The good news was that she wouldn't be the only visitor here; media transporters hovered outside, and several reporters had already taken up positions on the outside steps to file their reports. She turned her head away, hoping none of them would recognize her as she hurried for the main entry. They would have plenty of time for that. But for now, staying anonymous felt good.

See, Margus? she thought. *I'm not here for the fame.*

So why was she here? A minute later Oriannon joined Sola, who stood in front of a group of twenty or thirty media reporters crowded into the sterile, tall-ceilinged media room. Instead of ornamentation and carved stone that was found in so many other public Coristan buildings, here the walls and ceilings gleamed in no-nonsense titanium, trimmed with plain, sharp-cornered black marble. Built-in tech controls could be found on almost every wall. Oriannon shivered. Ever-present probes hovered in the corners, watching the reporters who recorded Sola and Oriannon.

"All right, people, let's get your attention up here." When Sola brought the group to order, no one could doubt who was in charge. Here she wore her Security ID with its holographic photo like a badge of honor. In keeping with the setting, she wore a trim-fitting black tunic, and her red hair was pulled back tightly.

An aide affixed a temporary badge to Oriannon's shoulder. Did that make her a Security employee? She wasn't sure. She didn't feel nearly as serious as Sola, but she would try.

"We're here to discuss the Peace Initiative, so you'll confine your questions to that area. By now you all know Oriannon Hightower." She gestured to Oriannon, who nodded at the small crowd. This time it felt a little easier, though still very weird to have media people know her name and face. "I've asked her to share some of her firsthand experiences in the Owling city. But we'll get to that in a moment. First I want to tell you that Coristan vessels will no longer force open the water lines that begin over in Owling lands. "

A flurry of hands went up as the media asked several questions.

"We're not doing that anymore," she explained. "It's heavy-handed, it causes problems, and it's dangerous besides. Oriannon saw Owlings who violently resisted our people, didn't you?"

"That's right." Oriannon nodded. She'd seen that much. "But only because—"

"So what we're saying is that we're trying new strategies to help these people, but that we're still facing resistance. In fact, every time we've sent probes into the area—and we're talking about all twenty-three Owling cities, not just Lior—Owling hunting birds are turned loose on the probes. It's quite destructive, really, and so very unfortunate that they don't seem to understand our motives. We've lost several probes that way, although we're continuing to upgrade their capabilities, making them less vulnerable."

That would explain why probes seemed so different these days. Of course the next question from the media was something like, "What do we do about it in the meantime?" Sola smiled in response, the first time of the day, and her teeth glimmered like the polished titanium walls.

"Very good question. This is where Oriannon comes in. With her photographic eidich memory, she's graciously volunteered to provide us with a better map of the Owling capital city. This will help us safely secure the area, and it will help us to help the Owlings. They are a superstitious people, are they not, Oriannon?"

Oriannon hesitated. "Superstitious" wasn't exactly the word she would have used. But Sola understood the situation better than she did. Sola did want what was best for the Owlings.

"Their customs are different than ours," she finally admitted, and the media of course recorded every word. But what she said was true.

"And the horrible conditions!" Sola went on. "Oriannon tells us that life in the city was primitive even before the recent earthquakes. But now that conditions are so much worse, it's imperative that we offer humanitarian aid as quickly as possible, without any misguided resistance. We don't want anyone to get hurt."

Well, that sounded good too. And what better way to help save her Owling friends after all. Of course! This was a practical way to do just that—something no one else could do. Jesmet would have approved.

Wouldn't he?

An hour after the media conference, Oriannon couldn't help shivering as she followed Sola down the darkened halls of the Corista Bureau of Security building. Her feet clicked on cold marble tiles, and she wondered if they kept it so cool and dark for a reason. Five steps ahead and not slowing down, Sola conferred with a huddle of three advisors.

Maybe she's forgotten me? Oriannon wondered. But soon enough, Sola glanced back over her shoulder and pointed at a closed black office door.

"Wait in there for me, would you, sweetheart? Make yourself comfortable. I'll just be a minute."

Oriannon nodded and stepped to the door, pausing as it whisked to the side. She stepped into the dim, sparsely furnished office and stood waiting.

Did I really agree to do this? she wondered. Of course by now it was too late to change her mind, and Sola would join her any minute. Telling herself not to worry, she looked around the titanium-paneled room and stepped over to the shaded window overlooking the city's green parks and multi-leveled avenues. From here she could follow traffic as it seemed to swirl about her feet, and see busy shuttles in the sky beyond. But even the spectacular view didn't set her at ease.

Away from the window sat a matched set of firm but comfortable brown leather chairs, obviously arranged for conversation, and behind them stood shelves filled with ancient books by Coristan thinkers. The titles included *An Alignment of the Planets*, *Principles of Power*, and *Destined to Lead*. She recognized none of the titles. But ... books? That did seem rather odd for anywhere other than a museum.

The equipment on one of the shelves looked vaguely familiar, as if she had seen it somewhere before. She ran her finger across a tiny blue screen and jumped when it flickered to life. A small, flat titanium box hummed, and a smooth voice told her, "Ready, Sola."

Oriannon choked back the dull feeling of recognition while she could not bring herself to sit or to make herself comfortable. Instead she stood fidgeting in the dim, filtered light from the window, still shivering in swirls of cool air. She avoided stepping on a black yagwar skin that decorated the floor, even as she averted her eyes from strangely shaped black carvings on the shelves that reminded her of frozen flames. The ones closest to her seemed to glow a deep red, as if alive, but they only made Oriannon shiver even more.

In here the only thing that gave any feeling of hope was the warm Stone deep in her tunic pocket, and she was glad she had taken it along, instead of leaving it locked in the usual hiding place back in her room.

The Stone brought back memories of the mentor who had stepped out of his banishment to save her, defying the religious leaders who had called him faithbreaker. The leaders who held to the teachings of the Codex so tightly, they had strangled all life out of it—and out of him.

Jesmet. Here in this office the name seemed strangely out of place. As she gripped the Stone, she pictured the way he had stepped into the star chamber for execution. As he did, he'd proven he wasn't just a music mentor.

The problem was, she still couldn't even breathe his name in public and certainly not in Sola's office.

I'm no good at this, she whispered to the window, as her words turned into a prayer. *They think I'm so smart when I memorize things. But Maker, you know I'm not! I hardly know who I am or how to follow Jesmet. I can't talk to Father about it. I can't help Wist or any of the other Owlings. I couldn't even help Cirrus Main. How can I—*

Behind her the door quietly opened, and Oriannon felt a draft of cold air at her neck. She released the Stone, and the memory of her mentor faded.

"Thanks for being patient, Ori. How do you like it?"

Sola's soft voice turned Oriannon around.

"Oh! You mean your office? It's very nice."

Without question she obeyed Sola's gesture to seat herself in the nearest easy chair. The soft cushions sighed under her weight as she sank deeper than expected.

"This is actually where I do some of my best thinking. Comfortable now?"

Oriannon had to nod her head yes. Extremely comfortable.

"Okay, then. I understand you've had a less than positive experience with neural transmitters in the past." Sola reached across to rest a hand on Oriannon's knee. "But believe me, this will not be the same. Far less intrusive. You don't have to worry, not for a moment."

"I'm not worried." Oriannon bit her tongue, not used to the feeling of lying.

"I could tell. But you would tell me if you had any concerns, wouldn't you, Oriannon?" When she looked deeply into Oriannon's eyes, the only thing Ori could recognize was concern, and as it washed over her like a welcome wave, she wanted it to be so. Sola was different, wasn't she?

"Honest." Oriannon gulped. "I'll be okay."

"Good girl. I know you will be. I also want you to know how much I appreciate what you're doing."

"I don't mind."

"No, honestly. You're making a difference. But remember, we're simply transferring low-resolution visual images, so it's nothing like those other clumsy machines you were used to, the ones that gave you so much trouble. This is completely new tech. Okay?"

Oriannon nodded and leaned back against the plush leather seat, as the equipment on the shelf once more told them it was ready.

I'll be good, she told herself with eyes closed and hands still shaking. *Sola won't let anything happen to me.*

An hour later Oriannon finally relaxed again, spent and completely drained from the effort of recalling every turn and passageway she had ever seen during her short stay in the Owling cliffside capital of Lior. With Sola's encouragement and a mildly annoying neural link that transferred vivid memories to a waiting computer, she recalled streets and buildings and passages, doors and locks, storefronts and alleys. If she had seen it even once, she mentally added it to the detailed schematic Sola's tech assembled as they spoke.

"Wonderful. That's wonderful." Sola smiled and nodded at the results, even swiveling a screen around for Oriannon to see. It looked as if someone had taken a detailed vid of the entire Owling settlement, which she supposed was the idea. When Oriannon began to rise from the chair, though, Sola held up her hand to indicate she should wait.

"Rest a minute before you get back up, Ori." Sola came over to perch on the wide arm of Oriannon's chair and asked about school, about Oriannon's parents, if she'd ever had a pet ... Oriannon answered as best she could, while Sola nodded with interest.

"You were fortunate." Sola finally stood and paced around the chair, arms crossed. "I wish I'd never known my mother."

Fortunate? Oriannon wasn't at all sure what she meant; her puzzled expression surely gave her away.

"Let me put it this way." Sola hesitated, as if searching for the words. "My mother was ... not the nicest woman in Corista. So my parents didn't get along, and as a girl I always thought it was my fault. Not anymore. Now I have—we have—a chance to put the world right. Can you understand that?"

"I think so." Oriannon nodded. She still wasn't sure, but for the first time she felt sorry for Sola.

"But enough of me." Sola straightened with a smile. "Ready for just a little more?"

Oriannon tried not to let her hands shake all over again. All she could feel was a slight tingle in her forehead, a vague headache, as the transfer continued. This wouldn't be so bad. Sola pointed to the fuzzy screen image of a rough-looking door hewn into the side of a cliff. Gradually it cleared into a more recognizable picture—the entry to the Grand Hall of the Owlings.

"That's it. We're especially interested in the Grand Hall." Sola leaned forward, checking an instrument that measured the transmission rate of the images. "Tell us about the passages that lead through the mountain and out the other side, and we'll see what else we can capture here."

These images would apparently be one of the keys to entering the Owling stronghold. As Sola reminded her, peace with the Owling people in large part depended on how well Coristan Security could access these sites. This was good for everyone concerned, and so the images flooded through the interface—hundreds, thousands of images.

"You're doing wonderfully, dear."

Was she? Oriannon struggled to concentrate, reached to bring back every memory she knew of—and perhaps some she wasn't even aware of. She wasn't sure how much longer she could keep it up, but when Sola smiled that way, she knew she was doing the right thing.

"I was just wondering, though." Oriannon didn't think it would hurt to ask. "When you said the Owlings were superstitious, did you really mean—"

"Don't get me wrong." Sola touched a panel to put her machine into standby mode, and it hummed expectantly. "When we're out there with the media, we speak in terms they understand. Conflict, you know. That's what they need for their stories. They need a problem, whether one exists or not. We give them one, and they're happy."

"So you didn't mean what you said?"

"Oriannon! I'm surprised at you for even thinking such a thing. I was simply attempting to express the fact that these people live in filthy cities under primitive conditions. You of all people should know how bad it is. We've seen it right here from the images you've given us."

"Yeah, but actually, I was wondering something else." Oriannon wasn't sure why she dared to bring it up, and why now. "I'd really like to go back to see what's happened in Lior. Do you think I could go with one of the teams that's been going over there? Just to see what's going on?"

Sola didn't answer right away. She shut down the machine and rubbed her chin as if thinking it over.

"Of course you can. I'd like you to. The thing is, it's still very dangerous, and your father would never forgive me if anything happened to you."

"I know what it's like. I wouldn't be in any danger."

"You know what it *used* to be like. Believe me, it's not the same. The poor Owlings are desperate, you know, under the stress of what's happened over the past weeks."

"They are?"

"Oh, yes. That's why they so desperately need our help to put things right. Everyone can use a little hope, no? Isn't that what the Codex requires us to do? To bring hope to the hopeless?"

Yes, that's what the Codex said. Sola was right. But by that time Oriannon had leaned back in her chair once again, and a nap sounded like a wonderful idea. New technology or not, the thought transfer had taken all she had.

"So let's give it a few more days," Sola told her, rising once more to her feet. Oriannon gazed up through droopy eyelids. "Perhaps a week or two. By then the situation will have settled a bit. That will give us an opportunity to speak with your friend as well."

Oriannon nodded her head slowly, barely aware of the fact that she could probably agree to just about anything at this point.

Please, she thought, *just let me sleep.*

"You see, I'm a little concerned about some of the influences in your life right now. One in particular."

"Uh-huh." Oriannon had no idea where this was going and no longer cared unless it allowed her to sleep.

10

here's Margus been the past couple of days?" Brinnin wondered aloud as the three girls walked home from school. They'd taken the long way home through the tree-lined Seramine Park, a haven of shallow ponds and manicured patches of soft grass in the middle of the city.

"Heard he's been sick," said Carrick, chewing on a raw stick of clemsonroot. Oriannon often wondered how a person could eat so much and still look so skinny.

"Maybe." Oriannon checked her comm just to be sure. "But he sure hasn't been taking calls, has he? I think we should go by his house and see."

As soon as she'd said it, though, she remembered what Sola had said about *influences* in her life. Had she meant Margus?

"I don't think we'll need to go by his house." Brinnin pointed behind them at a red lev-scooter jetting out of the bushes, headed straight for them. "Just my first impression, but he sure doesn't look sick either."

They nearly had to jump out of the way when Margus plowed to a stop right beside them. The thrusters on his scooter whined and stirred up a cloud of leaves. Oriannon backed up next to a large pond, not sure what to say. Margus barely looked at her.

"So what do you think?" he asked them as he climbed off the two-seater. It hovered quietly, and he patted the handlebars. "Just a few years old, but it sure is nicer than the one that got wrecked."

Oriannon thought it was nice of him not to say that it replaced the one *Oriannon* had wrecked. And she didn't really care to dredge up the whole story of how she nearly got killed following Jesmet over to Shadowside, lost her memory, destroyed Margus's scooter, and all the rest. But of course that was in the past. It wasn't her fault.

"Your dad really let you have another one?" Brinnin wanted to know.

"Sort of." He shrugged. "It's a long story."

They waited for him to go on, but it looked as if he wasn't going to volunteer any more details. Still, Oriannon had to admit it was a cool lev-scooter, metallic red overall with shiny titanium trim and a wraparound windscreen. She bent down to admire it just as it jerked on its anti-grav cushion of air, twisted like a living animal, and actually bumped her backward and off her feet.

"Oh, no!" She managed to windmill her arms and clutch empty air, but it didn't stop her from splashing backward into the pond. Almost before she could gasp in shock, though, Margus jumped in after her, grabbed her by the shoulders, and helped her to the surface. All very noble of him, but kind of rough, and not really necessary.

"Are you okay, Ori?" Margus asked. She'd rarely seen him act so quickly before. Here, though, it didn't matter much, since ...

"I'm not going to drown in waist-deep water, okay?" She sputtered and choked just a little. Then she pushed him away and stood in the pond's soft mud, hands on her hips, water dripping from her short hair. "And I'm fine, totally fine."

She reached for a rock to lift herself up, but he held her back with his hands on her shoulders. What in the world?

"Wait a minute, Ori." The serious look on his face told her more than his words. "I've got to tell you something."

"Fine, but can you let me get out of this water first?" Again she tried to climb out, but he wouldn't have it.

"Ori. We don't have a lot of time. Probably just a few seconds."

"What, before I hit you in the face or something else?"

He pointed up around them.

"No. Before those things come after us again."

This was getting worse all the time. Oriannon looked at him a little more closely, at his wet, matted hair and the water dripping off his nose. Funny. He didn't look crazed—just a little scared.

"What things are you talking about?" she asked him. "What's wrong with you?"

"You know where I've been the past couple of days?"

She finally gave up, her shoulders slumping.

"You haven't been sick, then, huh?"

He shook his head. "A couple of securities showed up at my house, and took me to their building downtown for a re-education session."

"Re-education?" Carrick was listening from shore. "What's that?"

"I'll explain it to you later." He brushed his hair back. "But I have to tell you what I found out about your medal, the necklace."

Come to think of it—Oriannon felt around her neck for the peace necklace Sola had given her, and a panic swept over her.

97

"It's gone!" She looked down through the partly cloudy water. "It must have fallen off in the water! You've got to help me find it!"

She started to crouch down, feeling in the soft mud around her feet. It had to be here, somewhere close by. They'd be able to find it if they all searched. What would Sola say when she found out? But once again Margus grabbed her by the shoulders and lifted her up.

"Oriannon! Listen to me!"

She might have actually hit him if he hadn't been holding her arms so tightly.

"You're hurting me!" She struggled to free herself, but he wasn't giving up.

"Oriannon, you've got to listen to me before it's too late. That peace medallion Sola gave you? It's a spy cam. They're using it to keep track of everything you say and do. Us too."

"What are you talking about? That's nuts. Sola wouldn't do anything like that."

"She would and she has. You've got to believe me."

"And you know all this because—?"

"No time to explain. I've just seen more over the past couple of days than they think."

"They. You keep talking about they. Who are *they*, anyway?"

"Come on, Ori! THEY! Those guys in the black helmets, remember? The guys that blew up the way station? The guys who broke into your house looking for the Stone? The guys who are taking over the elder Assembly? And you know who they work for?"

Oriannon wasn't sure she wanted to hear all this, not now. Because something still didn't add up.

"What about your parents?" she asked. "They just let you spend the last two days at this re-education thing?"

He sighed and finally let go of her arms.

"They've been listening to my dad at work, okay? They didn't like some of the things he said either. They said they were going to arrest him if he didn't—" Margus paused, his lip quivering. "I shouldn't be telling you this."

But Oriannon was still wondering.

"It didn't just fall off. You pulled it off my neck on purpose, didn't you?"

"I'm sorry. It was the only way I could think of to talk without them listening in."

"That's *if* they're really listening in."

"They are. I'm telling you they are."

"I still don't think that sounds like something Sola would do."

"You can believe it or not, Oriannon. I saw her there. She tried to get me to help with that Solution thing of hers, and I pretended I would, or they probably would never have let me go. So now I'm just warning you, Ori. I'm just telling you what I know."

"She wants to change things." Oriannon shook her head. "She wants to make things better."

"Oh, I know she wants to make things better. Question is, better for who?"

"That's not fair." Oriannon dug her toes in the mud, feeing it ooze through her sandals. No way did she want to hear this—from Margus or from anybody. Maybe he was still mixed up. Hadn't Sola said he needed counseling? What if he still did? She felt her head spinning.

Trust him, or not? He did betray Jesmet. And now?

"All right, don't believe me about the spy cam." He climbed out of the pond first, and his loose pants clung to his skinny legs. "But I'm telling you that in about thirty seconds you're going to see a whole flock of probes coming this way, because the only picture they've been getting from your medallion for the past two minutes has been a couple of curious gyt-fish plus a lot of bubbly water sounds. So they're getting nervous by now. You watch."

He held his hand out to her, but she ignored it. She could take care of herself, and she could climb out by herself. What was that? Though she couldn't see because of the silt they'd stirred up, her next step felt something small and hard, like a stone, or . . .

"I think I found it!"

She couldn't help it, even after what Margus had just told her. She stooped to fish the pretty medallion out of the water, just as a swarm of ten probes came buzzing over the trees, low and fast. As she stood there, dripping, holding the shining medallion up out of the water, the probes dropped to a hover just over their heads. She heard them clicking and saw their eyes focus on her, on Margus and the two other girls.

"Look, I found it." Oriannon felt her stomach sink as she blew a strand of lily pad from the dripping medallion. It sparkled in the sunlight. "Good thing, huh? Looks like it's okay."

She replaced the medallion around her neck as she climbed out. Margus was already back on his lev-scooter, and he gave her a look as if to ask, "Well?"

Margus. Now she felt the weight of what he'd told her, and she wanted to say something. What would have happened had she not found the medallion after all? With the eyes hovering above them, it probably wouldn't have made any difference.

Still, she couldn't make herself believe Sola would have been so underhanded, placing a spy cam around her neck. Maybe someone else was doing all this. Maybe somebody in Sola's office was doing things they shouldn't be doing. Maybe if she went to Sola, they could clear up this misunderstanding.

Or not. She squeezed the medallion in her palm, wondering once more what to do, whom to believe, and why it was so hard to figure out. All she really knew was that with this medallion around her neck—assuming Margus was right—she could not say or hear anything that would give anyone a clue about her doubts. If she really did have them. At least the probes drifted off once more to do whatever probes did when they weren't spying on people.

But as they started walking toward home, Brinnin came alongside and slipped her arm around Oriannon's shoulder.

"Boys are just like that, huh?" She shook her head as if she understood completely, the way sisters did. But then she leaned over to whisper into Oriannon's ear.

"We should meet back here tonight, after dark. I'll call Margus. We need a plan."

Oriannon could barely make out the words. Considering what probably hung around her neck, that seemed like a good thing.

"But leave the medallion at home," Brinnin added.

Oriannon tried not to shake at the shiver that went up her spine. She just nodded.

Tonight. After dark. No medallion.

Getting out of the house wasn't the hard part. Her father had already left a message on her comm that he wouldn't be home for another three or four hours. Another marathon meeting, it couldn't be helped, and Mrs. Eraz wasn't coming until the next day.

But getting away from the medallion was something else, especially when Oriannon started worrying what else the thing might be able to do. What if it had tagged onto her vital signs, as well as everything she saw, said, and heard? What if it also had some degree of thought monitoring?

If it does, she thought, *we're toast.*

At least Sola didn't expect her to wear it 24/7, just all her waking life. So it wouldn't seem so unusual that Oriannon parked it in a dish on her dresser, along with luminescent hair bands and a small vial of sand from Shadowside that reminded her of her friend Wist. The Pilot Stone lay safely buried beneath socks in the locked top drawer, where she hid it when she wasn't carrying it in her pocket, though she still didn't really know what to do with it. She slipped off the medallion and spoke into her comm.

"Oh, hey, Daddy? Yeah, I know. I've just been doing homework, getting ready for bed." She paused. "Sure. I won't wait up, no. Okay. See you in the morning. Good night."

She clicked off the receiver, hoping the performance had sounded realistic enough. If her father had actually called, she probably would have said those words exactly. She looked up as a light flickered and the ceiling shook when another flock of shuttles passed overhead. Tonight it seemed louder than ever. But it was time to leave.

Just to be sure the sounds would be right, she went through the motions of her nightly routine, right down to flushing the air-vac toilet and letting her bedroom door slip open. But instead of stepping back inside and crawling into bed, she took a step backward, let the door swoosh shut, and tiptoed for the back door.

Once outside, she hurried along the street and kept to the shadows as much as she could. She knew she would have to hurry before the artificial sunrise kicked in. Actually, having all the shuttles constantly passing overhead seemed to help keep the sky clear, so that helped. If only she could make it to the park without a probe stopping her and asking for ID. She took the long way around the park, pausing behind a clump of pink cerise bushes, coming up quietly behind the others.

"Thought for a minute you weren't going to come." Margus turned toward her before she could say anything. How had he seen her coming? She could hardly see their two heads, crouching behind an ironwood tree.

"I'm here," Oriannon told them. "Maybe I'm crazy, but I'm here. Where's Carrick?"

"She had to stay home," replied Brinnin. "Something about watching her little sister."

"How's your medallion?" Margus tilted his head to the side in a question, and she held up her hands in answer.

"It's back on my dresser at home. So if there's really a spybot on it—which is still not for sure—it's not with me now."

"Have you said anything about it to Sola?" he asked, and she frowned before answering him.

"Not yet. But I've been thinking about it. I still think it might be a big misunderstanding."

Or she hoped it would be. Oriannon wasn't sure what it would take to convince herself.

"Misunderstanding?" said Margus. "You're going to change your mind about that in a few minutes."

Why did he sound so sure of himself? She looked to Brinnin, who just shook her head in the dim twilight. Aside from the satellites, Seramine still had no outdoor lighting to speak of, and certainly not in a city park. Why would a city that once had perpetual sunlight even think of such things? They waited for another group of shuttles to roar overhead.

"Okay." Margus nodded at the other two. "It doesn't matter. We're ready."

"For?" Oriannon thought it might have been nice if they'd told her.

"I'm going to show you two what's really happening." He straightened up and walked over to a thick copse of cerulean trees, which hid his waiting lev-scooter. It hummed quietly as he made a few adjustments to the lift. "I don't know how we're all going to fit on this thing, but hop on if you can."

"Wait a minute." Oriannon still wasn't quite buying this. "Explain to me what we're doing first."

Margus sighed and faced her.

"Okay, listen. We couldn't tell you without, you know, someone else finding out. And I told you I was sorry about pushing you into the water, so if you're still upset about that—"

"I'm not upset. I just don't want to be dragged off somewhere and get into more trouble."

"Fine! You can stay here if you want. There's probably not enough room on the scooter for three anyway. I just thought you'd like to see what they're really doing to the Owlings."

He climbed on the scooter, moving forward enough for Brinnin to hop on behind him.

"I really want to see, Ori." Brinnin looked over her shoulder and motioned to the rest of the saddle seat behind her. "There's room for you too."

"What are you talking about?" Oriannon still wasn't sure. "What do you know?"

"Not enough," he replied. "Just bits and pieces from my two days of re-education, and it didn't sound real good. That's why we're going to take another look. You coming or not?"

Without another word, she climbed on the scooter behind Margus and Brinnin. With three instead of two they rode a bit lower than the lev-scooter was designed for, but that didn't seem to slow Margus down.

"Do you have to drive so fast?" she shouted, but he didn't hear her. And Oriannon had to admit it beat walking all the way down to where they could see the Plains of Izula broadened out in the distance and the city's warm stucco buildings gave way to prefabricated industrial gray warehouses and windowless metal buildings, two hours from the city center. Here the planet's precious water had not been used for watering, and it showed in the stark red rock outcroppings and tumbleweeds that scattered as they skittered just centimeters over the gravel road, kicking up a cloud of dust.

None of them had been to this part of Corista much, but it would be difficult to get lost. Every time they paused behind a metal building, another group of shuttles roared overhead, all heading the same direction as they were. When Oriannon craned her neck back, she could almost read the numbers on the underbellies of each spacecraft.

"Close enough." Margus finally found a dark spot between a storage shed and a ragged metal link fence where they could hide the lev-scooter. A pair of smaller shuttles touched down only a couple hundred meters ahead, where they couldn't quite see. But now Oriannon knew exactly where they were going. Margus held up his hand for them to pause in the shadows as four probes jetted by, right over their heads.

"Keep an eye out," he whispered. "There's a lot more security here. The site is up ahead."

"How do you know about all this?" wondered Oriannon. He smiled back at her for a moment before his expression turned serious again.

"Let's just say my re-education was good for something."

"They told you?" That didn't sound likely.

"Not on purpose. I just kept my ears open. Come on."

They crouched low on the dusty ground, running from building to building, and closing in on the landing site. But even with the darkness—which certainly must have helped them hide—Oriannon still wondered.

"Does something seem very odd to you about this neighborhood?" she asked Brinnin. The other girl wiped off a cracked window with her hand and tried to peek inside a ruined warehouse with gaping holes in its sides and roof panels flapping in the breeze.

"No people. Like a bomb went off."

Margus kept low as they stopped behind the corner of the building,

"Yeah, look up ahead," he told them. "It's been cleared out."

Past the next set of ruined buildings they could only make out barren roads and rolling hills stripped of trees and hints of foundations where buildings once stood. Here, block upon block of older buildings and storehouses had been pushed aside into tall piles of rubbish, leaving a gaping open space large enough for many huge landing fields—large enough for a small town.

What was going on here? Oriannon squinted to make sure she really saw it. Margus and Brinnin could only gasp at the enormous semi-transparent dome that stretched over the cleared area, crackling and shimmering with pure blue energy. She guessed it projected from scores of coffin-sized transmitters set up around the perimeter, each marked with black and yellow warning signs. It reminded Oriannon of a giant blue tarp, stretched thin across many hectares, larger than many domed stadiums put together.

"I've never seen one this big," whispered Oriannon. Small ones, sure; some shops used tiny force fields for security. Most prisons employed small-scale force fields across doorways or entries to keep criminals from escaping. But nothing like this. This kind of thing was far beyond the usual laser fences, even the ones that guarded the borderlands of Corista.

"And look at all those tents! It's a ... camp." Brinnin finally managed to whisper, and all they could do was stare at what the force field contained: Hundreds and hundreds of dome tents neatly arranged in row upon row, each one the size of a small garage dome, each one a dull green, and each one filled with a pale yellow light. They twinkled from behind the force field, shimmering and out of focus, and they seemed quite pretty in their own way.

They stared for several minutes, and Oriannon tried to understand the enormity of what she saw. Worst of all, more and more transports landed just outside the force field, each one directed into a vertical landing pattern by a laser-wielding flight crew. As soon as the shuttle touched down, side doors popped open and another crew surged forward to unload the cargo, as if orchestrated and planned just so.

Even at a distance, Oriannon could see this was no ordinary cargo. She looked over at Brinnin to make sure the other girl understood what they were seeing as well, and Brinnin nodded in wide-eyed amazement.

One of the black-suited workers shouted and motioned with
his laser pointer, showing the way to a opening in the force field, a doorway that led through to the inside of the tent city. Other guards waited inside, most of them holding either laser pointers or fully charged stun batons. And then the cargo exited one shuttle after the other: A disheveled, single-file line of Owling men and women, some holding small packages or crying children, most empty-handed, all long-faced and beaten down. Oriannon stiffened with shock, recognizing the pain written on their faces. And she couldn't help wondering — *What happened to Wist?*

A woman stumbled to her knees halfway through one of the lines, drawing an instant response from their guard. Oriannon discovered that the laser pointer had another use, as the guard focused a high-powered red beam on the woman's leg.

"No!" Brinnin gasped and clapped a hand over her own mouth, but Oriannon understood the cry. They ducked out of sight as they heard the woman's scream of pain. Brinnin dissolved into tears at what she'd seen.

"It's okay." Oriannon tried to comfort her, but the tears welled up in her own eyes while Brinnin shook her head.

"It's *not* okay. You of all people, you should know. I thought these were your friends. And this isn't just a camp. It's a *prison* camp. Don't you see what's happening?"

Oriannon wished she didn't. Even at this distance they could hear the cries of pain, the guards yelling for prisoners to hurry, the hum of stun batons and lasers used often and without mercy. When Oriannon finally dared peek around the corner of the building again, she froze again at what she saw.

"Not again," Margus whispered.

Only this time the horror came from within the dome, as a young man not much older than them broke from his line and hurled himself at the fence. But instead of breaking through, the poor Owling was caught up in the blue energy, yanked and twisted as the snarling force field pulled him into its grip. They could not see his face, only his arms and legs as they convulsed in helpless agony.

"We have to do something!" whispered Brinnin, still choking back tears.

Only, what? A second Owling man, much older and silver-haired, broke away to try to pull the young man clear. He only made it three or four steps from his line when a swarm of probes descended on him like angry veno hornets, jabbing and stunning him with sparks of energy. Though he covered his face and head with his arms, they kept at him, violent and angry, until he had fallen to the ground.

"I've never seen probes like that before." Oriannon still couldn't believe what they were seeing as they watched haggard lines of Owlings being hustled through the doorway, through the force field, and into the tent city.

"Why are they taking all those people in there?" wondered Brinnin, but Oriannon could only repeat what Sola had hinted at earlier.

"They say because of the earthquakes." The words felt bitter and warped on her tongue, and she knew them for lies. "They have to bring the Owlings here while they repair the damage back on Shadowside."

"Listen to what you're saying." Margus frowned at her. "This isn't disaster relief. This isn't humanitarian anything. You can't believe that."

By this time Oriannon's head was spinning, and she was only sure she didn't really know what she believed anymore. As they huddled in the shadows, the scene repeated itself over and over as more shuttles jockeyed into place and the emptied spacecraft took off once again with a roar. As they did, a flurry of probes circled the enormous dome, making wider and wider circles until they neared the warehouse behind which Oriannon and the others hid.

"We'd better go back," Margus told them, "before they spot us."

Without a word, they followed Margus back to his scooter. They held on in stunned silence until they reached the front of Oriannon's house and Margus brought his scooter to a jerky stop. They sat there for a minute as the lev-scooter idled.

"So that was the Solution, huh?" Margus stared blankly ahead. Oriannon didn't know how to answer. Her mind still felt numb after seeing what she'd seen.

"If that's what it was," said Brinnin, "maybe somebody should explain what the problem was again?"

"I should ask Sola," Oriannon finally replied, sliding stiffly off the back of the seat. "We need to find out—"

"Are you crazy?" Margus slipped off the scooter to face her, crossing his arms and turning his head to the side in a challenge. "That's the *last* thing you should do."

"But—"

"You tell her what you saw," Margus went on, "and you know what happens? To you? To us? To our families?"

Oriannon swallowed hard, and this time she knew he had to be right. The only thing was, how had she gotten herself so deeply into this mess, and on the wrong side? Margus paced now as he told her his plan.

"Remember what they did to your scribe friend? What was his name?"

"Cirrus Main."

"Right. So play dumb. Find out what she says, go to your banquets and your media things for now, but don't let on that you know anything. You'll be our insider. But whatever you do, don't you dare tell her what we just saw."

"And once you find out more," Brinnin added, "then we can, uh ... then we can, you know ..."

Her voice trailed off, but Oriannon nodded. At least it was a start. One way or another, they would find out the truth, and then they would help the Owlings.

They had to.

Ori?" The low, familiar voice brought her out of her nap, though in the first seconds she still wasn't quite sure where she was. "What are you doing still up?" her father asked.

Now Oriannon shook her head, clearing a dark dream that had brought her back to the edge of the refugee camp, the *prison* camp, and that was the last place on Corista she'd wanted to remember. Meanwhile, the media images floating in the middle of the living room flickered from cooking demonstrations and documentaries on the outer planets to fast-talking salesmen pushing the latest lev-scooters and a wrestling match that Oriannon would normally have passed over in an instant.

"Oh." She worked up a smile, sat up in the chair, and glanced over at the shifting colors of the wall chrono. That late? "I was just waiting for you to get home."

"You didn't have to do that." His forehead looked almost as wrinkled as his Assembly robe, and the shadow on his face told her he hadn't shaved for several days. How long could he keep this up? "Why don't you get to bed, catch a few hours. School today, right?"

Oriannon shook her head.

"It's Seventh Day, remember?"

"Yes, right. Of course it is." He scratched his chin and nodded. "I'll be at the Temple most of the day."

Without a doubt he had lost track of time. He turned toward the kitchen, changed his mind, and circled back. On the media screen, a Coristan prizefighter raised his fists and pranced about the small arena, his bare chest glistening and a look of animal vengeance on his face. At his feet, a bruised and bloodied Owling lay wounded on the floor, barely moving as the other man kicked him.

"No, stop!" whispered Oriannon, and though she wanted desperately to look away, she could not.

The cam cut away briefly to show more wild-eyed Coristans in the audience, pumping their fists and cheering their champion. She looked over at her father, who stood with his arms crossed and his lips pressed tightly together. He muted the sound, leaving only the bloody images to assault them in their own home.

"Looking for the goodness in everyone ..." he echoed Sola's familiar words before holding a hand to his temple with the same paralyzing look of fear that had gripped him since they'd returned from Shadowside. And now Oriannon was surer than ever that something — or someone — was taking her father away from her. In bits and pieces, perhaps more some days than others, but still ever so surely. And the worst part was that she had no idea how to hold him back from the growing darkness that threatened to consume them.

"Are you okay, Father?" Oriannon stepped closer, while his eyes darted about the room as if something was chasing him. "What's wrong? Your head?"

Something *was* wrong, even if he shook it off and tried to smile at her. Elder Tavlin Hightower didn't normally act like this.

"Headache, yeah." But the beads of sweat on his forehead betrayed him. He closed his eyes briefly, took a deep breath, and lightly ran his finger over the carved marble viria bird perched on the wall shelf. "I'll take something for it; don't worry."

"I don't believe you. Something's not right."

For a brief moment the father she knew spoke to her in a softer voice.

"Listen to me, Ori. I just want you to be careful, that's all. Things are changing. You can see that, can't you?"

"What ... what kinds of changes do you mean?"

The question seemed silly as soon as it left her lips. They both knew. He took another deep breath and finally shook his head.

"I wish I could tell you more. Look, you might just want to pack a small bag so you're ready for ... I mean, maybe we should plan a little vacation, real soon. Take a friend along."

"To where?"

He shrugged, as if he hadn't yet thought about it.

"Wherever you want to go — the coast maybe. You've always liked the sea. But listen, even though you've been working a lot with Sola lately, perhaps you shouldn't share all your plans with her. Do you know what I mean?"

Oriannon nodded.

"Is that Elder Tavlin Hightower speaking," she finally asked, "or my father?"

"I just don't want you to worry." He turned his gaze to a carved pair of moordoves, Oriannon's favorites because they reminded her of the real birds that lived in the Temple towers. "But if anything were to happen to me, I want you to know that ... I love you."

Oriannon shook with all-out panic as her father's words settled upon her. She wrapped her arms tightly around his neck, and the tears choked her words, but she had to tell him about what they'd seen, had to tell him now. She pulled back for a moment, only to see the dark fear had returned to her father's face, and his lower lip trembled as if he had just seen something horrific, beyond words.

"Father?" She reached up to feel his throbbing forehead, and she knew without a doubt this was no simple headache. But the father she knew had disappeared once more and she had no idea how to get him back, no matter how desperately she tried.

"Father, please don't talk like this. Can't we just—"

"Pardon me," came another voice. "Sorry to interrupt."

Without warning, their living room comm link viewer came alive, bringing up a holographic image of the last person Oriannon wanted to see just then, hovering in the middle of the room. The woman might just as well have stepped in through the front door. Who had disabled the setting that blocked callers from automatically popping up into their house?

"I'm so glad you're both still up." With her hair styled and makeup obviously in place, Sola looked as bright-eyed as the two of them looked bleary. Oriannon straightened her hair and noticed that her father stiffened as well.

"Of course we're still up, Sola." Her father put on a business tone now, as he spoke to the image in his living room. The fear in his eyes seemed to subside a bit, as if the waves had receded for now. But when would they return?

"Actually, I was hoping to speak to Oriannon about some very exciting news, but—" She paused for only a moment before smiling and continuing. "But you're more than welcome to listen in as well, Tavlin."

They stood awkwardly in the middle of the living room, and Oriannon wasn't quite sure what to do with her hands as Sola continued with her news.

"We have quite an announcement to make, and I'd appreciate it if you'd keep this just between us until we have a chance to announce it at the media conference."

"Another media conference?" Oriannon hoped her voice didn't betray her disappointment.

"Oh, yes, didn't I tell you about that before? You'll be there, of course, Oriannon, at the spaceport. But it's not for another forty-five minutes, so you have plenty of time to rest up and prepare."

"Wait," said Oriannon, trying to sound neutral. "On Seventh Day? You don't mean tomorrow?"

"No, actually it's far too big of an announcement to wait. We'll be bringing in media as we board the shuttle. Tavlin, you should attend the send-off as well. Why not? In fact, it might look quite good if an elder is present."

Oriannon's father nodded, and his jaw tightened.

"I'd be pleased to be there." His voice sounded strangely flat, and Oriannon noticed his fists were clenched behind his back, out of view, as he spoke. But if Sola noticed, she didn't let on.

"So here's what we're announcing." Sola smiled once more as if she was practicing for the real presentation. "We've initiated a large-scale rescue program for the poor creatures over on Shadowside, and we'll be transporting them here to temporary housing. In fact, we've already begun limited relocation operations."

We sure have, thought Oriannon, remembering the horror of what she'd already seen. Her gut knotted at the thought of what "limited relocation operations" *really* meant. But of course Sola continued.

"Wherever possible," she said, "we're going to encourage Coristan families to adopt orphaned and dislocated Owling children. I know this may be quite difficult for people to accept, given our recent dealings with the Owlings. But this is where you come in, Oriannon. I'd like you to travel with me to one of the disaster sites in Shadowside. I'll bring along a team, and we'll have you do a little on-camera work at one of the sites."

Go along with Sola? Yes, this was the plan Oriannon had agreed to follow with Margus and Brinnin. But now the prospect literally made her feel ill.

"Didn't you say it was too dangerous?" she asked Sola. Maybe there was still a way out of this.

"Did I? Oh. Well, we seem to have cleared up any difficulties. I'm assured now by my people that the situation on the ground is quite stable, though I must tell you that conditions over there are deplorable. Truly horrendous. How anyone ever lived on Shadowside, I'll never know."

Oriannon had a pretty good idea, but that was before the earthquakes. Of course, she had been to Lior after the quakes too. Perhaps she didn't understand Sola's definition of "horrendous."

"You'll see that it's simply chaos," Sola added. "And I must say that I am so grieved it has taken us this long to respond after the natural disaster. There's no excuse for that, but I promise you we'll make up for it. And you'll be proud of your daughter, Tavlin, for the way she's making such a difference. She's doing wonderful work."

Once, before she'd seen the landing zone, Oriannon might just have stood and smiled at compliments like that. Now she stood, smiled . . . and held back a scream.

"I am proud of her," Oriannon's father nodded and rested his hand on her shoulder, but she could feel it tense and trembling. The good news was that the conversation seemed to be winding down.

"Oh, and Tavlin?" Sola's smile still filled the room, as it always did. "Perhaps it's just a poor connection, but it seems to me that you look quite pale. You're all right, I assume? You might want to take a quick shower before your transport arrives, which should now be in just — "

She looked to the side, probably to check a chrono.

"Thirty-seven minutes. I'll see you both at the spaceport."

It was not a question or a request. Her image faded as a defeated Tavlin Hightower shuffled to his room. And once again Oriannon had the odd feeling that someone had replaced her once-powerful father with a timid old man, stiff and stoop-shouldered. He paused a moment as his door slid open with a swoosh, as if he might say something else to her. But the door quickly closed behind him again, leaving Oriannon alone in the front room with a smoldering anger.

Idiot! She gritted her teeth as she considered who she had become over the past weeks. *Did I really want a sister — or a mom — so badly that I would trade . . . everything?*

One last time she toyed with the nice warm feeling Sola always gave her. The smiles and the hugs. The feeling of being important in Sola's eyes. The feeling of being noticed.

The feeling of being lied to and used.

But what had it cost her? Wiping away a final tear of regret, she walked over to the little black box resting on their polished pluqwood table, where the comm signal projected into a holographic interface. She yanked out the network card and twisted it into a pretzel. When she tossed a few pieces to the floor, a pair of biomice scurried out from their docking port to gather the pieces of plastic, and she backed away so they wouldn't brush against her foot. They did their job, but she didn't have to like the half-alive creatures.

Right now, though, she wished they were big enough to carry her away, hide her wherever they took scraps of food, crumbs, and trash. A strange thought, perhaps, but no one would find her there—not her friends, not her father, and not Sola.

Especially not Sola. Oriannon stood in the quiet, feeding plastic scraps to the biomice, watching them scurry about. She heard water running in her father's room, and it reminded her that their ride would be here in a few minutes. What else could she do but get ready herself? Slowly she shuffled to her own room, picked up Sola's medallion from her dresser, and dangled it from her fingers.

"Here's a good snack for you guys," she whispered to the biomice, who still twittered around her feet. She dangled the medallion even lower, just out of their reach, as she thought of what her father had told her. Yes, she would pack a bag for that "vacation" he had mentioned. She just wasn't sure where they could go to be safe and away from what was happening here. Certainly nowhere in Seramine. Nor on the opposite side of their small planet, as the Owlings were finding out. Not even a remote outpost like Asylum 4 was safe.

"Ori?" called her father from the other room. "Are you almost ready to go?"

"Just a minute." Oriannon sighed before slipping the medallion back around her neck. Sola would expect it. Just for good measure, she quietly opened her drawer and slipped the Pilot Stone into her pocket—though she turned so that Sola and her Security people might not see what she was doing. They had probably seen and heard the whole thing with the biomice. But strangely enough, Oriannon couldn't make herself care—until she saw her father again five minutes later as they climbed into a waiting four-seat lev-transport.

He still looked haggard. Though Elder Hightower had freshened up in pressed white linen slacks and a sky-colored violet pullover robe, his own dark expression had changed little. She knew better than to ask him about it a second time, and they rode in silence through the streets of Seramine to their appointment.

Play dumb, Brinnin had said. Oriannon wished they had a better idea, but for now she couldn't think of one. So be it. She would go to the spaceport with her father, she would play dumb, and she would find out as much as she could to help her Owling friends.

Before it was too late.

13

ecause we're concerned for the entire planet, that's why." Sola
demonstrated why she was so good in front of a cam, smiling
broadly and standing at the top of a shuttle's boarding platform,
where she provided the perfect photo opportunity. "And I want to
personally make certain each and every survivor is accounted for."

With one hand Sola steered Oriannon's shoulder while with
the other she gestured casually to the gathered media, clustered
down on the tarmac. Three meters of height gave her the advantage
she sought, and she'd had a dark blue Coristan flag draped strategi-
cally behind them. All her props were in place.

"Now," she asked. "Other questions?"

When she paused, the media shouted out a flurry of questions,
and she seemed to pick one out of the air that Oriannon had definitely not heard.

"Yes, someone asked about Miss Hightower. Thank you for
mentioning that. She's coming along as my personal assistant on
this trip, and of course you already know that she will bring her
familiarity with the Owling culture and environment. It's a very
quick little flight, of course, but her father, Assembly Elder Tavlin
Hightower, sends her off with his blessing."

She waved at Oriannon's father, standing at the edge of the crowd, and a couple of cams pointed his way for a quick shot. The media would probably not point out the irony of the elder waving good-bye to his daughter as she boarded the very same shuttle that had once belonged exclusively to the Ruling Assembly, but that had now been painted over in the gleaming black of Sola's Security. Of course no one dared bring that up, the same way no one asked what had happened to the authority of the Assembly. It just wouldn't have been right, or so it seemed.

In any case, the shuttle's engines had begun to hum louder, a signal for them to hurry. Oriannon's hair stood on end in the ion backwash.

"Miss Hightower!" a woman reporter shouted over the growing whine of the engines. "Oriannon! Are you going to be able to recognize Shadowside, after all the damage they've sustained?"

Oriannon tried to answer as they boarded, but the engine noise drowned her out. She tried again, but it was no good.

"Thank you!" shouted Sola, waving a final time with her on-camera smile. A flight attendant in bright blue coveralls pulled Oriannon back through the doors as they slowly came together with a hiss of air.

"I don't know if I will," Oriannon answered through the window, and she peeked through as everyone outside scurried for cover, including her father.

Sola, of course, was only just beginning her role as hostess to the media for the flight on her "new" shuttle. There was no mistaking how much she relished being the center of attention for ten hand-picked media reporters—all young men eager to ask her more questions.

"If you'll come with me, boys." She signaled for the gaggle of admirers to follow. "I'll show you around. We've had this Security shuttle specially retrofitted for long-distance travel in comfort, with two complete levels, rest areas, a lounge, and a cruising range that's been extended so that we can reach any of the orbiting moons we choose. It was rather, er, *basic*, before."

The reporters followed her words pretty closely with recorders and cams. Of course, Sola expected nothing less.

"Now the galley is up this way ..."

Oriannon let them get on with their tour as she found a seat and pressed her nose to the plexi viewport. Now she could barely see her father standing behind a fence, looking over his shoulder at her as a black-suited security escorted him from the scene.

"I'm sorry, Father ..." she rose to her feet, but the grav field kicked in and she was jerked back into the seat. Red takeoff lights flashed as the shuttle jumped straight up from the pad. Now there was no turning back, even if she wanted to.

"Does it look like anything you remember?" One of the reporters, a dark-haired guy from Media712 with very straight, white on-camera teeth turned to Oriannon as they disembarked the shuttle less than an hour later. But she couldn't answer; she could hardly swallow as she took in what she saw.

How to describe it? A bomb had gone off here — if not literally then nearly so. And they'd found a perfect place to land, if the word "perfect" could be used in a horrible situation like this. Instead of touching down at the base of the cliff, the way Oriannon had expected, they'd found a clear area right up in the middle of the city, in what used to be the city plaza.

123

Only this hardly resembled the plaza anymore, with smoking piles of rubble, charred timbers, and broken doors. This looked nothing like the once-bustling Owling city of Lior, where little children had run up and down quaint, crowded walkways carved into sheer cliffs, or played in fountains that ran with warm spring water. She remembered so much life and light in each tiny home, the way they glowed like holiday lights in windows. Many homes had been tucked into caves and crevasses, many more balanced precariously on cliffs. She remembered mothers chatting from window to window, and fathers sitting out on stools, talking and drinking tea or playing their peculiar board game with polished white and blue stones.

Now Oriannon saw none of that. No shops and no schools. No snowy white owls sitting on perches tethered with tiny leather leashes. No homes and no Owlings. Only destruction and the awful smell of death that made her want to cover her face.

She heard a distant screech, and looked up to see a hunting owl still circling the city, waiting for the owner who would never again call him home. She whistled twice, the way she had heard Owling men do to bring the birds back down to their perches. But the wary bird only cocked its head and remained at a safe distance high overhead.

"I don't blame you," she whispered up at the bird. "Stay away from here."

In fact, barely enough remained to show that this had once been a living, thriving place. The owl's shadow passed over a broken pile of rubble, and with a powerful flapping of wings, it moved even higher, disappearing into a bank of fluffy gray clouds.

Now the sunlight those poor Owling people had celebrated only days before muscled between the clouds to cast lifeless shadows on half walls and shattered roofs. Here, out on the ruined plaza, Oriannon could almost hear the echo of the dancers, holding hands and winding around and around, with Jesmet smiling and clapping his hands.

Had it really only been two weeks ago? She wondered where Jesmet was in all of this, or how he had let this happen. Oriannon would have liked to have asked him, if he'd still been around. But now the deserted ruins only echoed with the haunted voices of memories, like unwelcome ghosts in a nightmare from which she could not wake. Even the Pilot Stone in her pocket seemed cold and lifeless for the first time since she'd pledged to keep it.

"Whew!" Another reporter wiped his brow as he set up his cam, ready for filming. Now the suns beat down on him as well. "Not much left, is there?"

Oriannon felt her head spin, and not because of the heat reflecting off the rocks. Rather, she couldn't stop thinking of what the place had once been. Here lay shards of a beautiful green mixing bowl with a pattern of white birds on the side. There, charred pages from a book blew over the cliff and fluttered out of sight. Very little else remained to remind her that Owlings had once lived, laughed, and celebrated here.

She picked her way through the rubble to the place where Wist's crooked little cliffside home had once stood, where her friend had lived with her grandfather Suuli. All that remained were piles of stone and splintered timber, tumbled and burned. She bent to pick up a small piece of polished wood, scorched around the edges but delicately curved in a way that reminded Oriannon of a musical instrument. An erhu, perhaps, like the one Wist had played. Perhaps it had belonged to her Owling friend.

She turned the scorched piece around in her hand, trying to hold back the emotions, feeling suddenly almost as scorched as the wood itself. Strange—though she supposed fire might have broken out when the earthquakes hit. The only thing was, she had been here when those quakes had first shaken the city. Yes, Lior had seen damage, but nothing even remotely like this. She stopped a tech specialist as he hurried by on his way back to the shuttle.

"Excuse me." She held out the charred wood. "But do you know what could have caused this?"

The tech hardly slowed down.

"Besides a disruptor beam, you mean? A high enough setting can set a fire. But ... hard to say without running tests."

"Wait—" Oriannon couldn't imagine who would order such a thing. Not even Sola. "Isn't there some way to tell for sure?"

"Sorry." He looked over to where Sola was standing in front of a ruined building. "I really can't say. But take my advice and

125

leave it alone. Things are getting strange these days. Just do whatever she wants you to do, then forget it and go home. That's my approach."

Oriannon nodded as she slipped the wood in her pocket. Forget it? Not possible. If there really had been a fire up here, or if a disruptor had been used to destroy Lior, she would find out.

"Oriannon!" Sola waved at her to join the larger group, which was assembling again. "I'll need you over here with the rest of us."

Oriannon followed a couple of reporters as they all gathered around. They shaded their eyes as several smaller transports landed next to their shuttle. More reporters?

"Here's what you'll be including in your reports." Sola scurried about like a mentor on a field trip, handing each of the reporters an e-tablet. All of them accepted the gift, though some with a puzzled expression.

"I know you're working hard to present this horrific story," she explained, "so this will make it as simple as possible for you. Each one is different, and my staff has carefully prepared it with your needs in mind. No need to worry."

So that's how it works, Oriannon thought as she watched the reporters set up, and she could hardly keep the disgust from showing on her face. *Sola chooses them. Sola brings them here. Sola tells them what to say.*

And by then, it was no surprise when Sola handed another e-tablet to Oriannon.

"What's this?" Ori did her best to stay in character. *Act dumb.*

"Just take a few moments to read it over and memorize it," Sola explained. "I'm sure you'll have no problem."

Memorizing wasn't the problem. When the reporter with the cam focused on her, Oriannon thought about what she was saying while her knees went soft and her voice went shaky.

"All right, dear, you don't have to be so nervous." Sola motioned for the cam to stop. "You're the spokesperson for all of Corista's youth, remember? Why don't you take a deep breath and let's try it again. But this time, I'm going to bring in the boy, so let's do get it right."

The boy? She wasn't sure who that would be, but now it was starting to make more sense. Oriannon nodded and looked around for help, wishing for an interruption. Playing dumb didn't work anymore. So when the cam's red record light started to flash, she took another deep breath and launched into the prepared script.

"We're here on Shadowside," she told the camera, "in the ruins of what was once a busy Owling city. I'm Oriannon Hightower, and I was held here before the planet's axis shifted and earthquakes destroyed this place. But thanks to ... Sola, there are survivors."

Survivors in this case meant the little boy they'd brought off one of the other vessels. As Sola would put it—their "guest star." The cam panned across the ruins where Sola was on her knees next to a frightened little Owling boy, trying to smile him into submission.

This is where the other narration would come in, edited later to explain how Sola never gave up, and personally clawed through one of the ruins to find the little abandoned boy. Oriannon knew the words; one of the other reporters was pacing up and down behind the camera, practicing quietly.

The more Oriannon saw of this circus, the more sick she felt for letting herself be a part of it. The only good news came when the camera stopped and Sola hurried off for a drink of ice water, leaving the little boy wide-eyed and on his own. Oriannon approached him slowly.

"Hey, little guy." She crouched down to his level. He couldn't have been more than five or six. "What's your name?"

At first he wouldn't look at her, wouldn't answer. So she slipped the medallion off her neck and offered it to him.

"You ever seen anything so pretty?" she asked. "My name's Oriannon."

Finally he looked up at her with his big, dark Owling eyes—eyes with a deep sadness that reminded her of Wist, even a little bit of Jesmet himself.

127

"Olim," he finally whispered.

"Olim? That's a nice name."

But he recoiled when she reached out to straighten his dark tousled hair—as if he was used to people who would hurt him. She pulled her hand back but still held out the medallion.

"I'm not going to hurt you, Olim. Here—it may not be as pretty as a Trion necklace, but mine's at home."

His eyes widened even more, if that was possible.

"Trion?" he finally whispered, and he cautiously accepted the medallion.

"Not this one," she admitted. "I got my Trion necklace from ..."

She hesitated, remembering that every word they said could be overheard somewhere else. But as the little boy fingered the medallion, it slipped from his grip, tumbling far down a narrow crevasse that had broken through the plaza tiles.

"Oh, no." The boy reached for the medallion, too late, and it clattered far down into darkness. "Oh, no!"

He looked at her once again with eyes of fear, shrinking away as if she was going to beat him.

"It's okay," she told him over and over. But when he started to cry, she finally gave him a hug.

"Trust me," she whispered into his ear. "You did me a favor. And you know that Trion necklace I told you about? I got it from Jesmet himself."

At the name of Jesmet, Olim pulled away with a look of shock. But Oriannon wasn't about to explain it all now. She held a finger to his lips instead.

"Shh," she whispered. "It's a secret about Jesmet, okay?"

He studied her face for a moment before nodding grimly. She believed he would keep it secret. She also believed he might have more of a story to tell—if she could only find a place to talk to him, away from Sola and her paid reporters.

"Good." Oriannon held up her hand in a pledge. "So listen to me. I promise I'll try to help you if I can. Maybe we can find your mom and dad. Deal?"

He looked at her with his head to the side, as if trying to decide if he could trust her. Finally he smiled faintly and accepted her pledge with two hands.

"Deal."

When she looked down at his feet, she saw that he wore ugly electronic security anklets to keep him from running. That had to mean he'd already been processed through Security back in Corista. She groaned in frustration, heard a clicking sound, and looked over her shoulder to see nearly every cam had been filming them.

Oh, no. Her heart nearly stopped. Even in trying to help the little boy, she hadn't been helpful after all. They'd been filming. Had anyone been able to tell what Oriannon said? She straightened up, careful not to signal to little Olim that something wasn't right.

"No, that's great!" Sola called out as she hurried forward. "Don't move. These are just the kind of shots we were looking for."

Yes, unfortunately. A moment later, Sola joined them, adding her own commentary for the cams. Each one followed her obediently, catching all her moves.

"And this is the little Owling boy we found amidst the ruins," Sola told the cams, her voice taking on a sad tone as she moved closer to him. "We couldn't find out what happened to his parents, though we searched desperately. We have to assume they were lost in the earthquakes. All we know is that we're going to work just as hard now to help find him — and the Owling people who used to live in this city — a better life. We're going to give them the kind of hope they never knew before."

Oriannon stood helplessly by while Sola's straight-faced deception made her feel she needed to take a long shower. All at once she wanted to grab Olim and run away screaming, but obviously she could not.

"There, did you get that?" Sola finally asked the reporters. "Let's try that angle over here."

Oriannon backed away while they took more close-ups and scripted backgrounders, all designed to convince viewers that they were moving heaven and earth to help this little boy. Sola even used that tired old expression.

Oriannon stumbled back to the shuttle, feeling ill for her part in this farce, and afraid of looking back. But she couldn't help watching three techs come in with makeup in reverse, dusting red dirt on the little boy's forehead and rubbing the hem of his little robe to make it look more worn than it already was. He would have to look dramatic for the camera all over again. Of course, now he tensed up once more, but even so he stood perfectly still, as if he knew he had a duty to perform. This time, though, he never took his eyes off Oriannon, and now she could see the pleading there. She finally had to turn away; her vision had so blurred with tears.

"Oriannon!" Sola called her again. "How about one more shot over here with the little boy in front of this building?"

But Oriannon couldn't, not even one more time. Pretending she didn't hear, she hurried toward the shuttle.

"I'm not feeling well," she told the security waiting by the open hatch, and every word was true. The only thing she could do now was lock herself in the restroom, fighting back tears that would not stop, and wait for the others to return.

14

It wasn't hard to see why all the reporters were enjoying this assignment. What was not to enjoy? Once safely aloft, everyone's grav seats released, and the reporters literally drifted over to the fully laden buffet table.

"Enjoy!" Sola played a perfect hostess. "We thought you might need some refreshment after all that hard work."

The reporters chuckled at the joke and seemed to know better than to question Sola. A chef in a floppy white hat stood anchored behind the buffet, carving off slices of bread and dishing up generous pieces of pie doused with cream. "Aren't you going to have anything?" One of the reporters paused to let Oriannon into the line in front of him, but she only shook her head.

"I'm not hungry," she told him, though her stomach growled at the scent of so much good food. But what she said was sort of true. She knew she could not eat, not after what she had seen down on the planet. She needed to find somewhere to be alone.

"At least have a bite," insisted another, the dark-haired reporter who had spoken with her when they'd first landed on Shadowside.

Ori had purposely not asked any for their names, thinking it better not to have to remember any details on this trip.

"Well ..." She paused for a moment, remembering her manners.

"Sure, go ahead." He held one of the flaky delicacies out to her on a fork, smiling a crooked smile at her as he chewed and swallowed another one himself. Goodness, didn't his wife feed him at home?

She gingerly took the pie with a napkin and nodded her thanks.

"We got some great shots of you and the Owling, Miss Hightower," another reporter told her. "My editor is going to be real happy when we put this story together."

Yeah, with all the help you got from Sola. But she kept the thought to herself, and looked around for a way to escape. With all the partying going on in this gold-plated, plush-carpeted extravagance, she thought it couldn't be that hard. She needed to get away to think.

"That's great," she answered. Without looking back she headed for the door at the end of the main cabin, near the restrooms but also off to the side near a spiral stairway. She waited for a moment while a flight attendant in a prim navy blue suit brushed by, then for another moment while Sola told another joke and everyone laughed far too loudly as they piled their plates high with more pastries and breaded fruitmeat.

When no one seemed to be paying attention, she ducked past the "Crew Only" warning sign, slipped down the metal staircase, and found herself alone on the lower utility deck.

She stood quietly for a moment, letting her eyes adjust to the dim lighting and the low ceiling of pipes and conduits. Down here, constantly thrumming engine thrusters caused the metal grate floor to vibrate, and she could feel their power through her shoes. Warm drafts drifting by her face smelled of burnt ion fuel and pneumatic lubricants. Only occasionally did she hear a faint laugh drifting down the stairwell behind her.

Kind of creepy, she thought, and the farther she got from the stairwell, the more intense the engine noise and vibrations became. Still she wound her way through narrow aisles between crates of supplies piled high and strapped to the floor. She wondered if there was any chance the little boy could have been taken down here.

She read some of the labels: diurnal generators, deconstituted consumables. Stuff for longer trips, probably when they went to the farther reaches of their system. Nothing too interesting. Lighted wall panels cast a strange red and blue glow, and she felt her hair stand on end as she stepped closer to the force field generators that powered their craft. She caught her breath at what she saw when she rounded a corner.

"Oh, no!" A large crate had been strapped to the deck, with holes in the sides like tiny windows, and a tight metal mesh nailed across the open front as a crude but effective screen. Four dark shapes cowered inside, huddling and shivering. At first she could not tell if they stood on two feet or four, and for a heart-pounding moment, Oriannon wondered if she should flee while she had the chance.

I shouldn't have come down here! No telling what kind of wild animal this might be or what it might do to her if she ventured too close.

So she held her breath and waited for an attack, ready to bolt for the stairs. But when none came, she straightened her back and took a tiny step forward. In response the creatures inside pressed themselves more tightly into the corner, in the way of trapped animals.

"I'm sorry," she told them, finally gathering her courage to step up to the crate and touch the mesh. "I didn't mean to startle you."

In truth, she was the one more startled—particularly when she got close enough to see these were not wild animals, but Owlings! She strained her eyes to be sure, hardly believing what she saw. In a cage? Three men and a younger woman looked as tired and haggard as the makeup artists had made Olim back when they were taking photos. They didn't answer her.

"Are you from Lior?" Oriannon struggled to keep from breaking down at the sight, barely managing to force out the words. They only looked at each other and shook their heads no. The woman muttered something she could not quite understand over the engine noise, so Oriannon pantomimed a mountain with her hands and raised her voice. "The cliff city? Lior?"

Where else could they be from? Oriannon knew the Owlings lived in a number of other villages and settlements; Wist had once told her that much.

"I have friends in Lior." Oriannon looked around and back toward the stairs, though she couldn't see them directly from where she stood. "Had. A girl about my age? Wist? Her grandfather's name was Suuli, and—"

That certainly got a reaction, and they now stared at her with eyes wider than ever. The Owling man closest to her stepped up to the mesh window, dragging a foot behind him as if to make a quick retreat.

"You're knowing of Suuli?" he asked, and she could barely make out his hoarse voice. That, and she had a hard time making out his words through his heavy singsong accent, heavier even than other Owlings she had heard. Maybe they had different accents in different parts of Shadowside. She lowered her eyes for a moment before looking back at him.

"I met him before he died in the first earthquakes. But I was with Wist just a few weeks ago, after Jesmet returned."

He turned back to the others, and they spoke to each other in hushed tones, eyes filled with fright. The woman still shook in the corner, crossing her arms and looking genuinely ill. The other two men shook their heads again before the leader turned back to her.

"We're not believing you saw Jesmet," he told her. "If you had, you would be in here with us, not out there with them."

"No, you don't understand. I'm your friend, not hers." Most certainly not hers. Oriannon unwrapped her pastry from the napkin and tried to push it through the mesh. "See? Are you hungry? Here, take some of this."

The Owlings made no move to take the food as it dropped to the floor of the cage. They didn't even look at it.

"Why are you acting this way?" she asked them. "I'm not going to hurt you."

The leader studied her more closely, as if trying to decide what to tell her.

"They said the same thing when they were attacking our village," he finally replied. "We fled to Lior."

The engines whined a little more loudly as they banked to the side. Oriannon grabbed for a handhold, and the Owlings fell inside their crate before scrambling back to their feet. She noticed for the first time that they all wore silver glasteel tracking anklets. Apparently the cage wasn't enough.

"Attacked?" she asked. "What kind of attack? You mean, after the earthquakes?"

"Earthquakes we survived. Stealing our water we survived. But when they came to Lior, they knew exactly where to find us. Every hiding place. Every doorway. Every alley. They even came up through the Grand Hall passageways! How could they be knowing? They destroyed everything. And for what?"

His voice trailed off while his eyes took on a glazed, faraway look.

"Sola said she would give you hope," Oriannon mumbled, ashamed that she had once believed it. She squeezed her own hands together, trying to keep from trembling, trying to keep from remembering how she had given Sola every detail of the city. She turned aside and held a hand over her mouth, ashamed to see how she had been used — and how stupid she had been.

"What are you saying?" he asked.

But now she knew just how twisted the words sounded, held up against the truth of Lior in ruins and these poor people captured in a cage.

"I'm so sorry," she managed, afraid to look at him. "I know that Sola said she would give you hope."

"Sola!" He spit the word back at her. "You're seeing what this Sola has done to Shadowside? You're seeing what her securities have done to us? We're house servants now. Slaves. This isn't hope."

Oriannon had to back up a step, away from the words. She felt her cheeks burn as she reached for the piece of scorched wood she'd slipped into her pocket next to the Pilot Stone. If this Owling was right—and he most certainly was—the wood could only have been scorched by a disruptor beam.

"Please," she begged him, though now she wasn't sure she could bear to hear. "I need to know what happened. I *must* know."

For a moment, the Owlings murmured among themselves, arguing, perhaps wondering if they could trust Oriannon. Finally their leader again approached the front of the cage.

"I don't think—" He winced now and held a hand to his forehead, blinking his eyes as if trying to focus. "I don't think you'll be wanting to hear."

"I do. Please."

She waited for him to answer, to tell her what had really happened. But this time he backed away with a new sense of fear in his eyes. Though he opened his mouth, only a low groan came out as he gripped his right temple and fell to his knees.

"What's wrong?" Oriannon pressed her face to the mesh, pushing as close as she dared. She grabbed and shook the simple electronic lock on the cage door, wishing for a combination to set them free. "Can't you tell me anything else?"

But he only waved her off, pointing in the direction of the stairway. He must have heard the footsteps coming their direction before she did.

"Hide!" he warned her. She hesitated only a moment before jumping into the shadows behind a large crate. There wasn't much room to squeeze out of sight, but it was the best she could manage.

Just in time. A moment later she could see a steward checking the cage. He double-checked the door and paused to examine the lock—obviously tampered with and hanging askew. Oriannon pushed herself back into the shadow as far as she could manage, but obviously it wasn't enough.

As the steward turned around he crossed his arms and stared straight at her. She remembered the same tight-faced look on Mentor Narrik's face, back at the academy, when she and Margus had once stepped in late to astrophysics class. This time, she slipped her trembling hand behind her. He touched a comm on his collar and reported back to someone upstairs.

"I've found her," he said. "Level one-b, cargo bay."

Had they sent him out to search?

"Just stretching my legs actually." She stepped out of the shadows wearing her most contrite look, knowing it would probably do no good. "Curious to see what was down here."

"Apparently you found out, and as you see, it's nothing of your concern. You're not to be here, Miss Hightower."

"Really? Well apparently there's nothing special about coach class. Glad it's for them and not us." She laughed to cover her unsteady voice. "Although, isn't there a restroom down on this level somewhere?"

She couldn't be sure the steward was buying her act. But with a straight face, he motioned her back toward the stairway.

"You'll find it back up on the main level."

She wasn't sure how much trouble she was in, but when she looked back over her shoulder she decided it wasn't nearly as much as the four Owlings probably faced. When she heard laughing upstairs again, she knew she had to do something about what she had just seen.

Only, what?

"Oriannon, dear!" Sola was the first to notice her as she made her way back to the media crowd. "I thought perhaps you'd gone off to take a nap or something."

Oriannon glanced quickly at the steward, who ducked away and said nothing.

"Actually," she told Sola with a hasty yawn, "maybe I am a little more tired than I thought."

"And you must be so upset about losing your medallion."

When Sola narrowed her eyes, a hint of an accusation showed through.

"Oh, yes." Oriannon gulped when she realized Sola knew what had happened. "It happened so fast."

"I saw, and I suppose you're not entirely to blame. I must say, however, you'll have to be more careful around those people. We'll get you a replacement when we return to Seramine." Sola beamed at the rest of the reporters, most of whom had drifted off in twos and threes to chat and nibble on their snack trays. "Meanwhile, get all the sleep you can. We have a long day ahead of us."

Oriannon was almost afraid to ask what she meant. What long day?

"Didn't I tell you?" Sola took a sip of her steaming clemson-root tea, then flashed a satisfied smirk. "As soon as we land we're scheduled for an interview program with our friend Meela. You'll be looking your best, won't you?"

Maybe Oriannon would be looking her best, and maybe she wouldn't. She hardly cared at this point. Even so, she checked the mirror in the media green room, the place where guests on Media240 got their makeup just before going on air. She made sure her Trion necklace was safely tucked out of sight, where no one would see it, especially not Sola.

"My, but we have some dark circles under our eyes, don't we?" The makeup artist dabbed a little extra translucent powder on Oriannon's cheeks and checked her chrono. "Still getting used to the dark like the rest of us?"

Three minutes until airtime. How was Oriannon supposed to answer?

That's right, I haven't slept for the past several days, and I've just seen all of Shadowside destroyed. The Owlings have been taken away to a nightmare prison. Other than that, I'm having a great day.

Oriannon sighed and nodded. She would just answer the interview questions and get it over with. Three minutes later, she discovered, Meela Rhon wasn't going to make it that easy.

"So now, this is fascinating, you two." Meela leaned forward in her interviewer's chair, looking from Sola to Oriannon and back again. The set behind them showed a moving Seramine street scene. "You went on this rescue mission to Shadowside cliff city, Liam, and—"

"Lior," Oriannon corrected her, and Meela Rhon stopped short.

"Pardon me?"

"Lior. The city is called Lior."

Meela smiled and nodded.

"Yes, of course." She turned to the nearest tech behind and muttered something about editing that last part out. Then she turned back to the cams. "And this, by the way, is the young woman who should know—after living through such primitive, difficult circumstances there."

"It wasn't difficult." Oriannon shook her head. "They saved my life."

"Yes, fascinating." Now Meela was frowning. "Let's take a look at how her father reacted to his daughter's bravery, shall we?"

The room darkened as a giant wall screen lit up with her father's recorded image, his name at the bottom for those who wouldn't recognize him: *Tavlin Hightower, former Assembly elder.*

Former? Oriannon nearly choked on the word even as she recognized their living room. When had this been recorded?

"I'm proud of my daughter," he told the cam, and his voice sounded as flat as it had during that conversation with Sola. Of course, Sola hadn't told them she was recording it to use on a national media program. But now Meela leaned over and lowered her voice a notch.

"Sola, is this what you want on the show?"

"Maybe you can enhance his voice," said Sola. "It's because of the . . . well, you can fix it."

"No, he's fine." Meela Rhon shook her head. "I mean his daughter."

"Oh, yes, of course. You'll have to excuse her," Sola whispered back. "We've been through a lot in the last day or two. I assume you can enhance that portion of the interview?"

In other words, *edit it out*.

"Of course." Meela turned the charm back on almost as effortlessly as Sola, as if they were competing for the smile award. "Oriannon, dear, please don't worry about a thing."

"But, did it say *former* elder by my dad's name? What was that all about?"

"Former?" Meela looked surprised, but glanced quickly over at Sola. "I'm sure I don't know, but we can certainly look into it later, if you like. Now why don't you just relax a bit, collect your thoughts before we go on."

Oriannon didn't need any thought collecting, but she knew by this time who was controlling the cams. What was the use? With the video clip over and the lights back up, Meela continued with the interview.

"So let's talk for a minute about the latest rescue. Sola, how were you able to locate the little boy?"

That's when Sola launched into her fictional story about searching the ruins, the dangerous wall that nearly collapsed on them, and the little whimper that led them to the young survivor. Of course she embellished it with details sure to bring a tear to their viewers' eyes. But by this time, Oriannon knew that she had only been brought on the show to make Sola's story look better. She glanced backstage when she saw a movement.

"And now we have a special surprise." Meela Rhon motioned to a curtain behind them. Oriannon caught sight of the little Owling boy, surrounded by make-up artists and techs. "We're going to bring in the little survivor that everyone is talking about."

Lights and recorded applause came up while a tech led the wide-eyed little boy into the studio. When he caught sight of Oriannon, he broke away from his handler and ran into her arms, sobbing.

"Hey, Olim," she whispered in his ear over all the noise.

He just clamped on and buried his face in her shoulder. In a moment she would be crying too.

"Shh," she patted him on the back. "It's going to be all right."

But he only squeezed more tightly as the cams circled like a yagwar coming in for the kill. How could she convince the little boy everything would be all right when she didn't believe it herself?

"I'm scared," he told her over and over. "I want to go home."

Of course he had to know his home was gone. But Meela Rhon kept up the chatter as if they had just brought in a cuddly little animal on one of the late night shows. Olim recoiled when she reached over to pat him on the head.

"Well, as you see, he's still recovering from the ordeal," she told the cams. "But there's more to come. Next up, we'll introduce you to the loving Coristan family that has agreed to adopt this little fellow, despite great odds. It's all part of the Peace Initiative."

The lights went down for a moment, the applause went up, and Oriannon still had no clear idea what was going on.

"Here, we need to calm him down a little more." Sola pointed at a tech, who nodded back at her from his spot behind a control panel. Instantly little Olim shook his head and gripped his temple with a free hand, and he began shaking in panic.

"I don't think he's feeling well," Oriannon tried to tell them, and she held him a little closer. What was going on? "Look, there on his forehead. He looks like he might have cut himself."

She pointed out the neat little pink scar on both sides, just below the hairline. Odd. She hadn't noticed them before. Just below the surface of the skin, she noticed a strange throbbing before Olim again covered his head with his hands. She couldn't help thinking back to the Owlings on the shuttle — how they had acted almost exactly the same way.

But no one was listening. When one of the techs tried to pry little Olim loose, he started howling.

"Thirty seconds," called another tech. Sola straightened her hair as if nothing was happening.

"I want to stay with Ori!" cried Olim.

"Here, I should hold him a little longer," Oriannon tried to tell them, but that only brought another tech, who pulled even harder at the little boy in a bizarre tug-of-war. When she gripped his ankles, she felt a pair of security anklets, hidden under the folds of his little pants. But finally Oriannon had to let go, while Olim eventually slumped in what appeared to be fear and exhaustion.

What was going on here?

A moment later they brought in a young, well-dressed couple from backstage and positioned them in chairs. Lights up. More applause. Olim seemed to settle down a bit.

"We're back again with Media240 Reports, where First Citizen Sola Minnik has just been telling us a remarkable story of courage, how she and her staff traveled to the far side of the planet on a humanitarian mission to rescue survivors after the devastating Shadowside earthquake. Sola, what's next for this little survivor?"

That introduction gave Sola the chance to talk about her new initiative to rescue young Owlings and place them for adoption with suitable Coristan families. With tears in her eyes, she explained how so many young Owlings were just looking for a chance, for a place to call home.

And the program continued, working up to the moment Meela Rhon introduced the young couple, and to another round of prerecorded applause. Here was the compassionate family that would take in the little lost Owling, she said. Wiping away a tear of her own, she explained how Sola had brought hope once more to a planet in crisis — one little Owling child at a time. After all, they had been through so much.

Meela let the obvious questions hang in the air. Who wouldn't get behind this? Who couldn't?

"They're different from us of course," explained Sola. "But those of you with pets know, you can get rather attached to them, can't you? And with the proper training, I believe Owling youngsters can find a useful place in your homes. It's the right thing to do."

The applause never let up. Olim had slumped back against a chair, a hand on his temple, fear rising again in his big round eyes. Maybe he'd given up.

"Looks like the little fellow is just a little overwhelmed by all of this," said Meela. "Maybe we should just let our new family take him home so they can get acquainted. What do you think? Touch the link on your screen if you'd like to respond the way this young family has. Find out more about being a sponsor."

Once again, techs turned up the applause. The lights clicked off, and they rushed in to escort the couple offstage.

"This way, Miss Hightower." By this time Oriannon had her own escort. She didn't reach out to Olim, afraid of setting off another scene. But she watched in amazement as the couple simply hurried offstage and through a sliding door, without a look back at Olim.

Another scam. Oriannon shook her head.

Olim, by now looking almost drugged, was at the same time shuffled away and into a small, padded crate. He looked back at her with a silent plea just before the door slammed shut and a tech snapped four latches, one after the other.

"Wait a minute." Oriannon looked around for answers, but Meela Rhon had already joined her techs to review the editing.

Sola, meanwhile, had a quick word of advice for her.

"Don't you ever embarrass me like that again!" she hissed, and her eyes narrowed to slits as she leaned into Oriannon's face. No one else would hear. "I did not give you this opportunity just to have you . . . stray from the script. Do you understand my meaning?"

Oriannon swallowed hard, considered the alternative, and nodded.

Act dumb, she reminded herself. *Don't let her know what you know.*

But right now she hated acting like a sweet innocent idiot, and she would tell Margus how much . . . as soon as she got out of here. But for now . . .

"I'm sorry." Oriannon nodded and looked at her feet, and she knew it would do no good to ask about Olim's security anklets, not here and not now. "I didn't mean to ruin the interview."

"Well ..." Sola paused for a long moment until Oriannon looked back up.

"That was some of the most wonderful footage I've ever seen." Meela Rhon came gushing by on her way out of the studio, putting her arms around both of them. "I just know our ratings are going to spike when viewers see the darling part when that little Owling boy grabs you around the neck, Oriannon. How did you get him to do that? Something you said?"

"Uhh ..." Oriannon fumbled for a lie that would make sense. When she looked over to check on Olim, his crate had already been taken away, and her heart dropped away with it. "He was just a nice little boy who was missing his mother. Where did they take him?"

"Him?" Meela acted as if she had no idea. "He's being well taken care of. Don't you worry about him." She turned to Sola. "You have plenty of others, right, Sola?"

"Of course." Sola nodded, and it brought to mind the parade of shuttles, ferrying so many Owlings away from their homeland ... to what?

"And you be sure to bring Oriannon along next time, my friend." Meela wagged a finger at Sola. "Her face lights up the screen, almost as much as yours."

"Of course it does." Sola smiled once again and shifted effortlessly back into her public-relations mode. "And of course I will. Right, Ori?"

Only my friends are allowed to call me that, Oriannon would have replied if she'd just felt a little more brave. Instead she nodded again, even more weakly this time.

With that, Meela was whisked away inside a small knot of handlers and techs, off to her next appointment, or show, or whatever. She did wave at them on her way out.

"We'd be honored to have you back any time, First Citizen!" she added. "Oh, and you too, Miss Hightower."

Oriannon thought she would rather die.

"We'll be in touch," Sola told her as she headed for another exit in an equal flurry of comm calls and assistants. That left Oriannon standing with the escort, trying to put together the pieces of what just happened. She didn't even have a chance to ask about her father. And once more she shivered from that feeling of wanting to take a long shower, of being a part of something so filthy that it had rubbed off on her in the worst way. The ugly weight of the lie they had just created crashed down on her so hard she could feel her shoulders slump.

There was no adoption plan, only Sola's Plan. No parents, only actors. And poor little Olim shouldn't be trusting her for anything—certainly not for the family she could never find—if they were still alive.

"Miss Hightower?" said the escort, pausing at the sliding door. Techs rolled by with cams on their shoulders, buzzing among themselves on their way to the next show. Station probes zipped about on their errands, ferrying information and equipment between offices and studios. Mission accomplished.

"Coming." She tried to shake the thought of what she had just done, but it would not leave her. There had to be a better way to get answers. She saw her father's image again on an editor's screen, and she knew where she would start.

16

"You're doing fine, Oriannon." Margus's voice crackled over a comm connection the next morning. "You looked like you knew what you were doing."

"You only saw the edited version." She shaded her eyes from the worst of the suns, kept walking toward the Temple, and lowered her own voice to speak into her tiny shoulder-mounted comm. "You should have heard what I said before they cut it all out."

"Wish I could have. But you should see all the shuttles still landing, Oriannon. I'm watching from those wrecked warehouses. I don't think they've stopped flying since the other day."

She looked past a low red roof in the direction of the Plains of Izula to see what he meant. Sure enough, in the distance a steady line of shuttles still headed toward the dome, which of course was too far off to see.

"I see them. But Margus, I've got to tell you what really happened at the studio. There was this family, right? A couple, really. And they—"

She bit her tongue as she rounded the last corner before the Temple square, where a probe hovered just in front of her, blocking her entry.

"I didn't catch that last part. Ori?" Her comm buzzed as Margus tried to re-up the connection. She turned her head to the side, though she knew the probe might still be able to hear every word.

"I'll get back to you after I see my father." She pressed the button sewn into the shoulder of her plain, off-white tunic, terminating the link. The traditional Coristan dress hung to mid-thigh over long black pants, and she casually brushed out a wrinkle in the material, pretending not to be concerned.

But how could she not be? She had hardly seen her father since she returned from Shadowside. No one would explain why he was called the "former" Assembly elder. And again he left home before she even woke. Concerned? Meanwhile the probe had already scanned her from three meters away.

They never used to do that, she thought. Well, and she used to be able to walk right into the Temple to see her father any time she wanted. But no more.

"Name and number," demanded the probe.

"Again?" She parked her hands on her hips, where a full water bottle sloshed from her belt. "You already know."

She almost caught her breath at her own impertinence. But maybe it was time to challenge these beastly little pests. Oriannon tried not to look at its ugly eye, but she could swear it blinked.

"Purpose."

"I'm here to see my father, Tavlin Hightower." Oriannon's voice cracked even when she tried her best to keep it steady. "He's an Assembly elder."

Or rather, he *was*. She waited while the probe checked its files, and it took longer than it should have.

"Still checking," it told her a minute later, and she wondered how far she would get if she tried to scale the tall stone boundary fence or push past the locked gate. Finally a green light blinked on the side of the probe.

"You may proceed."

"Really? Say, while you're checking, how about telling me what happened to a scribe named Cirrus Main?"

The probe only hesitated a moment this time.

"No such record. Please proceed."

"Didn't think so."

Oriannon didn't ask again as the locked gate to the Temple courtyard snapped open and she slipped through. She would have just hurried across the courtyard if she hadn't noticed a small movement out of the corner of her eye.

There — nearly hidden behind a hedgerow — two small men with shaved heads and ragged clothes tugged at the roots of a stubborn dead tomos shrub, while a young woman in a soiled gray robe pushed from the other end. They could only barely sway the thorny branches, but they kept at it doggedly — until the woman noticed Oriannon staring and they stopped to stare back.

"Owlings." Oriannon mouthed the words, and of course that fact was painfully obvious. None stood taller than the bush, and even at a distance their wide eyes gave them away. Their feet were bare, and all three wore shackle-style security anklets.

Not so obvious was why the Owlings were working in the Temple gardens to begin with, without protection from the searing midday suns, and especially without a probe to guard them. They glistened with sweat, and the smaller of the two men leaned on his friends for support. He looked to Oriannon as if he might topple over at any minute.

"Here." She stepped toward them, holding out her unused water bottle. "Looks like you need this more than I do."

Instead of accepting the offering, the Owling woman stood her ground and brought a hand to her face as if debating what to do. They looked at each other with the same uncertain fear Oriannon had seen in Olim's eyes, and in the eyes of the Owlings on the shuttle. It made her wonder if Wist had been put to work like this, perhaps somewhere else in Seramine.

"Here. Please take it," she told them, still holding out the water. "You have to drink something."

But when they would not take the bottle from her hand, she uncapped it, set it down on the ground in front of them, and slowly turned away. If they were as thirsty as Oriannon thought they were, they would surely change their minds.

Instead, a cry of alarm brought her around to see two probes descending on the Owlings as they cowered in fear. Where had the probes come from? Each one displayed dual attack arms, spanned from tip to tip by a jagged, threatening stream of bright blue plasma energy.

"Stop it!" Oriannon lunged forward without thinking. "They're not doing anything wrong!"

At the sound of Oriannon's shout, the probe spun to meet her. Unfortunately its plasma field caught the tip of her outstretched left hand, slapping it away with a withering sting that made her cry out in pain. Though the probe had only dealt her a glancing blow, a burning sensation leaped up her arm as Oriannon fell to the ground.

"This is not an authorized assembly," the probe told her, matter-of-factly. It reached down and picked up the spilled bottle, emptying the rest of the water on the gravel path. "You are not authorized to be here."

"Yes, I *am* authorized!" Oriannon gasped and got to her knees, cradling the injured hand. "What do you think you're doing anyway? I'm going to report this to the Assembly, and —"

"It's okay." The Owling woman raised her hand in a gesture of thanks. So she *did* speak. "No trouble for our sake. Please be going."

Oriannon stopped in mid-sentence, watching numbly as the Owlings returned to wrestling with the tomos shrub. The two men didn't look back, but the woman glanced over one more time and said a silent *thank you.*

The probes, now that they had intimidated these workers, made no other warnings but slowly retracted their attack arms and assumed a watching position several meters away.

"Just trying to help," Oriannon mumbled. Her poor left hand tingled with a thousand needles, and she could hardly move her fingers, but she dusted herself off with her good hand and hurried toward the Temple once again.

She just hoped she could stop from dissolving into tears, this time in one of the impressive, high-ceilinged Assembly meeting chambers where her father met her five minutes later. Here the wood-paneled walls were lined with holo-portraits of elders from past generations, and Oriannon couldn't help thinking they were watching her. She took a deep breath and slipped her hand behind her back as her father waved the sliding door closed.

"They told me you were on your way." Elder Hightower stood by one of the portraits, looking paler than the holo-image. "Actually, I hate to say it, but I'm expecting Sola here in a couple of minutes."

He must have seen her stiffen at the name. But this time she would not be sidetracked, she would not be interrupted, and she would definitely not cry, no matter what.

"Father, they're calling you a *former* elder. What are they talking about? Security can't just fire you, can they?"

"Oh. Is that why you came?" He offered a weak smile as he glanced toward the closed door. Sola, of course, could come marching in at any time. "I hope you're not worried about rumors."

"It's not just rumors, Father. But how can I know? You never tell me anything."

She fingered the Pilot Stone in her pocket, which reminded her she carried secrets as well. He looked so worried, she couldn't bear to give him more to think about.

"Look, I wish I could explain, Oriannon. All I can say right now is that the elders are going to be working with Security in a new way. It's mostly politics. Trust me. It's all going to work out."

Oriannon studied her father, trying hard to keep her jaw from dropping in disbelief.

"That's all you can tell me? Father, every time I turn around, something bad happens, then something worse."

"I know how it looks. I saw the interview, and I know a lot of things seem confusing right now."

This time Oriannon held her head in her hands, wishing she could scream.

"I don't think it's so confusing anymore. I just passed three Owlings out in the courtyard, working like slaves. But then a bunch of probes come down and nearly killed them, just because I was trying to give them a stupid bottle of water. That's not confusing. That's just evil!"

"Ori, Ori." He looked around the large chambers and sighed before lowering his voice. "I know you're concerned about those people, but you can't blow it out of proportion. It's Sola's Plan, and there's not much we can do about it right now. It's the Maker's will besides. You can't ask a lot of questions."

"But it's not right, and I don't think the Maker would want stuff like this to happen. Would he want all the Owlings brought over here as slaves? I've seen things, Father. I know it's not the way Jesmet would want it."

"Jesmet? You've got to let that go, dear. It's over and done. You've got to face the fact that Jesmet is dead."

"No, he's ..." She shook her head as tears now filled her eyes, wondering how she could tell him. If only he could see for himself that Jesmet lived! If only she could prove it to him! Instead she reached into her pocket, pulling out the scorched piece of wood from the ruins of Wist's home.

"This is from Lior, and it proves something." She held it out for him to see. "See? These scorch marks are from disruptor beams. I'm giving Margus a piece too. He could test it to make sure."

He took it from her hand, which by now was shaking noticeably. But she wasn't finished.

"See, I don't think the city was ruined from earthquakes or fires, the way the media — or Sola — have been telling us."

He narrowed his eyes at her and crossed his arms.

"I'm not sure what you're saying, Oriannon, but if you think Coristan vessels — "

"Attacked." She filled in the word. "What if they *attacked* the Owlings, just like the probes attacked those Owlings out in the courtyard? That's what I think happened. That's what I've heard. And now Sola is telling everybody about her big rescue, but it's a total lie. You have to know it's a lie. I don't know what she's thinking, but — "

"No, you stop right there." He raised his voice and held up his hand. "Stop. You can't go accusing Sola this way. You don't know what you're saying."

The holo images on the wall seemed to lean even closer, as if generations past wanted to hear her story too.

"But what if it's true?" She pointed to the evidence in his hand. "What if we can prove it? Can't you do something about her? What if ..."

She just couldn't make herself ask him, *What if Jesmet was really alive?*

"It's not that simple, honey. Believe me, I ... I wish it were."

For a moment he seemed to soften, as if he truly wanted to tell her something more. But then he dropped the charred wood on the floor and reached for his head as the horrible, faraway look crept into his eyes once again.

"Father?" Once again she wasn't sure which father she was talking to. The firm, loving father who always knew what to do — or the pained, distant father who shook in fear and who spoke in whispers. She wished she knew what she could do to keep him from slipping away.

"Daddy," she whispered, "please tell me what to do."

For a moment he was silent, until a soft chime sounded and the conference room door slipped open to reveal an aide pushing a

153

large lev-cart stacked high with probes. Oriannon gasped softly at the sight of so many, so close, though obviously they had not yet been powered up.

"Sir. Sola here to see you. We're going to be stationing more of these around the Temple."

Oriannon's father focused his eyes and seemed to return to himself for a moment. He waved at the aide and nodded.

"Please tell her I'll be just a moment. Park that cart right inside here."

The aide raised his eyebrows and sputtered something about remembering what happened last time when she was kept waiting.

"I said I'll be right with her, all right? Now park it over there."

He motioned to the corner of the room, and without another word, the aide did as he was told and hurried back out the door, allowing it to slide closed. When Oriannon's father spoke again, his voice sounded barely above a whisper. He gripped her by the shoulders, desperation in his eyes.

"I'm sorry I let you get involved with her, honey. That's all I can tell you right now. Just be careful."

He pointed toward the back corner of the room where the new probes were parked on their lev-cart, and for the second time that day someone asked her to leave. First the Owling woman, and now her father.

"Father," she couldn't stop the tears anymore. "You know I—"

"No more, Ori." Urgency filled his voice that she had not heard before. "I'm getting you out before she gets here. For your own protection."

He marched her past the carved conference table to the far wall, though it seemed to Oriannon he might be even more confused than he appeared. As they brushed past the cart, he accidentally knocked one of the probes loose with his shoulder, sending it bouncing to the floor. Instead of picking it back up, he closed his eyes and held his forehead.

"Where are we going?" She looked up at him to understand. "There's no way out here."

"It's a portal. Do you know what that is?"

"I've read about them, but I wasn't sure they were real."

Behind them the chime at the door sounded again, warning them Sola was about to step in. Her father trembled as he guided her toward the wall, and his words came in short bursts between breaths.

"They're real enough. Now go."

And then she stiffened in fear — not because of any portal, but realizing she had not finished what she'd come to tell her father. She dug in her heels and almost tumbled to the floor.

"Father," she blurted out. "I know you might not want to hear this, but —"

"Not now. Just hold on, all right? It may be a bumpy ride, because —"

"Father, I've seen him. Jesmet is alive!"

" — because the portal may not be quite calibrated for someone your size."

"Did you hear me, Father? I said —"

"But I'm sure you'll be safe."

"Jesmet —"

"Yes, I know." He guided her straight towards a portion of the paneled wall, his hand on her elbow. "We'll talk about it later. I'll be home when I can. Now go!"

"But, Daddy —"

This time she managed to trip over the stray probe. She put out her hands to keep from slamming into solid wall. Instead she felt her hands literally sucked into the wall, and she could only stare at the disappearing stubs of her arms. But before she could wonder too much, her shoulders followed into the fast-moving current, then the rest of her.

The effect was less orderly than she hoped. The portal pulled and yanked at her mercilessly, sending her spinning head over heels, off balance in a twilight in between the Assembly chambers and the outside world.

She instinctively grabbed for a handhold, but found nothing except dimly lit empty space that quivered and shimmered the more she tried to grasp it. Something hard and metallic slammed into her back, sending her spinning even more. She cried out as the portal spun her into the kind of dizziness that squeezed the breath out of her.

A moment later she tumbled out of the portal, literally spit out into a thick growth of bushes, still tumbling. She winced at stone and brick flying past from all directions, almost materialized but not quite, until she felt solid cobblestone beneath her.

Oriannon had somehow materialized in the middle of a city street, and while her arm twisted behind her, she managed to keep rolling and sliding until finally skidding to a rest on her back. A cushioned bump of air and a soft jolt of hair-raising energy told her a lev-scooter had nearly run over her.

"Where did *you* come from?" A woman looked straight down over her handlebars at Oriannon. Oriannon tried to sit up, but her aching head would not cooperate. "I nearly ran you over."

"Nearly?" Oriannon couldn't tell the difference. Finally she managed to lift her head slightly, just in time to see a stream of lev-scooters and other transporters zip by. Each one laid on its warning buzzer; several drivers suggested with startled yells that she immediately remove herself from the middle of the avenue.

"I was just driving along, and—" The white-faced scooter driver snapped her fingers. "Just like that, you rolled out of nowhere."

"Sorry!" Oriannon reached to pull herself up and took a quick look around. The chic boutiques and leafy street trees told her she'd materialized right in the middle of Ossek Way, Seramine's busy main avenue.

Behind her, the Temple stood bathed in a pink afternoon sunlight, and a quick visual measurement told her the portal had ended only a couple of hundred meters from where she'd entered. She got to her knees, tried to clear her head as she apologized again, and looked for a way through the crowded traffic. In the process she discovered what had bumped into her so hard in the middle of the portal. The probe that had fallen off the cart back in the Temple had rolled through and followed her here.

"Out of the way!" Another angry commuter yelled.

"Believe me, mister," she told him, but he had already zipped by. "I don't like this any more than you do."

"You need help," the woman finally decided, moving slowly back into traffic. "I'm calling Security."

"No!" That gave Oriannon all the motivation she needed. "I mean, don't bother them. I'm sure they have enough to do without worrying about kids who fall down in the middle of the street. I'm getting out of here."

She glanced down at the wayward probe again, and for a moment thought about leaving it there, but then had a better idea.

I wonder what Margus could do with it.

So she snatched it up, tucked it under her arm, and covered it as much as she could with the folds of her tunic. With one last look back at the Temple, she hopscotched her way through traffic, and headed straight for the only safe place she could think of to meet her friends — the Glades.

17

"This is the absolute coolest thing you have ever done, Oriannon."
Margus grinned and poked at the shiny black probe. Despite
its rough ride through the portal, it still looked brand new when
Margus laid it out on a blanket in the middle of the Glades. "But
I still can't believe you actually had the nerve to steal it right out
from under Sola's nose."

Oriannon was starting to think she should have left the thing
back in the avenue.

"Well even if I *had* taken it," she told him, "would that have
been so bad? At least it's one less probe to harass us, or attack the
Owlings. And you know what else? I was thinking maybe we could
use this thing to get closer to the prison camp, maybe see what
happened to Wist."

"I agree with Oriannon," said Carrick.

"You always agree with Oriannon," countered Margus. "She
could say you're a furry blue treb bear, and you'd say 'I agree with
Oriannon.'"

"You think she's wrong?" For once Carrick wasn't letting
Margus walk away with the argument so easily. "Nobody else has
a probe like this."

159

"True, but do you have any idea what it's going to take to reconfigure this thing? And even if we do, then what?"

"Simple." Oriannon thought as she spoke, which was different than making it up as she went. "First we find other probes flying into the camp, and we steer this one into the group. Then when we're in there, we just search tents until we find her."

"No problem, out of ten thousand tents, right?" Margus never took his eyes from his work. "Then Wist hops on the probe and rides to freedom, along with every other Owling who's been captured."

"Get serious, Margus," Oriannon told him. "We're talking about our friend in a prison camp."

"I *am* serious. I'm working on this thing, okay? I just don't think it's going to be that simple. Oh, and you know that piece of charred wood you showed me?"

He pulled it out of his pocket and tossed it back at Oriannon, offering his verdict. "It's coated with disruptor particles. Off the scale."

Oriannon nodded and pressed her lips together. Of course it didn't surprise her, but Margus still didn't look satisfied.

"So can you explain all this yet?" he asked.

Oriannon had no quick answers as Margus ticked off point by point on his fingers. "Okay, I'll tell you what I think. First, Sola and her securities go in and level all the Owling cities. You think just for the water? Maybe. Or maybe that was just an excuse.

"Two, they round up all the Owlings and bring them back to a fortified camp. Nobody's complaining yet. Not even the Owlings."

"They don't usually complain about anything," Oriannon explained. "They're not like that."

"Maybe they should learn. But anyway, three, Sola starts bringing in a few of the Owlings for work teams. She makes it look like they've been rescued from earthquakes or whatever, and she even asks people to adopt some of the orphans. Pretty sweet deal."

"Except for the Owlings," added Carrick.

"Except for the Owlings. Meanwhile, Sola takes down the Assembly of Elders, maybe so no one will get in her way. Everybody in Corista thinks Sola is their hero. End of story."

Not even a leaf rustled in the Glades around them. For a moment, Oriannon could say nothing about the awful truth of his words. She wondered where Jesmet fit in, or if the Stone had anything to do with it.

"And after all that," he added, "we're going to send in a stolen probe to look for one girl we think might be in the camp. Makes sense to me."

"How come you're always so sarcastic?" Oriannon thought she'd ask. "At least we're doing *something*. So do you know how to adjust the frequency so we can use it, or not?"

He sighed as he studied a set of instructions that flashed at him from his e-reader, the ones he'd hacked from his dad's work network.

"Just give me a few minutes, okay? You guys are so impatient."

It wasn't that they were impatient, really. Oriannon just hoped that after three hours of tinkering, he might be able to put it back together without leaving a handful of parts behind.

"Those are just extras." Margus tried to explain ten minutes later as he clicked the other half of the shiny black cover into place. "I don't think they do anything."

Whether they did or not, they were ready to test their borrowed probe — this time on a new control frequency. Margus held up a remote that had a keypad and a small screen, while he toggled a cursor for guiding the probe left, right, up, and down.

But Carrick still had her doubts. "You sure it's not going to wake up and, you know, hurt us?" she wondered. She stepped backward, putting a buffer between her and the probe.

Margus rolled his eyes.

"Look, I'm throwing it into a control frequency nobody else uses."

"Nobody?" Carrick obviously wanted to be sure.

"Of course." He paused. "Well, seems to me maybe city garbage collectors use it to talk to each other. But they hardly do that very much, so it's not an issue. We're totally safe."

"Hmm. Garbage collectors, did you say?"

"Right. But what I'm saying is that *we're* going to control this one. Not Security or anybody else. We can leave the weapon system offline, so this thing can't hurt anyone. Here—I'll do that right now."

"You're sure?" Carrick wasn't taking any chances.

"I told you, all right?"

Oriannon hoped he was right too. Because unlike Carrick and Brinnin, she had ridden along on one or two shuttle flights with Margus Leek at the helm. More than anyone else, she knew the considerable gap between what Margus said and what Margus could actually do. Maybe she knew even better than Margus himself.

Then there was still the small matter of the pile of spare parts, which Margus had simply shoved off to the side as he checked his remote.

"Here we go!" At Margus's command the probe came to life, humming and lighting up. Brinnin and Carrick clapped and cheered. Still the probe didn't rise from the blanket; it only turned circles while making grinding noises.

"It's not working." Carrick was the first to mention the obvious.

"It's powering up for the first time, all right?" Margus hit the power button with his thumb several times, causing the probe to lurch about. "Give it a chance—whoa!"

The probe suddenly decided to hover at shoulder height, where it continued its startup dance. As it spun slowly, its single eye came to life, once again giving Oriannon the unsettled feeling that someone had given their sight for the sake of a machine. She shivered at the thought.

"There, see?" Margus crowed as he entered several more settings into the remote. "Starts up perfect. With this thing, anybody can work it. I think it should have a pretty good range from here, and you know these things can shift into hyperspeed, which means you have to be extra—"

"Let's just see how it works," said Brinnin, reaching for the remote. But as she did Margus must have pressed something else, sending the probe into action—straight up to the surrounding canopy, where moss hung on treetops and flocks of viria fluttered about.

"Bring it back down!" said Carrick.

By now Margus was frantically working the remote. Oriannon just stood watching, her arms crossed. She could have expected as much.

"Anybody can work it, huh?" she asked. Margus bobbed and weaved as he punched every button on the remote, as if it might help guide their probe or coax it back down. Instead of responding, though, it only circled vaguely over the treetops and wobbled off in the direction of Seramine.

"Just needs some fine-tuning." Margus wiped the sweat from his forehead.

"I think we'd better follow," suggested Brinnin, and as usual she made the most sense. She didn't wait for anyone to agree; she just set out after it.

Oriannon arched her eyebrows and looked at Margus before following Brinnin. She didn't want to think what might happen if this probe simply wandered back to town straight into the hands of a Security detail. If that happened, there would be some explaining to do.

"All right, all right." Margus still tried working his remote as he joined the chase. At least the probe didn't seem to be in a hurry.

Oriannon caught sight of it a few times through the trees as it wobbled this way and that.

Fifteen minutes later, they all pulled up short in a neighborhood of midsize homes, attractive two-story stucco buildings that marched shoulder-to-shoulder down narrow avenues. In front of every house, a leafy tree provided shade, while bright flower boxes hung from hooks and stands on shady porches.

"Is that it?" Brinnin pointed as she caught her breath. And sure enough, the runaway probe seemed to have locked into formation around a couple of city garbage collectors, working their way down the street. One drove a large, hovering sled with a collection and sorting bin in the back, while another emptied trash collection barrels and tossed them into flower beds and doorways.

"Oh, no." Margus groaned when he saw what had happened.

"I can see now that was an excellent frequency to use." Carrick leaned up against a nearby two-story apartment building, arms crossed and watching. "I like the way you think, Margus."

The probe circled overhead as one of the sanitation workers spoke into his shoulder comm and dumped another load into his tired old lev-cart. He looked up and ducked, as if he expected an insect to attack. Instead, the probe just kept circling, almost close enough for the man to swat, but just out of reach.

"Don't do that!" Margus warned him, but from a half-block away, the man in greasy green coveralls obviously couldn't hear.

"So what do we do?" wondered Carrick. "Just walk over there and grab it?"

"Yeah," answered Brinnin, "while anyone in the whole neighborhood can see us."

They all looked at Margus, who threw up his hands.

"Don't look at me." He tried the remote again. While he did now seem to be able to control the altitude, he still couldn't get the probe to stop circling. Sometimes it dipped, other times it wobbled in its new orbit.

"This is pretty funny," said Carrick. Oriannon might have agreed—if she hadn't noticed what had just rounded the corner and started toward them.

"Don't look now," she said, lowering her voice and drawing back. She assumed they could all see the two securities on patrol, each riding a shiny black single-place lev-scooter.

"Bring it down to me when I get there," she called over her shoulder as she set out at a slow jog down the street toward the probe. If she hurried, she hoped perhaps the garbage sled would block their view and the securities wouldn't notice.

By the time she reached the sanitation workers, however, the securities had already covered half the distance between her and them. She guessed by then they had closed to within ten meters. Still they showed no sign that they had noticed her or the wayward probe. Despite their fast lev-scooters, she might still have a jump on them. So when Margus brought the probe down lower, she simply reached up with two hands and plucked it out of the air.

"Hi, there." Oriannon smiled at a husky sanitation worker who stood between her and the approaching securities. "Do you mind if I borrow that can for just a minute?"

"Uh—" He stared at her with a slack-jawed look of amazement. Without waiting for him to reply, she simply lifted the refuse can from his grip, stuffed the squirming probe inside, and added several bags of pungent household waste from the back of the sled as padding. *Very* pungent. She clamped the top on quickly, and the garbage can seemed to take on a life of its own as it tried to circle the men the same way the probe had done.

Oriannon kept a desperately tight grip on the handle, as the securities approached and then slowed to watch. She could almost feel their eyes on the back of her head.

"Crazy kid," muttered the garbage man, loud enough for everyone to hear. He grabbed the can and slammed it down on the pavement before leaning on it. "They have no idea what kind of toxic gas can build up when you leave trash out in the sun too long."

165

"Toxic?" asked one of the securities.

"Yeah, deadly, even. We run into methamine gas all the time. Peels the paint right off your fancy lev-scooter. Here, let me give you a whiff."

The garbage man started to unlatch Oriannon's can, but that was obviously enough for the securities.

"You don't need to demonstrate." The nervous security shook his head before twisting the throttle on his scooter and jetting down the street, followed closely by his partner. They disappeared around the far corner a moment later, leaving the garbage workers doubled over in laughter.

"Good one, huh?" The sled driver stepped down to slap his partner on the back. "Did you see how twitchy he got when you offered him a whiff?"

They nearly rolled on the pavement as they congratulated each other for outsmarting the securities. Methamine gas? What a joke.

Which was all very well, and Oriannon smiled her thanks, but she still had a probe to retrieve from inside an aromatic garbage receptacle.

"Careful there, miss," warned the first worker. When he flexed a muscled arm, he revealed a tattoo of the Trion. "That stuff in there is really toxic."

Which of course only set them up for another wave of laughs, while Oriannon carefully dug through a pungent pile of aged fish bones and other unidentified nasty items to extricate her prize.

"Margus!" she yelled. "Can't you shut this thing off? It won't sit still!"

By that time the garbage men must have realized what they had actually stumbled across. Both of them helped Oriannon hold down the probe while Margus ran over, flipped up a small access panel in its side, and powered it down. Their friend with the Trion tattoo gingerly dabbed at the side of the probe with a greasy rag from his hip pocket.

"Never been this close to a dead one," he muttered. "Usually it's in your face and none too friendly."

"Say," said the driver. "You wouldn't want to sell it to me, would you? It might look good back home, mounted on the wall. Long as it doesn't light up again, that is. Can you pull the power supply?"

"Yeah," agreed his friend. "Your wife would appreciate that a whole lot. Almost as much as the giant stuffed terramole head."

Which set them to laughing once more, and Oriannon sighed with relief as she and Margus carried off their prize.

"Thanks again," she told them. "I sure appreciate what you did."

"Yeah," agreed Margus. "You have no idea."

The two men looked at each other with a shrug, then back at the slick black probe.

"It's our duty as patriotic Coristans," said the driver.

"Ha!" the other man agreed with a chuckle and wiped his hands on his grimy coveralls. "But you kids be careful, eh? That thing's no toy."

"Right," answered Margus. The man squared his shoulders and faced Oriannon one more time.

"I'm not going to ask where you got it, young lady. But what do you think you're going to use it for, anyway?"

Oriannon caught her breath and wondered how to answer. The truth?

"We're going after our friends. One at a time, if we have to."

18

I don't understand it!" Margus threw down the remote and stalked off to the back window of Oriannon's house. "I did everything right. I even plugged in my dad's password. It ought to work."

Before the biomice could activate, Oriannon picked up the remote and examined the small screen, seeing what the probe saw: deck furniture and the little ceramic outdoor fireplace her father once enjoyed—when he used to spend time at home.

"This button for up?" she asked, pressing an arrow at the top of the remote. Brinnin looked over Oriannon's shoulder, watching every move.

"I tried that," Margus called back. "It's not responding. I think you might have broken it when you stuffed it into the garbage can yesterday."

"Of course. My fault." But Oriannon watched the perspective change as the probe rose to her command. Instead of seeing the deck railing, now she focused on the view across the darkened Rift Valley below her home, the twinkling lights of distant homes and farms. Far beyond that stretched the Plains of Izula, leading

169

to the borderlands between Corista and what was once known as Shadowside.

"Way to go, Ori." Brinnin quietly encouraged her.

She nudged the toggle stick forward with her thumb and caught her breath as the deck disappeared and the valley floor opened up below. A moment later, Margus rushed back to join Brinnin and look over Ori's shoulder too.

"How'd you do that?" he asked, looking back and forth between her monitor and the empty deck out the windows. "It's — it's gone!"

"Of course it is." She smiled and focused on the screen. "We're flying down Ossek Way right now."

"Wait!" He reached over and tried to grab it from her, but she pulled away. "You're going to smash it into that tree."

"I'm not smashing into anything," she told him as she guided it around another corner. "It has just enough force field to deflect obstacles if they get too close."

"You figured that out by yourself? But I don't understand how you got it to run. Unless . . . oh. Wait a minute. Put it in my hand for a second. I'll give it right back."

She shrugged and followed his directions. And sure enough, Margus frowned and handed it right back.

"It's keyed to a different set of biosigns," he told her. "Yours must be close to whoever it's personalized for."

The thought chilled her when she realized where this particular probe had come from.

"Hers?" she whispered.

"Congratulations," Margus replied. "You and the Head of Security seem to share biosigns. Or close enough."

"This is too weird." She stopped the probe. "And I don't like it."

"Just a gender biosign adjustment," Margus told them. "Now that I know, I can adjust the setting."

She still didn't like directing a probe that was designed for Sola Minnik. But maybe Margus was right.

"All right." She concentrated again on the screen. "But I'm tired of zipping around empty streets. I'm going to see if we can get inside the camp."

"Are you sure?" He glanced up at the sky. "The suns are coming up in a couple of hours. Barely enough time to get there and back, even at hyperspeed. After that it might get tougher to pull this off."

"Maybe, maybe not." She bit her lip in concentration for the next several minutes as she navigated a hyperspeed course to the camp and then guided the probe into position low into a clump of bright pink cerise bushes, not far from the camp.

"Now," she said under her breath, "let's see what we can see." She rotated the eye, taking in the landscape surrounding the camp.

Margus looked on. "The first test," he told her, "is to see if we can blend in with other probes without anyone discovering us."

In the distance she could make out the now-familiar force field bubble around the camp, shimmering blue like a huge glass bowl over a lamp. Row upon row of tents shimmered out of focus behind the bubble, while the occasional shuttle landed briefly just outside the main entry to load and unload Owlings.

"You see that?" Margus pointed out securities bustling about just inside the perimeter. Some rode scooters, others traveled about in lev-sleds packed with prisoners. But their real chance didn't come until some ten minutes later, when swarms of probes descended like insects from the city, all aiming for the only entry through the force field and into the camp.

"There, there!" Margus jumped at the sight. "There must be at least a hundred!"

"I see them." Oriannon fumbled with the eye-view, pointing it first into the bushes, before bringing it back out on the flock. "Now let's see if we can ..."

She eased up on the toggle stick as the largest part of the probe flock filtered by, and she watched for a chance to blend in. Then just as suddenly as they appeared, she found her probe sucked into their movement, bouncing against minor force fields, heading straight for the camp opening.

"Slow down!" Margus jumped up. "You're going to crash it again."

"I'm trying, all right?" As Oriannon maneuvered through the flock, she wondered if something or someone else had taken a hand to the controls. When she tried to move left, it stayed straight on course. Right, and it bumped a little but remained more with the flow.

"I'm losing control," she cried, biting her lip. Wrestling with the controls no longer did any good. But still she was on course for the opening, so what else could she do? Something else made her sit up even straighter.

"Uh-oh." Margus noticed it too, and he peered straight into the screen with her at the disturbance just inside the main gate. Even through the shimmering blue they could both make out what was going on. Oriannon wished she could not.

"We've seen this happen before." She dug in her heels, as if that could stop the probe short. Desperately she worked the controls, trying to pull to one side or the other, anywhere but straight. "Come on, please!"

But no matter how far she pulled back on the toggle, no matter how much she pressed the abort button, their probe had joined in the mind of the flock and could not be stopped from descending upon the Owling man at the entry. Just like the other Owlings before him, he had obviously tried to jump from one of the lev-sleds and run to freedom, but he'd only made it two or three steps before being hit and attacked by the first probes.

It did not stop there, as wave upon wave of probes descended on him and he fell to the ground, squirming and covering his head. Still they came like a horrible swarm of enraged rivin fowl, jolting him with visible blue high-voltage jolts. Surely this wasn't necessary.

"No!" Oriannon groaned and closed her eyes as she dropped the remote to the ground, terrified of what the probe was doing. She prayed hard and fast, but in a stinging flash of tears she knew that what she had meant for good had suddenly turned so evil. "Please, no!"

"Don't give up, Oriannon." Margus picked up the remote and held it out to her. "It has to drop out of swarm mode sometime. I think there's a built-in override when the probes all respond to an emergency."

"And we can't stop it?"

"I think it's part of the design. I'm guessing we should be okay again after a minute or two."

"You're *guessing?*"

"Look, I don't know any more than you do, okay?"

Of course there was only one way to find out. Still Oriannon was afraid to look or think that she had just taken part in such a horrendous attack. She could have thrown up at the thought of what they'd done, but still she had to know.

"Do you think he's still … alive?"

"N-no. I mean, maybe. I hope so. Depends." He jabbed the remote at her and raised his voice. "Here, would you just take the remote? How do you expect to know unless you look?"

Oriannon hesitated once more, but finally held out her shaking hand. She would look. She had to, though it was almost impossible to see anything through the interference of buzzing probes. She adjusted the view to a slightly wider angle, allowing them to watch two securities yank the Owling off the ground by the shoulders. Alive? With a little help he stumbled back toward the sled he'd jumped from. Finally Oriannon breathed.

"Good," she whispered. "Thank you."

"It wasn't your fault." Brinnin rested a hand on her shoulder.

"There!" Margus pointed to a small green light that popped up in the corner of the screen. "Try it now. I think the override is gone."

Yes—but this time she had to be careful of where she guided their probe. Ahead there was a confusing mass of buildings, tents, and probes just inside the entry. She pulled the probe away from the crowd and slowed it down as she explored between rows of tents.

"It'll be real easy to get lost in here." She did her best to keep it high and not to bump into anyone. "All the tents look exactly the same."

"Owlings too," added Margus, and she couldn't argue. Owlings in ragged dirt-gray hooded robes shuffled around the camp in twos and threes, some carrying heavy black buckets of what must be water. When an old Owling woman stumbled and spilled water all over the dusty ground, Oriannon paused the probe, even while realizing she could do nothing. Instead a young Owling man helped the old woman to her feet, looking over his shoulder at the probe with a frosty kind of disdain.

Most others wouldn't even raise their eyes to see what was passing by. As she continued through rows of tents, only the youngest children and some of the young men noted her presence—and then shrank back into the early morning shadows.

"If they only knew who we really were," said Oriannon, but then she realized again how that sounded and what the people were seeing. "Can't we tell them it's really not a probe? I mean ... you know what I mean."

"I know." Margus nodded, and he reached over to show her which buttons activated the audible feature. Brinnin seemed to be taking mental notes as well. "When it flashes green, you speak a message. It'll come out the probe so people can hear you."

"That bucket of water is bigger than the poor little girl!" she answered, causing a young girl just ahead of her to turn, scream, and drop her load before disappearing into a nearby tent.

"Oh, brother," Margus shook his head. "She heard that. I wish I could do this for you."

"I didn't mean to scare her." But when she approached another cluster of Owlings with the probe, Oriannon knew it wasn't going to be easy communicating through an instrument of fear. They turned around and hurried off as well. She knew she would have reacted the same way.

"No, please wait." She spoke directly into the remote, wishing she could do something to calm their fears. "We're just looking for my friend Wist. Please."

But the dusty path between tents had already cleared, and she didn't dare steer her probe into a tent. No telling what might happen. Instead she elevated a few meters to get a better view of the many rows of tents, simple shower huts, and open dining sheds spread across hectares of open space under the protective blue dome.

"Ori," Margus warned her, "Keep an eye out behind you."

But she swiveled her view too late. Already another probe had come up behind her, extending what looked like a small scanning arm in her direction.

"What's it doing?" Oriannon jumped back but didn't move her probe quickly enough.

"It's checking out your codes," replied Margus, stiffening and gripping his chin. "Probably it wasn't expecting you to be there."

"What's it going to find out?"

"Everything." He groaned. "My dad's password, the codes I tried ... and it's going to trace it all back."

"Not if I can help it." Oriannon jerked backward now on the toggle stick. But by then the other probe had clamped on and was extracting data like a tremonian leech. She worked the controls desperately, jogging her probe from side to side. In the process, she hit what she thought was a thruster control, only it wasn't.

"What are you—" Margus started to ask, but they could both see the ugly black arm projecting directly ahead, and the flash of blue energy.

"Whoa!" Oriannon held the control steady as the other probe spun away backward, sparks flying. It hit the side of a tent, bounced on the ground, and came to a rest. One side appeared visibly scorched, all its indicator lights had flickered out, and a thin plume of black smoke rose from the eye, though it still seemed to blink up at her.

"You knocked it out, Ori!" Brinnin cheered her latest move. "Yes!"

Margus, on the other hand, was pulling his hair. "What did you do that for? They're going to be all over us!"

"What else did you want me to do?" She maneuvered away from the disabled probe. "I was just trying to get away."

"Yeah, well you did that. Now get out of there, would you?"

Oriannon couldn't help noticing several Owling faces peering out from nearby tents, no doubt wondering what was going on. And she couldn't help trying to speak to them just one more time. She pressed the Speak button. Margus reached over and snapped it off.

"There's no time for that anymore. Don't you get it? As soon as the securities figure out what happened, they're going to be all over us. They may already be."

Oriannon knew he was right.

"I thought you said you'd disabled the weapon," she told him as she swiveled the probe back and up, looking for the way out.

"Maybe the swarm reactivated it."

Whether that was a good thing or not, she pressed forward and headed toward the floodlights illuminating the only entry they knew, the place where the Owling had been so brutally attacked. Several nearby probes bumped and spun off her force field, making her wince. How conspicuous could she be?

"Out of the way," she whispered. She had no idea what they might try to do to her at the entry, so instead of slowing down cautiously, she gritted her teeth, held her breath, and kept the toggle pressed all the way forward. She aimed for the lightest part of the opening. They might stop her, but not because she hadn't tried.

"Oh, wow." Margus made a tight face, squinting and holding up his arms as if he might fend off an imminent collision. If she hit anything at this speed, the probe's low-level force field might not keep it from being smashed to bits against another probe, or even the helmet of a nearby security.

Never mind. Oriannon focused only on the entry, the single spot in the shimmering blue force field that gave her hope of escape. Two securities, unaware of what was racing in their direction from behind, headed for the open exit on slow-speed sleds. She would press out just ahead of them. If she didn't make it out now, she might never.

"Here we go!" Oriannon could feel her heart racing but kept a hand on the toggle—easy now. They brushed against the first unwary security, whirling him off to the side. Right now that didn't matter. Once she made it past the next security, she squirted through the narrow entry and out into free air. Violet sky stretched in all directions as the prison camp receded behind them.

"Faster!" Margus knew they weren't home yet. They still had to reach the distant low hills where the Trion rose like sparkling diamonds. They still had to make it home to Seramine. She snapped to the rear view and noticed no one chasing them—yet.

"Clear for now," Oriannon reported through clenched teeth. No one cheered.

"For now," echoed Margus. "But we still don't know how much data that other probe downloaded."

"You think it did?" Oriannon already knew the answer.

"Even a little information will point a finger right back at us and our families."

If it did, Oriannon had a pretty good idea of what Sola might do.

"We're going to keep this thing at my house tonight," she told him, and the others didn't argue. They all knew what could happen if securities found it in their possession—especially to Margus, with his dad's password and ID coded into its electronics. She felt the sweat trickling down her forehead, but said nothing else as she kept the probe flying home.

"Okay." Margus headed for the door with Brinnin as the probe finally touched down on Oriannon's deck. "But tomorrow night we should meet at the Glades just to be safe. We'll try this thing again. Oh, and Ori?"

He paused while the door slipped open.

"Let's not use our comms if we can help it, okay? If anybody ever listens in . . ."

She knew.

19

The next evening at sundown, Oriannon and Brinnin sat waiting in their usual meeting place on a mossy log deep in the Glades while Carrick paced.

"I should have eaten something before I left," said Carrick, swatting at another bug as it buzzed her ear. "I would have, if I'd known it was going to take this long for him to show up."

"I can hear your stomach rumbling from here." Oriannon studied the trail to see if he was coming. "I'm sure securities will be able to track us just from the noise."

"Oh, stop it." Carrick frowned.

"It hasn't been that long." Brinnin kicked at the moss as the day's light began to leave them. "Just thirty-two minutes."

"He'll be here," said Oriannon. "He said he would be here."

"Maybe it doesn't matter." Brinnin came up with one of her ideas. "We can just have Oriannon fly it again. You know how to run that probe now, don't you?"

Oriannon sighed, stretched her legs, and checked her backpack.

"Mainly, but it's still not much of a plan. And after what happened yesterday, it's too dangerous unless Margus changes the ID. When they scan it, they'll know right away it's stolen."

"Who says they'll scan it?" Brinnin wanted to know. "That's not for sure, is it?"

"Not for sure," Oriannon answered, "but if it happens, we're toast. I'm going to call him and find out what's up."

Maybe calling was risky, but what choice did they have? Still Oriannon trembled a little as she touched the comm button woven into the shoulder of her blue tunic and gave the voice command to connect with Margus. Even if she'd done it a hundred times before, this time something was different.

"Doesn't he answer?" Carrick could hear the call tone over and over. Strange. Margus always picked up on the first or second tone. Oriannon was just about to terminate when the call picked up and a strange woman's voice answered.

"Yes?"

That was it. No hello, no explanation. Oriannon's throat went dry.

"Uh, Margus?" She wished she hadn't said it the moment the words left her lips.

"Actually, this circuit has been temporarily re-routed. Please stay connected, so we can—"

Oriannon quickly reached over to terminate the connection, but she knew it was already too late.

"Was that his mom?" asked Carrick. "She sounded pretty nice."

But the pale look on Brinnin's face told Oriannon she knew as well.

"That wasn't Margus's mom." Oriannon was sure now. She grabbed her backpack and started running. "That was a Security intercept."

Brinnin was right on her heels.

"And now," added Brinnin, "they know exactly where we are."

Carrick held back in the middle of the Glades, hands on her hips.

"Wait a minute," she called out. "How do you know? Why are we running?"

Oriannon only paused for a moment as Brinnin passed her on the path.

"All they needed was three seconds to fix our position with a couple of sats," she called back. "If you don't believe me, just stay right where you are."

"What are we, spies? How do you know all that?"

A distant crashing and two approaching searchlights made the hair on Oriannon's neck stand on end. It must have answered Carrick's question to her satisfaction as well.

"Okay, okay. Wait for me!"

As it turned out, Oriannon didn't have to wait at all. Carrick could run pretty fast with the right incentive.

"There, in the Glades!" came a distant metallic voice, while surrounding lights grew stronger each second. "Remain where you are with your hands in plain view!"

To Carrick's credit, she didn't slow down a step—except when she tripped over a root and went sprawling on the forest floor. Oriannon stopped to help her up.

"Don't slow down for me," said Carrick, gasping for air.

"Shut up and keep running!"

Oriannon helped Carrick to her feet just as an entire bank of satellite floodlights snapped on, turning the center of the Glades as bright white as day. A shuttle descended from above to hover over the exact spot where they had been sitting.

"Oh, wow," whispered Carrick, staring back through the tangled branches and trees of the Glades. Only a few hundred yards separated their dark from the curtain of light. "They really want to find us."

"Come on!" Brinnin grabbed their arms, spinning them around. Already the wall of light had widened, approaching as fast as they could run. "This way!"

"Margus's apartment." Oriannon decided in a panic. "We have to see for ourselves what happened to him."

The other girls nodded and followed her. Still, no one spoke as they kept a steady pace back through the Glades and finally broke out into a Seramine side street. No one reminded her of the obvious, but Oriannon's mind spun as she ran.

If they know where the call was made, she told herself, *they know who made it.*

Even so, they kept running, never looking back. They still had five blocks through the tree-lined streets to the apartment building where Margus lived with his parents.

"I just want to know," Carrick said between gulps of air, finally breaking the silence. "Since when is it a crime to call your friend?"

"Maybe ..." Brinnin gasped for breath as well. "Maybe since they figured out that friend is messing around with a stolen — er, a probe that doesn't belong to him."

"Or when they figured out we broke into the Owling prison camp," added Oriannon, just as they rounded the last corner to the apartment.

"You've got to be kidding." When Carrick stopped short, the other two nearly ran her over. But now Oriannon wasn't interested in getting a step closer either. In fact, her stomach turned almost the way it had when she witnessed the destruction of Lior.

Out in front, a fleet of Security cruisers with blinking blue emergency lights hemmed in the two-story apartment, while swarms of probes had taken up station above the roof. Three frightened-looking people were being led outside to waiting cruisers, and Oriannon thought she recognized them.

"Those are his next-door neighbors," she whispered to Brinnin, who nodded. What about Margus himself?

"He would have called us if he could have," Brinnin answered.

Oriannon could imagine him perhaps eating his evening meal or getting ready to meet them. She knew that if he'd seen what was coming, he would have called to warn them. Good thing he didn't have the probe.

"Where are you taking us?" The voice of one of the frightened prisoners rose above the crowd noise, and everyone hushed. "We don't even know Margus Leek or his parents. We hardly ever see them! You can't just—"

The security taking them away obviously wasn't interested in having a conversation, as he pushed the woman and two men into the backseat of his cruiser. But the words sent chills up Oriannon's spine.

A handful of probes descended to begin scanning the small crowd of curious onlookers that had gathered outside, while a tall security stood full and straight at the front door, directing the arrests.

"Show's over, people." His voice boomed over the crowd. "This building's locked down. So unless you live here, let's clear the area immediately."

Oriannon and the girls would have been glad to obey, but the probes seemed to have a different idea.

"Don't let them see your backpack, Ori." Brinnin whispered as she moved to shield her friend. Perhaps she hadn't acted quickly enough. While a probe moved in to scan Brinnin's eyes, she bent over and coughed, covering her face and delaying the search by a few moments.

"Get out of here!" hissed Brinnin, between coughs. "I'll catch up."

She probably shouldn't have said anything, but still Oriannon had no choice, and without a word she pulled on Carrick's hand to retrace their steps around the corner. Once clear, they weaved through the dispersing crowd and sprinted away.

"They must have arrested him too!" said Carrick. "They took him because of what we did."

Oriannon slowed down as they passed a series of terrace overlooks and hanging gardens, and for a long moment she was afraid to answer. But Carrick was right, and they both knew it. Even so, Oriannon wanted to kick herself for letting this happen.

"It's all my fault. None of this would have happened if I hadn't taken this stupid probe."

"I know," said Carrick, her face long.

"You're not supposed to agree with everything I say!" If Oriannon could have destroyed the probe in her backpack, if she could have smashed it to the pavement, she would have. But before she could, Carrick lifted it from her shoulder—as if she knew just what Oriannon was going to do.

"Here, let me take that for a little while," she said. "Your shoulder's probably tired."

Actually it wasn't, but Oriannon let her. Better someone else holding that cursed little ball than her. In fact, at that moment she didn't care if she never saw it again. How would it help them find Wist anyway? She leaned against a nearby tree, trying not to hyperventilate.

"This is nuts!" Carrick threw up her hands. "We're creeping around, running away from securities, tripping through the Glades, hiding behind bushes. When did we become criminals?"

She looked down at the pack tucked under her arm and paused, as if she had just answered her own question. To make matters worse, Sola's face gazed at them from holo-monitors set up at the nearest street corners. Her message was the same as always: "We're building a new world!" Sola's winsome smile spread across her face. "A new peace."

"A peaceful *prison* camp," Oriannon mumbled, wondering if Margus was now seeing the camp firsthand.

"Come on," she finally told Carrick, leading the way down the street once more. This time she knew exactly what she had to do to find Wist. "I need to get my dad to help before it's too late."

Or maybe it already was.

20

ather, wake up!" A few hours later, Oriannon shook her father by the shoulder as he lay deathly still on a couch in their front room. Only his labored breathing, rattling deep in his chest, told her he lived.

"Please," she whispered. "I need your help."

She touched the spot where his temple throbbed. His forehead glistened with sweat, and he shook and writhed, groaning as he did. Sunken eyes and pallid yellow skin made him look even more ill. She had almost decided to call their housekeeper, Mrs. Eraz, when he finally woke.

"What are you doing, Ori?" He looked up at her through slit eyes, licked his chapped lips, and swallowed with great difficulty. "Is it time to get up?"

"You're not well, Daddy." She hurried to the hall washroom and brought back a cool cloth for his forehead. "Do you want me to call someone?"

"No, don't." He tried to sit up but fell back into his pillow. "I'm just glad you're here. I worry about you."

You and me both, she thought.

He peered at the lighted chrono floating in the corner of the room.

"Oh, my. Looks like I've overslept a bit. See what a shift of the planet's axis can do?"

"Father," she blurted out, "Margus was just arrested with his family."

"Your friend?" His face clouded, and his expression turned serious. "Do you know why?"

"I'm not sure, but I think it was because of the probe from the Temple that went through the portal with me."

"Oh." He groaned and scratched his head. "I wondered what happened to it. Did you give it to him?"

"Well, he was working on it." She looked down. "And I don't know what happened exactly, but ... I'm sorry, Father. I didn't mean to—"

"What you don't mean to do will get you in a lot of trouble these days. Look, you *must* stay away from probes and from Margus Leek. You haven't tried to contact him, have you?"

"Well, actually ..."

"Oh, no." He groaned again and shook his head. "If you have, you're probably on a list of new security risks. I'll see what I can do about that when I get to the Temple."

"But what about Margus? Can't you help him?"

"Help him?" He held his forehead. "Ori, I wish I could. But now I'm a *former elder*. I still report to the Temple, but we're just ... Well, these days, it's all up to Sola. I can only do so much. Do you understand?"

Not really. She studied him for a moment as a growing fear squeezed the breath out of her and she realized her father would truly not be able to help her rescue Margus, much less Wist and the Owlings.

"I understand you should see a healer, Daddy. You don't look good."

This time he forced a smile.

"Well, Nurse Oriannon, I'll take your expert advice under consideration." He checked the chrono again. "Meanwhile, Sola wants to see all the former elders in another thirty-three minutes, so I'd better get moving. You'll excuse me?"

He allowed her to help him to his feet. He stumbled toward his room and paused at the door.

"One other thing, Ori. About what you said the other day." He turned to face her with a pained expression, still gripping the door for balance. "We're hearing some very strange rumors lately, and we think they may have something to do with the axis shift or a change in the planet's magnotronic field. It's affecting the way people experience reality."

She tipped her head to signal that she wasn't following, so he went on.

"All right, just to give you an idea how strange it is ..." He sighed once more, as if trying to decide whether he would tell her. "We're getting reports—unconfirmed obviously—from people who say they're seeing your old mentor again. There's actually a word for these kinds of delusions. Pedunc ..."

Now she knew what he was trying to say, and why.

"Peduncular hallucinosis."

"Right. Basically, people are seeing things, hallucinating. But the good news is we think it may be temporary, until things settle down, and people's bodies get used to the way the planet has changed. See, it's not your—I mean, it's not *their* fault."

"You're saying you think my friends and I are seeing things?"

He winced in pain, a hand to his head.

"Ori, don't take it the wrong way, please—"

"But don't you ever wonder if people aren't seeing things?" she asked. "What if they actually ... what if it really *is* Mentor Jesmet? What if, after the execution, something happened to make him ..."

Alive? She wasn't sure how to explain it, any more than she could explain the strange Stone she had promised to guard. Maybe she only imagined its far-off music, if that's what it really was. But she certainly hoped seeing Mentor Jesmet wasn't peduncular hallucinosis. A moment later, she also knew she wasn't imagining Mrs. Eraz out in the kitchen, dropping pans and screaming.

"Out!" cried their round-faced housekeeper. "Shoo! Get out of here!"

"Father?" Oriannon turned to see her father. He waved at her to see what was happening when a red-faced, wide-eyed Mrs. Eraz ran into the room.

"I'm sorry for the fuss, sir." She struggled to keep up with the words as they tumbled out, and she waved a towel about her as if to clear the air. "But they followed me in through the side door, and now they won't leave!"

Oriannon peeked in the kitchen, not knowing what to expect. She had never seen the plump little Mrs. Eraz this agitated—not even the time Margus had nearly set the kitchen on fire.

But this time her reaction was for good reason, as two probes had taken up positions inside their house—one just inside the side door, and one in the back, just inside the entry to the deck. A third positioned itself at the front door.

Almost instinctively Oriannon pulled back, expecting them to notice her. None made a move, but just floated silently.

"I tell you I cannot work in the kitchen with those things looking over my shoulder!" complained Mrs. Eraz. "What's it going to do, help me prepare your evening meal? They have no right to be here! Every time I see one of those disgusting eyes of theirs, it gives me goose bumps."

She looked to Oriannon's father for help, but he hobbled into the hallway behind Oriannon, his green fuzzy robe slung over sagging shoulders. He looked even worse standing up than lying down, if that was possible, and Oriannon thought of steering him back to the couch. Instead, he surveyed the situation through bloodshot eyes as he leaned against the wall for support.

"I'm sorry you were startled, Mrs. Eraz." He cleared his throat and tried again. "But I forgot to tell you that they were due to be installed inside the house. They're for your own protection."

That doesn't sound like my father, thought Oriannon. But then after what she'd seen of him lately, perhaps it should not have surprised her. Meanwhile, the probe in the kitchen began to wobble slightly, and he held up his hand, perhaps to keep it from drawing any closer.

"If I needed protection ..." Mrs. Eraz trembled as if she was about to explode. "I would ask for it. And I do tolerate these things out on the street, since no one asked me and I have no choice in the matter. Here, however, I believed it would be different, and in the home of an Assembly elder, no less."

That would be *former* Assembly elder. Oriannon didn't correct her, and her father still tried his best to make things right.

"Please don't say anything you'll regret, Mrs. Eraz. They're part of the new plan. For your protection."

"Yes, you mentioned that." By now her face had turned nearly purple, and Oriannon stepped off to the side, just in case one of the probes reacted to the outburst. "But no one has yet explained to me what was wrong with the old plan, if there ever was one. All I know is that I cannot work in a house where these horrid things are staring at every move I make. This is a gross invasion of privacy!"

Oriannon knew the feeling.

"Please, Mrs. Eraz." Oriannon's father held up his hand. "Before long you won't even notice. You'll get used to them."

"As a matter of fact, I will not!" She stomped toward the front door, throwing her towel right at the hovering probe and catching it in the eye.

"Mrs. Eraz!" Oriannon's father managed to jump after her, just in time to keep the probe from mobilizing its stun arms. It had already shaken off the towel and come to attention, blocking the door.

"Am I being held in this house—or this job—against my will?" The frost in her question would have iced the room had not Oriannon's father intervened.

"No, of course not." He remained between the probe and Mrs. Eraz, hands outstretched as if breaking up a fight. "I just wish you would reconsider. Please. You've been with us for three years, and you know it's not easy to find good housekeepers. In fact—"

"Three years and four months. And I wish you'd considered that fact before you invited these ... *things* into your home."

"I didn't exactly invite them, Mrs. Eraz." Oriannon's father retreated into the room as the probe finally retracted its attack arms. "I had no choice."

"Nor do I. I'm sorry, Elder Hightower. And by the way, I am not an Owling, despite what you might have heard."

By this time, however, the probes had focused directly on Oriannon's father, no doubt recording every word and reporting back to Security. Oriannon would have stepped forward, if she thought it would do any good. She would have taken Mrs. Eraz's biggest cooking utensil and batted the probe right out the window if it would not have brought down more wrath upon herself and everyone else.

Instead, Mrs. Eraz gave her a little nod that told her she understood, and stepped through the door for the last time.

"Take care of your father, Oriannon," she said, her voice soft and mournful. "He doesn't look well."

No, he didn't. But as the front door closed behind Mrs. Eraz, Oriannon's father wordlessly retreated to his room, leaving her alone with their three new probes. He hadn't believed her about Jesmet, and he hadn't given her reason to hope. Mrs. Eraz wasn't coming back. And she wondered, *Am I as much a prisoner as Margus now ... in my own home?*

21

"**O**h, wow." Brinnin repeated herself over and over as they walked down the colonnaded hall, their first day back in classes after the teacher break—or, as the media reported, a "mandatory planning period."

"Oh, wow." Brinnin said it again.

Oriannon would have said it too, except that Brinnin seemed to be providing enough wide-eyed astonishment for both of them. She tried not to gawk but nearly bumped into a limestone column as they walked.

"I had no idea they were going to add all these viewscreens." Oriannon really didn't care to look at all the floating, smiling faces—Headmaster Knarl on one side of the brightly lit hall and the familiar face of Sola Minnik on the other. But while one smiled, the other greeted them—like a tag team.

"Welcome back to Ossek Preparatory Academy," boomed Headmaster Knarl, looking down a rather lengthy nose. His dark moustache quivered as he spoke, the way it always did. "You're going to like the changes we've made in the past several days. With advice and guidance from Sola herself, your mentors have been working hard to build and enhance your new learning environment here on this beautiful campus."

Beautiful, yes. Sometimes Oriannon thought it actually resembled a Coristan Temple more than a school, with its graceful arches, columns, and long tiled hallways. These talking heads, however, shattered the illusion.

"Headmaster Knarl is of course right," Sola remarked from the other side. "You are the new Corista, and we're all very excited about the fresh start you'll be receiving here."

Oriannon got a crick in her neck from looking back and forth at the introductions—and she wasn't the only one. Everyone else stared wide-eyed at the projections on their way down the busy halls to their lockers. After an unplanned week-long holiday like the one they'd just been through, getting back to school would take a little getting used to.

But a new schedule? Seeing Sola at nearly every turn? This would take even more adjustment. Besides all that, Oriannon had to duck away from twice the number of probes as she was used to. Brinnin looked at one as they walked by and leaned closer to Oriannon.

"They're not chasing you, are they?"

"I think my dad called them off. Now if he could only call off these kids." A group of younger students stared at her as they walked by. "What's up with them?"

"Don't you remember?" Brinnin smiled and kept walking. "You're famous. You know Sola."

"Oh, yeah." Oriannon followed her friend into the multi-tiered orchestra practice room where even more changes awaited them—not to mention Carrick Trice.

"Where are all the instruments?" asked Carrick, but no one could tell her. Everyone sat in their old seats in the five-tiered practice chamber—everyone except Margus in the back-row percussion. No one sat in his seat. Oriannon tried not to look there as the other students filed in and stomped down to their chairs, chattering with excitement. She herself stepped past the woodwinds section, and past the viols, where Carrick occupied the third chair. Finally she reached her own front-row seat for the three-stringed erhu—first row, first chair—the chair reserved for the best string player in the orchestra. Only this time everything felt wrong, and empty besides.

Maybe Mentor Jesmet will somehow step out of his office, she thought, *and stride up to the front of the room, the way he used to do. Then he'll set everybody straight.*

Oriannon could see the memory before her, even as she imagined his voice and his easy laughter. So the reality of Nurse Anno standing before the class jolted her, and she must not have been the only one to be surprised.

"Funny, you don't look like Mentor Jesmet," said Carrick under her breath. That turned out to be her first mistake.

"Let's get one thing straight right from the start. This goes for Miss Trice and everyone else." The trim, well-groomed woman appeared to be wound up tight, ready to spring at them with claws extended. Several of the kids in the first row actually recoiled.

"That will be the last time we'll hear that name mentioned here. In fact, this gives us a chance to make our new academy policy very clear from the start: Mentioning the name of this convicted faithbreaker is disruptive and upsetting to the greater good, and thus will be considered hate-speak."

She crossed her arms and paced as she spoke, not at all like the old Nurse Anno would have done. Perhaps, Oriannon mused, Nurse Anno's body had been appropriated. But she definitely still had more to say.

"You all know what that is. Hate-speak will not be tolerated, and anyone disregarding this directive will be re-educated immediately. Does everyone understand?"

Oriannon could see eyes widening in shock and heads bobbing numbly. Was this what all the mentors had been working on for the past several days, as Headmaster Knarl had implied? Nurse Anno finally seemed to relax a notch, even showing them a thin smile.

"Now, I do regret we had to start out on such a negative note, but Sola recommended that we deal with the issue forthrightly and honestly."

Sola, not Headmaster Knarl? This was getting more interesting all the time.

"But now that the ground rules are clear to everyone, we can go on to more pleasant things. Changes and improvements for instance."

A boy in the back, one of Margus's percussion buddies, blurted out a question.

"Nobody can find their instruments, Nurse Anno. They're all gone."

A small chorus of murmuring yeahs agreed with him, causing Nurse Anno to hold up her hand for quiet.

"That's right. There are no instruments because there is no longer an orchestra in this academy."

"What?" asked the drummer. "You've got to be kidding!"

The rest of the class erupted as Oriannon tried desperately to hold back a growing feeling of panic that told her *this is all my fault!*

"Did you know this was going to happen?" Brinnin whispered to Oriannon.

Oriannon could only shake her head in shock as Nurse Anno once more held up her hand for attention.

"If you'll all quiet down, I'll explain."

Slowly the class complied as she went on.

"Now, I can tell you that it was a difficult decision. But as we all know, there are only so many hours in the school day. Sola felt it was more important for us to understand the New Coristan World Order during this time. So there was no choice, really."

"The new what?" asked a viol player sitting behind Oriannon. In this class she still imagined the rest of the kids with their instruments. Maybe she always would.

"The New Coristan World Order," Nurse Anno repeated. "You might have also heard it called the Solution, but we'll have plenty of time get into that later. The point is, I guarantee you're all going to enjoy this class, once you give it a chance."

"We'll enjoy it," added Carrick in a hoarse whisper, "whether we like it or not."

Fortunately Nurse Anno didn't hear her this time, because a few of the boys groaned just then from the back row. The woman frowned and pointed to the back of the room.

"Boys, do you have any constructive questions?"

"I have one." Carrick raised her hand.

"What's up with her?" Brinnin leaned over again to whisper in Oriannon's ear, and Nurse Anno paused before calling on Carrick again.

"Miss Trice?"

"I just want to know one thing. Was your old job taken over by probes?"

A couple of students couldn't help snickering, but Nurse Anno didn't seem to notice.

"I actually do appreciate that question, though you may have meant it facetiously. My former duties as a school counselor and health care practitioner have been integrated into an automated clinic. Any other questions? Good. Now, we'll—"

"Wait a minute, pardon me." Carrick had her hand up once more. "Does that mean we still call you Nurse Anno, or something else?"

By now Nurse Anno's face contorted in pain, and when she touched her forehead briefly, it reminded Oriannon of the strange way her own father had been acting. But their new mentor appeared to shake it off as she parked her hands on her hips and faced Carrick directly.

"Yes, from now on, Miss Trice, you will address me as *Mentor* Anno. And if you need to go to the academy's clinic for one of your frequent headaches, you will be well taken care of in every way—just not by me. Now, as there *are* no further questions, we'll begin by directing our attention to a message from Sola at the front of the room."

Without waiting for Carrick or anyone to interrupt her again, she snapped her fingers to turn down the room lights while a life-size, but translucent image of Sola Minnik floated down from the ceiling and came to rest at the front of the room, looking pleasant and composed as always.

"I'm glad we have a chance to talk honestly about what's happening to Corista," Sola told them. "And I know you're going to have questions about what it all means to you and how you're going to fit in. You might even be wondering, 'Why are we seeing so much of this Sola Minnik?'" She smiled. "Well, let me tell you where I come from and why I'm passionate about the future of Corista ... your future."

Of course Oriannon had heard it all many times before—leaving the past behind and looking for the greatness of Corista, building a peace together, a fresh start for all, blah blah. Ori could have delivered the speech herself without skipping a word.

But as she looked around the room, she had to shudder at the way most of the other kids hung on Sola's words. Oriannon couldn't believe it.

They're eating it up! she thought—and then it occurred to her that she would have done the same thing only a few days ago. For the next hour they nodded at all the right times, smiled at all the jokes, even clapped at the end. Maybe it was just Mentor Anno's eyes on her as the lights finally came back up, but Oriannon forced herself to clap with all the rest, though she purposely kept her hands from making any sound, and she nearly felt ill listening to Sola for that long.

But it didn't stop there. Mentor Anno led them through endless sensitivity workshops, brainstorming sessions, and three more vid lectures. Oriannon could have screamed. And when they were finally freed from the extended morning class three hours later, she couldn't help saying something to her friends in the hall.

"Need to watch what we say, Carrick." She covered her mouth and leaned away from the two probes patrolling the hall. "Now Anno's got her eye on you too."

"I know." Carrick slammed her locker harder than she needed to. And maybe she thought all the noise in the hallway would shield them. "I just thought she was one of the good guys. Now we know she's one of *them.*"

A glance at the probes eyeing them told Oriannon not to answer back. It wouldn't do any good to challenge them to their faces.

"I'm hungry," announced Carrick, and of course that was no surprise to anyone. "I wonder if Sola's Solution means we're finally going to get edible dining hall food."

"Let me know." Oriannon held back as her friends hurried ahead. "I'll catch up."

Brinnin looked at her as if to say, "Are you sure?" But Oriannon just nodded and waved them on. And she kept an eye on the doubled number of probes in the halls, trying to discover any blind spots where they wouldn't be watching her—not easy to do on the fly. Every time she turned a corner, another probe met her with its watchful eye.

"You mind if I go to the restroom?" she asked one, but it didn't catch her sarcasm as she stepped in to wash her hands—and think. Good thing everyone else had gone to lunch, and good thing the probe remained out in the hallway. She was ready to scream, actually. She turned to the sink, closed her eyes, and let the cool automatic water run over her hands. She much preferred the feel of water to any sonic cleaner.

Where do we go from here? she wondered. But nothing in the confusing jumble of past weeks seemed to add up. Not the returning of Mentor Jesmet, nor the Stone she kept hidden for a purpose she did not know. Not the brutal destruction of Asylum Way Station 4, nor that of Lior. Not her father's strange behavior — and now the disappearance of Margus.

Certainly not the remaking of this academy in the image of Sola Minnik.

She splashed water on her face, trying to clear her head.

"Jesmet," she whispered into the bubbles, trying to pray as disturbing memories of the past weeks swirled about her like a solar storm. Faithbreakers, Owlings, prisoners, liars, Sola, her father ...

Please. Please show me what to do! We can't just stay in this school not doing anything. I promised to take care of the Pilot Stone. Why? What do we do now? How can I help the Owlings?

But heaven kept silent, and instead of an answer from the Maker, she felt a wet cascade on her sandals as the sink overflowed all over the restroom floor. She screeched in spite of herself and hopped backward, but the water just kept coming.

"Oh, great!"

She hadn't noticed how clogged the sink had been. The accident activated cleaning biomice, but even a dozen of them scurrying about on the floor couldn't hold back the waters. All they did was clear the floor drain and bump into her feet, which made her jump even higher.

I hate biomice.

Soon enough, a cleaning woman came running into the restroom, wearing the ill-fitting blue coveralls of a tech. Oriannon would have escaped in embarrassment and without another word if she hadn't caught a glimpse of the tech's strained face.

Another Owling. The tech didn't even look at Oriannon though. She just stepped to the sink and buried her arms in the water, searching for the problem. A moment later she winced in pain, making Oriannon think her finger was stuck.

"Here." Oriannon stepped forward. "Let me help you. It was my fault."

The Owling only shook her head as water finally cleared from the sink in a whirlpool, leaving puddles on the floor. By this time the woman was soaked, and when she bent over to clean the floor, Oriannon could clearly make out an oversized Security anklet.

"Why do you have to wear that?" asked Oriannon, afraid she already knew the answer. "Did they make you? Did they take you to that big prison camp?"

She could ask nothing more as a red light blinked on the anklet and the Owling stopped what she was doing to try to cover it back up. When it vibrated, Oriannon could hear the thrumming sound. The woman turned toward the restroom door.

"Wait!" cried Oriannon, but of course it did no good. As she watched the Owling woman hurry back out to the hallway, Oriannon noticed she looked almost as tall as her, almost the same build—and it made Oriannon wonder. She looked at the loose anklet and wondered if the Maker had just answered her prayer.

It just might work, she thought.

22

"No, no, no!" Brinnin shook her head again as they navigated through Security and double scans on their way into the school building the next day. "It's a terrible idea, Oriannon. Horrible. Awful. It won't work and I won't let you do it."

"Why not?" Oriannon kept her voice down, pressing through the first-hour hallway crowds and past the projected faces of Headmaster Knarl and Sola Minnik. "You're saying you won't help?"

"That's not what I meant. I want to help. I just don't want what happened to Margus to happen to you, that's all."

Oriannon felt like throwing up her hands and screaming, even in the middle of all 657 students hurrying down the halls of Ossek Prep. Brinnin, of all people, should get it.

"Well," she told her, "in the three days since they took Margus away, what have we done to help him?"

Brinnin didn't answer right away, so Oriannon answered for her, counting on her fingers all the things that would not and had not worked.

"First of all, we know nobody here at school will help — not Mentor Anno and especially not Headmaster Knarl."

"Especially not him," Brinnin agreed, and they steered clear of a hovering probe. "He's so tight with Sola——"

"Right. And second of all, we definitely can't ask Security for help, since they're the ones who took him."

"Wait. How could you even think of going to them?"

"I'm just laying it out for you, you know, all the possibilities."

"Okay, then what about your dad? Didn't he help get you off the hook after we tried to call Margus?"

Oriannon shook her head.

"Yeah, but he can't help with something like this. Trust me. He just can't."

She didn't add that her father needed help himself, and Brinnin gave her a confused look but thankfully didn't press her to explain more.

"So I've thought it through, Brinnin, and it's up to us. I mean, look at what's going on around us. Here at school, at the Temple, everywhere. This is what Sola calls 'humanitarian!'"

Two Owlings shuffled by in janitorial garb, heads down. Out on the patio, at least a half dozen more Owlings labored in the sun, still wearing their traditional hooded robes, which must have been unbearably hot under three searing Coristan suns. No one could miss seeing more and more Owlings in Corista—all downcast and all working hard.

"And what about your friend Wist?" asked Brinnin. "You really think you can find her?"

"If she's at the camp, I will. I have to."

"But that's only one person."

"I told you, Brinnin. We start with one at a time. Wist. Margus—if he's been taken to that place too. Then we go from there."

Brinnin shook her head again. "I still don't——"

"You mean you just want to stay here, going to *Mentor* Anno's class on Understanding the New Coristan World Order, while they turn every last Owling into a slave? Is that what you want?"

"Of course not, but—"

"Okay, then." Oriannon pulled out her older special ID pass, and Brinnin grabbed it from her hand.

"But you're not serious, girl. You can't trade places with an Owling, even if you do give her the pass. She won't fool anybody."

"Why not?"

"Well, besides the obvious reasons, this pass is like, what, two years old? It's no good anymore."

"We'll see, won't we?"

"Yeah, but even if it *did* work . . ." They ducked around a corner, and Brinnin gripped her friend by the shoulders. "Do you have any idea what they'll do to you if they catch you inside the camp?"

"They won't catch me."

"Stop! Now you sound like Margus."

That brought a smile to Oriannon's face, never mind how serious this was. She wiggled free of Brinnin's grip.

"I'll take that as a compliment. But don't you worry; I can handle it. And when I find them—"

"Yeah? Then what? See, that's the problem with this. That's the huge problem: You can't even tell me what you'll do then!"

Mainly because she hadn't quite worked everything out yet. But in Oriannon's mind, now was not the time for retreat. Even here in the crowded hallway of Jib Ossek Preparatory Academy, the charge had begun. So she snatched back the old-style ID pass and detoured to stand in front of a nearby probe.

203

"Would you scan my pass, please?" She held out her old pass and smiled at the probe, as if it cared. "I just want to be sure it still works."

With her free hand, she dragged Brinnin along behind her.

"I still don't understand what you're doing," hissed her friend.

Not that she needed to show the extra pass, of course. Only a few places required the old-style ID anymore, mainly small businesses that hadn't yet converted to the new system. Now the probe could have obviously scanned her eyes and given her the same information in an instant. But this time she was—

"Just proving a point."

They waited for a moment before the probe flashed an "all clear" green light and reported back that the holder of the pass was, in fact, *Hightower of Nyssa, Oriannon, Special Clearance ID: 9907–2236–0021.*

"There, see?" Oriannon slipped the dog-eared plexicard back in her pocket with a satisfied nod.

"See what?" Brinnin didn't sound so sure. "They still recognize your old card. They recognize everybody. What does that prove?"

"It proves that it always helps to have a dad who's an Assembly elder, even if the Assembly is being shut down. Even if Sola won't let him make any decisions anymore, and even if she's in charge of the whole world. They haven't taken away my special security clearance yet."

"Must be an oversight."

"Maybe. But today's the day, before they figure things out."

Brinnin groaned.

"I still think we should find another way, Ori. This is just too dangerous. What if they discover me with the Owling girl who's using your pass to get around?"

But Oriannon set her chin as they marched down the hall to their first class. Now she was sure of it.

"I trust you," she told Brinnin. "But you know the only thing that's too dangerous is not doing anything, right?"

"As long as you don't try to do what only the Maker is supposed to do."

"I'm learning, okay?"

That still wasn't good enough for Brinnin.

"I don't care how much you say you're learning. If you're not back by tomorrow night, so help me, I'm telling your dad everything. About Jesmet, about everything. Do you hear?"

"Well, like Margus always used to say—" Oriannon grinned. "No worries."

●●●

No worries. When the mid-day meal hour arrived later that day, Oriannon repeated Margus's saying over and over, claiming it as her own. She wished Brinnin and Carrick wouldn't glance over at her as she did her best to blend into the moving crowd. She flashed a spread-fingered wave at them just to remind them.

Five minutes. They would get it right.

Meanwhile, she did her best to stay low, not even looking at the probes. When the meal line entered the busy dining room and snaked around the outside wall, she quietly peeled off to the right through the staff entry to the kitchen.

The only thing that would stop her now was if one of the supervisors didn't think she was a student worker. She grabbed a white apron off a hook, just in case, and slipped into it just before stepping into the main work area.

"Hey!" A woman called at her, and Oriannon wondered whether to freeze or turn around. She turned around but kept moving her feet toward the back door. The large woman pointed her way. "We need these serving trays moved out right now."

Oriannon tried to play dumb, but it didn't work.

"You mean me?" She pointed to herself, looking around the kitchen. Several new Owling workers huddled at a nearby counter, peeling mounds of prickly loanfruit. The supervisor woman frowned at her and parked her hands on her considerable hips.

"I'm certainly not talking to one of those Owlings, dear. Now don't tell me you don't understand me either?"

"Uh ... sure I do." Oriannon had no choice but to follow the woman to one of the front serving windows where her fellow students filed by for their meal. This was not what she had in mind, especially not when one of the Year One girls caught sight of her.

"Hey look who's working back there!" squealed one of the girls. "It's Oriannon! She must have gotten in trouble."

Not yet. Oriannon didn't even look to see who had spotted her; she just hurried back to the clean-up station with an empty serving platter. This was not the smooth escape she'd had in mind. She managed to slosh grease all over her hands and arms before finally dumping the deep-fry tray on a counter, then stripped off the apron and pushed through the back door as quietly as she could.

Did anyone else see me? she wondered and held her breath, waiting for the supervisor to come charging outside after her. But the only sound out in the loading area was steam whistling from power vents.

All right then. She crept around the corner to hide behind a tall bush. From there she could quietly keep an eye on the Owlings working outside on the academy grounds, without anyone noticing her.

"Three, four ..." She counted several others in the surrounding gardens, though it was pretty tough spotting the little people as they hunched over their work between hedges and bushes. Some worked on their knees, pulling weeds and such, while others raked paths or trimmed hedges with a simple blade. Obviously they'd not been given power tools.

A distant probe kept track of them all, occasionally coming closer to nudge them with a spark. Oriannon waited until the probe was occupied with a couple of young men on the far side of the garden to make her move, crouching low and crawling between two hedges. The nearest Owling woman worked quietly with a rake only a couple of meters away. She looked to be only a year or two older than Oriannon, at most a few centimeters smaller, and wore the loose-fitting hooded cassock typical of Owling men and women.

"I'm not going to hurt you. Please don't say a word." Oriannon put a finger to her lips, hoping the startled Owling woman would understand her and not attract the probe's attention. She couldn't take a chance, though, so she grabbed the woman by the shoulders and gently pulled her to the ground.

"I'm your friend!" Oriannon whispered, holding a hand over the woman's mouth so she wouldn't scream. "And I'm a friend of—I mean, I follow Jesmet."

At the mention of Jesmet's name, the Owling girl did stop struggling, though her eyes still darted about in fear.

"If I let go of your mouth, will you call out?"

Oriannon wasn't sure if the young woman actually shook her head, but there really wasn't time. One of the other Owlings or even the probe could come checking at any moment. She would have to take a chance, and she lowered her hand. The woman gasped but said nothing as they both crouched on the path.

"Please listen to me," Oriannon went on. "I need your help. I have to get into the camp, so I need your clothes and I need your anklet."

The young woman only stared at her, wide-eyed, as if startled by the odd request.

"Your anklet," Oriannon repeated, pointing at the ill-fitting silver glassteel ring, then pointing at her own ankle. "I need you to give it to me, or they won't let me inside the camp, right?"

Finally the woman opened her mouth, speaking softly and with a thick Owling accent that made it difficult for Oriannon to understand.

"You're not wanting to go there," she whispered. "A horrible place."

"I know, I've seen it." Oriannon reached for the anklet. "But look, can you help me?"

"They'll be knowing it's gone." The woman shook her head and pulled back. "A friend of mine tried to pull it off, and they knew."

"Not if it's on me instead." Oriannon hoped she was right. She knew she had no time to argue the finer technical points. "Please. I need to find my friends, and we need to stop what's happening with the Owlings. This is the only way I can think of."

"But where will I be going?"

Oriannon pointed to the back door of the kitchen.

"I'll give you my ID card, and we're going to trade clothes. You'll pretend you're me, a student here. You're going to be sick so you can check out from school through the digital nurse, and then you'll stay with my friends Brinnin and Carrick. They'll hide you until—well, you'll be safe. Do you understand?"

"Hide?" The Owling woman glanced at the school building, her eyes still wide in fear. "And how will I be sick?"

"Never mind that. Brinnin's over there, waiting for you." Oriannon took hold of the anklet. As she had hoped, it fit only loosely over the slight woman's ankle. Perhaps the kitchen grease on her wrists and arms would help slip it off a little more quickly. "They'll make sure nothing bad happens to you. Now, please, before it's too late."

Five minutes later, Oriannon had assumed the role of an Owling slave, hiding inside the robe of the Owling woman, pulling the hood up as far as it would go. The rough fabric smelled of Lior, of Shadowside—dark and musky, but full of its own strange life. That, and a bit smoky from all the open fires the woman must have tended.

At the moment, Oriannon had no fires to tend, only gravel paths to rake and weeds to pull in the gardens fronting Jib Ossek Academy. She tried to hold herself like the other Owlings, slump-shouldered and looking down, hoping that no one would look into her face too closely or notice she was slightly taller than the woman she replaced. Once in a while she stooped to rub dirt in her face, hoping to disguise her Coristan features a bit more. She pushed the gravel around with her rake, the way she'd seen the woman do earlier.

Would this work?

Not if the probe got too close, and certainly not if it managed to scan her eyes. Meanwhile she would say nothing, just do her work, follow orders, and follow the others. How strange that all her friends were in class only a few hundred meters away. She could hear shouts from a ragball game in the field on the other side of the building.

Come on, Brinnin. She wished she could see what was going on inside. *Get the Owling woman out of here!*

Oriannon slouched a little lower and turned away as the probe finally made its rounds, coming closer, hovering for a moment over each Owling worker.

Stay away! Oriannon's hands shook, and she feared her plan would unravel before it began. She pivoted with her back to the probe as it paused to check on her. As it did, her anklet vibrated distinctly, sending an unpleasant chill up her right leg. Not gentle at all, the jolt shook her to the bone, and she swallowed her scream.

But the vibration ceased, and the probe moved on to check on others, leaving Oriannon to gasp in relief and peek out from the hood that had hidden her so far. But if she had just passed her first test, she knew it was nothing compared to the next one. An hour later she followed the others as they quietly filed toward a waiting lev-platform. She would not be the first in line, and not the last. And no one spoke as they climbed on their waiting transport — to the prison camp.

23

At this point Oriannon's strategy was simple: Every time she felt a little too close to a curious Owling, she would back them away with her most horrendous-sounding cough and wheeze. The two securities assigned to transport them paid no attention to a potentially sick prisoner as they neared the camp. These Owlings were obviously a cheap commodity.

In fact, she was simply number fifteen of twenty-three. An hour later her anklet buzzed unpleasantly once more as they passed through the main entry and into the dome. She guessed that buzz simply confirmed the anklet wearer had checked back into the camp, almost like an electronic roll call.

This time it took a moment to register that she'd actually made it inside, and not just taken a virtual peek with the stolen probe. *Almost like when I saw it before*, she thought, forcing herself not to look about like a tourist. But in person and from the inside, this dome appeared much, much larger, with a vaguely burnt odor that seemed to cling to her. It must have come from the force field itself. She sniffed and tried not to sneeze at the way it scratched her nose.

Away from the force field, fearful shouts echoed, and all the smells of living and dying seemed to fester within the dome. Even worse, the despairing cries of unseen Owling children shook her almost immediately, bringing unexpected tears to her eyes. Remembering how they had danced and sang only weeks before, she could not help feeling their aching loss of heart. It weighed on her like the worst poison, so much more than the awful stench of sickness and exhaustion.

Even the Trion's fierce sunlight only managed to filter through the force field as a feeble glow. It did lend a strange black-and-blue tint to this bruised, captive world along with a pallid cast to her skin. Brinnin would have been mortified. Looking down at her hands, Oriannon wondered if by passing through the entry she had turned more corpse than alive.

The Owlings themselves appeared not far from dead. Some wandered aimlessly through the vast expanse of dome tents, others struggled to walk while carrying heavy plastic buckets of water. Still others simply sat in the dust, staring at their feet or at nothing in particular, muttering to themselves. She'd never seen Owlings act so strangely.

But Oriannon was not on a tour, and she started filing away information to get her bearings. The securities set down the empty transport at a staging area—a simple clearing scratched into the meadows, not far from the main entry and wedged between three simple, green prefab sheds and the first row of tents. Securities hurried in and out of the dull metal sheds, barking instructions at each other as if this might be an administrative center.

At first she mentally filed away the locations and layout of what she saw. Perhaps, she thought, it would come in handy. But as soon as the nearest security grunted and waved for the newly arrived Owlings to step away, she hurried off between two Owling women. Surely it would only be a matter of time before she would be discovered and punished. She would have to find Wist, quickly, and figure a way out.

"Out of the way!" roared a security, and as he jockeyed his craft back into position, a portion of the ion lifter caught her from behind, scorching the hem of Ori's long tunic and sending her flying headfirst into a well-worn patch of dirt. As dust flew around her head, he ignored her misfortune while she gasped to reclaim her breath. But still she kept her hood pulled tightly around her ears and said nothing as the lev-sled moved away.

So now what? she asked herself, taking small gulps of sultry air. Before she could rise, she felt herself lifted by the shoulders to her feet, where she wobbled uncertainly.

"You want to be staying out of their way," a boy told her, and she turned away with a dusty cough to avoid his gaze. But she noticed he stood with another boy about his age, younger than her and studying her curiously. Something looked familiar about them, and she knew in an instant she had seen them before.

"Thanks," she answered from behind her hand. She did her best to imitate the singsong Owling way of speaking. "I'll learn — I mean, I'll be learning."

Apparently satisfied, the two boys went on their way toward the tents, but the first one stopped short and turned back around.

"You're talking?" He scratched his head.

Ori remained silent, hoping she'd not already done something wrong.

"Most who are working outside are too scared to be saying much," he told her. "Maybe because you're so ... tall?"

Tall compared the Owling. She stepped into a crowded aisle between two rows of tents, sidestepping young Owling children and mothers with babies, but still the boys followed.

"Wait a minute," the first one called to her, but she did her best to disappear into the crowd. It would be better not to attract too much attention right away. Perhaps she should have asked them if they knew Wist, but for now she wandered the aisles of this makeshift prison, holding the hood in place and trying not to stare at the refugees.

At first she tried to compare the experience to her time in the Owling city, since many of these Owlings must have come from Lior. She actually did recognize some of the faces. There was a shopkeeper who had once presided over a proud collection of intricate pottery in his store. She remembered the intricate designs he added to his handiwork—stars and swirling clouds, beautiful and brooding, as mysterious as the Owling landscape. Now he sat in the dirt, holding his head and rocking back and forth.

There was a grandmother. Oriannon remembered her smile as she once hung out a long row of laundry from her balcony in the cliffside city. She'd had a charming, clear singing voice and had sung of the beauty of Jesmet's world. Now she stood staring up into the blue dome, wringing her hands in the air and groaning.

A woodworker? Back in Lior, he'd come to the window of his shop with sweet-smelling sawdust on his brow and a wide smile on his face. Now the sawdust had been replaced with mud, the smile with a long, vacant stare that looked right through her.

Oriannon shivered. Something unspeakably wrong had happened in this prison, and unfamiliar cries filled the air like the humid heaviness of a greenhouse. The hidden darkness of Sola's Plan had stricken these poor people hard and without mercy.

Even so, not all were affected—yet. Several young children chased each other between the tents, and their calls sounded almost like the old Lior. Somewhere, perhaps far off across the hectares of tents, she thought she heard quiet singing that reminded her of the happy music that once filled the Owling city. Here, though, it sounded painfully out of place. As Oriannon tried to locate it, a little girl brushed up between her and the nearest tent.

"Sorry!" The girl grabbed Oriannon's arm for balance as she looked up with puzzlement at her face. "Oh! But you're not Owling, are you?"

Oriannon wasn't quite ready for the question and stumbled over her tongue for the right answer.

"No, actually, ah ..."

"That's okay." A sparkle in the girl's eye testified she had not yet been touched by the brooding evil that swept through this place, and she held on to Oriannon's hand the way little girls do. "You don't have to be saying anything. A lot of people can't anymore. But are you knowing Jesmet? My name is Moya. You should be coming with us."

"Well—"

Oriannon let herself be tugged by the eager little girl, down one aisle of identical tents and across another, deeper and deeper into the camp. Before it was too late, she should ask about Wist or perhaps if she knew of a Coristan named Margus Leek. But right now something else seemed very important to this little sprite, and so Oriannon followed her toward the sound of singing. At the tent doorflap, a young Owling man with a scarred face nodded quietly as he stepped aside to allow them in.

"Shh!" Moya put a finger to her lips, but Oriannon had already seen enough to know she needed to remain quiet. For the singing had ceased, and she counted some twenty Owlings crammed into the tent, standing silently, eyes closed, while they took turns praying.

"Mama." Moya slipped to the side of a woman in the group, tugging on her tunic so she opened her eyes and noticed Oriannon standing just inside the door. The woman smiled and nodded her welcome but returned to prayer—for names Oriannon didn't recognize, for strength to face whatever the Maker allowed, for their Security captors, for the Coristan leaders who persecuted them. Several in the group mentioned Sola by name, but not with the kind of barbs or bitterness Oriannon might have expected. Did they really know who they were praying for?

Oriannon had heard prayer like this only once before, when she had visited the Owling city. Then, as now, it sounded so unlike the lofty petitions she had grown up hearing in the Temple. They hardly resembled the kind her father offered in a strange, otherworldly voice to a very distant and far-off Maker. Here it sounded different, almost as if the Owlings actually knew the Maker, the way they might know someone like Jesmet. It sounded so different, in fact, that she wondered if it actually could be prayer.

The words shook her even as they woke something deep inside her, and after a few minutes her legs shook beneath her so that she could no longer stand. Instead she fell to her knees on the tent floor and hid her face once more beneath the cloak.

If this is really prayer, she told herself, *then I've never really prayed before.*

Perhaps it was just coincidence. But for the first time in days, Oriannon felt the Stone warming once again in her deep pocket, and she almost jumped at the feeling. There it was! She heard once again its distant dream voices, only much louder this time, almost as if they were in the next room.

Or in this case, the next tent. In a way she could not explain, this Stone now sounded very much like the voices of the praying Owlings.

So she did not notice at first when one of the men stopped in mid-sentence, snapped open his wide eyes, and looked directly at Oriannon as if she had interrupted him.

Surely he had not heard the Stone as well?

24

hat had she done?

Oriannon wondered how the man had known she was even in the tent, the way he stopped in the middle of his prayer.

"It's okay, Siric," Moya's mother told him in a soft voice, barely audible above the continuing prayer. "Jesmet must have brought her."

Which Oriannon thought was an odd thing to say, since Jesmet was nowhere near, but it seemed to satisfy the man as he returned to his prayer. A few others joined him, and the soulful words gradually joined as they flew higher and higher, circling until they soared gently into a melody of their own. They needed no musical instruments, no priest in violet robes, and no orchestra leader, but Jesmet might well have been there, leading and directing these musicians from a single sheet of music.

Oriannon listened to the symphony of prayers, though she could not say where the prayers left off and the song began, or if there really was any difference between the two. Perhaps not. But now the music opened its gates so that others in the tent could join in. They did, softly at first, to a tune Oriannon knew in her heart but not by memory.

217

Oriannon wished she could join in as fully as the others, but knew that she must keep her place at the edge of the group. So she just hummed along quietly, choking back unexpected tears until the music finally came to quiet rest, like a tiny viria songbird alighting on a branch that would not bend beneath its weight. No one announced an end; they just all seemed to know the prayer flight had folded its wings once more. The Owlings lifted their heads to open their eyes, one by one, with a sort of peaceful contentment in their faces that made Oriannon wish she was one of them. Never mind that their homes had been destroyed and they had been dragged away to a prison camp to serve as slaves. She wanted to be able to pray like that.

Once again she felt very much the outsider looking in, and she hoped they might overlook her intrusion. *What am I doing here anyway?* Without thinking she scrambled to her feet and looked for the way out. Meanwhile, Moya's mother stepped over to greet her.

"We're glad you came," she told Oriannon, her arm around her daughter. Oriannon knew she had seen the woman before, on the street in the Owling city. "You're always welcome here."

"I'm seeing Moya brought another one." The man who had looked up from his prayer chuckled as he joined them. "That's three more, just in the past two days."

Moya smiled up at them with a slightly puzzled expression. "Isn't that what Jesmet tells us to be doing?"

"It is, Moya." He patted her head with a smile, and introduced himself as Siric Mil, originally from one of the valley Owling villages but more recently of Lior. Most of the other Owlings at this gathering, he said, came from valley villages, though a few had lived in the cliff city. He waited expectantly for her to respond, and she knew then that she could hide no longer. If the probes found her, they found her.

So Oriannon finally introduced herself as she slowly peeled away her hood. Though she left off her full family name, she heard a small gasp from several of the others.

"Oh my!" Moya's mother brought her hands to her face in surprise. "You're the daughter of the Assembly elder—the one who came to Lior! I'm so sorry I didn't recognize you at first."

"No, don't apologize." Oriannon didn't want to make her feel awkward, but the woman went on.

"It's just that all Coristans seem to be looking, well, they're all looking pretty much alike to us. I'm sorry."

If she hadn't been so serious, Oriannon would have laughed, since she might have once said the same thing about the Owlings. By this time Moya was tugging at Oriannon's robe.

"So why are you wearing Owling clothes?" she asked, looking up at Oriannon with her innocent Owling eyes. "Where did you get them?"

"Oh, of course. The robe." Oriannon looked around to see everyone in the tent waiting for her explanation. "Actually, it's a long story, but I needed it to find Wist of Lior. And my Coristan friend Margus Leek, if he can be found here. There are Coristans in the camp, aren't there?"

"Not many," Siric admitted. "We're thinking they are being taken to the far side, but we still cannot be sure."

"So you don't know where Wist is?" asked Oriannon. She looked at Moya's mother, still hoping.

"Everyone in Lior was knowing Wist." She nodded her head but paused before going on, which made Oriannon even more nervous.

"Was knowing?"

Oriannon fought away her worst fears as the woman looked at her feet.

"I saw her just before your ships—pardon me, before they came to Lior. Not since."

Oriannon nodded and closed her eyes, not sure how to react. She couldn't give up already.

"I'll keep looking for her." Oriannon took a deep breath and squared her shoulders. "For Margus too. If they're in here, I'll find them."

"I would not be a naysayer," said Siric. "But it may be too late."

Oriannon wasn't sure what he was saying, and her face must have shown it. He motioned for her to follow him to the other side of the tent.

"Here," he told her. "I want you to be meeting someone."

He led her to a young woman in the corner, sitting quietly with her head in her hands, rocking. She wrinkled and contorted her face, and it was all too clear that, like many others out in the camp, she lived in her own world of fear.

"This is my daughter Terit. When the Coristans came, she was separated from us, and the securities captured her. She was one of the first to be receiving the implant."

Another woman bent down next to her, offering a cup of water, but Terit would only moan and hold up her hands. Oriannon couldn't help recognizing the look of confusion and fear on the girl's face.

"Terit used to dance," he told her, his voice cracking. "And she truly had one of the finest singing voices in the village. Like a little bell. Now—"

His voice trembled as he reached down to stroke her hair. For a moment Terit looked up at her father with a flash of recognition, until the dark thundercloud of fear overtook her once more. Oriannon almost couldn't look as Siric continued.

"We watched our daughter as the fear began taking over her thoughts," he said. "More one day, less the next, until ..."

"I'm sorry." Oriannon looked again over at Terit. "The effects are ... permanent?"

"The implant cannot be removed without killing the host. Be staying with us and you'll be receiving one too. As will we all."

"Siric, please." Moya's mother scolded her husband. "You don't have to be saying such things."

"But it's truth, no? Our guest is wanting to know truth."

"Yes, but not necessar—" the woman still objected.

"It's all right," Oriannon told them. "I need to know. I *must* know. Please tell me."

"You want to be knowing?" Siric's voice rose in anger, as he looked from Oriannon to his daughter and back again. "Then here's truth: Owlings sent to work outside receive this implant—above the eye, there, in the side of the head. Everyone in the camp will be receiving one, once the securities fix their machine problems. I don't fully understand; this is what I am hearing. But I am knowing that soon we'll never be acting out for fear of being punished. Never be running away for fear of becoming lost. We'll always be doing just what the securities be telling us, for fear. In the end, we'll all be like our sweet Terit."

"Oh, Siric." Moya's mother turned away, her face red.

"Truth?" He wasn't finished yet. "Sometime I would like to ask Jesmet why this has all happened to Terit, and now to we Owlings. But ..."

He sighed and looked at Oriannon with the saddest pair of dark Owling eyes she had yet seen, and she felt the pain of what he was trying to say.

"But," he sighed once again, and this time he rested a gentle hand on Oriannon's shoulder. "Jesmet always does what he will, does he not? Always what is best."

Moya's mother finally stepped back.

"She's heard enough, Siric. I think Oriannon needs to be finding her friends, and we should be helping her, instead of telling her terrible stories."

"Only truth." Siric still faced Oriannon squarely. "But, Miss Oriannon, if you truly want to be finding your friends, why wouldn't you be first asking your father? Is he not an elder?"

"He was, but ..." Oriannon was having trouble seeing through a growing veil of tears. "See, I couldn't be sure at first. Now I know. He has the implant too. He ..."

She couldn't finish, just turned and buried her face in the Owling woman's shoulder as she finally cried for her father, and for all that he'd been through. How could she not have known?

Moya's mother wrapped her in a comforting embrace, letting her sob until there were no more tears. For the first time in a long while, Oriannon didn't feel embarrassed about crying. Here in this tent with these strange Owlings, she knew they understood more than she.

"I'm sorry," Oriannon finally managed to catch a breath and pull back a few minutes later. But Moya's mother just shook her head and wiped at Oriannon's cheeks with her own sleeve.

"As I am." Siric looked at his wife, who nodded. "It was not my wish to be upsetting you."

"No." Oriannon tried to smile. "You've been very kind."

"Does this mean you're going to be staying with us?" asked little Moya, and her voice sounded hopeful. Oriannon shook her head.

"Thank you, but no; I do have to go."

"Go where?" Moya wasn't giving up. "You're not knowing your way around the camp like I am."

"Of course not. But I still have to find Wist and Margus."

"And then?" asked Siric. "Moya is having a point, you know, that you won't be getting far without securities discovering you. I'm not even knowing how you made it inside, except perhaps they weren't expecting you coming the wrong direction."

Thought the camp seemed to be patrolled by thousands of probes, at least they weren't expecting her here.

"I don't know how I'm going to find them either," she finally admitted. "Once I do, I'll figure out what to do next. Jesmet said not to worry about tomorrow, right?"

For a moment she wasn't sure if they were going to let her go, but Moya's mother walked with her toward the door.

"You'll need to be hurrying, Oriannon, as we expect probes at any minute. Remember, if you don't check in for work, they'll be checking your anklets until they find you. It's unpleasant. But if this is what Jesmet tells you . . ."

Yes, she would hurry. It would not be good to be caught here in this tent with no way out. And yes, that's what Jesmet told her.

"Wait, one thing more." Siric stopped her. "I was feeling something when you came into the tent, almost as if you were singing aloud, words from the Codex. Very odd. But I'm thinking you knew what it was?"

Oriannon reached into her pocket, the way she had so many times, just to be sure the Pilot Stone was still there. So he had sensed the Stone and its music. She thought of telling him everything, even wished that she could. But right now she just hoped they would see how little time she had.

"That's a long story." She smiled at them and kept backing toward the exit. "And I don't mean to be mysterious, but . . . maybe after I find Wist and Margus?"

Siric studied her a moment and then nodded as if he understood, while his wife and Moya stepped up to give Oriannon a hug. How long had they known her, a half hour? It felt more like years. He told her to try searching in the far eastern corners of the camp, where hundreds of young Owlings without families had been taken, and where it was rumored that a handful of Coristan prisoners had been seen as well. He said that Moya could show her.

"Perhaps you'll be finding them there," he said. "Though I'm still not knowing what you propose after that."

Oriannon didn't answer. She still didn't know either.

"We'll be praying for you, Oriannon Hightower." Moya's mom rested a hand on Oriannon's shoulder in good-bye.

Wist had told her that too, once. Only now it was time to find her, if she still could—and if it wasn't too late, the way Siric had said. Oriannon thanked them and turned to go, but the young Owling man who had been watching the tent door burst in before she could leave.

"Probes are coming!" he announced in a hoarse whisper. "Just a few tents away!"

25

In an instant Siric Mil took charge of the group inside the tent, holding up a hand to calm the little girls who had begun to cry. Perhaps this kind of search didn't happen as much as Oriannon assumed.

"All right, everyone just be staying calm!" he told them, though his own daughter began whimpering in the corner, and his wife tried to comfort her. "Be holding on to Jesmet and we'll be all right."

Oriannon thought that was an odd but somehow comforting thing to say, considering where they were, and she remembered the last time she had seen Jesmet in the Glades. Where was he now?

"What about Oriannon?" Moya still held tightly to Ori's arm, as if her new friend would run away if she let go. Maybe she should have a few moments earlier. Now it was too late.

"Stand behind those girls!" Siric pointed to a cluster of three young women, one holding a baby and the other two pulling more tightly into the group. Oriannon nodded and didn't hesitate to slip behind them, stooping to make herself look shorter and pulling her hood up tightly as she did.

Not that it would make much difference. She knew the girls could not offer much of a shield against an aggressive probe, like the one that now pushed in through the tent flap, right past their guard. It hovered for a moment in front of the group, extending its charged attack arms in a way that everyone would understand. They stood quietly, waiting for the probe's next move.

One of the younger girls in her group started crying, so Oriannon reached out to rub her shoulders. She imagined herself, along with the others, as trapped animals, hunted and without a way of escape. Once again her anklet buzzed in that entirely unpleasant way, and it made her want to claw and kick at the thing to remove it. She thought she could have, only now it would certainly not have done any good. If the anklet was another way of locating Owling workers, she was found.

The probe moved quickly from one to the next, shining its fingers of red laser light directly into people's eyes, then repeating their name and assigning them a number. Perhaps they'd never had one before.

"Given name," it demanded. Siric Mil was the next to stand up to the probe and respond. The probe seemed to think about its newly gathered information for a minute before spitting back a response.

"Your new identification code is 239–45–0002," it finally told him. "You will report for further processing when summoned within the next 48 hours. Do you understand? Indicate by saying yes or no."

"Yes." Siric nodded, and the probe continued on. By this time Oriannon's hands had stopped shaking, and she found herself strangely calm. Many of the others had their eyes closed, their lips moving slightly in prayers. She heard her name whispered.

When the probe found her here—and that would likely be in just a few moments—she would not be able to explain it away by telling them she was the daughter of an Assembly elder or that it was all some kind of mistake. Not this time. But oddly enough, she didn't seem to mind. Maybe it was the Owlings, surrounding her with their prayers. Or maybe it was the Stone in her pocket, which now seemed to hum so loudly she was afraid the probe would hear it.

Thank you. She added her own awkward prayer, simple as it was. Right now that seemed like enough. *Thank you for keeping me calm.*

"Are you praying?" Moya whispered up at her. Oriannon closed her eyes with a little smile and nodded. Perhaps that was the reason she didn't see the young boy until Siric shouted a warning.

"No, Adom!" His sudden cry made Oriannon jump back in fright and snap open her eyes. "Don't do it!"

Obviously Adom wasn't listening. She opened her eyes just in time to see the boy swing some kind of club—a broken tent pole perhaps. He connected with a horrific shower of sparks, sending the probe spinning and tumbling across the tent. Instantly it set up a piercing screech as it bounced on the ground twice and twirled upside down on the floor, while the tent erupted in confused shouts from all directions.

"What's he doing?"

"Get it! Grab it!"

"No! Watch out!"

The wounded probe sent blue attack surges in all directions as it spun out of control. Siric tried to calm everyone down, but the boy swung his club wildly and connected two or three more times. He shouted and screamed in fury, adding to the utter chaos until Siric finally managed to grab him around the waist and wrestle him to the ground.

"Let me be going!" shouted the boy, sobbing and swinging at once. Finally Siric pried the club from his hands, but too late. The probe lay shattered on the tent floor, its two attack arms mangled and half severed. Several lights still blinked feebly, but it could do no more than turn slowly, its alarm now barely audible.

"Why didn't you let me finish it?" sobbed Adom, his face red with emotion and his fists balled on Siric's chest.

"That's not how we're doing things, Adom." Siric tried to stand the boy to his feet. "You're having no idea what you just started."

"I'm knowing that we need to be fighting back. That's what I'm knowing."

But the alarm had already sounded, and Oriannon knew what happened to anyone who resisted. She ducked as at least ten fully-armed probes swarmed into the tent, followed by a single security with a charged stun baton.

The probes asked no questions, coming at Adom with savage swiftness, their weapons charged. Siric tried to hold on to the boy, but Adom pried himself away while the probes came at him from all angles, stinging him again and again until he collapsed to the floor. Finally he rolled on his back in obvious agony, defenseless against the attack.

No! Oriannon felt the anger boil up inside her. This time she could not just stand by and watch, and she didn't stop to consider what would happen if she was caught. Instead she jumped straight into the melee—never mind what the probes, or the security, might do to her.

"You leave him alone!" she shouted, trying to peel away the attackers. When one caught her with the edge of its stinger, the burn made her yelp in pain, the way it had that day at the Temple.

She gasped at the intensity of the sting, but didn't stop until a particularly large jolt literally sent her spinning away from the fight. From there, Siric tried to hold her back, under the watchful eye of the security.

"How can you let this happen?" Oriannon screamed at the security, not expecting an answer. Now it truly did not matter what anyone did to her, and she swung with all her strength, missing her mark. "Do you go home to your wife and kids and explain what you do to defenseless kids? Do you?"

This time Siric gripped her more tightly or she might have jumped at the security too. He still held his baton ready in one hand, as he worked a remote with the other. One by one the attacking probes recoiled and left the tent, leaving him standing alone in front of them.

"Actually," said the security, his voice hoarse. "I'm not married."

He pulled back his visor, revealing a young, ruddy-cheeked face, and a head of stringy blond hair that stood up straight. Oriannon had to blink several times before she was sure, and even then she couldn't believe it.

"Margus?" she whispered, feeling limp.

An awkward silence descended on the tent, while the security backed away behind his baton and snapped it off. Adom still moaned in pain, and a couple of his friends crawled to his side to comfort him.

"I'm so sorry about this," Margus told them. "I tried to stop it. They're only doing what they're programmed to do."

"You know this person?" asked Siric, confusion written on his face. While Oriannon caught her breath, he finally loosened his grip on her shoulders. She felt like she might collapse on the floor.

"I'm not sure if I do." She gulped, never taking her eyes off Margus. He looked strange beyond belief in the black Security uniform. But now that she knew it was him, she could have spotted him from a kilometer away.

"Ori, I had no choice." Now Margus pleaded with her, and his face wore a trace of the same kind of fear she had seen all over the camp. "Please, you have to let me explain. It's not the way it seems."

"No?" She shook her head in disbelief. Margus, of all people! How could he? And then they heard the call come in on his shoulder comm, since his earbud had fallen out.

"What's your status, Leek? We show probe 778 offline. You need help?"

Margus looked around the tent again while every eye focused on him. Adom even tried to sit up, though he was shaking and glassy-eyed, and looked to be in the first stages of shock. Finally Margus leaned into his shoulder comm to reply, even as he took Adom by the arms and hoisted him gently to his feet.

"No help needed. Just a malfunction."

"Well, then report back to Zed–24. We need help over here with an altercation."

"Right away."

He paused to look at Oriannon again, and she tried to look away.

"Ori," he told her, "we need to talk. Can you stay here until tonight? I'm off duty then."

She shook her head, still unsure what to think of Margus in the uniform of a security.

"I have to find Wist before it's too late," she told him. "Maybe it already is."

"That's what I need to talk to you about, Ori." He turned his attention to Adom. "But look, I have to take this guy in. The probes all saw what happened."

As if on cue, two more probes reappeared at the tent flap. Had he timed it that way? Immediately Margus slipped his visor back into place, resuming his role as a security.

"Leek!" His shoulder comm sputtered once more with an impatient voice. "Are you coming?"

"On my way."

Now the security pointed at Siric with a warning.

"Everyone in this tent stays right here until tonight." His glance shifted to Oriannon's direction. "That means everybody."

Without another word, he pulled a pale-looking Adom outside, leaving them alone once more. Moya began to sob.

"It's okay." Her mother comforted her. "He's going to be okay."

Oriannon wasn't sure he would be, and she wasn't sure Moya's mother really believed it either. But everyone held their breath a little longer, until one of them finally checked outside.

"All clear," he announced, pulling his head back in. "For now."

That was all Oriannon needed to hear as she headed for the exit.

"Oriannon, wait." Siric called after her. "If that was your friend—"

Oriannon turned once more to look back at the group.

"I'm sorry for what happened," she told them. "But I have to find Wist."

And for the second time, she would try to leave the Owling tent. She slipped outside and headed for the far eastern corner of the camp as angry drops of rain splashed the worn mud and soaked through her hood.

She would find Wist, with or without the help of the security named Margus Leek.

26

O w!"

Hours later Oriannon fell to her knees as the pain shot through her ankle and up her leg. How would that not look conspicuous to the probes on patrol above their heads? She tugged at the glassteel ring around her ankle, wishing that she could tug it off as easily as she had taken it off the Owling woman. Problem was, her ankle was much bigger than the Owling's. And this time the anklet didn't budge, since it had locked itself on more tightly than ever. As Moya's mother had warned her, it now seemed to be responding to some distant, continuous signal.

Could Margus have helped her with it?

An older Owling man sitting up against a nearby tent eyed her suspiciously in the growing shadows, and she smiled at him through her pain. Trying to ignore the steady drizzle, she wiped a wet strand of hair out of her face.

"These things don't ever come in the right size," she said, "do they?"

He didn't answer, just pulled at a ragged beard and stared. Another electrified jolt of the anklet made her gasp for breath. The

233

searchers, whoever they were, were not giving up. This could not be good.

"Please, Jesmet." Now she wasn't sure she could put any weight on the foot, and it throbbed with pain even as her entire leg turned numb. She paused a moment to think through her options.

First, the securities were obviously still trying to locate her anklet's wearer.

And second, since they hadn't found it yet, they had to know someone with this particular anklet was out walking where she wasn't supposed to be. Right?

She didn't want to think about Margus or what his role could be in all this chaos.

A pair of probes flew by, barely clearing the tops of the nearest tents, making Oriannon wonder why they didn't find her more easily. Maybe it wasn't that simple. Trying to ignore the pain, Oriannon rose on her good foot and hobbled next to a couple of mothers, each with a young child in tow. She had to blend in, and she had to find what she came for. She wasn't sure she could do both.

"I'm looking for a girl named Wist," Oriannon told them, trying not to wince as she came closer. "She's from Lior. Maybe in the far eastern corner of the camp. Do you know where that is?"

The nearest Owling woman looked at Oriannon with alarm, then up at where the probes had just slipped by. She shook her head.

234

"I'm sorry. We're not being from Lior, and we don't know this camp well. But—you are all right?"

Oriannon swallowed hard, biting the side of her mouth to keep from crying.

"I'll be better when I find her. Thanks anyway."

She hobbled on as the anklet continued to vibrate—sometimes tightening, other times just sending jolts of pain. Was there a bright side?

They still don't know who I am, she thought, *or where I am.*

Except for Margus. She clung to that small consolation as the skies opened up in a way she had not experienced often in Corista. The planet's shift had brought weather changes as well; not just darkened nights, but downpours. The force field seemed to have no effect at stopping the incoming rain. Minutes later she lifted her face as muddy rivulets washed down in the cleared spaces between tents, carrying socks and a boot, scraps of wood, the wrapper from a meal ration. At the base of a steep hill, she slipped and fell into one of the torrents, grabbing on to the side of a tent for balance while muddy water mixed with camp garbage washed over her.

Gross! The smell made her gag, but she fought off the reflex the same way she tried to dismiss the throbbing pain in her ankle.

Get up! Keep walking! Wist has to be here somewhere.

Every few meters floodlights created pools of swirling light in the growing darkness, while the Owlings around her scurried for cover and sloshed through the deepening mud and mess. She stopped as many as she could, asking them the same questions about Wist and how to find her. And always she got the same answers.

"Sorry!" Or, "Wish we could be helping you, but no."

No one had any ideas. From where she stood she couldn't even see the other end of the camp, and the little markers she could read had names like Beta 12 and Gamma 14. Still the tents stretched on and on across muddy hillsides and flooding low spots. Oriannon began to shake in desperation.

"Why did I even come here?" she asked herself. "Why didn't I wait for Margus?" But she knew the reasons. She wondered if she might meet the same end as Terit.

"Margus!" she finally cried out, when she knew she couldn't walk many more steps, but of course Margus did not answer. She took hold of the cloak of a passing man and asked the question once more. "Please! Do you know of a girl named Wist? She's from —"

"I'm very sorry." He shook himself free and headed for cover. By now the rain had soaked all the way through her cloak, adding a heavy weight she could no longer bear. Soaked to the skin, she

235

had to get out of this cold rain somehow, or go back the way she came. Only . . .

Where did I come from? She thought she had passed through this section of tents before, but really couldn't be sure as her mind started to grow as numb as her feet. She stumbled over a root partially hidden in the mud and wondered if she had been walking in circles. By this time all those dull green dome tents looked quite the same. Unable to see where she was walking, she sank into mud up to her ankles.

"Please." Every step now had turned into a prayer, a plea to the Maker for help. A nearby awning collapsed under the weight of water, unloading on her head.

"I can't do this!" she finally cried, hoping someone friendly would hear. But the mud tugged at her as if with hunger, tearing at all the self-confidence she had brought to the camp. Maybe she had carried a little too much pride in her fancy name, tucked behind all the nicer thoughts that said, "I can do it myself!"

And right now, the mud told her she could not. What had she told Brinnin back in school?

Don't you worry; I can handle it.

But that was then, before she had stepped into this dark, muddy nightmare, where at least half the Owlings were hiding in their tents, and the other half's minds had been numbed into blind, fear-filled submission. She could handle this? Though she tugged with all her strength, she could barely move one foot in front of the other. Finally she stopped and lifted her head once again, this time in pure defeat.

"I'm sorry, Jesmet." Tears streamed down her cheeks, mixing with the cold rain. "If you're trying to get my attention, well, here I am. I can't do it. But you knew that from the start, didn't you?"

The rain stung her cheeks, making her feel as if she too might wash down one of the muddy rivers. Had she really thought she would find her friends this way? She looked up at the dark blue dome, wondering why the force field could keep so many Owlings trapped inside, but let through something as small as a raindrop. It made no sense, but then nothing made sense right now.

Still she tumbled on, fully expecting that she would trip once more or fall headlong into a sea of mud. If that happened, surely no one would ever know—unless a probe came along and finally identified her cold blue ankle sticking out of the debris.

Don't think such things! She chided herself, but she could tell her mind was going through serious stages of shutdown. She had to find help, or shelter, or both! Again, her anklet vibrated and clamped down hard enough to drive her to her knees, even in the mud. This time she was beyond tears, and she could only manage a jerking sob as she looked for a place to collapse.

A small light at the front door of a metal-sided service shed seemed close enough, and she didn't care if it brought her face-to-face with a security. As the rain poured down harder than ever, she crawled the last few meters and pulled herself to shelter beneath the steps and then into the pitch-dark crawlspace between the ground and the shed's raised floor. She bumped her head on unseen pipes, wondering if the shuffling sound behind her might be some disgusting rodent with sharp teeth and red eyes.

She turned around and clapped her hands into the darkness, which seemed awfully silly but was the best she could do. No matter what kind of welcome awaited her under this little building, she was not giving up her space. She was finally out of the driving rain and the worst of the mud, and she could even hide behind foundation supports. Maybe it would turn out to be a good place to spend the night.

The shuffling noise grew louder, but this time she decided not to fight back. So what if a rat nibbled her toes? She watched a security ride by in a small lev-sled, but he didn't slow down. Maybe the rain would slack off in the morning, and maybe she would find her way back into the camp crowds. Maybe she would find Wist in the morning. Somehow. She had to believe such a thing could happen. Beyond that she could think of no other choices.

237

She closed her eyes, fought away the pain in her leg, and wished for sleep that refused to come. She thought she heard distant singing again, and wondered if it might be Siric and his people. Perhaps it was only the rumbling of her empty stomach, now aching after so long a time without a meal. Or maybe it was the Stone!

For a moment she thought she heard someone calling her name, and she imagined Jesmet walking through the streets of this camp, searching for her. That of course would have been a hallucination, quickly dismissed with a shake of her head even as she huddled closer to one of the shed's foundation pilings.

Keep your head straight. Don't let your mind play tricks on you.

Not even nice, pleasant tricks. On the other hand, maybe the Owlings actually would be praying for her, the way Moya's mother had said they would. That, she thought, would be nice, and she could accept such a comfort. So she allowed herself to imagine just a little, tried to imagine what she would do in the morning, and how she would get out of this mess. She kept her hand near the Stone. The music might not keep her warm or wipe the mud from her face, but it would warm her inside and remind her why she had smuggled herself into this nightmare in the first place.

We can get out of this, she told herself, hoping it was true.

t first Oriannon had no idea where she was or how long she might have been asleep. She especially had no idea why someone was calling her name or why her back felt as if it had been cemented into one position.

"Would you wake up, Ori?"

I'm dreaming, she decided. *I'm in some kind of cave, and Margus is yelling at me.*

But when she tried to straighten out, the solid bump to her forehead felt very un-dreamlike.

"Ouch!" She fell back down, rubbing the point of contact. Then she remembered the night before, the shock of seeing Margus again, her nightmare slog through the mud, and the fruitless search for Wist. She heard heavy footsteps over her head and remembered where she had found shelter for the night. For a moment she slouched a little closer to the ground.

"Hey!" It sounded like Margus again. "Over on this side!"

She followed his voice toward dull blue light and tried to focus, but still wasn't sure how to react when a black-suited security reached under the building and grabbed her by the arms. She would have screamed, but couldn't imagine who would come to help her. Besides that, no one could see them in the service alley behind the shed.

"You are the most stubborn person I have ever known, Oriannon Hightower!"

This time the security pulled her out behind the building and stood her up straight. She had no choice but to stand there and look Margus straight in the visor. She reached up and pushed it clear, just to be sure the eyes belonged to him. He let her.

"How did you find me?" she whispered, shivering in her damp clothes.

"Well, I found a little Owling girl wandering around, calling your name."

"Moya?"

"She didn't say. All she would tell me was she'd tried to follow you for a while, then lost you when it started raining. She was pretty upset. So I took up where she left off, looked for infrared, and finally found you under the building."

"You make it sound simple."

"I don't know. But look, there's no time for that now. In a few minutes they're going to be wondering what happened to me."

"What *did* happen to you, Margus? And what happened to your parents? Do they know?"

He shook his head and wiped the tears from his face.

"They're both dead, Ori."

"What? Margus, no!" She couldn't believe it. "How?"

He turned away from her, arms crossed in obvious pain.

"Everything happened so fast when Sola came to my house that night."

"That night—when we were waiting in the Glades."

"Yeah. She wanted to know about the probe we stole. I had this great idea and told her I would help her, if she wouldn't hurt my dad."

"Don't tell me that."

"No—it's not what you think. I wasn't ever going to *really* help Sola. Are you kidding? I just thought I could get inside here that way, and we could help the Owlings."

"So she made you a security? Just like that?"

"No. Well, sort of." He paced to the corner of the building, peeked out, and paced back. "I'm actually just as much a prisoner as all the other Owlings. I can't leave the camp."

"Oh. But then what about your dad—your parents?"

"She promised they would be treated okay. But she lied, Oriannon. She always lies."

"But ... killed? That's—I mean, I didn't know she would ..."

He nodded. "Sola told me it was a terrible accident, that they tried to escape or something. I don't believe it."

"Oh, wow. I am so sorry, Margus." The words sounded trite, but she could think of nothing else. "I'm sorry too—for running off from the tent last night."

"Doesn't matter. I probably would have done the same thing. But there's something else I have to tell you, Ori."

She looked at him more closely. He was sweating inside the black helmet.

"They put an implant inside my temple. I didn't want them to, but they made me take it. Just like they made all the elders take it, and so many other people. And they can turn it up any time they want."

Now she understood the pained look on his face.

"Same as my father," she told him.

"Yeah, I think so. Same as all the Owlings are going to get, but you knew that. Only with theirs they keep it turned up most all the time, and with mine they just threaten me with it."

"Have they done it yet?"

"Just once, to prove it to me." He closed his eyes. "I don't want to tell you what it's like. Except I have never been so scared in my life. It's—"

"Don't," she put up her hand. "You don't have to tell me. I've seen it."

"Yeah, but until you feel it, you have no idea how much it grabs you. Like, the fear, it's everything. Huge. And you know what else? It makes me want to get these people out of here, more than ever."

"Okay then." She nodded. "But ... you don't think we can help all of them escape? Even the ones who are already processed?"

"Maybe we can't do anything about them. But if we can help Wist escape, maybe we can help the others escape before they're processed too. That's something."

"Yeah," she agreed. "Problem is, I can't even *find* her."

For the first time he showed her a tiny hint of a smile as he edged over to the corner of the building once more.

"If you hadn't run off, I might have been able to show you last night. Now Brinnin's going to have to show you the way."

"Wait a minute." Oriannon paused. "Did you say Brinnin?"

"Didn't I tell you?" He glanced around the corner and pointed with his chin. "See that probe over there, hovering above that building?"

She noticed a single probe, partially hidden behind the peak of a metal roof.

"I see it. But it's all by itself. Don't probes usually stick together?"

"Unless they're being controlled by someone."

"No way!" Oriannon wanted to run out into the open and flag down Brinnin's probe. Instead she held back in the shadows while Margus explained.

"You walk down that corridor a couple hundred meters. Don't look up, and don't act like you notice anything. Brinnin will steer down in front of you, and from there you can follow her to a section called Zed 65. You're headed in the right direction."

"That's where Wist is?" After all this, she wasn't sure how it could be so simple, and she wasn't sure why he hesitated.

"She's there. The question is, can you make it?"

"I'll make it." She flexed her feet and winced. "What about you?"

"Meet you there as soon as I can get free. We just have to be careful not to let anyone see us talking, or together, unless I'm dealing with you the way I would a prisoner. Okay? Now go."

Oriannon paused only a moment before limping out into the open in the direction Margus had told her. She didn't look up, and hardly even looked to the side. A moment later she felt rather than heard a moment of air directly behind her.

"Don't turn around." The probe's voice resembled Brinnin's, only softer and slightly more metallic.

"Is that really you?"

"Close enough. And I hate to say this, Ori, but you look awful. I have never seen you—"

"Never mind me. Can you believe Margus?"

"He's the one who let my probe through the front gate. Like he knew I was coming before I even got here. I couldn't believe it."

Oriannon forced herself to keep walking, never looking back. "You haven't been stopped by any other probes?"

"Not yet. I figured I had to take the chance though."

"You're crazy, Brinnin."

"Me and who else?" The probe moved around to the lead. "You've been gone all this time. Your dad's going nuts that you're missing."

Oriannon stopped to think about what her friend had just said, and did her best to not think about what was going to happen to her father.

"What about the Owling woman I traded clothes with?"

"She's at my house. Carrick has been entertaining her this whole time with me. We play skak, and Carrick taught her to bake loanfruit pies. She's pretty fun. Quiet, but fun. Oh, and actually, Carrick had to go home, which is why I'm the one running this thing, but she said to say hi."

"Okay, good. But now Wist. Do you know where she is?"

"Actually, I thought I was going to have to convince people I wasn't a regular probe, and then start asking around, but—"

"Brinnin! Tell me!"

"Right. Margus said Section Zed 65 is way off at the far end of the camp."

"That's what he told me too. You know the way?"

"Yeah, but ... there's something else you should know."

Oriannon stared at the probe, trying to imagine it was really her friend. Brinnin finally explained.

"I just heard that area is being processed, and I think Margus is supposed to help."

"Oh, wow. So you know all about that." Oriannon pushed on even faster, trying to ignore her feet. She didn't want to believe what she'd just heard, didn't want to think Wist was being processed, like so many others. But before long she had to slow down as the anklet clamped down once more. She paused to rest, leaning on her knees.

"Anklet," Oriannon explained, gritting her teeth. "It's been tightening. Really hurts."

By this time Oriannon had to assume the Owling woman who should have been wearing the anklet was way overdue to report for her work detail again. What would happen when she didn't show up? Perhaps she would be assumed dead. But Oriannon didn't want to find out, and hobbled on as quickly as she could after Brinnin's probe, zigzagging through the camp. Every step intensified the pain, but she pushed down the thought and counted silently to keep her legs moving. One, two, one, two ...

"How much longer to Zed 65?" she finally asked, and the probe flew a little lower as others passed overhead.

"Maybe another fifteen minutes, Ori. Keep going. It's straight ahead now. But listen, what are we going to do when we find her?"

An Owling girl looked at them curiously from the opening of a nearby tent. She'd probably never heard a probe say such a thing.

"I was wondering if there was a way for Margus to get Wist onto a work team, get her outside before she's processed, maybe—Brinnin?"

When she turned around, the probe had disappeared—or rather, lofted several meters above.

"What are you doing?" Oriannon wondered, and the probe swept down on her in a wobbly arc.

"There's a pack of securities headed straight for us," she told Oriannon, "so you'd better duck away somewhere. I'll go look for Margus and meet you at Zed 65."

Oriannon didn't have time to disagree as the probe peeled away and left her standing. Did she have a choice? She snugged the hood tighter over her head and looked to the side where a terrified Owling sat mumbling, not looking at her. Without thinking, she turned and limped through the maze of tents, anything to stay one step ahead of the oncoming sweep of securities. Just behind her she could hear the cries of frightened Owlings pulled outside. She put down her head and ran, praying it was still the right direction.

"Wist!" she cried out as she approached a small clearing marked by orange stakes stamped with Z 65 in dark block letters. She raised her voice. "Wist!"

28

Three steps into the Zed 65 clearing, Oriannon's ankles gave way and her knees buckled beneath her. She could not stop herself from falling face-first into the dirt, but picked herself up and stumbled into the nearest tent.

"I have to find Wist!" she gasped, and a small woman grabbed her by the shoulders before she could fall into the small cooking fire smoldering in the middle of the tent, about the size of a large living room.

"Here, sit down for just a moment." The woman guided her to one of the cot bunks lining the wall. She reached for a small styro cup, filled it with a steaming liquid that had been simmering in a pot next to their fire, and handed it to Oriannon. "Drink some of this."

"You know Wist?" Oriannon nodded her thanks and brought the cup of smoky, bitter tea to her lips. She didn't stop to think that here in the camp, such a tea would probably be in short supply. It tasted faintly of the Shadowside that had been lost, of wild berries and dark steppes, and Oriannon drank it with a thirst.

"Of course I'm knowing my own niece. Now wait."

The small woman paused for a moment and frowned at the sound of approaching cries. No doubt she'd heard the sound before, but Oriannon wondered how much time they had before the sweep reached them. Finally the Owling disappeared outside.

Alone in the tent, Oriannon leaned back and listened as she sipped her tea. Even with so many noises about, she could not keep her eyes open. A moment later she jerked awake to see Wist leaning over her with a look of concern.

"Whatever are you doing here?" asked the Owling girl. Her face looked scratched and her cheeks a bit hollow, but the sparkle remained in her eyes. "You look horrible!"

"So I've been told." Oriannon tried to get up, but could not make her legs obey. Wist gently helped her lie back down.

"Here," she told Oriannon. "Take a few minutes."

"No, I've come for *you*." Oriannon protested, though her strength had already left her. All she could do was reach out and grab Wist's hand. "There's no time to rest."

"It's good to see you too."

Now Oriannon could not feel her right leg—whether from the tightness of the anklet or the numbing effects of medicinal Owling tea, she could not be sure. Wist dabbed at her face with a rough washcloth. Of course this was way too much like the first time she'd come to Shadowside, needy and weak, and Wist had first cared for her. So their lives seemed to repeat, only this time they found themselves in a Coristan prison camp, rather than the safety of the Owling city.

"We have to go, Wist." Oriannon tried once more. "Margus is going to help you escape."

A shadow fell over her bed, and Oriannon recognized the bearded, reluctant leader of Lior by the serious look that only Owling eyes held with such depth.

"What is she talking about?" asked the man.

"Becket Sol." Oriannon forced a weak smile. "I found you."

Becket Sol didn't return the smile, just held his palm to his forehead and frowned.

"I'm hoping you're not here on some sort of rescue mission." The frown never left Becket Sol's face. "You are endangering your life by coming here."

"I was just going to ..." Oriannon's heart fell as she tried to explain, but Wist held another cup of Owling tea to her lips. Her foot stopped throbbing, for the moment.

"Be drinking more, Ori." Wist told her, and Oriannon was in no position to refuse.

"She's not knowing the anklet is the least of her problems." Becket Sol talked past her, but now more Owlings ran in and out of the tent, and he turned aside to confer in excited whispers.

"What's he saying, Wist?" Oriannon blinked back the numbing effects of the tea. "What's going on?"

A boy announced the answer when he pushed inside.

"They're processing everybody in Zed 63!" he told them, looking out of breath and wild-eyed at the news of the neighboring section. Of course the news came as no surprise.

"Oriannon." Wist adjusted a hard pillow of shredded rags beneath her head. "You should be resting now."

"No!" Oriannon shook her head and sat up, despite Wist's gentle hands on her shoulders. "I didn't come here to rest; I came to get you all out of here."

"Ori." Wist shook her head. "You know we can't."

"You say that because of all the horrible things you've seen. Well, you know what? I've seen things too."

The tent went silent for an awkward moment. But before going on, she took a deep breath and finally pulled herself to her feet, holding on to Wist's shoulder for balance. She had to say this, if they would only listen.

"I saw Jesmet do things no one else has ever done. He turned away a yagwar with his voice. He made our school food disappear, which everyone really appreciated, by the way. And when

249

a girlfriend of mine fell off the top of a ladder and … died, he picked her right back up off the floor—alive! You didn't see all these things, did you?"

Well, of course they had not, but Oriannon kept going without waiting for their answer. She knew that if she stopped to take a breath, she might never finish.

"I saw him step over the border to save my life, even when he knew he would pay with his own. And then I saw him killed in the star chamber, back home in my city." She pointed in the direction of Seramine. "You didn't see that either, but I did. We all cried because we knew he was dead, and we thought that was the end."

She paused at the dark memory.

"But then I watched him walk up to Lior just a few hours later. Remember that?"

This time several of the Owlings nodded. Even with all the commotion outside, every one stood still and stared at her. She couldn't stop now.

"After that we all saw him dance in the streets of Lior. Remember that? So I know who he is now, and I think you all know too. You know what it says in the Codex."

"The Maker himself will dance in our streets." Wist quoted the ancient scripture that most Coristans had forgotten. Oriannon nodded, and now she could feel her heart pumping again.

"That's right. So I don't know what's about to happen, and I don't know what Sola is going to try to do to us. But I'll tell you one thing: I'm not ready to give up just yet. Maybe you all are, but I'm not."

Her words brought quiet clapping from everyone standing close by. Oriannon, on the other hand, felt ready to collapse.

"So you think it possible your father will be standing up for us?" asked Wist, her soft voice echoing through the tent.

"That's what I thought, at first." Oriannon shook her head and tried not to cry all over again. "But it didn't turn out that way. My dad already has the same implant Sola wants to give to everybody here. Not as serious yet, but it's the same thing, so he can't help. But Brinnin, Margus, and I—we have a plan."

Even as Oriannon spoke, she wondered what had happened to Brinnin. She glanced around the tent again, looking into the dark eyes of all the Owlings who stared back at her. But something felt good inside now. She'd said what she'd needed to say for a long time—what she needed to hear as much as the Owlings.

Even so, she knew they didn't have much time. Suddenly and without warning, the Owlings all scattered in panic as a probe entered the tent. A little girl screamed, but Oriannon didn't move and didn't flinch. She knew.

"Did you find him?" Oriannon asked the probe.

"I'm sorry, Ori," answered Brinnin's voice as the probe pulled up beside her. "Not yet. He said he would meet us, but I haven't been able to find him."

"He'll be here," said Oriannon. "Just keep looking, and—"

"Oriannon." Becket Sol interrupted her, though his voice had softened now. She looked over at his square-jawed, determined expression. "I'm sorry, but this we can't be doing."

"What?" She wasn't sure what he meant.

"The only thing you need is to be returning home safely," he went on, "so you will be showing yourself to the securities. Be telling them you are Oriannon Hightower of Nyssa. This is what your father would be wanting."

"What?" Oriannon focused on the Owling leader. "Don't you at least want us to try?"

His expression turned even more serious, but with a hurt in his eyes.

"It is dangerous for you, Oriannon. Ori. I am appreciating what you say. And I'm knowing Jesmet will be here for us." He paused and sighed. "But you are Coristan, we are Owling ... and this is not your struggle."

She couldn't believe what he was saying, and she knew no one argued with Becket Sol. But he had to understand!

"After everything that's happened," she said, making sure they heard every word. "I don't know if I'm a Coristan anymore. I'm a Jesmet follower. Isn't that what you are too?"

"Wist, make our guest comfortable." He had already closed his ears, and he held up his hand. "We will be getting her to safety, but we're not having much time."

He hurried from the tent, leaving Oriannon dumbfounded.

He's making a huge mistake!

She shrugged off Wist's help but turned back to her.

"We're going to get you out of here, Wist, and then everybody else. I'm going to find Margus. Just wait here, and I'll talk to Becket Sol again."

"Ori." Wist looked her with her impossibly large Owling eyes. "You don't understand."

"I understand that I didn't come all this way to go back alone. I'll talk to him."

She pushed off uncertainly and hobbled out of the tent to find Becket Sol. If she could just make him understand. If he would just give her a chance.

"Oriannon!" Wist called out after her. Oriannon was not as careful as she should have been, charging across the clearing in front of Wist's tent. She did see the man she thought was Becket Sol, standing in the middle of a group of Owlings. She did not see the securities move in from two directions, leaving them with nowhere to run.

252   "This way!" The securities herded them away from the tent, stun batons drawn. "You're all coming with us!"

Ori wasn't sure if she heard Wist cry out in the distance, or if it was Brinnin, but it made no difference. Neither could save her from what she had just stepped into.

29

At first Oriannon thought struggling might be a good idea, despite her weak ankles and light head. However, force-field wrist cuffs put an end to any ideas of escape.

"Please!" she shrieked, "you can't do this!"

By this time she had a pretty good idea that, just as Becket Sol believed, nothing she said would help. Still she would try.

"No?" The security who had grabbed her outside the Owling tent was obviously not impressed. "And why not?"

"Because my father is an Assembly elder."

"Oh, so that's why you're here," he drawled. "We don't see too many Coristans in this camp. Your dad must have ticked Sola off good."

Oriannon couldn't see the face behind this man's helmet, but she didn't like the arrogance in his voice. She liked even less the way he dragged her through the muddy pathways toward a waiting lev-transport. She decided to try one more desperate angle, despite where it might take her.

"I know Sola," she told him. "You can ask her."

He only laughed in her face.

"You're not the first one to try that line."

"Then scan my eyes! You'll see my name is Oriannon High-tower of—"

"Don't need to." He pointed at the anklet. "You've got all the ID we need."

She had to try something a little more drastic, even if it only slowed him down. She just wasn't going to go along with this because they told her to. With a shout she lunged to the side, directly into a tent.

"What are you—?" The security yanked at the shoulder of her robe as she collapsed the tent and tried to roll. Unfortunately her arms remained shackled behind her, and all she could do was grab whatever came to hand. She heard an Owling shout, and small hands grabbed her as she tried desperately to scramble away.

"This way!" a young Owling boy wrestled her away from the security's grip and helped her climb through her shackled arms so she could use her hands out in front of her.

"Backup at Zed 64!" barked the security. Oriannon knew what that meant. Before she had taken a step, she was surrounded by three probes, barely centimeters away at every side. She looked at the Owling and nodded her thanks.

Her anonymous hero hesitated only a moment before bowing away. The probes let him go. Meanwhile, her Security escort kicked aside the partly collapsed tent and strode up to where she was checkmated by the circle of probes. He pulled back his face shield to reveal cold, bloodshot eyes and a tight-lipped frown, while two of the probes pulled back from their circle just enough to let him approach her.

254

"Hold out your wrists," he ordered, but she shook her head.

"I'm not doing anything. Not anymore. You're going to have to—"

"Quiet!" Without waiting for her to finish he grabbed her wrists and yanked them straight out. From a remote on his belt he pushed a small button to suddenly release the shackles.

"You're hurting me," she complained, but he only chuckled.

"We've got something new for cases like you."

Oriannon saw a sadistic smile cross his face, one that told her he surely enjoyed what was going to happen to her next. He looked at the two nearest probes and pointed at Oriannon.

"Immobilize her and deliver her to the Processing Center. Right away."

She flinched, waiting for the sharp jolts of current the probes would surely deliver. More than that, she knew that what had tormented her father would soon be hers as well—only worse. They would not hold back anything. She prayed quietly, but could not stop shaking.

Don't leave me now, Jesmet. Please.

Her hair stood on end as attack arms from all three probes extended to within centimeters of her face. This time she knew she could not escape.

"You don't have to—"

She started to object, but a moment later she could no longer move her jaw, could hardly make a sound. It didn't hurt exactly, just felt uncomfortable and tingly. Her hands would not move either. In fact, nothing would. And when she looked down she saw she had been lifted a meter off the ground, suspended upright and just as helpless as a fly in the web of an eight-legged spod.

No! In her desperation she looked for Margus, though she wasn't sure what he could have done if he had come by. Even worse, what if he were assigned to take her in for processing? At this point she knew she would do just about anything—cry, beg, break down completely—if only she could move.

Now she could only groan, but not loud enough for anyone to hear. So the probes simply paraded her unceremoniously through the camp and past hundreds of Owlings—a trophy for Security and a warning to anyone who dared to resist. Most of the Owlings—or the ones who still had their senses—looked at her with pity before lowering their sad eyes. They had to know where she was being taken. And they had to know they were next.

Oh, Jesmet! she thought. *Where are you now?*

Obviously not there in the camp, though she wasn't sure what he could have done. She simply remained on display as the probes ferried her to the heart of the camp—a sprawling, circular metal building with a wide entry into a big hallway that followed the windowless perimeter. Dozens of downcast Owlings lined the hall ahead, blocking the way.

"Move aside!" growled her attending security. As they paused, Oriannon noticed muddy handprints and scribbled signatures on the wall. One desperate Owling had hastily scrawled, *Save me plea . . .*

Oriannon was pushed forward and given the honor of cutting to the head of the line. No one objected, and most offered quick, furtive glances as she was pushed through double doors to a central clinic area.

Or perhaps clinic would be too nice a word to describe the pale green room illuminated by harsh floodlights. A glass-front cabinet held a mess of medical instruments, while three uncomfortable-looking patient tables featured force-field restraint cuffs for both arms and legs. Oriannon, of course, had already been sufficiently restrained.

"This one says she's an elder's daughter," the security announced in a loud voice. "How about that?"

"Not bad. I've heard better stories though." A small-statured tech in a Security-black frock looked up from a floor-mounted instrument Oriannon had never seen before. But it wasn't the sinister-looking instrument that made her catch her breath, it was the unmistakable round eyes of an Owling.

He went on as if they came to hear his stories, speaking with none of the usual singsong Owling inflections.

"Yesterday we had someone who claimed to be Sola's little sister. That was quite amusing for a short time."

"No, really." Her security crossed his arms, mission accomplished. "This one insists."

"Oh, I see. Well then that's perfect, since we've been able to modify everyone on the Assembly as well."

The tech turned to Oriannon with a smile that made her ill, but she could no more avert her eyes than she could speak or move.

"And I must say, that was one of my finest accomplishments. Er, Sola's, that is. Imagine an Owling putting down the entire Assembly, when they thought their implants were just a simple, harmless security measure. They had no idea what we had in mind. Pardon the pun. But after all those years, our coup seems like justice, does it not?"

A silent scream filled Oriannon's head as she understood for the first time what had really happened to her father, and to Corista. But that didn't explain how he could do this horrible thing—to his own people, no less!

"Of course you're surprised," he told her as he looked more closely at the side of her head. "But not as much as the Owlings are when they see me. After ten years, you think anyone recognizes me? Ha! My friends left me for dead, and it was a lonely Coristan Security patrol named Sola Minnik who saved my life."

Oriannon had no reply, but she was beginning to understand how a mind could be twisted by hate. And Sola had once served on the border, had she?

"Ah, but enough of my story." He adjusted his equipment, and it hummed as it came closer. "Look at it this way: Sola tells us it's all for the ultimate good of the planet, and now you'll be able to identify with your former leaders."

She wished the look in her eyes could tell him how little she appreciated his sarcasm.

"No need to track identity?" asked the security, but the tech shook his head.

"Hmm, no. We're at a point now where it doesn't matter any longer. With all the delays, well, you know how Sola gets. We proceed."

"On the table?"

Again the tech shook his head.

"Leave her as is. It's actually easier this way."

She would have kicked him in the knee or clawed his face—anything to get away. But she could only watch as he pulled a long, jointed mechanical arm closer, adjusting several more controls as he positioned his machine between the three probes that carried her here, close enough for a snug fit. A plate-sized attachment at the end of the arm opened into two, like the old-style earphones, and they closed around her head.

So this was how they did it. She nearly burst on the inside, struggling with all her mind to scream. But still no part of her useless body would respond.

"Now, don't move," he warned her, then chuckled. "Oh, that's right. You can't. Well, that just makes it so much easier, don't you think? We'll have this friendly procedure over and done with in just a moment, and then you'll be on your way."

The insides of the plates began to glow with a warm green light, and in a morbid sort of way it reminded her of a time when she was younger and all the pre- and first-year students lined up for inoculations at the school nurse's office. Of course that time Nurse Anno had only used a small hand-held instrument, and the vaccines had been injected painlessly into her arm. This was no vaccine.

"You're thinking it looks like the shots you used to get, aren't you?" the tech said. "At first that's what I thought too. You'll be interested to know that we started with the same technology. Only here it's been ... enhanced just a bit."

Still he prattled on, like a school nurse trying to set his patient at ease. And as the paddles glowed more intensely, the machine whined until a sudden release and a tiny prick in her temple made Oriannon flinch—as much as she could manage from where she still hung. The glow subsided, and the tech removed his machine with a proud look on his face.

"That wasn't so bad, was it?" he crooned, nodding to the security. "I think we can let these probes get back to their work now. I'm sure they have more important things to do than harass this poor girl. Go on."

The security nodded back, touching his remote so that Oriannon was slowly lowered to the rough wood floor, back to her own two feet. She tottered for a moment as she regained her balance, and her legs felt her weight once again. The probes disengaged without a sound and disappeared out the door, flying above the heads of Owlings who barely noticed or moved. And this Owling tech had the gall to smile at her again.

"There. How does that feel?"

Unguarded now, Oriannon knew she could have scratched the man's eyes out. Instead she lifted a hand to her temple. Other than a small raised bump, she felt nothing different.

"What have you done to me?" she lowered her voice. "What are you doing to all these people? How can you—"

But she could not finish her sentence. He touched a button on the machine's control panel, and she felt the first, intense wave of fear.

"Hold that thought," he told her, as the fear knocked her to her knees. She felt sweat on her forehead and her heart beating out of her chest. At the same time, she could not help hyperventilating to the point of dizziness as her temple throbbed with pain. She knew the fear would tear her apart in moments, if he left it on.

"Please ..." she gasped, knowing she had been pushed to the edge of insanity. Her arms and legs trembled out of control, and the darkest weight of the world pressed down with a force she had never imagined. "Please, help me!"

"Whoops, I'm so sorry." When he made an adjustment, the wave of raw fear receded as suddenly as it had washed over her, leaving behind a nauseous feeling. "Didn't mean to startle you there. Just wanted to see if you were online, and apparently you are. Am I right?"

259

Oriannon gasped for air, and her mouth felt cotton-dry.

"I don't know what you mean."

"Of course you don't." He nodded and patted her on the head. Any other time she would have slapped him, and inside she wished she had the courage to do just that. But another shadow had been cast in her mind. As much as she hated herself for doing so, she could only nod and look back at the line of waiting Owlings.

"I . . ." she struggled for words. "I didn't mean to cut in line."

The words could have come from someone else's mouth; they sounded so strange and foreign.

"Please don't concern yourself." He finished his adjustments. "Now . . . you'll feel a little different from here on, since your implant causes a certain level of ongoing anxiety. Don't forget the implant is permanent, so if you're ever tempted to have it removed, well, that would be fatal, I'm afraid. The good news is that your device is remotely adjustable, so it you ever find it makes you uncomfortable, remember that my Security associates can always pull it back a little. Or not. You just let me know. You feel fine now, don't you?"

Oriannon felt herself nod, and despised herself for it. She didn't feel fine; she felt dark and empty. But she had no words to describe what had just happened to her. Now she knew what Margus meant.

She also yawned, and leaned against the tech's machine to keep from falling over.

"Of course, as you've already discovered," he continued, guiding her to an exit. "Things could change drastically. It's all up to you. And oh yes, I forgot to mention. You're going to feel drowsy for the next few hours. It's a side effect we haven't yet been able to isolate, though you needn't worry—it appears quite harmless."

"Harmless." Oriannon tried to keep her eyes open and repeated the word as if it would make it so.

"So you go back to your tent and sleep, and in the morning we'll introduce you to a whole new activity program."

Even as drowsy as she was, Oriannon had a good idea what he meant. Back at Jib Ossek Prep, she'd seen Owlings in the "activity program." But he smiled once more and air-washed his hands, looking quite satisfied with himself. He did not know she had no tent to which she could return, and she didn't feel inclined to enlighten him. She would worry about the morning when it arrived. Right now the only thing she wanted was to find a place to lie down and close her eyes.

Any place.

30

The next morning Oriannon hardly remembered the blanket she used on the hard dirt floor. She did, however, remember an Owling woman's kind eyes, and the hard piece of doan biscuit the woman handed her as they were rounded up and marched out to the staging area by the camp gate.

"Thank you." Oriannon also remembered her manners. Despite the bread's staleness, she chewed it gratefully. Amazing what a person could get used to when she was this hungry. She wanted to strongly object to Security herding them onto an open lev-transport platform, but a twinge of fright kept her mouth shut.

That would be the implant doing its work, she reminded herself. Yet even though she knew exactly what was going on, she could not find the will to push past this locked gate of fear.

"Where are you being from?" whispered the Owling woman as they stepped up the stairs to the transport. Oriannon looked at her quizzically, and it seemed an odd question for an Owling to ask a Coristan. Still, she struggled to answer the obvious question.

"I'm from ... the city," she finally managed. That could of course have meant Seramine ... or Lior.

"Really?" The woman seemed interested. "I was never seeing it before it was—you know. But everyone is always saying how beautiful it used to be."

The woman's words brought back a rush of memories to Oriannon of the simple but beautiful Owling cliffside city and the precarious views of the valley below.

"Yes," Oriannon finally answered. "It was beautiful . . . once."

She watched as the main gate's energy field dropped and they all passed through its tunnel to the outside. Despite her fears, Oriannon found she could take mental notes. How long did it stay open? Who was watching? How secure was it? Perhaps the information might come in handy sometime, though strangely enough, the prospect of escape now seemed more remote than ever.

Meanwhile the open air of Corista had cleared, and a fresh wind blew in their faces. Oriannon knew it should have lifted her spirits, but all she could think of was what would happen if she leaned too far over the transport railing and fell out? Or what if an insect hit her in the eye and she was unable to see? She could think of a hundred things that now petrified her as the transport sped toward the far side of the Rift Valley, through a busy transport corridor, and finally came to a rest a few meters away from the main flow of land traffic.

This would be one of the main east-west corridors connecting Seramine and many of the outlying Rift Valley towns, where the dry rolling hills went on for kilometers and the only buildings were the occasional low-lying stucco home or domed farm. She'd traveled this way several times with her father, when she was younger and they used to explore the Coristan countryside.

"You work this piece of transport corridor," announced their security. Oriannon counted thirteen prisoners and only one security escort. Where were the probes? "Fill the trash bags, and in twenty minutes we move to the next section. Any questions?"

It must have been a figure of speech, since the security didn't wait for anyone to speak—if they dared. Instead he tapped a scroll button on a small handheld remote and, judging by everyone else's reaction, Oriannon wasn't the only one to feel the sudden, dark flood of fear. The girl next to her gripped her forehead and hid her face.

"That's more like it." The security chuckled as he lowered the ladder and motioned for them to climb out. "Get going."

The first worker out shivered and sidestepped up the shoulder of the corridor, muttering as lev-scooters and transports of all shapes zipped by. The slipstream nearly lifted them off their feet as the second Owling in line clutched her hair and mumbled something about bugs crawling up her back.

Meanwhile Oriannon fought off her own fears, wondering why they still didn't single her out as the only Coristan in the work crew. As the anxiety of being discovered and punished rose in her throat, she latched onto the nearest Owling woman's hand and never let go. They each received orange bags, and the bored-looking security leaned against their transport, stuffed a length of lakris root in his mouth, and waved them toward an empty stretch of corridor.

"See that bunch of trash up there?" he asked them. He spit a stream of brown lakris juice at their feet, not missing entirely. "I want to see it gone before Sola gets here."

If Oriannon felt intimidated before, now she hurried to find a place that might be out of view, away from everyone else. *Sola, here?* But she shivered as loaded lev-transports whizzed past. She wasn't sure what made her afraid of them, only knew for certain that she was.

She looked down at a wrinkled aplon snack wrapper and wondered what kind of disease she might contract if she picked it up with her bare hand. But what if she didn't pick it up? She looked back over her shoulder. The security and his stun baton seemed like a more immediate danger. Finally she closed her eyes, held her breath, and snagged the corner of the wrapper between two fingers.

What is wrong with me? she wondered, but the throbbing in her temples told her more than she wanted to know. She knew exactly what was wrong, and she knew exactly what was warping her mind. She just couldn't do anything about it.

Another convoy of transports flew by, barely a meter off the hard surface of the corridor, blowing trash around her feet. Oriannon felt her hair, still stringy and dingy from the camp's mud, and realized she hadn't been able to take a shower for days. The thought of a shower made her shiver, when it reminded her of rain coming down as it had the night she'd slept under the shed.

"Hey, you!" The security pointed at her from a distance. "Stop dreaming and start picking up."

She nodded lamely, but wondered how to pick up a discarded bottle of tart orange cider without actually touching it. A few steps away, her new Owling friend was scooping up enough trash for both of them.

"You get used to feeling scared," the woman told her, grabbing everything in sight. "It's how we live now."

"I'm not scared!" Oriannon managed to answer. She stood up straight, and her anger suddenly boiled over. In a strange sort of way, she enjoyed the momentary anger. It brought relief, like there wasn't enough room inside for both fear and anger. She forced the anger over the top to bury the fear, and it worked—for now.

"It's okay." The Owling woman shrank away, still stuffing her orange sack with wads of shredded paper and sticky wrappers. "I just meant—"

"And you know what?" Oriannon interrupted her, tossing her bag into the flow of traffic with a flourish. A lev-scooter swerved and sounded its warning buzzer as the driver waved angrily at her. "I'm not going to be scared from now on. This is nuts. This is—"

She didn't finish, as the fear hit her hard enough this time to send her crawling into the bushes, clutching her stomach and her head in pain and terror. She couldn't decide which felt worse—her spinning stomach or her aching head. But the sky fell on her and she gripped her knees in a fetal position, rolling and crying out. She bumped against the security's boots but was far too terrified to even look up.

"You don't want to do that again," he told her. "I have no problem adjusting your levels even higher, but I don't think you'd live through it. Understand? Now back to work."

She wasn't sure she would survive what had already hit her, and she had no idea how long she lay hiding and shivering. But the worst of the feelings slowly drained away, and eventually her Owling friend helped her back to her feet.

"You don't know what they can do to you," the woman told her. "That was nothing."

Oriannon finally caught her breath and straightened up. If that was nothing, she surely didn't want to find out how much worse it could get. But just then the security sounded a whistle and motioned for them to return. Oriannon and her friend both shouldered several sacks of roadside trash and made their way back to the transport.

They hadn't seen—or at least Oriannon hadn't seen—that another, much larger transport had landed on the shoulder of the corridor, causing a major backup. Smaller lev-sleds hovered nearby and overhead, while media crews descended even closer to get a good shot of Sola and her crew. In moments she was surrounded by a swarm of reporters setting up for their on-cam reports.

"In a surprise move," said one reporter, "Sola Minnik is personally visiting one of the worksites she has pushed to establish."

"Just another example," said another, "of her common touch and concern for the still uncounted thousands of refugees."

As the reporters introduced their stories, the work crew was lined up with bags in hand, waiting for Sola to look them over.

This is it, thought Oriannon, the now-familiar fear taking hold once more. *Even if I can't say anything, it won't matter. She'll recognize me, and that will be that.*

"In fact, Sola has been stepping up her public appearances," said yet another reporter. "Ever since the disappearance of Oriannon

Hightower, the daughter of a former Assembly Elder Hightower, whom she has pledged to personally locate."

Oriannon caught every word, and at this point she might have screamed for help if she had been able. Instead, she pulled yet deeper into her ragged hood.

"According to Security reports just obtained by Media240 Reports, Miss Hightower was abducted from her home by Owling terrorists, who —"

That's crazy! she thought, wondering who had made up the silly kidnapping story. Owling terrorists?

Give me a break.

"Whatever the situation," the reporter continued, "it's feared she's again being held as a pawn in the growing face-off between Coristan Security and Owling terrorists bent on destabilizing the planet."

Now Sola took center stage, as only Sola could do. This time, she was flanked closely by three hovering probes, like bodyguards. She could have reached out and touched each one, if she'd wanted to.

"That's been my goal all along," she told her audience, looking appropriately firm with a determined little pump of her clenched fist. No one would mistake the gesture. "To protect Corista and her people first, and then to bring security and prosperity to the entire planet. That's the kind of leadership Corista needs."

Now she waved at the work crew, who stood mute as Sola and her probes walked in front of them. She paused once, looking straight at the cam while resting a hand on a silent Owling's shoulder for another photo op.

"What's more, our new guest worker program will address many of these concerns about planetary security and economic growth."

Finished with her sound bites, she breezed past Oriannon. But instead of recognizing her, Sola seemed to look right through Oriannon before turning back to the cams and reciting more statistics about her recovery program and how important and forward-thinking it was, and how anyone who opposed it was anti-Coristan.

Oriannon paid no attention to the speech but her mind spun as she wondered how Sola could have just walked right past. Perhaps she had been thinking of something else. Planetary rulers probably tended to have a lot on their minds. Or perhaps she just didn't get a good look.

But what about the cams? If one had caught her picture, her father might learn where she was.

Wishful thinking, she reminded herself. Wishful thinking to imagine her father would come for her. Wishful thinking to imagine Brinnin had located Margus by now as well.

Still she trembled as the cams followed Sola back to her gleaming shuttle, the same one Oriannon had ridden in on that awful trip to Shadowside, to the ruins of Lior. How long ago had that been? Out of habit Oriannon dug her hands in her pockets, and it surprised her to rediscover the warmth of the Stone.

As she did, however, Sola stopped in her tracks and turned slowly around. The probes fanned out, and Oriannon froze, unsure if the Stone could have brought on such a reaction, and unsure if she should pull her hand out or grip the Stone even more tightly. By this time Sola looked as if she had lost something, and her eyes scanned the crowd while an aide gently ushered her inside. But not before Sola's eyes connected with Oriannon's — for just an instant.

Oriannon was sure it couldn't have just been a coincidence. Somehow Sola had felt the power of the Stone, or perhaps suspected its presence. It made Oriannon even more nervous to think that Sola could somehow track her now.

But Sola didn't seem to recognize her. Oriannon wondered how that could be — until one of the larger cams panned past her still face, probably taking background shots for the special news feature tonight. Oriannon tried to pull back as far into her hood as possible, but when the cam passed, she caught herself staring into the polished glassteel surface. And for just a moment she saw her own reflection and blinked.

Surely that's not me, she told herself. There had to be a mistake. Because staring right back at her, she could clearly make out a very dirty, almost olive-skinned Owling. There was no mistaking the especially large, wide-set eyes.

Her eyes!

She brought her hands to her face, trying to be sure of what she thought she saw. After what she had been through in the camp, her mind had to be playing tricks on her. But as Sola's black shuttle rose to take off, their security quickly pointed them back to work. All other thoughts made way before the man's stun baton.

"Back to work, Owlings!" he drawled.

Owlings? Did that include her? Oriannon bent over her work, her temples throbbing. Perhaps the implants had altered more than just her fear threshold. With the security's orders ringing in her ears, she could not bring herself to touch her eyes, afraid of what she might find out.

3·1

Hours later Oriannon dragged herself off the transport with the rest of the work crew. Fear and trembling mixed with the awful fatigue of hard work in the searing heat of the suns. In a twisted sort of way, coming back to the camp now seemed almost a relief.

She'd already begun to see a pattern—a lot of fear when the security grew impatient and turned up the volume, a little less when the work proceeded according to plan. So the fear came and went, depending on when the security wanted to turn it up or down. Other times it seemed to come out of nowhere.

"All I want to do is take a hot shower," Oriannon whispered to the Owling woman beside her. But just ahead at a makeshift open-sided food tent, she heard securities shouting, and it didn't sound good.

"You know the rules!" yelled an especially tall security. "One bowl, not two. What makes you think you're special?"

"It's not for me." A small Owling man cowered in the security's imposing shadow, and it looked very much like her friend Siric Mil, the father of Moya. "My wife is sick."

The security laughed.

"And I'm supposed to feel sorry? Every time we ease up on you people, you take advantage of it. But this time you ruined it for everybody."

That could mean only one thing. Even though Oriannon knew it was coming, the jolt of fear still made her cry out. It sent some scurrying for cover, while others simply squeezed their eyes shut and rocked. Oriannon lifted and shook her feet, one after the other, worried that insects might have crawled up on her toes. She leaned away from the Owling next to her, thinking only of lice and germs and horrible ways she might get sick in a place like this. Her entire body convulsed with fear. What would happen to Siric?

At the same time, she couldn't help noticing a black-clad security in the distance—and something about him looked intensely familiar. He ran from transport to transport, looking into faces, stopping anyone who would talk to him. Even with his face-shield down, and even from a distance, she could tell. As he worked his way closer to Oriannon's side of the crowd, she knew without doubt that it was Margus.

But instead of running through the crowd toward him, Oriannon shrank back behind a tent, and her mind raced through her worst fears: *I can't let Margus find me like this, since he's already in too much trouble and it must already be my fault or I wouldn't be here. Surely the Maker is punishing me, or at least Margus would have come earlier, and so would my father, so I can't let him find me like this!*

Somewhere deep inside she knew how contaminated by fear her thinking had become, and she fought hard to bring her right mind to the surface. But this time not even anger would chase away the overwhelming fear that controlled her actions. This time her fear masked everything else, and like a person with a terrible addiction, she didn't have the strength to break through.

Now Margus stood only meters away, raising his face shield and studying the open lev-transport she had just left. Did he suspect she was this close? She would have shouted his name but her voice would not obey. Instead she fell back even more, looking for a hiding place, and another security told Margus to move along to a different sector.

I have to say something now! She knew she might not have another chance for a long time. And as Margus turned to walk away she forced her legs to step out of the shadows, willed herself to follow him even as her entire body trembled in protest.

"Margus!" she shrieked, and her words came out garbled at best, but she managed to hold up her hand. Unfortunately, she managed to attract the attention of the same security who had hustled Margus away from the lev-transport.

"Wrong way." He pivoted her around by the shoulders and pointed her toward a larger tent. "Meal tent is over there."

She mumbled a protest and tried but failed to dig in her heels. But her fear of the man in black trumped all other fears, and she did as he said, falling into line with a hundred other Owlings. Her twisted mind began worrying about worms in the food and about what that would do to her stomach. She worried that the water would make her sick. She studied her feet again, wanting to brush off the mud but afraid to touch it.

And the tears streamed down her cheeks when she realized how much she hated who she had become.

She did manage to look over her shoulder, catching a last glimpse of Margus still searching the crowds. Now he was moving away from her toward the opposite end of the camp, and then he disappeared entirely in a growing crowd.

"Margus," she cried, wondering if she would die like this—paranoid and fearful of all the wrong things. She wondered if she would live her life hiding from the people she wanted so much to find, paralyzed and helpless. Oriannon had become the prisoner she had come to this camp to rescue.

She even wondered for a moment what Jesmet might have done if he were caught in such a terrible situation, but she really had no idea, and it hurt to think that way. Instead she lowered her shoulders, pulled her hood over her now-matted hair, and tried not to touch the people around her in line. What might happen if she did? She'd heard how horrible diseases could spread in a place like this.

They're not going to get me, she decided. She closed her eyes because it hurt to see and not be able to act. Instead she hugged her arms to her chest and began rocking back and forth on her heels, thinking back on good memories with her dad. She remembered the times they'd gone on picnics in the Glades, before all this trouble. Before she'd even known Owlings existed! She rocked and remembered, letting the anxious thoughts disappear into the past.

It felt better that way.

Oriannon did find a plate to hold out for a scoop of runny stew, which looked worse than she had feared. The rancid odor made her wrinkle her nose with disgust, but since she feared upsetting the server, she said nothing and moved away. She found a place to stand in the corner of the busy dining tent, where trash had been piled in overflowing cans and no one talked to each other. She noticed Siric Mil and Moya in the distance and wished she could call out to them, but shied away before they could see her.

So this is what my life has become. She tried to swallow, but gagged and nearly threw up all over her plate. A young Owling nearby must have noticed the reaction and came up closer.

"Aren't you the Coristan girl?" he asked, and she recognized him as one of Moya's friends. "You don't look very Coristan."

Maybe that was because she wasn't Coristan anymore. Oriannon honestly wasn't sure. She wondered how he recognized her as she nodded quickly and started to turn away, but he held on to the plate.

"So are you going to eat that?" he asked, looking hungrily at the stew. But though her stomach had been growling with hunger earlier, now she shook her head and dished the contents of her plate onto his.

"Knock yourself out," she managed to whisper.

He grinned at the unexpected double portion as she fretted about what kinds of bugs were stirred into their food and what diseases she might contract from malroaches. She closed her eyes once more to try to imagine herself somewhere else—perhaps her warm, soft bed at home, far from this nightmare. But in the middle of worrying where she would sleep that night, she heard a murmuring sound and opened her eyes to see what was happening.

Margus had followed her into the tent! He'd started at the far corner, looking into the face of each Owling he met. And he must have been asking them a question to which they did not know the answer, because each one shook his or her head ... until Margus reached the little boy who had begged her dinner. She heard his voice even from across the room.

"I know who you're talking about," said the Owling boy. Obviously unafraid of any security, he turned and pointed directly at her. "That's her over there!"

Of course Oriannon knew what she wanted to do. This time, though, her fear reflex took over much more quickly, and she turned away in confusion.

What if he finds me now? She worried all over again, even though she knew how irrational it was. Dropping her plate and fork, she pushed past several Owlings and slipped out the side exit, even as her mind screamed for her to stop.

Instead she weaved through a crowd, keeping her hood tight and trying to blend in. But someone tackled her from behind, sending them both tumbling between two tents.

"Ori! Why are you running?" Margus tried to hold on to her, but she scrambled behind a tent. "It's me, don't you see?"

He pulled back his visor to show her his face. And though her fear still overwhelmed her, she felt she could either scream or cheer at having been cornered this way. Maybe both. Her hood slipped off to the side as she crouched in the dirt, panting.

"Whoa. You look ..." He looked closer, while she found it in herself not to turn away this time. "You look terrible. Look what they've done to you. But *is* it you?"

Leave it to Margus to recognize her, even through the grime and whatever the implant had done to her face — if that's what really happened. She couldn't be sure anymore. And leave it to Margus to keep trying. Leave it to Margus to find her.

She finally nodded. "It's me."

She looked at the tents, wondering how soon the probes would fall upon them and force Margus to hurry away. It would be all her fault if he got in trouble too.

"Ori, did you hear me?" Margus's voice brought her back to reality, and he grabbed her shoulders.

"I'm sorry," she managed. "But how did you ..."

How did you know to look for me? she wanted to say, but he must have guessed.

"Brinnin told me you'd been taken. You know, our probe?"

He nodded over his shoulder to a probe hovering at a safe distance. Brinnin!

"But listen, we're going to get you out of here, and Wist, and as many others as we can. Do you understand me?"

"I understand, but Margus, I'm scared. Everything scares me."

Which reminded her all over again that they had to get out of this place of death, while they still lived. Only escape seemed more remote than ever.

276

"I know," he said. "But first we've got to get you back to your friends at Zed 65. Wist is waiting for us, and I've been able to delay the processing a little."

"How?"

"Doesn't matter."

He helped her to her feet, looking as if he was about to cry.

"We're in a mess here," she said, "aren't we?"

"I'm so sorry, Ori. I was too late to help you. I tried."

"I know you did, Margus. I just wish you'd been there too."

He looked away, but not before she saw him squint in pain. "But now just stick by me, okay? We'll find help. Do you hear me? There's got to be a way out of this place, and I'm going to find it before they dial up the fear factor on me."

Hadn't she once said the same thing? And now look at her. But she nodded her head and followed him, gripping his hand but then letting it go when she realized what it would look like. And she trembled again.

What if Margus couldn't get them to a safe place, the way he said he would?

Zed 65." Oriannon paused a moment as she tugged at Margus's hand. Next to a stenciled Z 65, someone had painted three dots on the tent flap next to the door, a dark stain that reminded her of blood. Perhaps it was. The dots were arranged in such a way that the artist's intent was unmistakable.

They had painted a picture of the Trion, their three suns. The symbol of Corista—and of Jesmet.

"Look familiar?" Margus smiled at her for the first time as he pointed at the blood suns, then looked around quickly for probes and waved her inside. As he followed her into the tent, Oriannon could have predicted the shocked reaction.

"It's okay," Oriannon told them, holding out her hands at the frightened Owlings inside. By this time her own fright had subsided just a little. "This is my friend Margus. He's not really a security. He's here to help us."

Margus removed his helmet, which worried Oriannon. What if a probe came in and saw him like that? But never mind. Within seconds, Wist pushed through the small, gathered crowd with a shriek and wrapped her arms around Oriannon in a big hug.

"We knew he would find you!" Wist said with a huge Owling smile. Several others gathered around as well—Owlings Oriannon knew by sight if not by name. "It was just a matter of time."

Yes, just a matter of time before they would all be processed like her and Becket Sol, who sat off to the side, his eyes closed, rocking. Another man sat next to him, his arm resting on Becket Sol's shoulders, comforting him. At first Oriannon couldn't see the man's face inside his Owling hood. But something about the way he held himself made her catch her breath.

"It's going to be all right, Ori. Trust me." Wist wouldn't stop smiling, which, at a time like this, seemed out of place. Naïve, even. How could she say that? Oriannon knew the securities could come crashing through the door of the tent without warning, hauling away anyone who had not yet been processed. The fear would overtake all of them—it was only a matter of hours, or maybe minutes.

Just a matter of time, just like Wist had said.

"How?" Oriannon found the courage to say the word, as her fear subsided a little more. "How can you say that?"

"Because," came another voice, "that's what I told her."

Oriannon froze at the sound of the voice, and she shook so much she could hardly look over at where he sat with Becket Sol. But now he pulled back his hood and looked at the crowd with laughing eyes, as if they should have known all along that Jesmet ben Saius would show up at this prison camp. He patted Becket Sol's shoulder and stood.

"Jesmet!" Margus was the first to make a sound, though Oriannon would have if she could have. "I never thought we'd see you again."

"Oh? What made you think that?" asked Jesmet. He smiled a greeting in return, and his electric blue eyes took them all in. Despite all he'd been through, his eyes were still the same. "I've been all over this camp. You just have to know where to look."

Oriannon heard the words but didn't quite understand what he meant. Had Jesmet really been here? She could hardly find the words to ask him questions, the way they'd always done when he was their music mentor and they were his students. This time, everyone in the tent knew this was no ordinary Owling.

"I have to tell you, Oriannon, that if I had been grading the past several weeks as an assignment, I'd have been disappointed in some of your work."

Oriannon studied the floor. Did anyone else in the tent, besides Margus, know what he meant?

"I'm sorry, Jesmet," she blurted out. "I just wanted to do the right thing."

"That's in your favor. Unfortunately, the only right thing I expected from you was to wait."

She felt her stomach ball up again, and she knew where this was going. "But—" When she tried to argue it just sounded weak and foolish. "For how long?"

He threw his head back and laughed. "You could have counted the days on two hands, Oriannon Hightower. I wasn't asking you to wait for a long time. But you know what? You would have saved yourself a lot of time and trouble if you'd listened. Your impatience fails you."

This time she could only swallow hard and nod. The familiar fear was all tangled up in her awe of Jesmet as he went on.

"So I have a new assignment for you, Ori. Margus. Wist. And Brinnin, when you see her. Isn't Brinnin still piloting that probe just outside our tent? No one's discovered her yet."

That would be Jesmet's doing too. Oriannon nodded while her chest tightened so much she could hardly breathe without thinking about inhaling and exhaling. Nothing seemed to happen without Jesmet anymore, maybe not even her heartbeat. But they all stood quietly as he explained.

"In any case, our friend Sola Minnik has been doing a rather good job of getting her message out."

Several of the Owlings in the tent shifted nervously, as if the mention of that name would instantly bring probes and securities down on them. Oriannon shrank back as well, hoping the fear would not descend on them again. But when he smiled once again, it seemed the brightness lit their tent so much someone outside would have to notice.

"That's all going to change now," he announced. "And what you have to say is going to shake Corista more than any earthquake ever did. You're going on a quest, spreading the word, sharing how to live life to the fullest."

"But we, ah ..." Oriannon stuttered. "We're stuck here. How would we do that?"

Jesmet's shoulders slumped.

"You always knew the right answers, Miss Hightower," he told her. "And that would normally be the right answer. But a lot of your right answers are about to change."

Margus raised his hand slowly, the way he would have in class.

"Mentor?" he asked. "Do you think you could remind me again what we have to say?"

Once again Jesmet leaned his head back and roared with laughter, much too loudly. After a moment he pointed at Oriannon.

"Show him the Stone you've been holding all this time, Ori. The Pilot Stone."

Oriannon had not forgotten, though it took her a moment to reach into her pocket and hold it up for all to see. She thought it might drop and break into a thousand pieces, or that a probe would rush in and snatch it. But this time the colorful rock glowed as never before with a pulse of life and with the songs of an ancient past.

"That rock had not changed for ten thousand years," he said, "until you took it into your hand."

"Did I do something wrong?"

"No, no. You kept it, the way you promised you would that day under the waterfall. But now you must take it out of your hiding place. Now it's for others to hear."

"But we never did figure out what it was saying."

"Didn't you listen?"

"All the time. I couldn't make out the voices. They were always too faint."

"Then give it to Wist." He pointed at her friend. "She'll tell you."

Oriannon did as he asked, reluctantly handing over the smooth Stone to Wist. The Owling girl didn't have to hold it up to her ear as Oriannon had done.

"It's the Maker's Song," she told them, loudly enough for everyone to hear.

"I heard it," said Oriannon. "but I never knew."

"Don't worry, Oriannon," Jesmet walked from one Owling to the other. "Everything I told you in class, every song we played together, every dance—Oriannon, what happened? Do you remember them?"

"Of course." She nodded. "I can't help remembering."

"Then all that you know of me is written inside you. Is that true?"

She nodded.

"So now you're my song, my letter to Corista, and to all the planets."

"Me?"

"You." He nodded. "Once I hid these songs inside the Stone, but now they're on your heart. The beginning of the planets? It's there. Cirrus Main's lost book of Joeb? There too. Now it's up to you and your friends to sing the songs. It's your job to send the letter on, so everyone can read it."

This time she held her head, afraid that the tickle of fear she'd been nursing would come tumbling back, the way it had so many times since she'd received the implant.

"But you don't understand, Mentor. It might be up in my head, but I'm too afraid to do anything about it. You know what they did to me." She waved her hand around the room. "To a lot of Owlings. Actually, I think I'm more of an Owling than a Coristan now."

"You believed you were because of your fears, Oriannon, and you saw yourself that way. But Owling, Coristan — it doesn't matter anymore. That's not an important question. Look around this tent: There's no difference. Just listen to the music. It's for everyone — even the people outside who have enslaved you. And speaking of outside, Brinnin, please quit hovering outside the door. Steer that probe inside, would you?"

Oriannon wasn't sure how he knew where the probe was, but it entered silently and hovered this time just inside the door. By this time Wist had gripped the wildly glowing Pilot Stone and swayed gently in time to the music they could all hear, every one of them. A little girl joined in with words too soft at first to understand. But then Becket Sol opened his eyes and joined in with a low, gravelly voice. His eyes had cleared, at least for now.

That opened a floodgate of song, with lyrics of stars and faraway systems, all bound by the Maker's strong hand and Jesmet's harmony. Oriannon knew she had never before heard the words, but she opened her mouth and sang along without hesitating. So did Margus. It sounded like the music she had heard in the Stone, once so faint but now clear, strong, and more beautiful than she had ever imagined. It flowed through the tent as if without a beginning, as if it would never end. Strange and familiar at the same time. Yet they sang the music, ancient and primal, from the beginning of everything they knew, but also newborn and fresh, as if they were singing together for the first time. So they were — with Jesmet's resounding deep voice leading them.

Without warning, the gentle breeze turned into a hurricane, hitting them with all its power. A rush of song descended that came not from their own voices, but carried them along just the same. Everyone in the tent stared at each other, some smiling in wonder and others gripping each other in bewilderment. Oriannon held on to Jesmet's arm as if her life depended on it, as if she might lose her footing any time and be swept out of the tent and into the camp, or beyond.

"Is this what you meant?" she shouted over the sweet sound, which was like music and like the strongest wind. It had to be Jesmet's promise from the Glades, and it came rushing back to remind her that he had told them to wait for that power they had never before understood . . . until now.

"This is the Numa?" she asked.

To her shame, she had charged ahead on her own. To her shame, she had confused Sola's evil intent with Jesmet's good. Even so, this Numa blew away everything in its path, with no regard for wrongs in the past. Jesmet smiled and nodded.

Yes, this was it. And without ceremony he reached out a hand to touch her forehead, softly, right at the place where the implant brought so much pain and fear. She closed her eyes and waited for a tingle, or perhaps some sign to let her know what was happening. Instead he just rested his touch there for a moment . . . and sang.

As he sang, the root of fear that had burrowed into her mind flew away. She breathed deep the cool breeze of Jesmet's song. She knew then it was the same as the one from the Stone, the Maker's Song . . . all the same.

"Will the fear ever come back?" she asked as she opened her eyes. But Jesmet had already stood to join the others. She felt her forehead just to be sure, and the implant remained, only now surely powerless.

Wist handed the Stone back with a smile, and it seemed pleasantly hot to the touch, like a mug full of clemsonroot tea.

Becket Sol jumped to his feet too, clear-eyed and singing at the top of his lungs with his arms outstretched.

Two securities appeared at the door, as Oriannon had been expecting, followed by another probe. "They're looking for me," Margus whispered in Oriannon's ear.

So now they had found him. One of the securities raised his visor, pointed at Margus, and opened his mouth to say something. Then he must have changed his mind. Instead he just watched, gape-mouthed, at the wonderful storm of pure music that swept through this place. Their probe did nothing, only observed. Finally they both pulled back their visors and relaxed. Though Oriannon had rarely seen a security do such a thing, it seemed entirely appropriate now. One looked very young—not much older than Margus and herself—and very much puzzled. She even thought she saw them mouthing the ancient words to the song, and she wondered if they could know the meaning as well.

Even the probe seemed to be affected by what it saw and heard. As if caught in the powerful wind, it spun once and then parked, its indicator lights flickering before it went dark. And as it powered down, it slowly descended to the tent floor, quivering. Perhaps it hadn't noticed Brinnin's probe, or perhaps it had been caught up in the force of the Numa as well.

The Numa finally lessened, leaving Oriannon breathless and certain in what she had only once hoped for. Becket Sol embraced Jesmet with tears in his eyes, as the two securities replaced their visors and backed away slowly. One of their comms crackled before they looked at each other and stumbled back through the door—perhaps embarrassed, perhaps something else.

"Eighty-one eleven, report!" the comm insisted. "We have a huge disturbance reported in your patrol area. And none of the implants are responding. What's the problem?"

33

From outside the tent Margus pointed toward a distant clearing near the front of the camp, far away and down the slope, where a constant stream of transports ferried in load after load of helmeted securities. Even at a distance Oriannon could see how they jumped from the idling crafts and assembled hastily in ordered lines, some twenty to a line, line after line. The last of the day's sunlight glinted off their steely black helmets.

"What do you think they know?" asked Oriannon. She looked over at Margus, who had hidden his security helmet in the tent and covered his black suit with a loose-fitting Owling robe.

"They know that our implants aren't working anymore," answered Margus, "and they know that if we're not scared, they're in big trouble. None of this works if people aren't scared."

Hence the show of force. It seemed as if every Owling in the camp was now standing outside their tents, watching battle lines being drawn. Of course, only one side was wearing riot gear, and only one side carried stun batons and laser pointers. It reminded Oriannon of another lopsided contest.

"Just like Asylum 4," she whispered, hoping she was wrong. But the way the securities were preparing could only mean one thing. She turned to look at Jesmet, who came up next to them.

"You'll remember what I told you," he said, his hand resting gently on Oriannon's shoulder. This was his way of saying good-bye. Even Wist and the others knew and begged him to stay.

"You can't leave yet," Oriannon told him, pointing at the gathering storm of black uniforms. Above their heads a swarm of probes gathered as well. "If you talked with them, maybe ..."

Her voice trailed off as he shook his head.

"Just because I leave," he told them, loud enough so they could all hear, "that doesn't mean I won't be here with you. Don't forget what just happened. Every time you sing, I'm singing with you. I'll be here."

"I know." Oriannon was quick to agree. "You'll be here in spirit, but—"

"No!" When Jesmet raised his voice, they all stopped murmuring. A storm brewed in his eyes. "I did not walk through the star chamber just to become a sentimental memory. There's much more to it than that. Did you not feel the Numa?"

No one dared answer, until finally a little girl's perky voice drifted out of the crowd.

"Was it to keep us from getting scared?" she asked.

Finally he smiled, spreading wrinkles across his fire-scarred face.

"Something like that," he told them. "But not being scared is only a start. There's much more, but you won't understand until after I leave."

"You're not leaving now, are you?" asked Oriannon.

He cocked his head to the side with a remnant of a smile— maybe yes, maybe no.

"I'll be back," he finally told her. And with that he stepped away and into nearby tent, following Becket Sol.

In the meantime, Margus was focused on the distant securities, who were shouting and lining up. Shortly they would come marching up the aisles between tents, accompanied by hundreds of probes. After what Oriannon had seen them do before, she could guess how ugly it might become.

"We could use a few more of those things on our side," Margus whispered, looking at the gathering probes above them. "I'd like to even the odds a little."

Surely Jesmet didn't intend a battle. But when Oriannon looked back at the tent from which they had all just emerged, she wondered if they could do something. Maybe it was a crazy idea, but as more and more securities massed at the front of the camp and more probes swarmed into the area, she didn't know what else to do — except what Jesmet had already told them: sing.

And just as it happened in the tent, the song began with a lone voice, joined by others, until tens of thousands of Owlings were thundering out the words to Jesmet's song, and the camp was filled with music that echoed across the low hills. Oriannon thought the sound of it might rattle a landing shuttle right out of the sky, while every assembled security stared. How long could this go on?

She wasn't sure, but she pulled Margus aside, back to the tent, and motioned for Brinnin's probe to follow.

"I have an idea," she told them, stepping over to the disabled probe and picking it up. "Whoa. This thing is heavier than I thought."

"I wouldn't touch that," Margus held out his hand in warning. "Securities might come back for it, or it could restart any time."

"Not if you reprogram it to our frequency." She tossed it at him, and he caught it like a sack of aplons, grunting at the weight.

"How am I supposed to do that? Maybe if I was operating the probe, but from here, I don't know."

"What do you mean, you don't know? You're the tech guy. Can't Brinnin help you, and you two can do whatever you did before?"

"Ori!" Brinnin spoke up for the first time, through the probe. "What are you volunteering me for?"

"I'm not volunteering you for anything, Brinnin. I'm just saying that if you two can work together, maybe you can unlock the access code to this other probe. Do they all work on the same master frequency?"

"It's not that simple, Ori." Margus shook his head, but he had already pried off the probe's main access cover with the end of a spoon. "Besides, I don't have any tools, and the last time I tried this, it took me days to figure out."

"Oh." Oriannon shrugged. "I don't think we have days. But I thought you wanted to work with a few more probes."

"You're crazy, Oriannon." Margus blew the air out of his lips and shook his head.

"But a nice kind of crazy." She smiled at him. "Right?"

Crazy or not, Oriannon left them to see what was happening. The Owlings had not stopped singing, but the song had taken on a more somber tone, and Wist stood in the middle of the group with tears running down her cheeks.

"What's going on?" Oriannon asked. But when she looked around the group, she knew the answer.

"He's not in the tent." Wist folded her arms to her chest as the others continued singing. "He's gone."

She looked up again with a soft smile mixed with tears.

Just like that? The securities appeared to have had enough of the concert, and they began staging once more. A swarm of probes flew overhead, broadcasting a warning message.

"A shutdown of all movement has been imposed," they announced, flying low enough for everyone to hear. "Return to your tents immediately."

The music softened a bit at the first flyover.

"You will all be reprocessed!" said the probes. "Return to your tents or you will be restrained."

"We will not!" Oriannon shouted, looking to the sky. Everyone who heard her cheered, while no one showed any sign of moving back into their tents. Instead, the singing continued even louder, while none of the faces around her showed any of the dark fear that had once made this camp so grim and so hopeless. This celebration obviously wasn't over yet.

Just down the hill from their tent, a group of about ten young Owlings stood in their own small circle, clapping and singing. Above them, two probes broke off from their formation and dove directly into the group, blue sparks flying. Screams of pain broke the peace, and Owlings everywhere cried out as if everyone in the camp had been attacked.

"Into the tents!" Several Owlings yelled at once, the confusion rising. Owlings ran in all directions. Oriannon looked for Wist and saw her out of the corner of her eye before she was bowled over from behind and tumbled to the ground between two tents. Looking up, she could see was an angry swarm of probes descending on the camp.

"Oh, Jesmet," she whispered. "Is this what you wanted?"

How could they be swept up in the Maker's Wind one moment and on the verge of destruction the next? The strange thing was, she felt no fear, even if this was the end. She would stand up this time to the machines sent to destroy them. This, she knew, is what Jesmet would have done.

And now she heard Sola's voice being broadcast through the attacking probes, screeching in anger, ordering everyone who breathed to lay face down on the ground. When Oriannon heard the words, something snapped inside.

"Stay standing!" Oriannon yelled, running through the camp, lifting Owlings to their feet. "Stay on your feet! Don't bow to these machines!"

At the same time, Owling men all around her ran through the camp, shouting and waving homemade clubs, tent poles, or any other weapon they could find. Only a couple of meters away one of them swung hard with a broken-off pipe, connecting squarely with an attacking probe. It exploded into flames and melted a gaping hole through the nearest tent. Owlings cheered.

So it began. Oriannon groaned at the sight of a battle she had not anticipated. Surely the peaceful Owlings had never fought like this, so savagely. They had always turned the other cheek. Even so, she picked up a pole herself, looking for a probe. She didn't have to wait long.

"Behind you!" someone yelled. Oriannon spun just in time to see a probe, attack arms extended, flying straight for her. She stepped to the side, swinging hard. She might have connected if the flimsy wooden pole not been sheared in half by the probe's energy field, and she could only stare helplessly at the stub as the probe veered back around to take her out.

That's when a brave young Owling boy joined the fight, leaping up from behind a tent and literally grabbing the probe bare-handed and pulling it from the sky. He rode it down into a crumbling tent, screaming the entire way. Meanwhile Oriannon lunged at the attacker, thrusting what remained of her jagged pole directly into the probe's eye. The explosion sent both her and the Owling boy flying backward on top of another tent.

"Yes!" the boy yelled as he scrambled to his feet, fire sparkling in his eyes. "One more down!" He ignored the fact that his face and arms were badly scorched, that he held no real weapon, and that thousands more probes would soon take this one's place.

So many! The sky darkened as probes hovered overhead, selecting their targets and dropping to take them out, one by one. The air smelled of burnt ion weapons and charred flesh, while Sola repeated her demands for their surrender.

"Face down!" she screamed at them. "Now! You will be dealt with even more harshly if you do not surrender immediately!"

"How much more harshly than this?" Oriannon wondered aloud. Just up the hill, she recognized Siric Mil, roaring like a wild animal and swinging a broken piece of pipe in each hand. As he spun he took down first one, then another, before a third probe caught him from behind with a flash of blue energy and he sprawled on the ground.

"Siric!" Oriannon picked up a pole from the wrecked tent and raced over to help. Using her pole as a long spear, she caught one of the probe's arms and twisted it to the side. From the ground, Siric's well-placed kick sent the probe spinning to the ground. He smiled as she helped him to his feet, though he doubled over in pain.

"Perhaps this is a better way to die?" he asked.

Of course he meant better than what Sola had planned. Oriannon wasn't sure how to answer. Siric simply nodded his thanks and hurried off to another nearby skirmish, leaving Ori wondering what to do next. All around her Owlings fell to the onslaught, while others took their places, bravely battling the attacking probes.

As the battle wore on, there was no avoiding the fact that more and more Owlings were falling as thousands more probes fell from the sky. One of them chose Oriannon and dropped from directly overhead.

When Oriannon caught the movement, she barely had time to cover her face with her arms. She recoiled at the powerful bite of its attack arms. She managed to roll under part of a ruined tent, forcing the probe to follow, and cried out at the fierce jolt on her elbow. Maybe she could entangle the probe in the tent fabric.

At the same time a living, breathing attacker screamed just over Oriannon's head. She felt the dull blows, over and over, as someone joined in the fight and pummeled the life out of the probe.

"Ori!" yelled Wist a moment later. "Are you in there?"

Oriannon stared at the remains of a shattered probe, speechless for a moment—but still alive.

"Here!" She poked her arm out of the tangled mess so Wist could pull her out. As they stared at each other, Wist clutched a glassteel pole and panted for breath. Her face looked bruised and bleeding, but Oriannon smiled with relief.

"Thank you," she told Wist. But this battle was far from over. Two nearby Owling girls had fallen in the probe attack, and they lay crumpled on the ground. Oriannon ran over to check their breathing.

"They're alive!" she called to Wist. "Help me get them inside!"

As Oriannon's duty changed from warrior to medic, they repeated their rescues over and over, losing track of time and victims. Though most turned out to be Owling men of all ages, some women were hurt as well. Many were even younger than themselves. Over and over Oriannon and Wist dragged them into the tent where they had experienced the Numa, though the brutal reality of the battle numbed the memory of what had happened there.

"Please don't leave me here!" A little boy reached up to grab her hand, and it worried her that he didn't cry, though his face was covered with the cruel red blisters of a probe's attack. She kneeled at his side and tucked a rough blanket around him, praying quietly.

"Don't worry." Oriannon smiled at him. "We'll be back."

But by this time securities had started marching into their tent neighborhood, probably to mop up any remaining resistance. Of course, fighting probes was one thing; fighting real men quite another. This would end soon, and not in a good way. When Oriannon and Wist rounded a corner between tents, looking for more injured, a security with a drawn stun baton blocked their way.

"What are you going to do," asked Oriannon, parking her hands on her hips, "kill us all? Then go ahead! But we're—"

"Stop." The security interrupted her with a raised hand. He lowered his baton and removed his visor to look at them directly. "I don't want to hurt anybody. This isn't right. None of this is right."

Oriannon looked from his young, tear-streaked face to the number on his helmet—8111—and gasped in recognition.

"You were in the tent," she said, and he nodded. He'd seen what happened when the Numa swept through their camp. He'd seen Jesmet.

"I just want you to know." He took a deep breath and coughed. "I'm sorry about all this, and—"

He didn't finish his sentence, and they didn't see the probe before it hit him full-force, as fierce as anything they'd ever witnessed. Wist screamed, and they both jumped to pull him away, but the probe kept coming, striking at one of its own. He fell to the ground, unprotected, and his stun baton rolled out of his hand directly in front of Oriannon.

She didn't stop to think, just grabbed the handle of the stun baton with two hands and swung it at the attacking probe. She missed the first time, nearly falling off balance, but connected the second, sending blue sparks showering in all directions.

At first the probe wavered but kept up its attack. So Oriannon swung again and again, sending the probe spinning out of control with the attack arms flying in several directions. The baton buzzed unpleasantly in her hands.

"Let's get him out of here!" shouted Wist, looking overhead for more attackers.

Oriannon paused, wondering if the probe would return for more. She wasn't sure she'd knocked it out completely. And though the young security didn't look as if he was breathing, they each took an arm and dragged him back to the tent.

"This is one of the boys who came into the tent," Wist explained to another Owling woman who was tending the injured. "He's not like the others. He was attacked by his own probe."

"Alive?" wondered the woman.

Oriannon couldn't answer until she heard a low groan. His eyelids fluttered once, and he seemed to focus on her face. She leaned closer to hear what he was saying.

"I know who you are," he whispered, barely audible above the shouts and screams outside. "I used to guard your dad in the Temple before—before all this."

"That's okay." She patted him lightly on the shoulder, afraid to touch him in the face where he had been badly burned in the attack. "You don't have to say anything."

"My belt." He reached down to a clipped-on remote, pressed his thumb on the release, and managed somehow to remove it. He held it out to her. "Take this remote."

She cupped her hands around his for a moment, unsure what he meant or what to do.

"Go on," he said, his voice fading. He pushed it toward her, but weakly. "Take it. It might help you."

He closed his eyes again, and his hands felt limp and cold in hers. She wasn't sure if she was holding a dead man's hands, but she had a good idea what he meant for her to do with the remote. She thought she could make out a tiny smile on his face.

"I knew the words to the song," he whispered. "I'd never heard it before, but I knew the words. Did you know them too?"

"I knew," she replied.

He didn't open his eyes again as she pulled away and heard more shouting outside. There wasn't much time.

34

oments later Oriannon caught her breath in the tent where Margus was still working on the probe. He threw up his hands and tossed the spoon tool against the tent wall in disgust.

"Forget it, Ori." The desperation shone in his eyes. "We just can't—I just can't make it work. Maybe with the right tools. But we tried everything, and it still doesn't—"

"Here." She extended the security's remote to him. "Would this help?"

His eyes widened as he took it in his hand. "How did you get this?"

"Long story."

"But these are only issued to regular securities. I don't know—"

"Margus!" She brought him to attention. "Can you make it work?"

He shook his head and took the remote.

"I'm not sure. It might take me a while to figure out."

She closed her eyes, wishing she could do something else. That's when the strange peace settled inside her once more—as pure and simple as the fear was dark and confusing.

"Ori!" Wist poked her head into the tent. "They're setting fire to some of the tents down the hill from us. We need to get out of here."

Oriannon looked back at Margus, who had stripped off the Owling robe again, and who already had the remote taken apart. He nodded and waved at her without looking up.

"I'll be good," he told her, licking his finger and pulling out a tiny circuit board. "Just leave me alone for a few more minutes."

"We may not have a few more minutes," she replied, but he waved her off.

"Go, already!" He never looked up from his work. "You're not helping."

She swallowed hard but left with Wist to see a wall of flames claiming several tents below them, sending billows of smoke into the evening sky. If it got much closer she would warn Margus. But now all the attacking probes seemed to be returning to the staging area while securities set up stations every few meters, standing tall with the indifference of bored guards on a parade route. Many of the injured had already been dragged away.

"This wouldn't have happened if Jesmet had stayed," murmured a young Owling standing next to them. "We shouldn't have made trouble."

Oriannon wasn't going to let the loose comment go.

"You don't know what you're saying," she countered, facing him down. "After all that just happened, you want to go back to eating their slop and being scared? Not me. Jesmet left so we could have the Numa, and if you don't believe that, you might as well go down and turn yourself in right now!"

As the Owling turned away, Oriannon wondered at her own words, since her tongue seemed to have a found a mind of its own. But she knew Jesmet's freedom had been worth it — even if they were only meant to enjoy it for this short time.

"Ori, look." Wist poked her in the side and pointed down a long row of tents toward the camp's main gate. "Isn't that ..."

She didn't finish. In the distance they could see that Sola's familiar all-black shuttle had landed near the administrative huts, but that wasn't what sent a chill up Oriannon's spine. Even this far away, she recognized the robed man being held between two extra-large securities. As she watched, horror struck, they wrestled him to the ground and beat him mercilessly with stun batons. He tried to shield himself, but there was nothing he could do.

This can't be happening!

Without thinking, Oriannon sprinted down the hill as fast as her legs would carry her, tumbling once but still waving and screaming.

"No!" she cried, scrambling back to her feet. "Stop!"

She didn't worry that securities stood on either side, allowing her a clear path all the way down. She only knew she could not just stand and watch.

"Father!" she cried, and she didn't care that every eye was on her as she ran. A small lev-scooter had crashed off to the side, and it still idled and sputtered. Perhaps her father had used it to get here. Oriannon paid it no attention, nor did she care that Sola Minnik and her three guardian probes stood at the door of her shuttle, presiding over the scene.

"Let go of him!" cried Oriannon, as if they would listen to her. She tore at the back of one security's uniform, grabbing at his helmet. He just laughed and threw her off, a minor annoyance, as they continued the beating. But she must have pulled the security off balance enough so that her father could turn his head and peer up at her from the dirt.

"Ori, no," he managed, his voice hoarse. But the next moment the security hit his face back down to the dirt as he struck again with his stun baton. Beyond panic, Oriannon turned back to Sola.

"Why are you doing this to him?" she screamed, still looking for a way to stop the attack. While the rest of the securities watched and laughed at the spectacle, she pounded her fists into the back of her father's two attackers.

"Enough for now. Let her see her father." When Sola finally spoke, the securities looked up at where she stood in the safety of her shuttle's open hatch. Perhaps she didn't want to get her feet muddy. But when she nodded, the two securities shoved Oriannon aside and backed away, leaving Oriannon's father face-down in the dirt. With deliberate contempt, they powered down their stun batons and sheathed them with a flourish before standing off to the side.

Oriannon was past caring what would happen to her as she knelt at her father's side and turned him gently over to cradle him in her arms.

"Oh, Daddy." She rested her forehead on his chest and cried. "I'm so sorry for the way it's turned out."

He looked up at her through puffy slits of eyes, and his voice sounded far away.

"I'm the one who's sorry, Ori. You tried to tell me, but I didn't let you. Now I ..."

He collapsed into coughing.

"Don't talk. It's going to be okay." She helped her father sit up, trying not to wince at the sight of the horrible welts on his face and neck. She looked directly up at Sola and raised her voice.

"You notice he wasn't afraid of you, Sola? Nobody's afraid of you anymore."

Sola shook her head sadly and stepped carefully down the boarding ramp, looking as if she had just arrived at a funeral.

"That's your mistake, young lady. One that you'll regret."

"No, you don't understand. Your implants don't work anymore."

"So you think. I'm so disappointed these — these *Owlings* — deceived you, and now your father. A real shame."

"But you're the one who did this," cried Oriannon. "Not the Owlings. What did he ever do to you to deserve this?"

"To me personally?" Sola raised her eyebrows. "Oh, please. If you only knew how difficult it was for the Assembly to accept change. In fact, your father is the last of the elders to face reality. It's a tough lesson, but you understand now, don't you, Tavlin?"

"I understand evil now." Oriannon's father raised his weak voice. "And she's standing in front of me."

"Tavlin, please. You're not well." Sola's voice hardened and she touched a button on the shoulder of her black suit. "I must say, however, you were quite brave to come looking for your daughter—without my approval, which of course landed you in all this trouble."

"I'm here to shut this place down," he said, and she laughed.

"Shut it down? Hardly. Look at you. On the other hand, I'm gratified you've been reunited one last time with your daughter. It's so fitting. But now it's time we clean up this mess and return a little order to an unruly planet."

She touched the shoulder button over and over, agitation clouding her face. Finally she pointed at a nearby security.

"There's something wrong with my three probes. Call yours."

He pulled a small remote from his pocket, much like the one Oriannon had received. But though he pushed every button over and over, he received the same response as Sola had.

"We've got an issue here," he mumbled, looking up. It appeared that every probe in the camp—a considerable number—was gathered a hundred meters overhead. Even Sola's three personal drones had drifted away. "We're not getting any response, ma'am."

"I don't want to hear that." Sola planted her hands on her hips. "Just fix it!"

He might have if he could have. Instead he shot quick glances at the sky, then waved his remote over his head in a last desperate attempt before diving for shelter under the nearby admin building.

"What are you *doing?*" asked Sola, her voice breaking in exasperation as she stepped toward the building. But even Sola's eyes grew wide when she looked up to see every probe in the sky falling like a sudden hailstorm. With nowhere to hide, she dropped to her knees, shrieking and covering her head with her arms.

Oriannon tried to hold her own arms over her father. The rest of the assembled securities scattered at the sight too, diving for cover anywhere they could find it, while Sola kneeled in a puddle of mud and moaned in abject fear. But instead of crashing or hitting their targets, the probes came to a sudden, choreographed halt just over their heads, bobbing innocently just out of reach.

"Tell me this is not happening," said Sola, finally peeking out from behind her arm. "I am going to absolutely *strangle* whoever is responsible for this!"

She might have if she could have, and likely would have chosen the first security who dared to approach her. In fact, when she finally noticed a pair of sandaled feet standing next to her, she struck out with a vengeance.

"What are you just standing there for?" she cried. "Help me up out of this mud, idiot!"

"No, Sola." Jesmet answered her in a voice that cancelled out all others. "It's best that you stay right there for now."

Slowly she raised her head, and her fiery gaze steamed when it mixed with visibly cold terror. She knew him, yet dared enough to unmask her red-faced contempt.

"Is someone going to help me up?" she finally sputtered. Not one of her staff moved, not a single security—not while Jesmet stood over her that way. Her eyes widened in even greater fury.

"I'm sorry we had to meet like this, Sola." Jesmet's voice came steady but strong. "Next time—I promise you—your position will be very different."

"Perhaps you'll be the one kneeling in the mud, and I'll be—"

"I only meant ..." he interrupted her. "I only meant that your life is going to change drastically. And the people you've enslaved will be free."

"Enslaved? We're helping them to—"

"No more! You're not fooling anyone but yourself, and you're not doing a very good job of that. But once you're able to see again, everything is going to be very different, I promise you."

"I see just fine right now, thank you. I just don't care much for the view from down here. So if you're quite done with your little demonstration—"

"Then you're free to stand. And Sola? I want you to know it's still not too late for you to change."

At that she dissolved into snide laughter, finally managing to grab a loose fold of his robe to hoist herself up. Gaining her old composure again, she nearly lost her balance but dared to wipe her muddy hands on his robe. He didn't stop her.

"If I ever feel the need to change," she told him, a sneer coming to her face, "You'll be the first to know. But I wouldn't hold my breath if I were you."

He didn't move to stop her, just watched with a sad expression as she wheeled and marched away toward the nearest security, spewing commands with every step.

"Are you fools just going to stand there like statues?" she screamed and pointed back at Jesmet. "I want these people put away, and I want this entire facility secured! Immediately!"

35

Oriannon didn't know what Jesmet was doing, but she knew with-out a doubt Sola's retribution would be swift. The probes began circling, and one broke away to make a line to where Oriannon crouched with her father.

"Margus said to tell you he's got it figured out," came Brinnin's excited voice. "Sort of."

"Too late," Oriannon said, looking up to see a detail of five securities approaching with stun batons drawn and charged.

She turned her head and waited for rough hands to grab her away, or for the sting of a baton across her back. Instead she heard a shout, and looked up to see the securities halted in confusion only a few steps away. One of them pointed as dozens of probes launched skyward.

"Uh-oh," said Brinnin's probe. "Looks like . . ."

She didn't finish; her probe was yanked upward as if on a string, joining hundreds of others. With one mind they acceler-ated, faster and faster, until they collided with the bubble dome's blue force field in a horrific burst of sparks.

"Daddy!" Instinctively Oriannon shielded her father with her own body as the force field shimmered and wavered, while tiny shards of the probes drifted down to cover them in an awful blizzard of titanium flakes. Her father squeezed her hand weakly.

"Time to get out of here with your friends, Ori."

"No!" She gripped his hand as if she could keep him from slipping away. "I won't leave you."

"Yes you will, Oriannon. Do what Jesmet says."

"What?" She wasn't sure she'd heard him.

"Don't worry." He smiled and looked up at her. "Your friend Brinnin already told me everything—even about Jesmet."

He gasped once more for breath, and she tried to shield him from the falling titanium snow as Jesmet hurried over to them.

"To the shuttle, Oriannon." Jesmet scooped her father's limp frame in his arms, then stood. "You must hurry."

"But ..." Oriannon looked around at the confusion as more and more probes exploded overhead. Sola's screamed orders could barely be heard above the pandemonium.

"Oriannon, listen to me carefully." He paused only a moment. "You need to go, you need to go quickly, and you need to go *now*. Brinnin and Carrick will be fine, so don't you stop until you've reached the Asylum way station."

"Which one?" she asked.

"The Pilot Stone will take you. Understand? Now follow me."

"But Jesmet, I belong here. This is my planet. Don't you want me to—"

"Haven't I told you? Going is your concern. The Owlings are mine. Do you want to see your father killed here?"

"I'm coming."

Oriannon and Wist ran to keep up with Jesmet's strides. Unfortunately, two securities still stood guard at the open hatch of Sola's shuttle. But Jesmet didn't slow down.

"You'll step aside," he told them, and with wide eyes they obeyed—as if their bodies were doing what their own minds had not commanded.

"What he said." Oriannon glanced at the confused securities as they looked from Sola and back to the shuttle. She stepped up the extended ladder between them, then helped Wist strap her father into the seat where Jesmet had placed him.

"Jesmet," she forced out the words. "My father? Can you—"

He knew what she was asking. He could do it. After all, he'd brought Brinnin back after she died, hadn't he?

"I'm sorry, Ori." His eyes spoke sadness and he patted her on the shoulder. "Sometimes it works that way, and sometimes it doesn't."

"But . . . why not? I don't get it."

"I know you don't. Just remember your father was willing to give his life for what he believed and for those he loved. That's a good way to live. Now go!"

"Jesmet!" She watched him jump off the shuttle, disappearing into the confusion and the dust below. Then she turned to Wist.

"You don't think they're going to just let us fly this thing out of here," she asked, "right through the camp entry?"

Wist shrugged. "Jesmet just said to go. So we go."

Oriannon nodded as the sky outside lit up in vivid blue and gold flashes of lightning and the rolling thunder of so many self-destructing probes. At the same time a swirling blanket of dust made it hard to see even a few meters away. Dark figures darted in and out of visibility, until Oriannon jumped back in shock.

"It's her!" she yelled. "Sola's coming back!"

"Ori." Her father tugged on her sleeve and she turned. His face looked more desperate and drawn than before, as if he was barely conscious. "We have to get out of here. She'll kill me, like all the others."

Oriannon bit her lip and looked out the fold-up doors. No way could she or Wist fly this shuttle away from here. Only Jesmet thought they could.

"How do we close the door?" she asked Wist. They should certainly do that much. Maybe it would buy them a few minutes.

They pressed likely buttons just inside the entry, but the controls only beeped back at them.

"We're sorry," came a mechanical woman's voice. "You're not authorized to take that action at this time."

"Ohhh!" Wist pounded at the buttons in frustration, but it only brought back the insistent mechanical refusal.

"We're sorry . . ."

Outside, a half dozen Owling men tumbled into view, blocking the way while Sola and her guards tried to shove them aside. Only a few more meters, and Sola would climb right in.

Thump! Something slammed into the outside of the shuttle, just below the entry.

"Wist!" Oriannon shouted. "It's a security!"

Not knowing what else to do, Oriannon grabbed a compact red fire extinguisher off the wall and aimed it at the pair of hands clutching the side of the doorway. When a black helmet followed, she squeezed the trigger and aimed for his visor.

"Ori, wait!" shouted the security. "It's me!"

But it was too late; she sprayed Margus full in the face with a foul white foam that smelled like curdled wye-milk. He managed to shout and hang on while Wist pulled him aboard and a horrified Oriannon threw the extinguisher to the side.

"Oh, no!" she tried to wipe the foam from his visor. "I thought you were—"

"Forget it." He threw the helmet back outside. "I'm glad I made it before you took off without me."

But they'd run out of time for talk, a fact not lost on Margus. He crawled forward, still gasping and rubbing his eyes.

"We can't close the doors, Margus," yelled Wist, pressing any button she could reach. "All it does is tell me—"

"We're sorry," came the voice once again. "You're not authorized—"

"Never mind!" Margus took charge as he slipped into one of the two pilots' seats. "Let's get some altitude. Maybe we can punch it through the entry."

Unfortunately, he wasn't having much more luck than Oriannon or Wist. As he wrestled with the controls, the shuttle lurched to the side and more warning voices told him how unauthorized he really was.

"Wist!" Oriannon pointed at the open door. One look told them three or four very large securities had just grabbed the lower rungs of the step and were crawling into the craft.

"Get out of here!" Wist unloaded the extinguisher in their faces, forcing them back out with a cry of alarm. But from somewhere outside in the dust and confusion, Sola Minnik still shouted instructions and threats as the shuttle began slowly spinning in place.

Again they lurched and tipped to the side, plowing a furrow in the dirt. Oriannon looked out the front viewports to see securities diving for cover on either side.

"Up!" she shouted. "We have to pull up!"

"I'm trying!" Margus had pushed or pulled on every control he could reach, but still nothing worked. He threw up his hands in desperation. "I thought I could pilot this thing, but—"

"Pilot?" Oriannon shouted, and everything Jesmet had told her came to mind. "The Stone!"

Of course it would take too long to explain. So she just dug deep into the pocket of her robe, pulled out the Pilot Stone, and handed it over to Margus. He took it, but looked at her with a question written on his face.

"What am I supposed to do with it?" he asked.

But he had no sooner asked the question than the Stone began to glow a deep, pulsating crimson.

"Ow!" He quickly set it down next to the bright blinking panel of nav controls, shaking his hand as he did. "It's hot!"

"We're finally moving up," Wist reported from the still-open entry. They could feel the dusty air sweep through, tugging at them as they rose. "Way to go, Margus."

"I'm not doing anything." He proved it by holding his hands up, away from the controls. "In fact, I'm still not doing anything. It's flying itself. Is that what this Stone was for all this time? To get us out of here?"

"Partly." But Oriannon knew they still had a problem — or more than one. As hundreds of probes incinerated themselves in the force field, explosions covered the camp with an orange glow, then yellow, then turning transparent white. A hum of surrounding force field generators turned to a high-pitched whine, even louder than anything on the shuttle. Several probes grazed the shuttle on their way up, shaking them each time.

"This can't be good, Wist." Oriannon grabbed her friend as they watched out the door. The high-pitched whine grew louder and louder, until they could hardly hear each other yelling.

"We need to get this entry ladder up," Oriannon yelled, "and the door closed. Or we'll never get away from here."

"Maybe it's just jammed," suggested Wist, and as the wind whipped their hair around their faces they both reached out to try to muscle the stairway back inside. But Oriannon nearly fell out when she saw who clutched the ladder's last rung, hardly a meter way. Wist must have seen at the same time.

Sola!

For an agonizing moment they looked at each other, and Oriannon guessed the same moral dilemma flashed through Wist's mind. Some twenty meters up, would they be wrong to let her fall?

Oriannon wondered what Jesmet would do, and remembered the way he had let Sola insult him, just minutes ago. Now Sola Minnik stared up at them in desperation from the end of a ladder, her lips blue and her knuckles white, dust swirling around her face.

Her eyes pleaded with them as another series of probes shot up on every side.

"Help me!" she mouthed the words.

Both girls lunged out to grab her hands just as a probe glanced off the ladder, tearing it from Sola's grip with a horrible flash of light. Seeing stars, Oriannon closed her eyes and grabbed for the woman's wrist. Beside her, Wist grunted with the effort as well.

"Pull!" yelled Oriannon, as Margus's strong hands grabbed them by the backs of their robes and they all tumbled back into the shuttle. At the same time the sky overhead flashed like a supernova, followed a split second later by an ear-splitting blast of power that violently shook their craft and nearly rolled them over.

"What happened?" Wist groaned as the shuttle righted itself. She held on to her friend as they both lay on the floor, gasping. "Are we alive?"

"I think so." Oriannon shook her head and got to her knees. For the first time since arriving at the camp she could see bright stars replacing the steady blue haze of the force field. The titanium snow had stopped entirely, and the air that still whipped through the open hatch made Oriannon shiver — but not nearly as much as the thought of what they had done. She was almost afraid to look at Sola where she lay on the floor, moaning quietly, her hands on her face.

"We need to take her down again," Oriannon announced, looking at Margus. "Can we let her off?"

"Wish we could." He shook his head as he slipped back into the pilot's seat. "But it looks like the Stone has locked everything in. I can't budge the controls at all. I tried."

As if to confirm, the entry door finally folded back into place with a hiss of air. Triple locks tightened down with a reassuring click.

"But the force field's gone," Margus told them. "We're on our way."

Below them Oriannon could still see Owling survivors as they stepped away from their shredded tents and hurried past securities. Some carried children in their arms, though most left empty-handed. All of them streamed out of the camp to freedom, just as Jesmet had said. And without Sola down there, Oriannon knew they had a chance.

Sola, however, still writhed in agony on the shuttle floor. Margus nodded at her, then at Oriannon.

"Think you should see what's wrong with her?" he asked quietly. Sola didn't give them a chance.

"I can't see." Sola finally faced the direction of their voices, and she looked blankly from one to the next. Her voice had dulled to a monotone, and she held a hand in front of her face, wiggling her fingers. "I can't see a thing."

Of course she couldn't. Once again Oriannon remembered Jesmet's words.

"Here." Oriannon approached her. The anger that had burned in her against Sola had turned to pity. "Do you want to sit down in a chair? It's probably—"

"Don't touch me!" Sola raised her voice. "Don't anyone touch me!"

Margus looked from one to the other and shrugged.

"I think she's along for the ride. Nothing by chance, right?"

"What?" Wist backed away. "You've got to be kidding. Do you know how far we're going?"

"I think I do." Margus nodded, rechecking a glowing blue and red touch screen in front of him. "Looks like the coordinates match for one of the Asylum way stations. Asylum ... One, I think. Assuming it hasn't been destroyed like the other one, it's pretty far out. Maybe a week away."

Oriannon caught her breath at the thought of a week in the same shuttle with Sola Minnik, who was blind in both eyes as well as in her spirit. She wondered if this was what Jesmet intended, and guessed it probably was. But in the silence, they looked back through the viewports as they left Corista behind. Wist wiped away tears.

"We didn't get a chance to say good-bye. Not even to Brinnin and Carrick."

Oriannon held her hand to the viewport and nodded her agreement, though she knew as well as the others they'd had no choice. Finally her father's grav-seat clicked as he woke and tried to rise, disoriented, from his forward-facing chair.

"Relax, Dad." Oriannon turned and did her best to keep him seated, but he obviously wanted to see their progress, and he focused on Margus.

"I see we have a real pilot on board."

"Actually, sir, we do." Margus nodded and looked out the viewscreen at the darkening sky ahead. "Only I wish it was me."

"Margus destroyed all the probes in the camp," Oriannon told her father.

"Good boy." Apparently satisfied, Elder Hightower leaned his head back with a smile and closed his eyes once more. No one spoke as they continued to climb through the atmosphere, leaving their homes and their memories far behind. Sola sat huddled in the back corner, her jaw set, wiping a stray tear.

"Are you going to tell your dad?" Wist whispered, "or are you going to let him find out himself that she's here?"

Oriannon sighed. "I'll tell him when he wakes."

Until then, Oriannon went forward to sit in the co-pilot's seat next to Margus, to watch the stars emerge from violet darkness, as if born one by one, glowing brighter with every passing second. She reached out to feel the warm Stone as it piloted them, and she listened to the soft music of Jesmet's Song. Funny how the music came through so clearly. Here the stars even seemed to know the tune. Margus looked over from checking their course and finally broke into her thoughts.

"We've never been to Asylum 1."

"No." She shook her head. "Never that far."

"But we might have some friends up there, don't you think?"

"Hmm." Oriannon smiled and looked up to the stars. If Cirrus Main still lived, they just might.

BEYONDCORISTA

ROBERT ELMER

Read chapter 1
of *Beyond Corista, book 3*
in the Shadowside Trilogy

"What's going on?" Just after the impact, fifteen-year-old Oriannon Hightower of Nyssa pulled her way hand over hand out of the back room of the shuttle, making her way forward to where her friend Margus Leek had been thrown to the floor in the control room. Eye-watering black smoke made her choke on her words and gasp for breath before a burst of argonite gas snuffed the fire out.

"Did we hit a mine?" she asked.

Their spacecraft shuddered and tipped to the side. Gravity stabilizers must have taken a hit.

"You mean, you don't know?" came a low, mocking voice from the back of the control room. Huddled in the corner, a defiant Sola Minnik waved her hands for balance as an even larger explosion ripped through the underbelly of the craft, and the overhead lights flickered out. The darkness would make no difference to a blind woman, however.

Ori ignored Sola's question and glanced up at the Pilot Stone—which still glowed a faint gold and blue from its place next to the directional displays. The array of multi-colored screens still glowed steady as well, taking their coordinates from the Stone. Or so Oriannon assumed.

"Ori!" Their Owling friend Wist shouted from the darkness of the passenger area. "You guys okay up there?"

"Um ..." Oriannon gripped a handhold to keep from being thrown about. "Can't say for sure."

Oriannon couldn't be certain if their craft might explode at any instant, or if they'd been less than fatally wounded. She flinched at the sound of grinding and twisting metal all around them, the smack and shudder of raw impact as something hard hit the outer skin of their craft—three, four, then five times. The engines shrieked in protest, and she felt their forward momentum slow, then come to a complete stop with a rude jerk. Margus struggled back up to his chair, holding his forehead.

"What's happening now?" asked Oriannon, rushing to help him.

"It's like a huge hand just closed around us." Margus pointed at zeros on a screen that normally marked their forward speed. "I don't know how, but we're being pulled backward!"

Never a whiner, Margus ignored the blood trickling from a gash above his eye, then throttled back so the ship lurched and they leaned to the other side.

"Backward?" Wist struggled forward to join them as the ship jostled from side to side like a hooked fish that knows it's going to die. But looking out the forward view ports revealed nothing but the emptiness of space. Then, slowly, the nose section of a dark, silver-black Coristan Security cruiser pulled into view. It might have blended into the blackness if the windows had not been brightly lit from behind. Oriannon groaned.

As emergency lights flickered on, she wondered how much time they had left before this escape was all over—before they were dragged back to Corista to be executed as rebels and insurgents.

"They're all around us," reported Margus. "Five cruisers. They've caught up."

"But how?" Wist looked around the control room as if black-suited securities might step in through the skin of the shuttle at any time. Another metal-on-metal impact shook them nearly off their feet, and Oriannon worried about her father resting in one of the two tiny passenger cabins aft of the control room. Margus checked his instruments once again.

"Grappling hooks." He didn't need to yell. "They're using grappling hooks!"

That would explain the grinding noises as large metal hooks burrowed their way more deeply into the ship's outer skins. Since the hooks had certainly been fired from several of the Coristan Security vessels at once, there would be no way to shake free.

"Ah, I see they've finally arrived. Have they?" Sola smiled as she felt her way forward, turning her head each time a new hook penetrated their hull with a sickening shudder. Even if the shuttle was built with multiple skins and air locks in between, they could not long survive this kind of brutal attack. From her own twisted perspective, Sola had reason to smile.

That didn't mean she was easy to look at, however. The woman's eyebrows and eyelashes had been singed completely away, while her once full head of red hair had been reduced to ugly, twisted wisps here and there. Worse yet, her face looked as if someone had blackened it with a blowtorch, while angry red blisters rose across her nose and cheekbones, framing sightless eyes still wet with rheumy, coagulated tears. It could have been worse, considering the flash bomb that had blown up in her face only hours before back on Corista. In an instant, she had gone from someone who had always prided herself on her well-kept good looks to a snarling, helpless apparition.

Now Sola blindly reached out and grabbed Oriannon by the collar of her tunic. "You didn't answer," hissed Sola.

"Let me go!" Oriannon tried to pull away, but she literally had nowhere to escape. Maybe it didn't make any difference if they reached the way station ahead of the pursuing Security vessels. Maybe it was better to end this way.

"Why don't you just enjoy what little time you have left?" Sola challenged her again. "Have a snack. I've stocked plenty of supplies. A cup of clemsonroot tea?"

"Why don't you shut up!" Margus yelled her direction. "Why don't you just keep your mouth shut and mind your own business?"

"Oh, but that's just it." She returned another crooked smile in the direction of his heated voice. "This *is* my business, just like this is my shuttle. My beautiful shuttle."

"You stole it," answered Oriannon. "It belonged to the Assembly."

Oriannon couldn't think of anyone she wanted on this "borrowed" interlunar shuttle less than Sola Minnik, who had served as former Security advisor to the Ruling Elders of Corista before promoting herself to First Citizen. Dictator, by any other name. Why would anyone want to travel with the fiery woman who had deceived and then nearly killed Oriannon's father—and probably all the other six elders as well?

"I'm very sorry you feel that way, Oriannon." Sola's sarcasm dripped through her words. "There's so much you don't know."

Oriannon didn't answer. Oh, Sola was probably sorry, all right. Sorry they had caught up with her and destroyed the death camp, where hundreds and thousands of the Owling people had been imprisoned while being prepped for forced labor all over the planet. Sorry the Owlings had escaped. After all the work Sola and her Security forces had put into setting up the camp, she would naturally be very sorry about that.

Sola might also be sorry they'd saved her life by pulling her up off the shuttle landing ramp as they took off from the chaos of the camp with probes blowing up all around them. She would be sorry they'd had to escape in the same luxury craft Sola had once used to travel around the planet.

But most of all she would be very sorry the flash bomb had exploded in her face, blinding her completely and instantly. Yes, she would be very sorry about that.

"Dear Oriannon." Now Sola shook her head. "You simply have no way of understanding. Neither does your common friend Margus, here. And besides, who's left of the Assembly, aside from your father?"

"Because you killed them all!" Margus yelled at her again. "You have no right!"

"But that's just it. I do indeed. That's exactly why we've been pursued all the way from Corista, and that's why this little game is going to end in my favor. Because it's my right to decide what happens next for Corista, and it always was."

By this time, Wist stepped forward to face their unwelcome passenger. The olive-skinned, short-statured girl tried to push Sola away. "You be leaving her alone!"

"How noble of you to defend your friend." Sola finally released her grip on Oriannon, but didn't move away. "And you know, I should thank you for saving my life back there on the planet. Quite unexpected. I did get a good look at your lovely Owling face, by the way, before the explosion. I've always admired your people's distinct eyes. But then, you're probably already regretting what you did for me, aren't you?"

"Are you being okay, Oriannon?" asked Wist. Oriannon didn't know what to say as Sola went on with her tirade.

"In fact, by this time you're probably thinking, *I should have just let that red-haired monster drop off the side of the shuttle back when we had a chance.* Isn't that what you're thinking, sweetheart? Well, it's a little late for that. Even if you dumped me now, you still can't get away, and I imagine that must be a lovely, sinking feeling."

Her laugh cut short just as a bright flood of light suddenly illuminated them from outside, and a tremendous shockwave knocked them sideways. At first Oriannon thought the light came from one of the Coristan vessels.

A moment later, she knew this was no searchlight and not from any other vessel. This light shone bright as any sun in the Trion system, and Oriannon had to turn away as it poured in through the observation window.

"What in the world?" Wist cried as she shielded her eyes. Margus ducked his head to the side. Obviously Sola would be the only one unable to see. However, she most certainly felt the overpowering force that had just gripped them.

Now their ship trembled as if caught in an awful, confused tide, much stronger than before. One of the Coristan ships scraped past them in front of the observation ports before tumbling away like a stray toy. That couldn't be right.

Neither were the powerful explosions that rocked them. Oriannon wondered how they had not yet been shredded or destroyed. Then something else exploded inside their own ship. The ship yanked and spun as if someone was now pulling all the grappling hooks into a tangled ball, while shockwaves from a firestorm of explosions rocked their world, pummeling them from the outside.

This would certainly finish them off, Oriannon knew, and she whispered a last word to the Maker as she gripped the back of Margus's chair to keep her balance.

"If this is what you will," she whispered, falling to her knees and bracing herself, "then I'm your servant."

She squeezed her eyes shut, fully expecting to open them up and see her Maker, or perhaps even the Maker's Song, Jesmet, standing before her. She wondered if it would hurt to die. She hoped not.

Only her ears hurt. Every warning buzzer on the ship sounded at the same time, screeching an unholy symphony to rattle her eardrums.

"Please, no!" She held her ears and peeked through tears to see her first view of heaven, which looked surprisingly the same as the control room of the interlunar shuttle in which they had been riding. She gagged on a toxic blend of smoke and sickly sweet argonite gas.

I'm still alive? she wondered, unsure if she should be relieved or terrified, or if she could be both at the same time. A quick glance around confirmed that if she was *not* alive, then Sola Minnik had come with her. That could not be a good development. She ducked her head, searching for air to breathe closer to the floor.

"Ori!" Margus shouted through the confusion. Beads of sweat lined his bruised forehead as he struggled with his controls. Obviously he was doing everything he could to control their craft, pushing buttons and pulling up star charts on his viewers. "I need help with this!"

Though Oriannon had no idea what she could do, she swallowed her terror and worked her way around the chair. The shuttle writhed and turned, buffeted about like an insect swatted by an unseen hand. Artificial grav came and went, pulling them in all directions.

Together they did manage to silence the alarms, though that should have had no direct effect on their survival. But as the alarms quieted, so did the rough ride and the explosions.

"Is everybody okay?" asked Oriannon after several long moments. By "everybody," she mainly meant Wist, who nodded slightly and looked at them with eyes watering. Sola had slithered off to her spot in the corner, while Margus kept himself glued to the shuttle controls.

"Look at this," he told them. "Asylum Way Station 1 was there on the screen just a minute ago — before all this — and now it's not there. No station, no Coristan ships ... nothing!"

"You sure your sensors are working?" Oriannon shaded her eyes as she gazed out the view window. For a moment longer they could see nothing but that brilliant white light. Then solar filters finally kicked in and shaded the window. "There has to be something. The securities?"

"Just debris," he answered, looking for himself, "and that crazy bright light. It doesn't show up on the scans. But the ships are gone for sure, and so is the Asylum station. Very weird."

Oriannon still wasn't sure what he was saying. Gone? Where would they have gone all of a sudden? But as quickly as the bright light had appeared, now it faded quickly from view. It flickered one last time in the distance like a sideways bolt of lightning, leaving them alone and drifting in the cold expanse of space — as if nothing had happened.

"It can't be just *gone*." Wist pressed her nose against the view port as the grav field kicked in again, only several degrees crooked this time.

"Like I said," Margus replied. "That was weird. Very weird."

Weird, yes. But that still didn't explain what had just happened to them, or why.

"Maybe it was some kind of black hole," suggested Wist.

"Only it wasn't dark," added Oriannon. "It was light."

None of this made any sense.

With the shaking seemingly over, Oriannon hurried back to check on her father, finding him still unconscious and tied into his bunk. He'd missed all the excitement, which was probably a good thing. She returned to the control room.

Meanwhile, Margus rested his cheek in his hand as if trying to figure it all out. "The thing is," he said, "if that ... that light — whatever it was — did something to the Asylum station, it took four big Coristan Security ships with it."

"Only not us," added Wist.

"That's what I don't get." Margus scratched his head, and green light from the primary nav screen made his face glow as he leaned closer. "They had ten or fifteen grappling hooks into us, and we're the ones who got left behind. We should have been dragged away with everything else."

324 Maybe so. But when Oriannon looked at the Pilot Stone, still glowing in its place near the main control panel, she thought she had a clue.

"We're moving again," she said, "aren't we?"

Margus raised his eyebrows when he noticed numbers changing by the second on the velocity gauges.

"After all that." He whistled in disbelief. "I'm amazed we're moving at all."

"And let me guess." Oriannon didn't even need to look at the nav screens—just the Pilot Stone. "We're headed to the next Asylum way station instead?"

It took Margus a moment to confirm his numbers, and he checked several screens to be sure, but finally he squinted at Oriannon.

"Asylum 2. Looks like it. I'd ask how you knew, but I have a feeling it has to do with that Stone of yours."

He didn't really need an answer.

"Anyway," Margus continued, "we're pretty beat up. So if we want to go anywhere else, it's going to take awhile, and we'll need to do some patching. Looks like point two five is as fast as we're going to go—quarter speed."

Wist pointed to a monitor, cocking her head to the side.

"What's that?" she asked.

A view cam trained on the outer tail section revealed shredded chunks of titanium outer skin, gaping holes, and miscellaneous pieces of hardware peeling away.

"Oh, no." Margus groaned, bringing the focus up a little and panning the cam around to show ten sharp grappling hooks still partly embedded in the outer skin. Several hooks still trailed hundreds of meters of braided cable, strangely frayed at the ends. If there had been any wind in space, the cables would have been flapping like flags.

"Just be telling us what to do," said Wist.

So for the next several hours the three of them shut off systems and made repairs as best they could. While Margus rerouted power and electronics from dead systems to backups, Oriannon checked for hull breaches with a handheld meter and Wist fetched tools and equipment from storage cabinets and downstairs. Through all this, Sola seemed to have fallen asleep again in the corner.

Margus inchwormed out from under a control cabinet with a grunt. "Duct tape." He held up a roll. "Don't leave home without it."

Oriannon couldn't help smiling, despite the danger that clung to them. No, the situation did not look promising, and she knew very well they might not make it to Asylum 2 in one piece. Margus couldn't duct tape all the gaping holes in the skin of their craft, and what systems remained online couldn't be trusted. He tapped at the deep amber warning light of an atmosphere monitor and frowned.

"Not good?" asked Oriannon. He shook his head.

"Looks like we're leaking life support air faster than onboard generators can produce it."

"It's still going to be okay," Wist said hopefully. "Right? We'll be fixing it somehow."

"You go right on believing that, dear." Sola called over to them, her eyes still closed. "I can hear every word you're saying, by the way."

"Then you can hear this." Oriannon lowered her voice to a near-whisper. "Jesmet cares about what happens to you, no matter what you do. Even if I don't. Even if you can never see the gardens of Seramine again or the way the Rift Valley sparkles in the sunlight or the red flowers of a flamboyan bush. Even if you can never look up into the sky again and see the Trion with your own eyes. Even then, Sola, he cares."

Oriannon felt a twinge of guilt for reminding Sola of her blindness in a way she would never have done to a friend. But if it did any good, maybe it was okay to rub that kind of salt in this pitiful woman's wounds.

Sola grunted and brushed the sleeve of her dirty green tunic to her cheek as she stepped out of the room and felt her way aft to the second of the two small sleeping rooms. She kept her face pointed away from them, perhaps to shield the tears ... or not.

"I think she's had enough of our company for now," said Margus.

"Or maybe she doesn't like where we're going." Oriannon checked the nav screen to make sure they were still headed for Asylum 2, and glanced at the Pilot Stone as it glowed. She wondered if it would really guide them all the way.

Margus tapped the atmosphere monitor again and frowned, but said nothing.

Wist straightened up with a hopeful smile. "Maybe when we make it to Asylum 2," she told them, "they'll be explaining to us what just happened."

When, not *if.*

She is the optimist, thought Oriannon, ripping off a piece of duct tape to patch a run of wiring back into place. She tried not to keep staring at the rapidly declining numbers on the atmosphere monitor, even as she tried not to wonder what would happen if even more Coristan ships took up the chase.

When, not if.

Forbidden Doors

A Four-Volume Series from Bestselling Author Bill Myers!

Some doors are better left unopened.

Join teenager Rebecca "Becka" Williams, her brother Scott, and her friend Ryan Riordan as they head for mind-bending clashes between the forces of darkness and the kingdom of God.

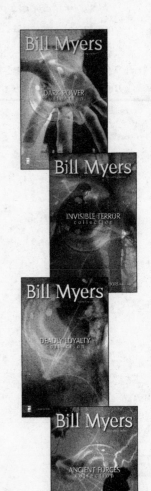

Dark Power Collection
Volume One

Softcover • ISBN: 978-0-310-71534-4

Contains books 1–3: *The Society,*
The Deceived, and *The Spell*

Invisible Terror Collection
Volume Two

Softcover • ISBN: 978-0-310-71535-1

Contains books 4–6: *The Haunting,*
The Guardian, and *The Encounter*

Deadly Loyalty Collection
Volume Three

Softcover • ISBN: 978-0-310-71536-8

Contains books 7–9: *The Curse,*
The Undead, and *The Scream*

Ancient Forces Collection
Volume Four

Softcover • ISBN: 978-0-310-71537-5

Contains books 10–12: *The Ancients,*
The Wiccan, and *The Cards*